DIGGING
FOR PHILIP

A NOVEL

DIGGING
FOR PHILIP

GREG JACKSON-DAVIS

**GREAT PLAINS
PUBLICATIONS**

Great Plains Publications
420 – 70 Arthur Street
Winnipeg, MB R3B 1G7
www.greatplains.mb.ca

Second Printing

Great Plains Publications gratefully acknowledges the financial support pro-
vided for its publishing program by the Government of Canada through the
Book Publishing Industry Development Program (BPIDP); the Canada
Council for the Arts; as well as the Manitoba Department of Culture,
Heritage and Tourism; and the Manitoba Arts Council.

Design & Typography by Gallant Design Ltd.
Printed in Canada by Friesens

CANADIAN CATALOGUING IN PUBLICATION DATA

Main entry under title:

Jackson-Davis, Greg, 1972 -
    Digging for Philip / Greg Jackson-Davis.

    ISBN 1-894283-42-2

    I. Title
PS8569.A275D53 2003   jC813'.6   C2003-910809-0
PZ7.J1385Di 2003

For my father, Dan Bryan Davis (1935-1998) --
My protector forever from the burning sands...

Author's Note

When I first began work on *Digging for Philip*, one of my greatest fears was that I would offend. But this book is meant to show respect for and to honour the Anishinaabe people and Native cultures of Canada while addressing some important issues. Research has been done to ensure the story be as authentic as someone in my position could make it. It does not pretend to be a "Native" story, but a completely fictional one of a white boy whose mind slowly opens to a new culture. When I told friends of my worry, the advice I heard most often was essentially, "It's your story, you write it." So I have.

Acknowledgements

I would like to extend special thanks to my first very encouraging early readers and editors: my wife, Khalie, my mother, Fran, Tish Connors, Graeme MacDonald and Maurice Mierau. I would also like to thank Dennis Jones for his initial encouragement and Ingeborg Boyens for similar support at the end of the process. Thanks as well to my best friend Roman Bamberger who housed and encouraged me while I finished the manuscript in Innsbruck, Austria. I am also greatly indebted to The Lake of the Woods Museum, various libraries, collections of stories, Ojibway histories, the works of Basil Johnston, Peter Gabriel's *Passion* CD, which has been played upward of a thousand times during the writing of this story, and a memorable, tempest-tossed and sometimes frightening June 1996 day trip to Shoal Lake with my Uncle Jack. Thank you also to my grandfather, Lloyd Wheeler, whom I never met, and my mother once again for the gift of my lifelong love, Lynn Island, Lake of the Woods. A final, personal thank you goes out to my wife and partner, Khalie Jackson-Davis, for all the intangibles, love and unwavering support. And if it's not already obvious, I thank you, the reader, for joining me here.

Lexicon

Amik: Beaver

Anakun: bulrush

Ani-maudjauh: He is leaving

Anishinaabe: The Good People (actual term for the nation of
people who have been called Ojibway, Saulteaux & Chippewa)

Anishinaabe-aki: Anishinaabe territory

Cheeby-meekunnaung: on the Path of Souls

Chekaubaewiss: "poked in the eye," dwarf who overcame a giant
in legend (see Mishi-naubae)

Coocoocoo: Owl

Gitche-Manido: Great Spirit

Kawaesind: The Feared One, a bully

K'cheeby/im: your spirit

K'd'ninguzhimim: You leave us

Kego binuh-kummeekaen: Do not stumble

K'gah odaessiniko: You will be welcome

Kinozhae: Pike

K'maudjauh: You are leaving

K'neekaunissinaun: Our Brother

Manido: Spirit

Manomin: rice

Migizi: Bald Eagle

Mishi-Coocoocoo: Great Owl

Mino-waunigoziwinning k'd'weekimmigoh:
You are invited to the Happy Land
Mishi-naubae: a name for a giant
Mong: Loon
Mudjeekawiss: Starting Son
Numaegos: Trout
Needjee: My Friend
Neewi-goon cheeby-meekunnuh: Four days on the Path of Souls
Negik: Otter
Saemauh: tobacco
Saugaushe: British people
Shaudae: Pelican
Tikumiwaewidung: He whose voice echoes across the lake
Wauh-Oonae: Whipporwill
Waukweeng k'd'izhau: To the Land of Souls you are bound
Waussee: Sunfish
Winonah: nourisher, originally an important mother figure
in Anishinaabe lore
Zaugitau: Emerging Bud
Zunugut ae-nummook: Difficult is the road

Northwestern Lake of the Woods

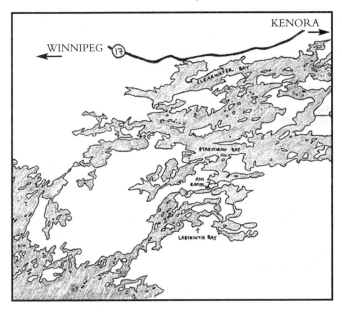

ONE

What Mother Doesn't Know, the Birds Do

The seagulls shrieked a protest as Philip's shovel struck the ground for the first time. Or maybe they were egging him on. They hovered above him, squawking rude remarks through the sheltering white pine branches. He could track their movements across blue gaps in the dark green needle canopy. The yellow-billed scavengers circled over him, but showed no intent to land, no desire to take part.

The boy shut out the disconcerting cries and heard only the water lapping on the bedrock shore. He gripped the shovel for a second thrust. His first effort had barely broken the wispy grass combed over the hump. He concentrated on a balder spot and jammed the shovel blade into the earth. His thin, undeveloped arms were hardly a match for the hard, packed crust. He threw down the shovel in frustration and the metal handle whacked against his knee. A jolt ran up his leg. But he stifled his cry with a quick hand, ashamed. He turned and sat on the hump. Fumed hotly, lips pursed, the air whistling out his nose. Idiot!

The gulls increased their volume.

"What the hell do you want?!" he yelled up at them.

Philip pulled up a corduroy pant leg and pushed on his throbbing knee with a testing thumb. He examined the spot where it hurt most, then pushed on it as hard as he could. Maybe if it hurt enough, he would learn better. Somehow satisfied, he covered the knee again. Glaring at the menacing gulls above, he pushed himself up off the hump. Had to gather himself and get back to work!

With his third try, he broke through the layer of yellowing grass and nicked the crust below. The shovel had a smattering of dirt stuck to it now, at least suggesting he had done something. But the ground seemed to get harder the more he attacked it. His desire was fading already. The surface barely looked different, but it sure felt like quitting time. He never finished anything anymore, provided he even started in the first place. But what was this...thing he was doing? Not some chore forced upon him, not even something he should do. Or that he really wanted to do. He could stop whenever he felt like it. Didn't even need an excuse this time.

He laid the shovel down more carefully. Sat on the hump, deep in his own rationalizing, barely hearing the boat buzzing out of the narrow east channel behind the island. He focused in on the gulls again, but there was no point in glaring. Despite their persistent circling, they seemed also to be actively ignoring him, half-curious to see what was happening, but nothing more.

Philip peered out through the old, mossy oak branches at the water. The brittle, craggy boughs swayed in the thickening breeze. Their funny-shaped leaves flipped pale underbellies to him. The growing cool against his budding sweat was a new west wind. Maybe the start of another 'Three Day Blow,' as his father had called them. Gusts flirted with the weeds growing in the bedrock cracks between him and the water. They looked happy, just two shelves down—moving, really dancing. Water squeezed through crevices and shot into the air, splashing the weeds and the expanse of flat rock. Philip lowered his head and grimaced at feeling so divorced from that fun.

Suddenly, over the din of waves and gulls, he heard voices, bites of sound broken by the blowing trees. He looked south-east across the rock to the water, but saw no one. He figured the people must be somewhere along the west shore on the other side of the thicket. Maybe even on the island. The voices grew louder. Other kids. At least two of them. Squinting, he could see flashes of florescent, life-preserver orange and the glint of an aluminium boat through the brush. His heart rushed with the excitement. Could these be friends? But its racing slowed almost immediately. The old irritation came to his eyes. He shook it off and blinked as things became even more blurry. The voices came more clearly as the boat moved along the shore until it was directly upwind from him.

He heard something about watching out for the reef.... He knew that reef well. Then more clearly: "The guy's a friggin' geek!" His heart leapt and sank at the same time. That feeling grabbed hold of his face again. Underneath his t-shirt, a bead of sweat ran from his armpit down into his pants. His body went heavy. Disappointed, but not surprised. You should be used to this by now! He rubbed his face briskly, but kept listening. Tried desperately to convince himself they were talking about someone else. The voices had to be the Emery boys. Todd and Bren. They barely knew him, so how could they know he was a geek? It had to be someone else.

"And did you see the way he looked when I said 'What's up?' to him at the Gunters' party last summer?" Maybe Bren. "He looked like I punched him in his ugly-glasses-face!"

Philip wanted to slap himself for forgetting what he was, what everyone knew he was. What he had been for fourteen years now. What he had become even more of over the last year and a half. Wanted to yell through the trees that he no longer wore glasses. But he did still wear them, or at least he should have. His mother insisted he was still too young for contacts, so he tried simply not to wear anything at all, with mediocre results. It wasn't too bad without them, except for reading and drawing. Too bad the great, gawky metal braces on his teeth weren't optional too. Images of the past year of grade eight in Thunder Bay clouded his mind. All the angry looks that met his eyes when he dared raise them. The loud voices. The hours spent alone in his room. He wished now he had kept count. That school sucked! So did this place! He swore Winnipeg had been better.

The voices faded out as the boat roared and sped off to the south. Philip watched it disappear around the tip of Gleason's Island and out of earshot. He stamped his foot with a brisk shake of his head and charged over to where he had left the shovel. He picked it up like a vaulting pole and lunged at the mound. Crashed into it with a grunt, readjusted the shovel and began jamming it into the unwilling earth. Stood on the blade, balancing for a moment, then fell over. The more it resisted, the harder he pushed his skinny body. If he stopped, what else was there to do? Nothing! This place had driven him to it. His cold, anxious sweat warmed up with a new flurry of activity. Every thrust came with a grunt and a jingle of the silver charm around his neck. But the mound was far more stubborn than he could pretend to be. The sweat ran from his brow across his face, making his acne sting. He winced, but did not stop his onslaught. Spanked the mound with the flat of the blade. Then went back to jabbing. Again and again, the shovel struck the earth with Philip's channelled aggression.

Within five minutes of continuous digging, his t-shirt was soaked and stuck to his back, heavy on a ripe pimple on his shoulder. He paused and leaned over the hump, out of breath. The sweat rolled off his nose to darken the disturbed dirt. Then he started up again. Digging into all those people's faces, knocking out their teeth, crushing their skulls. All of Thunder Bay. He never wanted to stop. Something had to come of this.

The boy righted himself with the help of the shovel against the hump. He let it fall and stretched out his cramped back. As he leaned back, he looked up at the blue sky and saw that even more seagulls had gathered there. The number was so large now that it no longer just annoyed him, but made him wonder. He shielded his eyes from the sun and tried to estimate how many. Fifteen.... Maybe sixteen....

"Phil-lip!" The voice jolted him from his counting gaze.

Mom! A sudden gaping hole in his stomach. "Damn!" he grunted. He gathered himself and answered a purposely loud, "Yeah?" He ducked under an oak branch, climbed over a granite boulder, down the dusty, ant-infested bank onto Swimming Rock. Down the sloping slab and up onto the worn path. Had to catch her as close to the house as possible. Had to keep her away from the hole. A clumsy brisk-walk to make up the time. Sweat, cold again.

Suddenly they were face-to-face. His mother smiled. "I heard you shout. Are you okay?" She pulled off one of her dirty gardening gloves and reached for his shoulder, but he pulled away. "Why are you all sweaty? What are you doing down there? Where are your specs?"

"Nothing. It was the Emery boys."

"No, it was your voice, I'm sure. I heard you yell."

Philip frowned as he thought back to hitting himself with the shovel. "That was ten minutes ago, Mom!" If I'd been shot, I'd be dead by now, he thought. "I'm fine," he insisted quietly. She doesn't give a crap anyway.

Her well-groomed eyebrows rose sympathetically, and she gave him that look like she knew how far from fine he was. But he turned and began walking back down the path toward his new project.

Jane Reddy shouted after her son, "I'll be calling you for lunch soon. Try to enjoy yourself in the meantime, dear."

He glanced furtively at her as he made his getaway.

Her mouth opened to say more, but an uncertain hand stopped the words.

Silly bitch!

Philip's hands felt more certain now, anticipating the shovel again. He let himself slip into an easy jog back down the path. His feet slapped down against the hard-packed bank as he burst out onto the rock. The continuous whirling of the wind above made him check the sky again. The gulls were gone. Finally! A sign that it was time to move on with this. He picked up the shovel and prodded the hump with the blade, as if to awaken it. Then he thought of what his mother would do if she found out. She had said it might be an Indian burial ground but was probably just a root from the pine tree. Nevertheless, she had told him not to touch it when he asked about digging it up a few years ago. So had his father. It would piss her off big-time if she found out. He tried to imagine her metamorphosing into an evil Hulk who would chase him around the island knocking over trees with oversized fists, trying to kill him. He would have a hard time explaining himself. Not sure there was an explanation at all.

It didn't matter that she didn't beat him or even shout much. She hates me. I hate her. It just made him want to dig faster, fiercer, deeper. It was her face he saw and thrashed at. Each breath stalled inside him, held as the shovel swung up and back to gather momentum. Then the air rushed out of his lungs with a heave as he thrust himself at the hump again. "You can't make me forget him! You can't!" he gasped, his jaw set.

A shriek pierced the rhythm of his thrusts, gasps and thoughts. Philip stopped and cocked his head to listen. Another shriek, then a clucking laugh. The boy looked up to see that four seagulls had congregated to circle overhead. What the hell?! Two more joined the group as he watched.

He shuddered as the wind gusted, cutting clear through the shelter of trees. The bushes seemed like they might just blow away. The sun still shone, but a new cold blew away its warmth. The wind had swung to the north. The lake went goose-pimply. A strong north ripple slid across the rollers crashing in from the west.

Someone had set up these distractions to slow him down! Sabotage! But there was no excuse to quit under pressure. No real goal to fall short of. Another monotonous seven weeks would pass before he and his mother needed to be back home. If he went so far as to call Thunder Bay home. His mother expected no more from him than to mope around all summer and maybe do some drawing. Like last year. Drawing was the only thing he could do well, but lately that too seemed to be souring on him. Day after boring day on an island in the middle of nowhere was killing him! And it was just the end of week one of being here! Any goal, however fabricated and stupid, would help to pass the time more quickly. He would try to finish the job before lunch....

A sudden south gust broke a branch from one of the rotten oaks which hid Philip and his work from the world of passing boaters. A staccato ring as something from above struck his shovel blade. He stared down at his feet to find the twig that had fallen but heard a greater crack and looked in toward the centre of the island in time to see a large birch branch crash down into the bushes below. The old birch had always looked dead and a little rotten, but not quite ready to collapse so easily. White pine needles above him whistled in chorus. The thick-needled branches caught the wind like a ship's sail now. Waves thundered against the west shore with increasing ferocity. Others crested as they rolled over the Swimming Rock shallows. The cold wind ran its rough fingers the wrong way through Philip's thin, reddish-blond hair, flipped it forward into his eyes. He pushed it aside, but it wisped right back. He kept digging. Shovel-load after shovel-load of dirt and wiry roots thrown into the air and blown back into the underbrush.

Philip felt what he had to call real fear. His fears over the last two years had been somewhat irrational, self-inflicted, or from dreams. He knew that. But this was different. He didn't need to exaggerate anything to liven it up. He didn't need to do anything at all. It was a fear for his life that came unexpected despite this clear-skied storm. But with it—the digging, the gulls, the wind—came a euphoric excitement, something close to fun. His temperature rose. Finally, there was nobody around to make him nervous: Philip versus the torrent, one-on-one.

A rare smile formed on the boy's face as he paused to examine his work. One end of the lump was simply gone, a foot-deep hole in its place. Another unfamiliar sensation came over him. Was it success? Whatever lay beneath the hump, he would find it. He would finish this. Finish it for all the sketches he had left half-done, all the disappointments on his record. He wiped the sweat from his forehead and pressed his restless hair down on the back of his neck. The wind wrapped itself around him. He felt it was about to rain, but a bright blue sky still framed the branches and the birds above promised otherwise.

He tried to sustain his excitement about the dig, but he felt a darkness setting in. The mounting fear overcame his forced smile. Almost involuntarily, he began digging again. The birds, waves and wind pounded at him. He fought them as hard as he could with the shovel.

A glance above between each thrust of the shovel allowed him to see the sky's blue intensify to a deep ocean shade. Mottled dark colours raced over him at a fast-forward pace, continually fading to sunlit-white, then blue again as they evaporated just south-east of the island. Like there was cloud over him only, yet it wasn't cloud at all. Was it one of those freak twisters like the one that had demolished a few houses down the lake a couple of years ago? Immediately above him a soot-black locomotive boomed. A churning hole in the sky. Philip looked into the earth, then back at the sky. Felt a connection. This was more than a twister, or certainly something other. The sweaty t-shirt went cold on his chest and a shiver shot through him. The mass exodus of gulls to the south caught his eye. He wished he were not alone here. Wished desperately for the shrieking again, that he would not be alone. Being alone usually meant boredom, but this version of it was pure terror. But if he had been a gull, he would have flown too. He yearned to make a run for the cabin and forget this thing, start all over. He felt his feet itch to sprint, but he could not complete the move.

Breathing heavily, with that sick, hollow feeling back in his stomach, the boy stared into the hole. It seemed deeper now, as if it were digging itself. The darkness above was tricking him. His eyes focused on the deepest point. It drew him. He changed his grip to hold the shovel like a spear. The wind howled one final protest. But all the frustration of these unsatisfying days raged like a brush fire inside him. He hoisted the spear above his head in his left hand. Concentrated briefly on the blade above him. Felt its power. His flesh prickled as he inhaled and pressed his lips together. The shovel shot from his hand into the bottom of the hole. The act overcame him with a fleeting feeling of confidence and power.

The blade clanked against something hard. Should have been a rock, but the tone was somehow wrong. The sound sapped all his harnessed energy. Had he hit bedrock? He spotted a hint of dark yellow surrounded by the earthy blackness. Pulled the shovel out of the hole, reached deep down, and found a surprisingly hard, smooth surface. He tried to brush it off. Then pressed his finger against it. The object was roundish. Or cornerless at least. Pitted, with holes. Fred Flinstone's bowling ball, like on the cartoon network.

Not enough light down the hole to see the object clearly. Philip planted a shoulder and his face against the ground as he reached in again to fumble in the dirt and identify this thing. His fingers stretched around edges, and he yanked the thing from the earth's grip.

He held it in front of him, by its…eyes. A human skull.

He tried to scream, but the battle cry of a full-grown man seemed to shake the island and rattle the air. It came not from the skull, but from everywhere. The sky. The lake. The island. The echo of the great, omnipresent shout rang off the shores. It rang even louder as the wind suddenly died and the band of furious clouds slipped off and faded away into brightening blue.

In Philip's head the cry rang on and on. His lips trembled and the taste of vomit crept quietly up into his mouth. He shook the skull off his hand and broke for the cabin.

T W O

The Reckoning

H is head still whirling, Philip whipped open the green screen door by its tiny handle and threw himself inside the house. He exhaled with a shiver. Stood just inside the doorway and closed his eyes. The door slammed shut behind him.

"Philip?" his mother called to him as she peered around the partition from the kitchen. "It is you! Well, I was just about to call. Isn't that just perfect?"

He looked down at the refinished softwood floor. His eyes fluttered to refocus the world. Then he stretched them as wide as he could, letting air into the sockets. Had to snap out of this waking nightmare. The sleeping kind had been more frequent lately—car crashes and broken glass again. Flashbacks to what the scene must have been like. But he preferred them to this too real horror.

He turned and dipped his head to peer at the south sky between the propped shutters outside the old French window. Blue and clear. The day was pristine and perfect. But the texture of the skull lingered on his right hand. He stared down at his outstretched palm.

"Come on. Sit down and eat your sandwiches. Peanut-butter and jam, like usual." Once she had intruded on his worry, Jane sat down at her place facing west and poured a glass of water from the pot-bellied jug. Her features were thin, with an angular jaw. She rolled her eyes slowly upward and plucked away a stray eyebrow hair. She sighed. "Philip! Aren't you coming to the table?"

He slowly moved toward his seat, his mind gripped by the texture his hand still felt. The skin tingled with new awareness. His pale knuckle-hair stood on end. He sat down across from his mother with his palms pinned to the wooden chair beneath his legs. He stared at the waxed wooden table just beyond his plate of two diagonally-sliced peanut-butter and jam sandwiches. The sandwiches meant nothing. It was still that cry! Its echo was still alive, reverberating off the walls inside his head. He swallowed, but his spit caught in his throat, making him cough. His glasses were folded neatly beside his place setting. He looked up at his mother. She had begun eating, oblivious to the disaster at hand. He had little idea of it himself, but he felt sure that it was just beginning.

Jane ate on but seemed to be making periodic checks on Philip. It was the same as ever. She hung over him. He felt her separateness and lack of understanding. Knew today she was even more puzzled, that she could sense there was even more wrong than usual. He couldn't hide his shock completely. He also knew that she wanted to say something. She would insult him and then pretend to be nice. Between bites of a dripping half-sandwich of onions, tomatoes and salami, she was rehearsing the openings.

It didn't occur to Philip to tell her what had happened just behind Swimming Rock. What did she care what he did all day?! More to the point: she would not react well. Even if this turned out to be really dangerous, she would just dwell on his deed. Even more in his interest to be silent this time.

His eyes shifted to the south windows again, toward the mound. All he could see was the closest layer of bushes and trees. An innocent hummingbird feeder was swinging in the ash tree just beyond the dried-out twisted wooden poles holding up the shutters. But he knew too well that only a few hundred feet from where he sat lurked the hole he had made. The skull he had unearthed. He wished he were back home with his satellite TV or his comic collection. He could block this out completely. Never would have left the house in the first place.

Jane put down her last bite's worth of sandwich. "Philip, you haven't touched your sandwiches. You usually take at least a few bites before losing interest." She went on, asking what was bothering him, but he blocked her out.

Just stared at his food with his mind shut down. His hand still buzzed. Mouth hung open and saliva gathered behind his lower lip, bubbling around his braces. He pulled his right hand out from underneath his leg and began rubbing it fiercely on his corduroy pant leg. Skull fingers!

"What are you doing, Philip?!" his mother broke through. "Did you get bitten?"

Philip gave a negative grunt. Barely caught the drool about to roll. He looked around him, suddenly no longer sure where he was. He could feel his legs tremble slightly beneath the table. The right one started to bounce on his toes the way it did in class. His hand reached out and grabbed a sandwich-half and thrust it into his mouth. He ate ravenously. His stomach suddenly cried out for food.

His mother made a move for his plate which he intercepted with an elbow. She gasped. "I'm just pushing the plate underneath to catch your crumbs. My God!"

He grunted angrily this time.

"Philip, honey. What's wrong? Please just tell me. You're always quiet nowadays, but I can usually read you better than you think."

Hopefully not! He picked up a second sandwich slice, and his mother seized the moment to push his plate up to his chest. He had no response to offer.

A gust hummed through the south screens. The windows waved back and forth on their hinges. One struck the lamp hanging on the wall. The curtains flailed about helplessly. Philip turned his head to the south and noted that the trees were almost still. Perplexed by the contradiction, he turned back to his food and tried to forget about it.

He finished his sandwiches and brought his plate and glass out to the extension. Put his dishes down on the drawbridge counter next to the sink and turned to look out the window at the north-west corner of the house. The windows at this end of the house were smaller, actually modern and waterproof. He pressed his forehead against the screen. Grandpa Frederick had built the extension only two years before he had died. Right after the power lines had been brought in. The work was not as precise as in the rest of the house—the roof leaked and the ants were already feasting on the wood.

Frederick Caplan had been over eighty-years-old by that time and died not long afterwards, when Philip was just four. Philip could barely remember his Grandpa, the island legend. Just the pipe and the missing pinkie finger on one hand. Instead, he had created a kind of friend from the old pictures he had seen, someone who never judged him and never made him nervous. Grandpa's ashes were buried near the east end of the island. This was his place.

Even from here, Philip could feel the cool wind gusting through the south windows, as it brushed the backs of his ears. His thin hair tickled the back of his neck. He rubbed his hand on his pant leg again. Wished he could just walk around the island like he always did before today, wandering aimlessly. It was boring. It sucked. But it was safe.

This was not.

He pushed his head harder against the screen. The tiny squares would imprint themselves on his skin. He rolled his head side-to-side and listened to his hair crunch, something he had never noticed before. Everything could be normal if he pretended hard enough and ignored the chill blowing in on him. But it seemed to come from everywhere. He closed his eyes, brought his hand to his mouth and bit down on his index finger until the skin creaked with the pressure. Stupid! Why did he have to be so stupid?

His mother walked into the kitchen carrying the mayonnaise and mustard. She put the jars into the fridge and turned back to the main room to finish clearing the table. As she came through the kitchen with another load, she leaned out into the extension, "Why don't you go down and bail the boats, Philip? It's not safe to have them full of water like this." Something for him to do.

Philip turned toward her and stepped away from the window to the middle of the room. He could see through and past her now, straight to the south door. His eyes wandered. Past the kitchen, the main part of the house was really one big room as none of the walls reached the peaked roof. A small section of actual ceiling that allowed for the attic over the living room space interrupted the view of the beautiful, original wood rafters and beams. The only solid, top to bottom part of the house was the stone fireplace and chimney. There was no panelling anywhere, and the outside walls were just the back of the fake log siding and two-by-fours, all a maple syrup colour. He refocused to look his annoying mother in the eyes for a split second, then down at her feet.

She smiled. "Go on now. Make yourself useful, boy!" Half joking, although it was true that he rarely helped out.

He stared at her blankly.

She gestured toward his empty plate on the drawbridge. "By the way, congratulations on eating both sandwiches. Outstanding!" She was just trying to get any rise out of him now. She waited for it for a moment. Then turned and checked herself nervously in the circular hand-mirror propped up at the sink. Frowned as she rubbed away smudged eyeliner from her cheekbone.

Still passively looking in her direction, his eyes caught a glimpse of something else. A movement behind her.... The screen door slammed loudly.

Jane turned. "Well, the wind certainly is kicking up." She laughed. "I don't know if it's ever opened the door by itself like that before. Not in all my years here." She turned to look at Philip, still chuckling, taking a sip of wine.

But his eyes had fixed themselves to the door, no longer passive.

"Don't you find that at all funny, Philip? Come on!" She pointed to the door. "It slammed all by itself!"

He was already too aware of this. Did not answer. His skin prickled.

"Philip?"

He bit his lip. Christ, there's somebody in here!

Somewhere outside his fear and confusion he saw her waving a hand back and forth in front of his eyes. "You are such a space case! Now go bail the boats before it rains again and they sink! Go!" She pointed briefly to the north end of the house, then spun back toward the main room.

Philip took a step backwards. Then, panic-stricken, he fumbled for his father's old rubber boots. He hopped on one foot as he slid the first boot on. Then sat on the old plank floor for the second. Pulled as hard as he could, but his heel stuck to the rubber lining through the hole in his sock. Finally, he forced the boot on. The heel burned from the rubbing. He sprang up to escape and smashed his head against the wooden wall unit cabinet above him. The dishes clanged in unison. He squeezed his eyes shut and put his hand to his head as he slowly stood up again. There was no time for this! He swung open the north door and ran out, still holding the top of his head, already aching. He stumbled down the railway-tie step and up the rock slab onto the main path. The slab tilted and clicked against the uneven rock below as he pushed off it to the upper level. After a few more clumsy, big-boot steps, he stopped and turned to look back at the house.

Christ, there's somebody in there!

He thought about his mother inside, but fear led him away from her. He began stepping backwards down the path. He swung around to sprint to the beach, but a balsam twig poked him in the eye. His hand moved to grip his new injury. No time to stop to nurse this wound either. He ran one-eyed past the old outhouse to the beach, boots clunking loudly. A chafing heel to add to his list of grievances.

He stopped himself at the end of the ramshackle dock. Out of breath. It was about as far away as he could get without leaving the island. He looked back up the path toward the house no longer in view, glad it was out of sight. His gaze shifted high and to the middle of the island. Eyes followed the sky-scraping white pines along the far side of the island to the one overlooking his excavation site. It had to be that one. It swayed menacingly in the wind, but he felt strangely safe at this distance.

The dock was usually one or two feet deep in water, but this summer low water had rendered it useless. Only bone-dry sand below. The water barely touched the outer-most crib, except in a strong north wind. The three boats were all pulled high up on the beach. The old aluminium fishing boat with the six-horsepower Johnson. The old, swimming pool blue fibreglass powerboat with the fifty on it his father had dubbed "The Ugly." One on either side of the eyesore dock. The canoe, just beyond the powerboat. The bank above the beach and all of its growth leaned toward the water as the erosion of the high water years slowly swallowed the land from the bottom up.

The boy jumped off the dock. Rubbers thudded loudly as he landed. He straddled the powerboat tie. Bent down and picked up a stray rock and threw it as far as he could. The rock landed almost noiselessly just twenty feet out into the choppy water. Just like a girl! He kicked the beach. Then dug his heel into the sand until he reached the wet layer below. Getting started was always difficult, especially if the activity was not of direct benefit to him. He looked at the canoe, its blue painter tied with a reef knot around a leaning balsam. He would start with it, the easiest. He remembered how his father had promised to teach him to solo a canoe when he got bigger. Those words were just two summers old. Now he was bigger. He kicked the aluminium canoe as hard as he could.

Philip's nose twitched as it caught a foul smell. Garbage. Or a dead bird. Following the strengthening stench, he stepped into the canoe and peered over the opposite side. Slipping in and out with the lapping water, a dead jackfish. The flies hadn't got to it yet, but the rot had begun.

More death.

The image of the skull returned to him. The seagulls. The band of black in the sky. He could barely believe it had been real. Had to go back just to see for sure.

He stepped gingerly over the thwarts of the canoe toward the stern where the rainwater was deepest. The seasoned, cut-plastic motor oil bottle, now a bail, floated just below the stern seat. He sat down on the last thwart, facing the stern and the open lake with his feet up on the gunwales and began bailing. He worked at his usual slow pace. After dumping exactly ten containers of water, he stopped. He pressed his eyes shut because he felt sure and he let the words slip out:

"Jesus Christ, I set something free!"

13

THREE

To Reconfirm

Philip realized he had been daydreaming when the bail clanged against the thwart and fell to the floor of the canoe. His eyes fluttered, then widened, and he bent down to pick up the old piece of plastic to finish his work. He bailed quickly enough that it required some concentration, but not so fast that it drowned out the fear.

When the canoe was nearly empty, it dawned on him that he couldn't keep busy indefinitely. There were only so many boats to bail. He wished for something to happen. Anything. He tried to calm himself. More than anything at that moment, he was lonely. He was scared, had that mix of excitement and dread inside him, but he was scared alone. A normal kid would have dug up that mound with friends. Only a deranged fool would attempt it alone.

Timmy had been his only friend in Thunder Bay during the grade seven school year, but even that had been by default. Timmy was obese, disgusting. It wasn't glandular either—the kid simply stuffed his face all day. But he was there. And like two opposites they were shoved together. Timmy had bounced off all the kids who rejected him and ended up in Philip's lap like a sick dog. Philip had been new and silent. He tolerated Timmy and his endless streams of hopeful conversation, but rarely responded to the things he said. All of it was the stuff of family get-togethers—the weather, food, collectable figurines.... Philip could hear the other boys, and what they said was usually significantly more amusing than Timmy's verbal diarrhoea. But he made no attempt to integrate at the new school. The more time he spent with Timmy, the more he hated him, the more he became his best friend. Everything had been better in Winnipeg. Everything had been better when his father was still alive.

A powerboat appeared from behind Blueberry Point. Philip's heart leaped. He waved impulsively, then realized his mistake and pulled back with a suddenly tight stomach. Shouldn't have done that. Big mistake. He knew it. The powerful engine droned baritone as the boat swerved into the bay directly toward him. He could see almost the entire bottom of the boat as it slowed down, losing its plane, rearing up to hide the passengers on board. The wake increased, then folded down into nothing. The high bow pointed at him like a gun. A tank coming at him. He reconsidered his wish for company. This boat did not belong to the innocuous Timmy.

"Hey, dickweed!" Philip heard a boy's voice over the engine. "What are you wavin' at us for, bitch?!" Then came that girl's raspy laugh. He hated that. The boat slowed to a drift, a swish of water drowned out the great inboard engine, and the bow dropped to expose Max, Rupert and Franny. Then came the higher whir of the motor being trimmed. Rupert drove the boat, Fubu stamped across his chest. Big Max stood up in the middle of the bow compartment with a sneer on his face. Franny behind Rupert, cigarette in hand. She tapped her ash overboard. Thick, black eyeliner. Poisonous.

They always seemed to come at him from Grouse Inlet. Rupert had a place in there for sure, probably one of the biggest. His dad was some kind of superstar lawyer or something in Winnipeg. Franny's family had a place somewhere in there too, but they might have been from Kenora. She was just a little different, as well as being the devil. Philip was pretty sure that she was cousins or something with Max. But he was from Winnipeg and a hockey friend of Rupert's. Maybe not too swift either. If he wasn't spouting off about great hockey hits he had made, he was boasting about something they had done "back at Symcoe Bay," so it was safe to assume he had a place there, but Philip wasn't even sure what lake that was. Whenever the three of them hadn't been cruising around the island last year, Philip had assumed they were at Max's, hopefully very far away and enjoying it so that they would never return. But they always did.

Rupert clunked the boat into reverse and they all jerked forward as the boat kicked up at the stern and stopped just inches from the bow of the canoe.

Philip braced himself with a squat, anticipating the impact. Then he stood up straight and motionless in the nearly dry canoe as the kids hovered above him like a swarm of hornets. The bubbling rumble of the inboard engine below didn't ease the feeling. The boat shifted sideways with the breeze and the three kids just glared at him. He studied the peeling grey paint under his boots. Kicked a flake away.

"Dork!" Rupert taunted coolly, throwing out his chin at him.

"Asswipe!" Max leaned on the side of the boat and spat into the water, just missing Philip's canoe. Franny tapped her cigarette and laughed her horrible laugh. She never said any of the things the boys did, but she didn't need to. She did it all with her eyes and that snicker. The boat rocked back and forth in the wake recycled off the Blueberry Point cliff. Philip could see the white mass of expensive boat just below his brow as he examined his foot, scraping at the canoe floor again. Would have loved to paint graffiti and crap all over that clean white surface! He felt his acne begin to itch at the sweat building beneath his skin.

"Man! You gotta to be the biggest wimp ever!" Rupert stood up from the plush driver's seat. "Haven't you figured out that I stole your cheap Styrofoam surfboard last summer?! Are you stupid? Now I'm telling you:" He shaped a megaphone with his hands. "I STOLE YOUR LOSER-ASS SURFBOARD!! And you don't even say nuthin'? Freak! Man, if you stole anything of mine, I'd freakin' kill you!" He laughed. "Yeah, so I guess it's a good thing you didn't do nuthin'. You'll live longer that way, piece of crap." He spoke like a hoodlum, although it seemed a little forced, but he was likely the smartest of the three, unless Franny was the silent leader.

Rupert's boat shifted around and toward the Blueberry Point shoreline in the choppy mix. But the kids turned to face him. A rise in the engine's tone as Rupert reversed the boat and spun the steering wheel like a pro. The boat bucked, swung and settled back as it had been. Bow pointed at Philip. Max smiled. Philip glanced up at him. Rupert gave him five seconds worth of his middle finger while revving the engine. He brought the throttle down again and popped the boat into gear. Forward, with a risky but cool U-turn away from the end of the canoe, nearly swamping it. If it had been any more shallow, his propeller would have struck bottom even trimmed up. Philip's knees buckled again, and he lowered himself down to grab the gunwales for balance. The displaced water jostled him and smacked against *The Ugly's* stern and the old dock's crib. And off sped the boat, complete with its three spoiled, asshole visitors, rearing up like an unbroken horse. Franny flicked her cigarette out in Philip's direction from the stern of the boat. Their eyes met, and she finished her flick with her index finger pointed at Philip's eyes. The bay went brown with the churned up mud bottom.

If only the water level were even lower so that they might have hit the reef on the way out of the bay. They weren't far from the worst part of it either. The big, heavy boat hitting the rock.... He could see it in his imagination.... Under water, the slow-motion approach of the untrimmed pro-

peller toward the bedrock slab. Then they meet: a water-muffled crash and
the screech of folding metal as the propeller and shaft are mangled beyond
repair. The whole craft kicks up from behind and Rupert's head smashes
against the windshield and bits of glass shower into the boat and water.
Max falls over the bow, head first into the shallow water. And Franny is
thrown violently into the back of Rupert's seat, burning her face on her
own cigarette. Wait—scratch that. She had dumped her cigarette
already.... But it would have been perfect! The boat sitting there adrift afterwards, lifeless. They deserved that end. Bastards!

Instead, Philip listened as the boat's hum faded out of range. He sighed,
trying to accept his fate as a born victim. But part of him raged. If he wasn't
such a retard, he could get them back for this, for everything. People were all
so stupid, but he could never show them he was better because he couldn't
even look at them anymore. Everybody sucks, but I suck the most. It was a
slogan he had developed over the last year.

Philip threw the bail down into the canoe. It bounced once loudly and
leaped out onto the beach. He stamped a frustrated foot. It made him even
more angry to watch himself react this way, like a big baby. Nothing he did
turned out right, big or small. At least he could count on this fact of life
and avoid living with any false hope. He bent down and leaned over to pick
up the bail, barely a foot from the dead fish. He put it back into the canoe
gently and walked back to the dock. Sat down on the edge, feet dangling and
clunking inside his boots.

He looked down at the sand and thought about Rupert and the surfboard. Last summer was still just a fog of grief except for a few notable low
points like that one day. He had barely used the board, so it didn't matter
much. But he had been watching while Rupert stole it. From the bush
beside the mound, just up from Swimming Rock, he had seen the whole
deal. It was near the end of the summer and Rupert had figured Philip out
from rumours around the bay about his weird behaviour and one actual
meeting between them where Philip simply didn't respond. When Rupert
and his little brother had landed on the shore in more modest boat than the
one he was driving this summer, little Fred had stayed near the boat, looking
nervous. Had to have been about seven and seemed to lack the evil genes of
his brother. Philip remembered distinctly Fred calling after Rupert in a loud
whisper, "This is not our island!" After Rupert had finished throwing
the Reddys' toothbrushes into the woods, he had held the surfboard
triumphantly over his head, then bowed, as if to a cheering crowd. Fred had
asked him, "You're not going to steal that boy's toys, are you?" And Rupert

had explained to his brother that they were not dealing with a boy, but a loser who deserved no toys. Fred had looked sceptical and just said, "Oh." Philip was so used to ridicule that Fred's reaction to Rupert's attitude touched him. But it seemed that only people who didn't know him actually came close to respecting him. Was it a pattern? Philip never missed the surfboard, but having it stolen from him was another knife in his heart. He wished he had the guts to get Rupert back. Or even kill him. Sneak into the inlet and plant a bomb under his cottage. But he wasn't even sure which one it was.

He lifted one foot up to dock level, then the other, planting his boot heels precariously on the edge, and pushed himself up, knees knocking. He looked out at the lake again and turned to walk back up to the house, so absorbed in his own history that he had forgotten about the mound.

F O U R

One More Bird

He was jarred back to the immediate when the house came into view. He inspected the walls and roof from where he stood just past the sleeping cabin, still above the step in the path, expecting some telltale sign. But there was no difference to be seen. The tattered, old green shingle roof and the simulated log walls were still intact. Even the long-forgotten, silvery, three-foot tall propane tanks stood obediently in place. Maybe he had blown this whole thing out of proportion, become paranoid. Big deal—just some old bones. Nothing could come of that. He coaxed himself down the path and walked carefully in the front door.

His mother peeked around the partition from the kitchen, paring knife in hand. "There you are. Did you bail the boats?"

"Yeah," Philip said just loud enough to hear as he kicked off and flopped his father's old rubbers into the corner of the extension. He remembered now he had only bailed one. Who cares? He walked past his mother in the kitchen and let himself fall into one of the old canvas rocking chairs in the main room.

He stared ahead at the colossal fireplace Grandpa Frederick had built. The very epicentre of the house. Massive, seemingly immovable rocks formed the base and even part of the floor as they extended a few feet in front and to the sides. The rocks had been taken from all over the island and the nearby Indian Reserve. Everybody who came to the house went on about how rustic and homey it was, how the fireplace was like no other. He would have traded it for a satellite dish or even a lousy black-and-white TV in a second. Then his mother would tell the entire story of how her father built it and how the roof around it used to leak so badly. Philip couldn't get excited about a pile of rocks no matter how difficult it may have been to put

19

together. Even with Grandpa Frederick in on it. He would take electric heating along with his TV any day. He moved his eyes up the chimney to the ceiling. And to the back of the house between the rafters where no attic floor boards hid the shadowed, water-stained roof. That roof still leaked around the chimney when it rained, regardless of his mother's claims. He had heard the pings every twenty seconds or so just last night. Why didn't they just put on a real roof? Cement or something. Man, this place sucks!

He examined the south screen door again. It had slammed on its own. His theory seemed pretty stupid now. When things enter houses through doors you are looking at, you can see them! There had been a really strong gust at just the right angle, period. Nothing else would make any sense anyway. And gusts could come from any angle. He had seen it before. He shook his head and stood up briskly. The smell of fried onions sifted into his nostrils.

At the table, Philip ate silently, still absorbed in how to somehow undo what he had done, erase his big mistake. The hole in the ground. It was important that his mother never find out because he knew how angry she could get, although he had never really witnessed it. He thought of how he might get topsoil and grass-seed to the island without being too conspicuous. He would steal it from his mother's gardening shed except he was sure she counted every grain of fertilizer or peat moss or whatever. Gardening seemed to be all that she did here now that it was just the two of them. It was like a disease. Maybe he could just pile a lot of deadfall wood over the hole. He slowed his plotting down. A glance up at his mother made him wonder if she wasn't reading his thoughts as fast as they came to him. She caught his eye. Maybe she sensed his plan. He tried to think of something else to throw her off. He knew his face was likely not as blank as usual, and it certainly hadn't been at lunch either. He coached himself to just keep eating, never looking up from his food, avoiding any opening for conversation.

But after a few minutes of silence, Jane smiled and forced it. "So what's up, sport?" She waited, but nothing came. "Philip?"

"Huh? What?" Startled by the interruption. But when he remembered who was speaking to him, his brow furrowed.

"Just wondering what's on your mind." She looked at him hopefully, trying to catch his eyes already falling into his food again. "Come on. I'm your mother...."

"It's nothing!" he almost shouted. He told her very little, and this was certainly not the day to change that. Why couldn't she just leave him alone?

"What is wrong with you, Philip?!" she exploded. A real shout. But all she got was a murmured reply. "What?!" she cried as she dropped her utensils loudly on her plate, a burst of tears, her eyes wide and waiting. "What is it?!"

His small protest had been too much. With his head still down, but his eyes finally addressing hers from beneath his brow, he turned the question around in his coolest, hardest voice, "What the hell is wrong with you?" His heart had shaken at her surprise outburst, but he couldn't let her get him. It hurt to finally hear a harshness similar to what he had always just pretended came from her. For a moment he acknowledged his bad casting of her. But she was being rough for real now, so it didn't matter. He gathered himself—now he had proof.

Frazzled by the blatant retort, she yelled at him across the table. "You don't talk to your mother in that tone, little man! This is my house! My island!" She stopped and gasped.

You can have it! He tightened his lip. Said nothing.

She took a deep breath. "I'm sorry, Philip. I'm so sorry." She covered her eyes, then pulled her cheeks down with her nails. The watery green eyes emerged again, make-up smudged. "I'm sorry but I can't bring your father back. I really can't. I would have done it a thousand times if I could. You have to believe me." Really weeping now. "But I need you to start moving forward again. Your shell seems to be just getting thicker, Philip. And I need you." She stopped and their eyes met. "Do you want to start seeing Doctor Southland again?"

No. Was this a threat or an offer?

She began closing the lids of the mayonnaise and butter, and collecting utensils. But the tears ran down her mascara-blackened cheeks so quickly she had to stop. She caught them with the clutched napkin. She looked up at the ceiling and squeezed her eyes shut. "I miss him too. So much. And when I go out with a man like Glenn, I'm not trying to replace your father. I promise. It's just so hard to be alone."

Philip stared at the table just in front of her place and tightened himself against the words. He was alone and just fine.

Jane stood up and turned toward the kitchen, condiments in hand, as if frustrated at having nothing useful to say. "He's irreplaceable. But he's not coming back." She turned to her boy. "I'm lucky to be alive. We're lucky to be here on this island together." She mumbled something in a whiny voice, laid down the two jars again and turned to leave the house sniffling, with a hand over her face.

Relieved to have something to scorn again, he exhaled disapprovingly through his nose. Lucky? Yeah, very funny! His mother's outburst had annoyed him. That was all he would allow it to do. Why couldn't she just leave that stuff alone? He knew he had. Just didn't feel like talking much lately. Especially to her. She had been at the wheel and survived. It didn't matter that the truck-driver had been at fault. If she had swerved just a little more quickly, his father would still be here. Or if she had swerved the other way, he would be here instead of her! If only he could have chosen who would die…. He had always worried about them when they had gone out and left him with Uncle Pete, and finally all his worries had been legitimized. He still wished he could have been there to warn them, to see the headlights coming, to yell, "Watch out!" Instead he just dreamed it again and again. A hell maybe worse than actually having been there. He shook his head, hoping it might all just fall out.

She seemed to think that his father's death had turned him into what he was now. But that was all wrong. He stuffed a piece of meat in his mouth and chewed hard to erase any doubts. He pushed his mind back to the real problem: the mound, the hole.

Within a half-hour, his mother was back and things seemed normal again, or as close as they could get today. She must have been out walking. She touched his shoulder and smiled to tell him she was okay, annoying him further.

That night Jane made sure her son was in bed by ten. Weighed down by the fatigue from digging and trying to convince himself the hole meant nothing, Philip put up no resistance and fell asleep easily.

His eyes flipped open again once it was dark. He waited to see or hear what had woken him, frozen to the bed. Then came the crowing of a large bird, a deep vibrating sound. Philip sat up and looked behind him out the window. Black. The bird crowed again. Sounded like a raven. He turned and put his feet on the cold, smooth floor. After a fourth crow, he stood up and carefully pulled aside the curtain to his room. He tiptoed across the main room to the south door. The floor creaked, as always. And the door opened with a biting squeak. She mustn't hear him leave! He carefully closed the door behind him, flipping the outside rubber stopper by hand. Turned to stare into a path of black.

A slim, weak moon pushed through heavy clouds overhead. But he couldn't see more than two or three feet in front of him. A heavy flutter of wings beckoned him down the path. The clothesline was just barely detectable against the sky's lighter shade of black. Philip took a few steps down the path, but the feeling that he had forgotten something overwhelmed him. He turned and retraced his steps back to the house. Leaning against the screen door he had just so carefully shut was a brand new shovel. The blade and handle seemed to be silver plated, unbelievably shiny. He didn't stop to wonder how it got there, but grabbed it and headed down the path again.

The birdcalls seemed to come from the direction of Swimming Rock. He heard the wings again, then stubbed his toe on a rock. His thin white legs goosebumped with the cool night air. He stopped at the end of the path. A line of white spots topped the rippling water stirred by a slight east breeze as the moon poked further through the clouds in the south.

Then a rustling to his right. Another flap of wings and a raven appeared, perched on an oak branch in front of him, just a few feet away. The immense bird crowed at him with deafening volume and swooped away, back into the darkness. The boy had to follow. He crashed aimlessly through the saplings and bushes until he saw the raven's glinting eyes again. This time it was down on the ground. Philip looked down at his bare feet and realized he had made it out of the brush and stood in some sort of clearing. He approached the raven. The shovel, dragging behind him, scraped loudly against something hard. Philip tried to scan around his feet, but saw nothing. He bent down and patted around on the ground with his hand. It all seemed familiar. His hand brushed against something. He tried to readjust to get a hold of it.

Something bit him! Like a mousetrap might snap, only more solid. It wouldn't let go. He let out a cry. Tried to yank his fingers away from the jaws, but they only clamped down harder. It had to be the bird! But the raven's eyes still shone in the moonlight. It was perched on a low branch ten feet away from him now. Whatever it was gnawed its way through his skin. He felt the warm blood run down his fingers, along with the pain.

Philip dropped the shovel and grabbed his left wrist with his right hand, tried to pull the hand free. After a few yanks, his hand shot up from ground level with far more power than he could have mustered on his own. Soundly attached was a brilliant white skull with jaw intact. Almost luminescent like the shovel. Around the skull hung a dark cloak. The figure had sprouted from the ground. The jaws released his fingers as the skull rose high above him. Cold, bony hands gripped his arms and threw him to the ground. The impact knocked the wind out of him, rendering him immobile. The spectre straddled him and the raven swooped overhead, crowing loudly. Philip felt that his lungs were about to cave in as he writhed about on the ground. He tried but could not scream. Turned his head to look up just in time to spot the shovel blade catching the moonlight as the spectre held it above him like a dagger. He squeezed his eyes shut and crossed his forearms in front of his face.

A crippling thud followed. His eyes opened to find the shovel in the ground half way up its shaft just beside his chest. He looked up at the face of the spectre, confused. The skull flashed familiar faces. His mother, Timmy, Franny....

Another miss on the next thrust. Each time the shovel plunged impossibly deeply into the ground. But the bony hands pulled it out again with ease.

It's digging!

Philip turned to look at the fast-growing hole next to him. Then up at his assailant who promptly hissed, "Not a hole. A grave." The voice was the raspy whisper of a man who had lived to be far too old. Philip tried to move, but panic kept him glued there. The spectre moved to the side and kicked him in the ribs, rolling him into the hole, suddenly easily three feet deep. Philip landed on a sharp rock at the bottom. He felt the pain, but could not react to it. It just froze him even more deeply. Felt the dirt creeping into the open wound on his hand. Wondered for a moment if he had been kicked by skeleton feet or army boots.

Soon his vision was obscured and he was spitting cold earth from his mouth. Between shovel loads, Philip could see the spectre above him. Just before each load of dirt fell onto him, he stared through the flying bits at the deathly grin looming above. As the weight on his chest grew, the boy realized what was happening to him. Then there was only earthy blackness—

His eyes sprang open. Panicked at seeing nothing. But the weight was gone. He reached out and up, and touched something metal. Then his fingers sent the message through. Bed springs! The upper berth! He gasped. Lips trembled. He pressed a clenched fist to his sweaty forehead. Safe. But he swore he still felt the grit between his teeth.

FIVE

Reparations

The next morning, he sprang from his bed immediately, grazing his head on the sharp metal edge of the upper berth. His t-shirt and pyjama bottoms were pasted with cold sweat against his skin. He thought for a moment that it might be piss. Right after the accident, he had started peeing the bed all over again. Like a baby. But it hadn't happened in the last half-year or so. He was relieved to find his t-shirt as wet as his bottoms. Just sweat. His fingers hooked onto the shirt neck, dangled his arm there. He stood staring out his window to the east. Started flapping the shirt's neck to dry off his chest. The day was clear, blue and windy again. He knew what he had to do.

He pulled off his pyjama bottoms and put on his bathing suit. Left his sweaty shirt on. In his cupboard he found the cursed blue and yellow Velcro running shoes everyone had made fun of at school. She had picked them out without his input. He could have found better at the recycling depot! He pulled a twig from between his toes and put them on. Picked his watch up off the night table: 6:30 am. Left the house as quietly as he could.

On the way down the Swimming Rock path, the morning sun streamed down on him through the east forest. Little spots of warmth hit his left side as the sun's light flickered on him through the mass of east trees with each step forward. He passed the entrance to his mother's garden. At the end of the path, he remembered the dream. For a moment, everything went black and the raven crowed. He looked to the right for where he had crashed through the brush last night. His eyes were drawn to the ends of freshly broken twigs. Had someone really taken that route?! His mother? That meant she would have found his hole! Or had he been here last night?! For real!

25

Mouth agape, he turned away in disbelief. Remembered the twig he had found between his toes.

He could remember waking up this early with his father and going down to Swimming Rock before his mother was even awake. Dad used to tell him that the sun was really just one big orange and that the rays were sweet juices squirting out of it. The stand of tall pine and spruce to the east shielded him from its juices now. On the water just out from the rock, ran the border between light and shadow, between morning heat and the leftover crispness of night. He remembered how it would slowly inch toward him. He shuffled down the bank to the rock. He paced the flatness, back and forth, mumbling, trying to make sense of the puzzling dream. No point in delaying any longer. He darted back toward the wood, up two steps of bedrock and the ant-infested bank, over the mossy boulder and under the oak branches to his excavation site. He braced himself for the worst. For a great black bird and a shiny new shovel. But things were just as he had left them yesterday noon.

Yesterday's ever-so-ordinary shovel lay half in the bush, holding down a few flowery weeds. Its blade glistened with morning dew, but it was most certainly not silvery or new. The old yellow-brown skull lay facedown in the pile of dirt dug from the mound. It too appeared wet. The sight of the skull made Philip start. He checked for any returning gulls, but the sky was clear. He picked up the shovel and leaned on it, surveying the ground around him. His eyes shifted over to the skull in the dirt—he had to bury it and do it right now! Although its rotten look assured him that last night's gleaming white face with intact teeth had been quite another, he walked cautiously over to the pile of dirt and lightly tapped the skull with his shovel tip. Had to check it for life and biting power. He remembered the gritty scraping sound well from his first strike and cringed to hear it again. Thinking for a moment, he rolled the skull over to the hole with his foot and watched it fall. It landed facedown there as well. He tried to remember what position it was in when he first unearthed it, but then decided he didn't want to touch the thing again. Just finish this! He started feverishly kicking dirt into the hole just in order to obscure the old bone. Then he used the shovel to return all the dirt to its rightful place.

After a dozen shovel loads, the hole was still one foot deep. Most of the earth he had removed yesterday was gone—not nearly enough now to refill the hole! The nightmare was continuing! Someone must have removed at least half of his pile. A conspiracy. His mother had secretly taken it to her garden. But he remembered how he had unwisely flung the earth to the wind. He leaned his chin on the shovel handle and wondered what to do.

The beach! Sand from the beach! He had it! If he took dirt from anywhere else, he would leave another hole. Just scrape a layer of sand off the beach and no one would ever notice the difference. Yes! He let the shovel drop and made his way back to the house. On his way up the path, he tried to figure out how to move the sand without being conspicuous. He only had one person to avoid which was a definite plus, he had to admit. She can't find out! Had to pull it off without a glitch. The wheelbarrow would be most practical, but how would he explain it? There had to be another way. He entered the house and saw that his mother was up. He let the screen door slam behind him.

"Hi, Sunshine! What a beautiful day!" Jane smiled at Philip as he walked past her to the extension and washed his hands. She was untying the bread bag for toast. "On a morning like this one, I'm so glad to be alive!"

Oh, please! Shut up!

She seemed to be waiting for a response, but he walked past her again and sat at the table without a word. "Did you go for a swim?" she ventured, looking quite shocked to see him wearing his bathing suit.

Philip grunted a "no" and pulled the popped toast from the toaster. He dropped the two pieces on his plate and then pulled a large mound of jam out of the jar and slapped it down, almost completely covering one piece. Then he took a huge bite of it. His glasses had been placed neatly within view on the table again.

Jane laughed and said, "Philip, that's disgusting!" She spread a thin layer of marmalade on her toast and took a dainty bite of it with her pinkie finger pointed straight up. Once she finished chewing, she said, "You should have gone swimming. Your hair is just awful! Let me fix it for you."

Her son glared at her from behind a glass of milk.

She pulled back. "Have it your way, you grouch!" Still trying to get some reaction.

You better believe it!

Philip finished his second smothered piece of toast and left his dishes for his mother to clean up. Before she could call him back, he had grabbed his knapsack and darted out the north door. He tore down the path to the beach. Had figured it all out over toast: make a couple of sand trips with his knapsack and be done with it. He got so excited on the way to the beach that he tripped over his own feet and fell forward onto his bare forearms, still gripping the blue and black bag tightly in his hands. Despite being alone, he groaned more with embarrassment than pain. Stuff like this just happened too often. One of his elbows really burned, so he tilted it up toward his face. The blood was a shocking deep red next to his pale skin. He must have cut it on the zipper of the bag. He got up and walked more carefully the rest of the way to the water. Someone should pave this path.

At the bay, he walked out to the end of the dock and looked about to find the best sand for the hole, ignoring the water-filled boats he should have bailed yesterday. Finally, he jumped left off the dock toward the shallower, reedy side of the bay, just clearing the painter attaching the beached fishing boat to the dock. His mother would never count the grains of sand, especially beyond the tin-can boat where the beach became bedrock. The water's edge there was littered with dead reeds, bits of wood, half a Styrofoam fender.

He dropped to his knees and began scooping sand into the bag. Remembered that dry sand was much lighter than wet. He kept pushing more into the bag until it was so full that sand rushed out between scoops. When the bag was upright it didn't look so full. Philip shrugged his shoulders and pulled the drawstring to close the bag. He grabbed a strap and yanked upward. The bag barely budged. He grasped it with the other hand and pulled again. The bag hovered precariously just above the beach as Philip bulged and sputtered with effort. He let it drop and exhaled. No way he could make it around the island with that! Would have to make more trips. He loosened the drawstring and kicked the bag onto its side. Decided to be realistic and scooped out about half the sand. Cinched the top again and lifted the bag onto his back. He had to lean ridiculously far forward to keep his balance. He made a mental note: Next trip, even less sand.

Right from the beginning, he sweated fiercely with his struggles. His body was not used to this exertion. The sweat dripped from his hairline, across the acne on his forehead into his eyes as the path took him uphill. He pushed himself up the abrupt level-changes and concentrated on each step around the roots and rocks through his salt-blurred vision. Could not afford to fall with all that weight on his back. He pushed himself to keep climbing this steep section. Little brush grew there, mostly just a bed of pine needles and a huge white pine tree every few feet. The holes between the roots that crossed the path were deep and treacherous. He forged on, past Blueberry Point to the east end of the island, the landscape changing as tall grass and leafy brush replaced the rock obstacles and hole-filled pine carpet. The colour of everything went suddenly from dark orange and brown to a brilliant, lush green. The mosquitoes came in larger numbers, feasting on the back of the boy's tender neck at this deserted end of the island.

At the south-east tip of the island, the path opened up to the shoreline. He had to stop. The straps slipped from his shoulders, and he let the bag drop to the ground. He fell onto his back right next to it. Hot, wet, and out of breath. He wondered if going the long route was really worth it. But this was the only way to be sure his mother wouldn't see him. He reached for the bag and pulled it under his head for a pillow. Tucked in his chin and pulled the silver canoe paddle charm into his mouth with his tongue. Lay in the sun, eyes closed.

The warmth brought him back to a day when he and Dad had taken the canoe into the back swamp. Just a few hundred metres from the island, but its own world. It smelled disgusting, but held many secrets. A picture of his father and him paddling quietly down the main channel of the bay and then stopping, letting the canoe drift. The water was a tight cellophane wrap, shiny and motionless. Sitting at the bow, turning and looking back over his shoulder at his father. A kind, bearded face smiling back at him. Philip pictured his five-year-old self who still happily wore the puffy red lifejacket he would later learn to hate.

A great splash just ahead. "Dad!" He remembered the jolt it had given him, then turning around to his father again for some reassurance, finding him laughing. "What was it?!" he had squealed, taking his cue and laughing too.

His father gathered himself and answered finally, "It was a beaver, Phil. Just before they dive, they slam their tails down." Bruce Reddy had been a good-looking man with bright red hair, little John Lennon glasses and a well-trimmed beard. Had carried some weight around the middle, but was relatively thin. His eyes always smiled. "Beavers are territorial. They don't like it when big goofy humans like us come around." He pointed to the right. "That's the beaver hut there. And if that's the mama beaver, she probably wants to get our attention away from it. She wants to protect her babies. I'll bet she splashes again. But over there." Pointed left.

"You wanna bet? Go get a Corvette!" Uncle Dixon had taught him that one. He looked over at the hut. "Dad? Can we make the beaver splash again? Can we get a piece of nice wood from his house?"

"Sorry, guy. That's a bit like if some huge monster came and took the roof off our house on the island. You wouldn't want that, would you?"

29

"No." Philip giggled as he pictured a one-eyed ogre removing the roof from the island house between a thumb and forefinger, and the tiny Reddy family looking up as their roof moved skyward. Smiled at the thought. Understood now.

"We shouldn't try to bother the beaver, but watching is okay. We don't want them to move out, right? I'll bet we can find one of those chewed pieces on the—" He gave a short hiss and pointed to something dark moving quickly along the surface of the water. Small, but it created a discernible wake as it moved across the bow of the canoe and disappeared. One second later a black tail appeared and then crashed down, piercing the silence. It had been exactly where his father had said it would come.

Philip opened his eyes and propped himself up on one elbow. He looked across the water to the swamp. He felt the muscles in his face twitch and pull downward. A tear slowly oozed out of the corner of his right eye and ran down his cheek. His nose filled up and he gave a quick gasp, spitting out the silver paddle. He swallowed hard and crushed the tear against his chin with his forearm. Everything had changed since then. Now there were too many beavers and people shot them. And he had not touched the canoe for the last two summers, except to bail it.

Enough baby stuff! Philip forced himself up briskly, rubbed the elbow where the grass had left its imprint. Then struggled to mount the bag of sand onto his back again. The brambles and the thistle patch scratched at his bare legs. The path wove away from the shore, then back again. As he went by his grandfather's grave, he stole a glance up toward the rocky burial site. It was the last thing he wanted to think about. One grave at a time.

Finally, he arrived at Swimming Rock from the south side path. It was seldom used and he could feel the spider webs break across his face. Checking for his mother, he cautiously walked to the path's opening. She was nowhere in sight, so he stole across the rock up to the mound area. He looked down at the hole, hoping that he wouldn't need too many more loads of sand. He pulled the bag over his shoulders with his thumbs and let it fall back onto the ground. Grabbing the top edges of the bag with two hands, he waddled over to the hole and tipped the bag over. Most of the sand spilled neatly into the hole. It had been a good idea, but he would need a couple more loads. He thought of going back to the beach and making the same trip again and let out a groan. Just wished he was better put-together and co-ordinated, so all of this would be easier. Max or Rupert would have no problems with any of this. Dicks! He bent down and picked up the empty bag and began his journey back around the island.

The sand should come from a different spot this time. Had to be careful not to leave anything that might catch his mother's eye. He patted down the upturned beach with his shoe and swung the bag onto his back. He began the same struggle onto the dock and up the path. But he stopped abruptly when he noticed a separation in the brush. It began from the spot just off the path where an old rowboat was entombed, and appeared to cut a good way through the island to the south side. He thought of the incline ahead and all the rocks and roots, and decided in favour of bush-crashing directly over.

He slowly followed a weaving path created mostly by fallen trees. The bugs were thick. He felt he must have swallowed one of the tiny ones. Most of the trees were balsam with new growth only at the very top and only brittle, needleless twigs at eye-level. He reached out and snapped them off as he pushed on. The ground was a firm blanket of old leaves and small twigs snapping underfoot. Also growing around him were cherry trees gone wild from a garden his grandmother tended something like fifty years ago. His mother's garden was closer to the house and had no berries or anything good in it—just flowers and vegetables.

He pushed a layer of branches aside and his path seemed to simply stop. He stood at the base of a small bedrock cliff. He could feel the cool damp coming off the heavily-shaded, mossy rock. He looked back and saw the old rowboat, the boats, and the water through the trees. He sized up the rock face and located a handhold. He reached up and brought his left foot up until it found something solid to push off. Philip strained to mount himself up onto the rock, his muscles trembling as they held his weight and the bag's. When he had made it halfway up, he stopped and realized that he had stumbled onto his Grandpa Frederick's grave, but from the north side. Not part of the plan, but at least he knew which way to continue from here.

After hoisting himself up completely, he stood and brushed his dirty hands off on his swimsuit. Wiped new sweat from his brow. The sun shone down on him from directly above and the moss beneath his feet now was of the crunchy, dry variety. Looked like cauliflower-coral. It was as if he had just jumped from a rainforest to an arid plateau. From here Philip could see over a good deal of the island, especially to the east where fewer white pines obstructed his view. Grandpa Frederick had asked to be buried on the highest point on the island, and now his ashes lay there, underneath a pile of huge rocks. Philip remembered arguing that his father should be buried next to Grandpa Frederick. No one had taken him seriously. But Dad should have been here too. Not in some field in Winnipeg. But his father had never made the specific request. And he was related only by marriage, they had said.

Philip's mind was jolted from his father as he took a closer look at the grave: The top rock was missing....

No. It was there, but it lay with its damp, unbleached side up, next to the pile. Philip forgot about the straps cutting into his shoulders. What had happened?! It looked as if someone had pulled the rock right off. He tried to think of another explanation. Maybe the spring thaw had done it. Maybe the old man had come back. But he remembered coming up here when they had first arrived for the summer, no more than five or six days ago.

Grandpa Frederick was the only one left who never got down on him, never criticized. Grandpa Frederick didn't deserve this. The grandson stood dumbfounded at the mysteriously placed rock. He tried for a moment to blame his mother, but he knew that even she would never do such a thing, especially to her own father. Although sure somehow that this problem was somehow even more serious than it seemed, he made himself move on.

S I X

Immovable Stone

Philip dumped the sand into the hole. Just needed one more bag of it. Then he could get away with topping it off with leaves and twigs.

Through the oak branches, the surface of the lake seemed now to be charging steadily eastward. Philip pictured all the water and fish in the lake migrating toward the swamp behind the east end of the island, then flying off some hidden waterfall. The waves moved with unstoppable force, the odd one capped with white. The second day of the famed 'Three Day Blow.' He remembered playing in the waves with his father. How they had tried to stand on the submerged air mattress together for as long as possible, always going for the record. Eight seconds. Nine. But the waves and buoyancy always prevailed. And falling off was really the best part. The game lasted for hours on the hottest days.

Philip looked at his watch: 1:15 pm. He felt hungry, but wanted to get the job done as soon as possible. He looked at the hole again and coaxed himself to continue. Just one more bag.

Then came his mother's voice. Singing. She was walking down the path, almost on top of him. Flustered, his head swung around quickly, his mind straining to find a way out. He looked across the brush and caught sight of her fast-moving bright pink bathing suit through the branches. She sang that stupid song about a kiss just being a kiss. He hated that hundred-year-old song, although he had never heard the real thing. He dropped to the ground, on his stomach, with his face uncomfortably close to the hole. Then rolled away from it onto his back. Her song went shrill and rose to a scream as she must have put her foot into the water. That shriek always annoyed Philip. She knew how cold it was going to feel, so how could she be surprised? Another yelp helped him map out exactly where she was. He raised his head slowly to look again for the best escape route. Or just lie there and wait.... But what if today was the day she decided to reminisce and look around. Even just the shovel was too obvious a sign of what he had done.

Had to get out before he was caught. And with the shovel. The oak branches were too sparse to risk getting up to sneak away through the brush, the route of last night's dream. He sat up cautiously, swivelled around on his bum, and his eyes located his means of escape. Just to the west of the mound area was a little drop-off which led to another clearing below. From the lower clearing he could get to the west shore path which would take him back to the house without incident.

He raised his head slowly to check for his mother, and dropped quickly when he found her head facing the shore from the large swell. He grabbed the shovel and his bag and shoved them toward the drop-off. A bead of sweat rolled down his forehead as he turned onto his hands and knees. Then another shriek came. After an initial start, he realized she must have slipped a bit while getting out. No time left! Philip scurried across the ground and half-jumped, half-rolled over the edge.

The shovel struck the side of the miniature cliff as he landed. He winced at the sound as he pulled himself off the ground on the lower level. Safe, except for the noise. He turned around slowly to see if his mother had heard the sound. Through a crevice he could see her head cocked as if to listen— she must have heard it! But she bent down to dry her legs, unconcerned.

The wind! It must have drowned out most of the sound! Or blown it away. He stood up carefully, checking his height and visibility, and walked across the pine needle bed toward the din of crashing waves on the west shore. He smiled with satisfaction for a moment. A close call. He had made his escape. For a moment he wondered how angry she would be if she did find out what was happening. She had told him not to touch the mound and now he had. He had to assume the act was unforgivable. He pushed through the layer of young pines that hid the old play area from the west path. A thorn lodged itself in Philip's thigh as he passed through the last layer of brush. He made his way through the rest of the bush layer very carefully, holding back the thorny branches between his fingers. When he got through the treacherous wall, he stopped and looked back. Soon this will all be over. He sighed, and walked back to the house, shovel in hand.

Philip did his best to ignore the crash of the waves on the shore next to him on the way up to the house. This west shoreline defied the years of pounding water with small but stubborn vertical cliffs. All rock on the island slanted eastward. Pieces lay like huge fallen dominoes, toppled and carved by glaciers millions of years ago. Or maybe an east wind had blown the slabs over once upon a time. Today's noise would surely overcome a scream. Or the clang of a shovel. Every few waves came one of particular power, cresting just before the shore, splashing high, making hollow clunking noises in the rocky pockets. The waves could easily overpower a man or boy on an air mattress, but only slowly wear down this island. He didn't like to swim in the big waves anymore. Without his dad it wasn't fun, didn't even feel safe.

Philip shook his head to snap out of this daze, eyes glued to the meeting of water and rock. Remembered now his mother was already out of the water and might well be on her way up to the house by now. He sped around to the north end of the house to avoid the merger with the regular Swimming Rock path. Up the step to the front door and down the other side, up the rock step which rumbled beneath his weight, and turned left off the path to the sleeping cabin.

This more ratty-looking cabin was mostly used as a tool shed, but had been a guesthouse in the days when more people stayed at the island. It hadn't been used for its title in the last few years. He was sure no one visited anymore because his father was gone. Everyone loved him. Philip looked over his shoulder again to make sure his mother was not watching him from the main house, then stepped inside the cabin. It was dark, shutters down. Dad, Uncle Pete and Grandpa Frederick had built it in anticipation of a continually expanding family. But they had never properly finished the inside. Now it smelled of a mothball overdose. No doubt his mother's doing. No wonder no one sleeps in here! He pictured all his relatives nodding in agreement at the disgusting smell of the cabin and the disagreeable nature of his mother. He laughed to himself. Pete and his family, who rightfully owned half the island, had moved all the way out to B.C. to get away!

To his left, a mini-stove and fridge, a double bed, an old dresser with a tin kettle sitting alone on top, a wall-full of books. On the right workshop side, cobwebs held the tools on their hooks and shelves. In the corner, picks, spades and handsaws leaned against the wall. Now the shovel rejoined them. He hoped he would never have to deal with it again. Philip turned and left the cabin, closing the door behind him. All he needed to do now was haul one more bag of sand....

He marched down to the beach, filled his bag, trying not to be overzealous, then began his trek toward Blueberry Point. Turned at the new rowboat grave path, like the last time. It had saved him time and effort, plus he felt a need to see Frederick Caplan's grave again. Wanted to take a closer look at what had been done. He pushed through the branches on his way toward the damp rock face he had learned to scale.

Brant from across the bay used to come over and the two of them would climb miniature cliffs all over the island. Brant lived in Toronto and stayed at the lake for at least a month every year. They had got along so well. Both liked to play pretend games in the woods. Their favourite was "The Terminator." The woods were the battleground for Arnold Schwarzenegger and the slippery Terminator II, stalking each other with driftwood pistols. But Brant didn't come over anymore. The last time he did, Philip couldn't look him in the eye. Philip could still remember when Brant had asked about his school year and about coming over for lunch almost exactly a year ago. He had just stood on the dock like a statue. Couldn't seem to answer, and especially a question which probed right to the heart of everything. Brant had probably felt unwanted, and told Philip he would see him later. He had hopped into his fishing boat and sped away from the island. That was early last summer, and he hadn't been back. Philip knew better than to tell himself it was Brant's loss.

With his mind back in the moment, he could spot the footholds where his shoes had scraped off the moss during his first climb. He carefully grabbed the same ledges and cracks as last time, and hoisted himself up the rock to the higher level. The brightness of the sunlight after being in the wild garden's shelter blinded him momentarily. Then he lifted his eyes to see that two more of Grandfather's gravestones had been toppled!

More! Now three stones lay dark and earthy side-up next to the rest of the grave, one covered with ants and their white eggs. The cavity in the grave exposed a silver box where Grandpa Frederick's ashes must have been kept. The box lay open and empty now.

It had only been an hour since he had passed through here the first time.

SEVEN

Not Done

Without thinking any further about how this might have happened, Philip began frantically trying to right the gravestones. He fought with their weight unsuccessfully, managing only to roll them back to the base of the grave. He brushed a layer of damp earth and white eggs off the top of one rock with a sweep of his hand. At least he had the box closed and out of sight now, wedged between the remaining rocks. He was pretty sure that his mother never visited the grave, so she would never know.

No real indignation at this act of vandalism raged in him—he was far too frightened and confused. What were the odds of two graves on one island being upset in less than two days? And one of them twice! He stumbled down the south hill from the grave and hurried around the island to the mound. Was this someone's idea of a joke? He filled in the rest of the hole and covered the disturbed ground and hijacked sand with pulled long grass and fallen white pine branches. The strange tomb was sealed, repaired. He could rest easy, he decided.

That night he turned and woke to find he was no longer on the mattress. Under him was a cold, alien hardness. A claustrophobic, metallic sense and sound. He was somehow surrounded. His adjusting eyes widened with shock at the painted grey floor of a canoe startlingly close to his face. And the spider webs and grains of sand along the wall in front of him were clearer to him than he would have expected. He lay on his side. The echoing, metallic chime of the thin aluminium sheet separating him from the water rang in his ears. The sun blinded him for a moment as he rolled onto his back, and his eyes slowly established a thick black line obstructing his vision of sky. He reached out quickly and jammed his thumb on the thwart that seemed to be shifting above him. Only then did he put the movement together with the ringing metal to realize he was afloat. He tried to sit up quickly, but hit his head on the forgotten thwart. The canoe lurched to one side, then returned to normal. Minutes seemed to pass as he tried to figure out how to free himself from this cage. He squirmed on his heels and shoulder blades toward the stern of the canoe, then cleared the thwart with his head.

Sitting upright, the confused boy scanned his surroundings and quickly recognized the familiar lichen-covered cliffs just behind the island. But there was something wrong. He waited for an answer. The cliffs looked shorter. Smaller? Watched the island shoreline as it passed by, but found no comfort in it. As the canoe swept past the south-east tip of the island, he absorbed its wicked clip. But he was not paddling.... He had no paddle. No wind, no waves. Felt like he was being pulled along from beneath by some sea creature. He looked over the edge of the canoe at the swirling around the hull. A current!

Once he had uncovered the first part of the mystery, he stumbled on the next: the water level was at least six feet above normal. Most of the island's familiar sloped bedrock shores were submerged. Now it was lake meeting directly with the woods. Didn't make sense. He wondered what his mother would have said if she had seen the water this high. It was at path-level at some points! A cloud of brown and debris covering the water's surface told of the swallowed earth below. The canoe swung neatly around the points of land, hugging the south shore now. The water rushed along the shoreline and enveloped the trunks of trees. The pace seemed only to increase. The water lapped in a quick rhythm against the canoe, and the wake swished as it folded behind.

In the distance Philip could see something else floating. Maybe a log. Wherever it went, he supposed he would follow. The log was way out in the open bay toward Gleason's Island. He looked for the rock islands off Swimming Rock and laughed at how the high water made them so wimpy, almost erasing one completely. Once nicknamed the 'Whales' because of their size and shape, they barely looked like fish now. Philip's eyes moved over to the log again. But it was closer to him now than before! Then his ear twitched at the sound of rushing water coming from a submerged Swimming Rock, just a bit further. He blinked hard three times, concentrating on the impossible sound. Sounded like white-water almost. Powerful, like a waterfall. Philip squirmed uncomfortably at his total lack of control. The log came closer, and both he and it seemed to be heading for the infamous white pine that marked the mound.

Philip realized now exactly where he was heading and why, in some strange way. The canoe, the log, as well as bits of weed and the rotting carcass of a dead fish closed in on the landmark. The whole lake was being sucked in that direction. Philip considered jumping ship for a moment, but he knew it was far too late. He stood up unsteadily as he approached the mound. A whirlpool swirled madly where the hole had been. He saw the log approach the pool and disappear in an instant. Should have been paddling the other way with his hands all this time! His skin burned beneath the sun and he felt dizzy. When the canoe was only feet from the whirling, Philip reached out for the old oak branches, but they only crumbled in his hands. In a mad panic, he ran and jumped off the opposite end of the canoe. He swam frantically, but he knew everything was going down. Everything.

But then the water became warmer. Philip reached down to find he had peed his bed. "Damn," he said out loud and wiped the sweat from his face. He hadn't sealed that hole in the ground at all.

EIGHT

Calling a Spade a Spade

Philip woke again later to his mother's hysterical shrieking. The night's dream came to him vividly as his eyes flipped open. Then the memory of wetting his bed, and now the cold. The smell overpowered him as he lifted the blankets to take a look. Sleeping in my own piss. He shook his head.

"Philip! Philip! Help me!"

He realized that this might be some kind of emergency. Swung his legs out onto the floor and stripped off his soaked underwear. He stood up and grabbed his swimsuit from the rafter above.

"Philip!" His mother again, sounding terrified.

His heart pounded. She was being sucked down last night's whirlpool! Or maybe he had been too mean to her and she had gone and slit her wrists. He knew the balance was delicate, trying to keep the wall up between them. A shot of guilt washed through him briefly. But he stopped for a moment after tying his shoes. Crossed his arms on his knees. It would be simpler to stay inside and let his mother get sucked down than to go outside and try to save her. Sometimes it was better not to start something if it was going to be hard to do. A small explosion and another shriek! He swallowed hard and headed for the north end of the house.

His skinny legs buckled when he saw the flames through the screen door. He stood inside for a moment, staring into the heart of the fire. The old tool shed: a great inferno of brittle old wood and metal tools falling from demolished shelves onto the ground. Jane Reddy stood ten feet from the fire with her forearm shielding her eyes. She held an empty bucket in her other hand. A fire extinguisher lay on the ground next to her feet. Philip opened the door and stood on the step.

"Oh, Philip! There you are." She rushed toward him. "You must go over to the McGinnises' to get help." She looked frantically back and up at the flames reaching towards the spruce tree above.

Philip stood mesmerized.

"Now!"

Aware now of the request, but sure he was not the man for the job, he continued to stare into the fire. It was much better if she went and he stayed here. He was too embarrassed to go to the McGinnises' anytime, but today he simply couldn't go.

"Philip!"

Just stay put, he coached himself.

Jane groaned in frustration. Knew he couldn't do it. She brushed by her son, ducked into the house to grab a lifejacket and the keys to the power-boat. Philip stood like a stone. Then the door slammed and Jane called, "Don't get too close. And fill that bucket again!" as she hurried away and down to the boats.

But Philip was lost in the flames. They seemed to dance. It was an angry dance, crackling and loud. The wind flirted with it. Powerful. One by one, the old asphalt shingles and two-by-fours toppled, blackened and weak. It had to have been burning a good while already. He picked up the bucket, but got no further toward helping. Just stood there holding it. What could he do? Every few seconds he was sure he saw a figure in the flames. The figure was orange like the rest of the fire, but seemed to have a head and appendages, fists that raged about. The image was clear even to his naked, far-sighted eye.

Philip was too involved to be useful. It did not occur to him to wet the grass and shrubs around the shed to prevent the fire from spreading. When the last three horizontal beams fell, the fire died down considerably. The roar of a boat made him turn. His mother out on the water watching the fire from the opposite side. She stood with her hands on her hips as the boat rode the growing morning swell, day three now. She must have decided the fire was dying and not gone to get help after all. He saw from the corner of his eye that she sat back down and put her hand to her forehead. At that moment he remembered he had bailed only the canoe. His mother was probably ankle deep in water if she didn't have the bilge working overtime. A moment later the boat swung back around toward the beach. Philip still watched from the step, not having moved since his mother left him there. By the time Jane returned to the house, there was nothing left to burn. A paper-thin platform with eight black, crumbling studs pointed stupidly up into the air. A pile of smouldering debris. Tools in there somewhere.

"It's like the shed was never here," Philip said out loud.

His mother came up behind him, lay her hand on his shoulder. "You okay?" She gave him a moment to respond, which he left blank. "I'm sorry if I scared you. I was sure it was going to spread. I was scared. Your father could have—" She looked back awkwardly at the smoking ruins, trying to pretend not to have mentioned him.

Philip felt her stop short. He felt like running. Felt like crying. But stood stoically as ever.

She looked at him again. "Philip, I know there are some kids around here that you don't get along with.... You don't think they would do...something like this, do you?"

"No!" he barked and pushed her away. He spun around, stepped inside and closed the door behind him. They couldn't possibly have hated him that much. Was it even possible to hate someone that much? But maybe they could. Or maybe it was somebody mad at her. He stormed to his room and the stench of old urine. Forget her!

He yanked the soaked sheets off the bed and rolled them into a ball. How dare she hint that he was somehow even indirectly responsible for this! Pulled fresh sheets from the cupboard and laid them on the top bunk. The mattress had to dry. He hadn't made any kids set the shed on fire! He took the ball of sheets to the north end of the house and threw it in the corner, next to the washing machine.

But he knew somehow the fire led back to him. He had done something to provoke it.

When he was about to leave the room, he stopped, squeezed the bridge of his nose between his thumb and forefinger, and went back to pick up the sheets, furious with himself, his mother, everything. She shouldn't wash them. She shouldn't know. She shouldn't know anything! Ever! He picked up a bar of old laundry soap and marched straight from the sink through the south door down to Swimming Rock, sheets under an arm and soap in hand.

At the water, he checked around him, glad to see the water level was back to the normal low level. As he was about to throw the sheets into the water, he remembered how close he was to the mound. With a brief hostile glare in its direction, he picked up the soap and climbed up the escarpment at the opposite end of the rock and walked east along the shore to find a better spot. It was still early. By the sun's level, maybe 8 am.

Who would set fire to a tool shed this early in the morning? Who would do it at all? Philip's mind dwelled on the fire as he worked his way along the same seldom-used path he had broken in on his sand trips yesterday. There was a logical link he was missing. He tried to jump over the thistle patch where this path met the regular one and struck his foot on a hidden stump. The pain set in a moment later, but he gritted his teeth and kept walking. Finally, he found a point which was far enough from the mound and flat enough that he could get to the water. He skidded down a dusty bank to the rock and laid the sheets down. He picked up each piece and examined it closely. Right up to his face. The pillowcase was okay, but both sheets needed work. He dropped the bottom sheet into the water and a balloon formed. He pushed it under and attacked parts of the sheet with the soap. He wasn't sure what he was doing, but rubbed the sheet hard with the bar. Wondered for a moment how he would dry them afterwards…. The rubbing took on rhythms. In his mind, he followed a beat that went with the sound. Sometimes the rhythm changed, but it seemed to come from inside him, yet somehow was out of his control. The rhythm was ever building even as it changed. It grew to a crowd of whispers. Words came, but he couldn't pick them out. An unidentified phrase hid amongst the whispers, rubbing, and swishing water.

It was something or other and "bobber." Philip laughed to himself. Rhythms often came to him in his drawings, especially when he would shade or use charcoal. But no drawing had ever produced words this clearly. He laughed out loud this time and stopped his work.

Then Philip heard clearly, in a harsh whisper, "Grave Robber!"

He didn't need to hear it again to know it was real. He leaped up in a panic. Turned to check for someone behind him, up along the path. Or a kid in a boat. Anybody. His hand clutched the soap and his eyes squeezed tightly shut. The soap shot out of his trembling fist onto the sloped edge of the rock. The sheet lay in the water, holding another large air pocket. Nothing moved. The whole world stopped for a moment. No one was even present to say the words he had heard! The soap slid off the rock into the water. It sank straight to the bottom and lay there like an old wreck. The more he tried for control, the more things seemed to slip away, to operate on some other level. He looked down at the soap. Should he go in and get it? It couldn't be more than three feet deep. He swore under his breath and dragged the sheet from the water. He felt like a piss-soaked sheet himself.

Wrung it out as best as he could, soaking his Velcro shoes. Clutched it to his chest. Then picked up the other sheet and pillowcase.

Grave Robber. The truth in the words made them even more frightening.

He stumbled back toward the house, tripping over the tangle of wet sheets that kept slipping from underneath his arm. The awkward twist of fabric was one more thing he didn't want to think about. He spotted a rotten log in the brush a few metres off the path. Crashed through a tangle of balsam branches and tried to lift it up. The moss-covered log disintegrated in his grip. He kicked a hole beneath it and jammed the sheets into the ground. Then threw odd pieces of the log on top to hide the white cotton. From the path, he looked back. He could barely see the sheets. Good enough.

His mother made him a large bacon and egg breakfast when he returned to the cottage. Trying to win him back, but with little success. He was hungry though, so he ate. It was almost eleven and he had been up since 7:30. There was no more discussion of the fire. Maybe it never happened. The tool shed simply no longer existed. The stuff in there had been useless: an old rusty push-lawnmower, a pair of ancient wooden cross-country skis, the old set of tools, some outdated steel gas cans.... It was a good thing his mother had done all that organizing last summer, putting all the current and gardening tools in the sleeping cabin shed. Otherwise she would have gone ballistic.

Mother and child ate and tried to move on.

But the boy could not.

After breakfast he walked out to the north point where a ten-foot-high cliff faced the open lake. It was a favourite place on this island. He had spent many hours on that point, thinking or drawing. It brought him peace, maybe because it had been his father's perch. But the point could do nothing to calm him now.

The fire. The gravestones. He could almost imagine Rupert doing something like this. But how would he even know about the grave? And the whisper.... Who would have called him a grave robber except.... Impossible, he told himself. He didn't want to think about it. Still, it could be Rupert. If it was, he had gone way too far. Then it struck Philip that even the skull could be a plant. All of this might be some awful trick. Maybe even his mother knew about it. That was doubtful. But some kids could be behind it all. He had to hope so. If it was a trick, he wanted to be certain.

He sat at the edge of the cliff with his head down, eyes passively watching the water crash below. The final day of the blow played with his thin wisps of hair. Played with his head. He scraped at the bedrock beside him with a piece of bark he had found. Watched it wear down. The rubbing reminded him of the rhythm with the soap. And the whisper. He stopped. Crap! That soap was still in the lake! He had hoped he could lull himself into one of his pleasant daydreams in his familiar seat. Maybe the one about Alissa Parker and her C-cup bra.... But concentration was elusive. There was finally something to keep his attention in the here and now, however horrid. He threw the shred of bark off the cliff in frustration. Even it mocked him as it swung back around with the wind and landed behind him.

This was doing him no good. He walked angrily back up to the house, swearing to himself. Went into his room and pulled the old, green curtain closed behind him. The bed was made. It must have been his mother. But on his pillow was a book, opened, facedown.

He strained to read the title: *Soul Catcher*, by Frank Herbert. He didn't recognize it. He picked it up and tossed it on his dresser. Lay down and closed his tired eyes.

"White Devil!"

The harsh whisper again. At first Philip opened his eyes and thought he must have said it himself. But he had done no such thing. The link was suddenly too clear. He lay on his lower berth, eyes wide, paralyzed.

NINE

The Chase

The sound of gunfire was deafening and the smell of powder strong. Women and children ran screaming past Philip as he crouched on the ground. The forest was densely wooded and the terrain rocky, familiar yet not quite. Old leaves carpeted a treacherous forest floor, hiding sticks and holes that would trip a careless foot. All around him people seemed to be running aimlessly, screaming. They wore leather skirts and furs, even the men. Philip felt a stick poke into his bare foot and looked down to find he was completely naked. And he could see perfectly.

One of the bronze-skinned men stopped on his way past him. His eyes were almost black. Troubled, but strong. He looked at Philip with pity for a moment and seemed ready to carry him away from whatever he himself was running. But he glanced over his shoulder and pressed on. Philip suddenly missed the sounds the forest was supposed to make—the whitethroat, the crows, leaves whispering in the wind. Just the thunder of footsteps and din of breaking twigs all around him. Slowly, there seemed to be more order to the chaos—everybody was running in the same direction. He watched as these people faded out of sight between the trees in the distance. He swivelled around in his crouched position and saw fully-dressed men approaching with guns. They seemed to be white. Through the trees he could see sudden bright flashes, puffs of smoke followed by great echoing explosions. More and more often. Each one louder than the last. Without thinking again, he jumped up and followed the darker-skinned people.

He ran as fast as he could. His feet found unexpected logs and dark wet holes, but he felt this run was for his life and did not slow down. He followed the shadows of the people, but never caught more than a glimpse through the trees. Philip looked over his shoulder as he ran and tripped over a fallen sapling. Fell on his side and his cheekbone bounced solidly on a rock. The pain shot through his body and his head seemed to spin. His groan cut short as a woman who had fallen behind the others made eye-contact with him as she passed with a carefully-held bundle in her arms. She averted her eyes and scampered off.

She was definitely an Indian, an American Indian. He guessed they all were now that he had had a moment to absorb where he might be and what was happening. He had seen more of them than he had liked in his life, usually drunk downtown in Winnipeg along Portage or around Langside and Broadway. But she seemed somehow different. Beautiful. Most of the ones he had seen were ugly to him. But even the man who had stopped was different than the faces he had seen so often in Winnipeg or Kenora.

The gunshots grew louder. Philip pulled himself off the ground and staggered onward, cheek burning. He didn't know why he was running except that guns made men dangerous. Instinct. He was barely conscious of his nakedness except for the blood running down his hip from his fall. As he ran faster, he could see the quick-footed woman ahead of him. Her feet moved nimbly atop the rocks and holes up an incline. Every one of his own steps was an adventure. He would never catch up to her. Then there was a shot louder than the rest. It was so loud that Philip thought he had been shot until he saw the woman ahead of him facedown on the ground. He kept his course in her direction, not thinking of anything but helping her. Then he was upon her. Somehow that wild shot had made it between the trees to strike her squarely in the back of the head. Blood. He had never seen so much of it up close. Then Philip's eyes were drawn to something a few paces ahead of the woman. A baby, its head had been smashed open on a rock like a melon. Oh, no! She must have let go of it when the bullet hit her. Only its tiny right-hand fingers were unstained by blood.

The misplaced white boy suddenly felt ill. He had never seen anything like this. It had to be a dream. But there was another shot and he turned to see a man in some sort of dirty uniform running toward him with a strange looking gun. The man ran clumsily in big boots. Philip scampered off in the direction he thought he remembered. But he saw no more Indians. Just prayed he would find them and that they knew a way out of this. His body was numb to all its injuries and the abuse against the soles of his feet. He pushed it onward at its maximum speed.

This had better be another dream, but I'm not waiting around to find out.

TEN

Blood for Blood

"I can't believe the shed burned down!" Jane exclaimed to no one in particular, still struggling with the puzzle. She sipped her wine and tilted her head. The setting sun streamed in the window behind Philip into her eyes. She always sat there squinting, but never said anything. She must have enjoyed it or was too stupid to do anything about it.

But the shed being reduced to ashes seemed like old news to Philip, used to sinister events and prepared for more. He had been ready all day.

"When do we get to leave this place?" he asked abruptly. He didn't look up from his beans and wieners, avoiding any harsh glare she might send him. His spoon flipped and dragged his wieners around the bowl.

Jane pushed air through her nose at length and closed her eyes in disgust. Her tongue clicked to start. The words came out hard and sharp. "Philip, we just got here! We're not leaving until at least August 20th." Her tone softened. "You've got more than a month and a half left. If we didn't come here, I'd have no break at all, you know." She delicately cut another piece of her perfectly cooked filet of pickerel that her son refused to touch. With her mouthful almost gone, she added, "And what would you do back home? You think you're bored now? Ha!" Chewing. "Summer in Thunder Bay would definitely be a version of hell, however tame."

Apparently she didn't like their new home either. They had made the move last June, just before they came out to the lake for a summer that was even worse than this one. Jane had said Lakehead University had a job with something called "tenure track," and this somehow made it better than the one at the University of Manitoba or back when she used to teach high school. Philip could barely remember her teaching high school; she had been

48

"working on her doctorate" since he was in grade two or something. When they moved, it was all about the job. Philip was sure it was more like trying to forget and start over. Maybe it was both. Whatever it was, it was no good. She swallowed the last bit. "If we were there, you'd wish you were here. Trust me." She sighed and took in a forkful of rice as Philip churned his full bowl with a crooked expression. Then she half exploded. "Philip!" Calmed herself before saying more. "When are you going to snap out of this...funk? I'm going absolutely crazy over here! Please, please try to enjoy this place. You used to see its magic. Please try. For me!" She stopped. Rethought her last words.

Yeah, right. For you!

Definitely a mistake.

Philip acted as if he didn't know what she was talking about, screwing up his eyes and eyebrows. Snap out of what?! She was so boring. And even when she was right, it was all crap. Didn't help him at all.

After the meal, Philip decided to take a walk around the island by himself. He was on edge about hearing the whispers again, but had to get out. He grabbed his glasses from his place at the table. Brought his sketchpad and pencil with him in case he felt in the mood. As he held the materials in his hand again, he realized he hadn't touched them in days, since before the dig. Before then, drawing had been all that kept him sane, even if nothing much came of it. His sketchbook was filled with unfinished work. Half of the pages had been torn out and thrown away. His skills were ever improving, but as with everything else, something had been missing for quite a while now. Nothing was good enough to finish. Each drawing either bored or bothered him instead of inspiring him. Until he ended it. But he drew beautiful lines. He drew trees, animals, but mostly cartoon superheroes. Daredevil. Wolverine. Mercury—his own creation. But the beauty of what he drew eluded him—it was just shading and contour. He kept his work to himself, but his new art teacher Mrs. Wright back in Thunder Bay knew what he could do.

He walked past the beach in the fading light where the canoe, powerboat, and fishing boat waited to be used, the last of which was still filled with water. He was surprised that his mother hadn't bitched at him about it yet, especially after taking the big boat out that morning. She must have run the bilge while she was out there. Out on the high, rounded rock, he laid down his pad and sat down, looked out over the water. Blueberry Point was the north-east tip of the island. From it he could see into the swamp bay on the east shore and almost all the way around to the great expanse of water in the west. Directly in front of him, Grouse Inlet, where his dad said people with money put cottages on top of swamp, hid itself behind a point of land. The water was calming down for the night. He had heard that the inlet had once been a great fishing spot for the Indians, but the last thirty years had seen fewer and fewer native boats in and out of there. In his own experience, especially on the weekends, the inlet just roared with powerboat life and water-skiers scraping dangerously close to the shore. And the multiplying seadooers his mother had cursed the past few years. He wished he had one. Ride it full speed out of here until he ran out of gas!

But he hadn't seen one Indian on the lake that he could remember. They were all drunk in Kenora. Dirty and drunk. Philip was glad they never came close to the island. He knew his mother thought they were pretty gross too. His father couldn't have had much use for them either, although he couldn't remember him saying anything much about it.

The eyes of the Indian woman from his dream flashed at him. They were glazed and open too wide. Her head bled dark from a large wound and her baby lay smashed on the ground in front of her.

He shook his head to make it go away, but the gruesome image stuck with him. He had wondered if the dream was about Indians, but now he was sure. The Indian dream was worse than the ones that had come before. And these Indians were certainly not drunk or lazy. Somehow not even dirty.

Overwhelmed by the vision, he stretched back onto the rock and stared up at the wasps working the young white pine above, hoping to take his mind off the dream. But images still buzzed around him. He reared back up, snuck on his glasses, picked up his pad, and selected a stump and rock scene to sketch. Anything to stop his mind's wanderings. He had used drawing to stop his father's face from haunting him. He had used it to quell the boredom in Thunder Bay and here. It was just as necessary now. His steady hand brought the stump to life on the paper. The perspective was perfect—this was Philip's gift. Still enough light to draw the blueberry bush next to the rock, but his concentration failed him. And the scale screwed itself up. He tried frantically to erase the imperfections. But the dirty eraser just smudged it all. The better one was back at the house. Maybe he was just out of practice. He hadn't drawn in a few days, but he couldn't remember when he had been this off. A total loss of control, like his brain had left him to do something else.

A voice intruded.

This time it was more than just a curse. A harsh whispering grew ually louder, but the words remained indecipherable. Articulated c' not in English....

He tried to drown them out by humming. He swallowed ' tried to draw again. His pencil slid across the paper aimlessly his bush.

He stopped his humming abruptly. He felt a gust ̣ ̣ ̣ ̣ not noticed before, much cooler than the air had been. A ̣ ̣ ̣ age! He shivered. The vicious voice seemed to be swearing at ' ̣ ̣ ̣ge tongue. Nothing he recognized. Definitely not Italian or F ̣ ̣ German. The boy's eyes widened and his brows rose. He felt a tingle ̣ nose. The fear was real now. His frantically clenched pencil. Drew anything just to keep him from being swept away. Trees, people, animals all over the page. Pressed hard, used grinding strokes to drown out the whisper. Then it came again. Keep drawing, he told himself. A tear dropped onto the page. He brushed it away, smearing a little boy's face.

Then it all stopped and he heard in perfect English, "You are a coward and a fool."

At that, Philip froze. He was a coward. He knew it. A burst of teary laughter pushed up through his throat, grabbing at the possibility that he had whispered the words himself. He let his pad drop from his knee to the ground. Maybe I'm just crazy, he thought. Maybe I just need help....

He could dismiss it all if he tried hard enough. A year and a half of solitude and mourning were finally taking their toll. He should have expected this. Anyone would be bound to crack sooner or later. He inhaled and held his breath for a moment, ready for something he felt was coming.

No longer a whisper now, it came: "This is real. Make no mistake. You are the White Devil. You will pay for your crimes."

Philip shrieked and ran down the path from the point. Crimes? His pad and all the world drawn on it lay facedown in a mix of tears, pine needles, and earth. Abandoned, like the soap. He nearly fell off the path as he tore down the hill into the surprising darkness of the woods. No thought as to where he was going. Reckless, oblivious to the roots and rocks underfoot. At the opening to the beach, he changed course with a cut to the right. Ran out to the end of the dock and leaped into the water. He landed in the cold, cloudy water up to his waist. The bay was still churned up from the heavy wind and looked even darker now as the day's light faded. His shoes eased themselves down into the clay bottom. His soaked t-shirt stuck to his body. His lenses fogged. Fists clenched in frustration, he held in the next cry. Wished the water would just wash it all away.

Philip stood in the water looking across to the inlet until shivers took him. He was not sure whether he was crying until he tasted the salt rolling into his mouth. His bottom lip trembled. His head bowed in defeat. Finally, the cold was too much and he pried himself from the clinging bottom. Must have been in there twenty minutes! Back out on the beach, he looked down at his corduroy pants, gripping him heavily, and let out a groan. How would he explain this to his mother? He laughed at himself for worrying about something so inconsequential. How could she compare to the hellish voice chasing him around the island?!

On his way up the path, Philip heard more insults, but none as clear as before. He could barely hear them because the words overlapped in the darkness, but he knew the content. Then he heard himself say out loud, "This island is haunted." A deep shiver shot through him as his words soaked in. A terrible discovery. He hoped again that he had gone mad. He would be glad to know it now.

As he approached the house, he heard his mother in the kitchen, so he went around the house and tried to sneak in the south door. He carefully opened the screen door and turned to let it close without the usual slam. As he turned around again to go his room, he found his mother staring at him from the kitchen doorway.

"What the—?" she gasped. "Look at you! Are you okay?"

Her hands left her widening hips as she looked at him in shock. He couldn't help but notice how pale she looked without her usual thick layer of make-up.

"What happened?" She moved toward him and reached out to stroke his matted hair.

He let her touch, but only long enough to think of an answer. "I slipped on a wet rock." He pulled back further and looked down at the puddle forming at his feet. His lame excuse made him cringe. But the brief hand on his head had felt good.

Jane smiled at him. "Well, get changed. We'll hang your pants up by the fire." As he dripped across to his room, Philip heard her chuckle to herself. "And I'll start bailing the house."

He closed the curtain behind him and took off his cold, wet clothes. He dried himself and put on a clean pair of underwear.

"Ready, Reddy?" Jane asked, trying too hard to be cheery, her hand signalling in through the curtain for his wet clothes. "Speaking of bailing, you didn't get very far the other day, did you?"

Philip should have known she wouldn't let that slide too long, but appreciated her not freaking out on him about boat safety or taking responsibility. Annoyed, but aware it could have been worse. "It's called a bilge pump. You flick a switch," he mumbled.

He saw his mother's servant stance through the curtain with the full-moon overhead light behind her. Might have heard him. Not sure. No wise-crack answer. He laid his pants, t-shirt, underwear and socks on her waiting arm. Caught the balled falling sock, pulled it to full length and laid it carefully on top of the shaky pile. Then watched her silhouette stride out in the living room, trying to organize the lump he had given her. "Next time you fall in, do it in the middle of the day so I can line-dry your clothes."

Another joke, deliberately away from boats and bailing, but he chose to take it seriously. "Okay." Heard her sigh disappointedly at the wasted effort.

He sat down on his lower bunk and spread his arms out behind him to lean back. His hand touched something. A book. He fumbled to turn on the lamp, the room almost black. When he heard the click of the switch, he looked down at the book. Cleaned his glasses on the clean shirt he had put on. *Soul Catcher* again. Open, facedown. He remembered finding it a couple of days earlier and throwing it somewhere. But here it was again. He hadn't put it here. Hadn't seen it since yesterday. It was a new looking, dark yellow, soft-cover book with black trim. Most of the books in the house were old hard covers from Grandpa Frederick's time. This book must belong to his mother, but Philip did not recognize it. He closed it and took a first real look at the front cover. He slipped on his glasses. The fierce eyes of an Indian wearing a multi-coloured loincloth bored right through him. Across the Indian's chest was the shadow of an eagle or raven and some kind of bee or wasp. Philip's heart started throbbing. He flipped the book to examine the back cover. He read carefully: "The Spirit World knew him as Katsuk, the avenger, balancer of heaven and earth. Blood for blood." The boy closed his eyes and released a long breath. The coincidence was too much. The grave he had stumbled on had to be an Indian burial ground. The book slipped off his thigh back onto the bed.

Blood for blood. It stuck in his head. Revenge for his dig.

Tomorrow he had to ask his mother about the book—if she had been reading it or put it out for him. The answer would help decide what was going on. He braced himself for anything.

ELEVEN

One of Whom?

Philip hid in a thicket along the shoreline and watched as the Indians rushed their families off into canoes and out onto the lake. A moment of relief hit him when he noticed how sharp his vision was without his glasses on—another dream.... He looked down to see what he was wearing.... Not again! The full birch bark canoes floated low in the water, five or six people crowded into each one. From the flat rock point, an old woman and young man directed people to the means of escape. Philip stared as they hurried the silent serious children away. The expressions on the children's faces showed that they understood the urgency of their situation better than Philip did himself. The launched canoes disappeared quickly around a nearby island that Philip suddenly recognized as his own. The growth on it was thicker then he remembered, but the shoreline was the same. The scraggy oaks looked a little fresher. The canoes followed each other in a single-file line. The people only a few feet away from Philip were starting to panic, whispering urgently in some strange language. Just one more canoe and at least fifteen people. Once the last canoe had been filled and was off, the two leaders directed two women and four children down into the water. The leader woman led them as they waded along the shoreline and out of Philip's view. The men hid themselves behind rocks and brush near Philip. He counted nine. They were armed with rocks and heavy sticks, three with bows and arrows.

Philip didn't move. He didn't trust these or any Indians.

Then he heard the first shout: "This way!" The strange English voices came from the woods, and then came the footfalls and branch-breaking of the white men. The sound grew louder and louder until a punctuating gunshot sounded and the first man appeared on the rock. He wore dirty clothes that might once have been blue and carried what Philip would have called a musket.

His mind flashed a picture of the dead baby in the woods. Just moments ago....

The man wheeled around looking for an answer to his vanished enemy or prey. He peered across the vast body of water he had probably never seen before. A young Indian man jumped up from behind a boulder and threw a baseball-sized rock which caught the white man in the side of the head, sending him toppling over without more than a grunt. The young man yelped in celebration only to be yanked down by an apparently older, stronger man. Philip thought he could hear a few harsh, whispered words from behind the rock. The element of surprise was lost and the white men coming from the woods began shouting loudly at seeing their man facedown on the rock.

In a moment all the Indian men were up and slinging arrows and rocks at the oncoming whites. The whites fell, writhing in agony or silently crumbling like sand. But they kept appearing from the forest as if there would be no end to them. As if there was a factory producing them just out of view. And after a strong stand, the Indians were on the defensive with nowhere to run. The arrows were spent and the clubs useless as the muskets shot bloody holes in the remaining brave men. Philip wondered why they didn't just run away. All but three of the Indians fell. Stupid, but brave. Somehow admirable.

The looks on the faces of the Indians shot by the white men varied from extreme pain and anger to utter disbelief. Some lay still and open-eyed. Others thrashed about on the rock. Philip watched from his hiding place, looking out from between the fingers covering his face. One of the three remaining Indians suddenly shouted something and all three made for the water. And were gone. It was about time they gave up!

The white men seemed baffled at this sudden disappearance. Five men stood with muskets ready, looking for an emerging head. One shot, probably at bubbles. Then more silence. Nothing. They spoke amongst themselves, just out of Philip's range.

Philip pulled his hands away from his face and scanned the carnage. His eyes stopped on one Indian who was still alive. The man lay on his stomach and bled badly from his back. The face was turned towards Philip. His eyes fluttered and squeezed tightly closed every few seconds. But the man maintained eye-contact with the naked white boy through the twigs, leaves and distance that separated them. Philip thought the Indian might cry out so that Philip might be shot too. But the man just looked at Philip with an almost kind face. The eyes closed more often now and Philip realized he was watching a man die. Still could not understand why he had not been given away. If Philip had been shot, he certainly wouldn't want anyone else to escape it, especially not a dirty Indian. Maybe from that distance the man thought Philip was one of his own. Philip looked into the man's eyes and ignored the rest of the scene. The eyes squinted completely shut for an instant and there was a great thud and a spray of red. Philip adjusted his gaze and saw that a white man had slammed the Indian's head with a thick piece of beaver wood.

"So you'd hit us wit' one of these, eh?" The hairy-faced man stood above the fading Indian. He took the Indian's hand and laid it out in a natural curled position, then smashed the hand with the club. Philip's eyes shut hard with the sickly crunch.

He felt sympathy for the Indian, although he could not explain it.

"Still breathing!" The white man gripped the club with two hands and smashed the Indian's back and arms repeatedly, like a woodsman chopping a downed tree. The Indian made no sound. Just the sickening cracking of bones. His eyes still focused on Philip when he could manage to open them.

Maybe Philip felt the sympathy because this Indian didn't do anything wrong. Or at least nothing that he had witnessed.

He could hear the white man giggle. "This is for wat you did to my father, dirty savage. And I don't care if it wasn't you! Ha!" He spat on the Indian, who must have been dead by that point. "God-damned savages," the man mumbled as he wiped the foam from his mouth with the back of his hand. Philip felt a bit less upset knowing that the Indian had been a bad man. There was one last blow for good measure, and the Indian's eyes opened again, but the stare was blank.

Philip's gaze was interrupted when he heard from just behind him, "Aye, look at wat I found!" A toothless, bearded man pointed directly into the bramble where Philip cowered, naked. Philip shuddered and sat still as the men came over one by one.

"Yeah, look at 'im. He's scareder than a babe in a windstorm."

The men all laughed heartily.

Then another voice said, "He's not a savage."

A long silence followed. They seemed to be slightly disappointed as well as shocked.

"Let's kill 'im anyway!" A loud shout piped up from the back.

An authoritative, apparently more educated voice answered from almost directly in front of Philip. "No, he's one of us." He looked down into the boy's blue eyes. "Give him some clothes and get him out of that bush. Maybe he can tell us something. Give him some of the meat. The Indians have starved him and used him as a slave. He may well have been kidnapped from a family in the east."

Philip was relieved, although confused. He hadn't been a slave.... He couldn't believe these men would spare him just because he was white. Just because he looked like them....

Three men helped him out of the bush and gave him a scratchy fur blanket. He could hear the comments flying. Maybe there would be a reward for the boy. Maybe he was an Indian spy. Maybe he was French. But no one spoke to him. Through the rumble of shouting and talking, Philip heard again clearly, "He's just like us."

Just like them?

TWELVE

Another Puzzle

The next morning Philip lifted the covers up to check that he wasn't naked. He was relieved to find his pyjama bottoms intact and dry. He stared up at the old mattress on the bunk above him. It was just blurry enough that he knew this was real life again. He could still see that it was badly stained and bits of stuffing hung from the springs. Remembered once finding the head of a smiling elephant in the pattern of stains. Today he looked at it differently for the first time and found a powerful human face with evil, angled eyes. He squinted to change his vision to find the elephant, but the angry face remained.

At the breakfast table he didn't wait long to ask last night's burning question. He looked up at his mother. A trickle of milk ran down his chin and dripped back into his cereal bowl. "Did you read *Soul Catcher* ever?"

"Yes...I did," Jane said, as if trying to remember how the story went. "Why?" When Philip didn't answer right away, she added, "It's not a bad book. A little hokey though."

"Did you read it yesterday?" he finally asked cautiously.

"Umm...No." Her brow furrowed and she gave him that big-eyed you're crazy look. "A friend of mine taught it maybe ten years ago back at Grant Park. The kids really liked the story."

"Do we own a copy?"

"Sure. It's on a shelf somewhere in the house...." Then her eyes lit up. "Would you like to read it?"

"No." He couldn't bear the thought.

"You should read it. It would do you some good to read something for a change, especially if you're so worried about passing the time here."

"You didn't read it yesterday.... In my room?"

"No! I didn't read it yesterday, in your room!" Jane mimicked, smirking and incredulous. "I'm sorry Philip. Is there a game going on here? In a box with a fox? I don't follow—"

"One more question."

"And what would that be?"

"What's the book about?"

She looked at him almost suspiciously and strung together an answer. "Well... It's about a crazy Indian who kidnaps a boy from a summer camp. I think he's a university student, the Indian. He learns about his people's history in a course or something, and decides to kill a white child as a sort of sacrifice. It was a bit much, I thought. I really don't remember the end. But I think—"

"Thank you," Philip interrupted, and he left the table with his cereal bowl. He laid his milky bowl into the sink and walked out the north door. Stopped and stood on the step. He had left the house to escape, but it was the entire island that was the trap. And perhaps even running away from the island wouldn't solve his problem now. The ghost might follow him all the way back to Thunder Bay, all the way to school. He didn't know anything for sure, but there was nothing good in any of this. He started down the path toward the beach. Still had one boat to bail.

"Hey, asswipe!"

Philip stopped in his tracks. Not again! Why wouldn't it just go away? Stupid question.

"Hey, penis wart!"

It was something different this time. The voice sounded more normal, younger.

"You can't hide from us. I can see you through the trees."

Rupert! Philip turned and finally spied the white of a boat on the water through the thin layer of woods. Those bastards again. He breathed relief, but was annoyed that they would bother him now. He stamped his foot like an angry bull, and made his way to the shore, resolved to kill at least one of them. He charged through the brambles and stumbled out onto a spine of rock along the shoreline.

"Oooh! What's he gonna do?" Max taunted. "Hey, punk! What ya gonna do? Gonna come and get us? Gonna squirt some of your zit puss at us, little piss-ant?"

Franny giggled and passed Max her half-smoked cigarette. If she weren't so mean, she would be almost pretty. Even hot. That made Philip hate her more.

"Hey, what did you do with your canoe? Did you put it on your head and get struck by lightning?" Rupert shouted. "Or did somebody steal it?"

Rupert had asked a question Philip couldn't have answered even if he could speak. He turned toward the beach and saw only the fishing boat and powerboat moored there. His legs faltered with the initial shock and he almost fell into the lake. A suddenly huge space gaped between the powerboat and the far bedrock wall. The three kids laughed while Philip stood there looking stupid and confused. Then Franny gave Rupert a subtle nod and the boat sped off. Philip barely noticed Franny flipping her middle finger at him from the stern of the boat.

The canoe! He opted to scale the shoreline toward the beach, not wanting to lose sight of the empty space for a moment. If he got closer, it might suddenly reappear. But his eyes weren't that bad! The canoe had belonged to his dad. Maybe Max, Franny, and Rupert had stolen it, like they did his surfboard. Maybe they had told him just to rub his face in it. To see how soft he was. That was like them. The thoughts flowed freely in his mind as he crossed the last flat rocky point onto the beach. But he stopped himself.

Kids around the lake knew two things. One, Philip Reddy is a loser. Two, never cross his mother. He had heard that she had been a real bitch about the power easement from the mainland ten years ago, almost ruining it for them and the next island, and everyone around the bay knew about it. Not to mention all her fussing about the main road. It was her canoe now, not his. They wouldn't have dared ruffle the feathers of the fierce Jane Reddy. Philip was glad to eliminate some suspects, until he realized he was now left with a yet another inexplicable occurrence.

The perturbed boy walked around the inside of the bay, over the fishing boat tie, and up onto the dock. Beyond the powerboat, he spotted the long slim impression left in the sand by the keel of the missing canoe. He jumped clumsily down onto the beach again to get a closer look. The leaning balsam to which the canoe had been tied showed no sign of strain, no wear marks. Someone had to have come up on shore, untied the rope, and pushed the canoe out into the water, or towed it away. There were no noticeable footprints around, but they would be impossible to see in the dry, debris-filled sand anyway. But the canoe had been pulled too high to simply drift away.

Would a ghost want a canoe? Would a ghost want to burn down a tool shed...? Maybe just to cause trouble. When his mother found out, there would be more than enough trouble. She actually used the canoe, especially when Aunt Gladys came down from Winnipeg. He had to find it. Now.

Without another thought, Philip leaped onto and over the dock as best he could, untied the old aluminium fishing boat and started to push it down the beach into the water. It was heavy, still full of water. A junky, oil-filled swell of water swished up toward the bow, then back down again. Should have bailed it when there was time! He stepped onto the bow seat and walked down toward the stern. He squatted and started bailing at a furious pace, a good part of the water ending back in the boat because of his rush. With only an inch left in the stern, Philip threw down the plastic bail and hopped back out onto the beach.

Usually, he had a hard time with the weight, but he barely noticed it now. He jumped into the bow of the boat as it left the shore and felt it bounce once off the sandy bottom, then float free. The boat turned on its own from the jerk of his entry. He stepped over the two front seats to the stern of the boat. It moved beneath him like an escalator going the wrong way. He pumped the gas-line bulb and set the little engine on START. The old six horsepower started on the first yank. He shifted it into forward and swung around and out of the bay to the east, hedging Blueberry Point. The bow reared high with the acceleration, then slowly levelled out on top of the smooth surface. Around the east end of the island, he drove dangerously close to the back reef, completely unaware. All he could do was think of the missing canoe.

As soon as he turned to check in the back swamp, he saw the sun glint on aluminium. A rush of relief—his mother would never have to know. He drove full speed almost all the way to the back of the shallow bay. The outboard motor struggled as it wrestled with a thick patch of weeds. In a panic, he turned it off and tilted it out of the water—the propeller smothered with swamp bottom. Just as he turned around to see which direction he was gliding, the fishing boat rammed into the side of the canoe, jerking the boy forward onto the middle seat. A strong smell floated up from the snarled and muddy propeller. The fishing boat somehow ended up parallel to the canoe. Philip nearly fell overboard grabbing for the canoe's painter as the boats began to drift apart again. He had a second start when he remembered he wasn't wearing a lifejacket. He tied the canoe painter to one of the ropes from the stern of the fishing boat, searching for some knot that would hold, a quadruple half hitch, and started the engine again without clearing the weeds. Couldn't remember the knots his dad had taught him. The smell grew strong again as he shifted into forward, now towing a precariously angled canoe.

With the near disastrous problem solved, he felt a sense of pride. It wasn't so often that he saved the day. Actually, it was never.

That night at dinner, Philip smiled discreetly. Twice.

THIRTEEN

The Message

The canoe went missing twice more in the next four days. Philip found it in the marsh the first time, but the second time he attempted a search, the little outboard motor wouldn't start. He tried to sneak out with the big powerboat, but his mother saw him leave and nailed him when he returned. She reminded him of the rule that he must ask before using the boats, especially that one. Luckily, she hadn't seen him come back with the canoe trailing behind, so this third rescue of the canoe got lost in the shuffle because taking the powerboat without permission—and into the swamp, no less—was both irresponsible and inexcusable. Philip kept reminding himself that his mother's wrath was the least of his worries.

The dreams worsened. Indians shrieked in the night and Philip watched them from bushes, always naked. He saw children held under water until their little arms and legs stopped flailing about. He saw white men in uniform slowly pick apart another ill-equipped group of warriors. He saw one kind of Indian kill another. He saw the white men rape the Indian women. He saw a ghost escaping from the mound and rising up to a fire-red sky. He saw drunken Indian men with pock-marked faces gesture to him. Some offering him whiskey. Some shaking angry fists. One claiming to be an "Ojibway," not an "Indian." Another claiming to be "just a man." Philip couldn't close his eyes without these images confronting him.

After the third straight night without sleep, he could barely function at all. Even as he lay awake in the dark, visions flooded his eyes and his mind. And the insults raged on. They always came to him at the same volume, in the same harsh whisper. But they seemed louder in the darkness when his other senses were at rest and there were no distractions.

Objects fell from shelves spontaneously and doors slammed even when the wind was calm. A knife went missing. The sleeping cabin tin roof had been all but torn off in a storm and had to be fixed by contractors. Even Jane was on edge. When she went to Kenora one day for groceries, Philip almost asked to come with her despite his people-fear. Thought whatever ghost this was might just finish him off if he were alone.

Eleven days after the earth had first been broken, its digger hadn't slept in three nights, and had not slept well for a week before that. He spent the daylight hours stumbling about the island, trying to concentrate on anything, to fill up the space in his head that seemed reserved for nightmares. He tried to read, but couldn't concentrate for more than a few minutes at a time. At night he pinched himself so he wouldn't sleep. Painfully aware that this couldn't go on indefinitely.

After a sugar-laden bowl of oatmeal on the twelfth morning, Philip set out to walk around the island. His objective now was to kill time as best he could, make it pass as quickly as possible. Last night he had tried drawing again, but his eyes, let alone his mind, could no longer focus. He had already started considering faking that he was sick, to get out of here. But it had to be believable.... And serious enough to warrant the trip home, but not to the hospital.

"You are not worthy of this place. This land is stolen."

There it was again. He stopped in his tracks. The sweat of frustration beaded on his forehead. He stood straight and clenched his fists at his sides.

"Screw you!" he exploded, gesturing violently up at the sky with a thrust of his middle finger. He ran blindly down the path. Swore, grunted, screamed. "Why are you doing this to me?!" He ran until he crumbled. Then asked weakly again, "Why?" Finally, deep anger empowered him as he located a head-sized boulder on the ground and wrenched it from its resting place. He screamed, "Go to hell!" at the top of his lungs and ran to a great white pine with the rock held above his shoulder. Rammed the rock against the tree. He slammed the tree with the rock again. The sound came from inside his head again....

"Stop!"

He stopped, leaning against the tree with the rock pinned between. Starting to pant.

"Stop. You are hurting the tree."

Philip let out a gasp. The island was strangely silent in the wake of this deeper, full voice invading Philip's world. Instead of threatening, its tone was almost pleading, although still grave. Concern motivated every word. Philip waited to hear more, but nothing came. He leaned on the tree and gazed through a cluster of leafless twigs of bush and out over the water. The surface was mirror still, charting the cloud scheme above. More curious than scared, Philip tried to provoke the voice again by hitting the tree again.

"Stop!" it thundered again before he could bring the rock back to strike. Immediately, he fell backwards onto a hard protruding root. He didn't understand how it had happened. He hadn't slipped. But now he lay at the foot of the pine tree with the rock by his side. It was as if he had been thrown over.

"I told you to stop, fool! And you will stop!"

The composed and powerful voice was even clearer now. Philip just wanted to run. He squirmed on his shoulder blades, trying to escape the sight of the moist, white wound in the tree's trunk. The tree stared him down. He couldn't seem to co-ordinate himself to stand up, flailing around on his back in terror.

"This struggle is of no use. There is no way out for you."

The boy mustered a tiny voice. "Who are you?"

"Who am I?!" A short silence. "Who on earth are you? And why do you behave this way?!"

Philip's insides shook at the volume of the voice in his head. But couldn't answer. It became apparent that the voice really was inside him as the deep tones echoed against the walls of his skull.

"You think this is your island, do you not? You think you deserve to continue your miserable life in peace. You think I am the invader. You are mistaken."

Philip's ears rang with the voice's rage. He wondered how crazy he had really become and how much worse it could get. But answers came before he could ask anything.

"You have not gone mad. I am real. The only false thing here is you. And if you think life has been hard since you made your mistake twelve days and nights ago, then wait. The fine is not yet paid, pale-face. You will pay in fear, torment, and sleeplessness. You will pay in dreams. Your dreams will tell you why."

An increasingly blanched boy lay immobile.

"You did not listen when your mother told you to keep away from my grave."

Tears streamed down Philip's face and under his ears as he lay paralyzed, eyes still fixed on the tree's wound. All the pieces were falling in place, but the picture was far worse than he had thought. He wished now that it was the tree who was speaking. "You have no right," he moaned between gasps. "No right!" the voice bellowed. "No right?! You people and that word! I have no right? Ha! I never did, according to you. Nothing has changed. A fool like you playing the oppressor.... I am the right! And I will turn you inside out if I feel it is warranted. I will deal harshly with you. Your words will not help you. Be the ignorant, self-righteous being you were made to be. I shall show you truth."

"Please.... Stop.... Please. I can't," he struggled, out of breath and strength. "You're killing me."

"I may kill you, but not yet. You have not yet met with discomfort in your spoiled, pathetic life. You have no heart. A lump of white flesh. Useless. I tire of you quickly."

Philip cried loud and hard. A child's scraped-knee cry. It didn't seem he could do much else, so over-tired and overwhelmed. He squeezed his eyes shut as hard as he could until he could feel the fluid leaking out between his eyelids. The worst part was that he agreed with the voice. He knew it was all true. He was both a coward and a fool. Too familiar. Fogged lenses again.

"This is not over."

Philip could feel the presence disappear from inside him, leaving his head stretched and empty. The pine branches above him began to howl. Of the three trees in the stand, the wounded one howled loudest. It shrieked angrily and shook its craggy branches at him for his deed. The wind was not only around him, but encircling him.

That bastard Indian ghost! How could it blame him for something he did by mistake? His mind flipped for an instant to his mother killing his father. A mistake? And who would have believed there was really an Indian burial ground on the island? He was just a kid! But the wind swirled on, throwing dust in his face. His fluttering eyelids fought with the dirt, but he still lay there half-blinded. Through his clouded vision, he swore he could see the shovel and the mound again, that he was back on the other side of the island, not having unearthed this hell yet.

He looked up to the sky with a hopeful newfound faith, and pleaded to the heavens out loud, "Save me. Save me, please." He had never believed in God, but it seemed to be a good time to start. He had not tried to pray since just after the death of his father when a friend of the family made him go to church three times. Please help me. I know I haven't always respected you the way I should. But I will, if you help me. I promise. Just make this whole thing go away. Kill that Indian voice!

"Like the fickle white men of many years ago," the voice attacked. He could feel someone inside his head again, pushing things aside to make room. "Your god will not save you. No god worth anything would save you now. You deserve no salvation. None of your people ever have or will. Death is not kind to men who do no good in their given time. Some pay later. You start now. You will not sleep and you will lose your mind. And you will understand why, but you will not be able to change it. That is true pain. Seeing you crawl back to a god you despise makes me see how weak you are. Stupid child. Your god has long ago forsaken you and the rest of your people."

"Shut up! Shut up! Shut up! Shut up!" Philip could not hear another word. He pulled himself up off the ground and ran down the path toward the house. But he could not elude the spirit.

"A white man will always run unless he knows he can win."

The voice was clear, even over Philip's heavy footfalls and sporadic grunting.

"Your forefathers ran away too. They ran away or feigned friendship until they so outnumbered us that they had a chance to truly conquer. You have not fallen far from that sick tree."

Philip arrived at the house and dashed through the south door, out of breath. He walked quickly past his mother sitting in the rocking chair in the main room. He pushed through the curtain to his own bed. Let his body fall facedown onto the lower bunk. His breathing still quick and deep. The clock read 11:40 am. All of this happening before noon!

Boredom was a fond memory. After a few minutes, Philip held his breath for a moment to listen....

"I am still here. And I have you."

Philip closed his eyes, but not to sleep. He just wanted to hide for a few moments.

Then he heard his mother's voice through the curtain. "You all right, Philip?"

He pondered her question. It seemed a cruel thing to ask at that moment. He wondered about telling his mother the whole story. Maybe it had gone so far that he should. Then they might actually leave the island earlier. But she would never believe it. And he couldn't blame her either.

Even with the shed fire and the roof incident, an explanation like this would still seem crazy. She would probably just think he was even more disturbed than she already did. He did not need any more friction with her.

"Yeah, I'm fine," he answered after a pause that lasted far too long. "I'm okay," he lied, "I just finished running, that's all."

"Running," his mother repeated in disbelief. She walked to the kitchen over creaking floorboards, calling over her shoulder, "Lunch in twenty minutes?"

"'kay." Philip turned onto his back and looked above him through the screen at the upside-down happy blue sky. He stared at the sky for twenty minutes, avoiding the angry face in the mattress above. He thought back to what the voice had promised. 'I may kill you, but not yet.' Right out of a movie! He shook his head.

He ate his lunch in silence.

If his father had been around, he would have helped. Things would never have become so desperate. He never would have touched the mound. Not in a million years! And if he somehow had done this, there would be someone to talk to at least. Someone to tell. How much longer could he endure the torture by himself?

If only Dad were still around....

F O U R T E E N

The Past

The boy dreamed himself into uniform and committed acts he had never even considered before. He recognized himself from bird's-eye view as a man of about twenty, wielding a gun and having his way. Had the feeling he had already killed a few people. On a rampage. He watched this young man strut over to a cowering young Indian girl trying to hide against a tree trunk and throw down his gun. Philip noticed a scar on the tree, but his older self had other things on his mind. A small part of him shrieked at this man to stop what he was about to do. He felt the man's intentions inside himself, but couldn't counteract them. Now the something inside screamed louder, but no sound came. No hesitation in the actions. There was a knife. Tearing of clothes. There was blood. Only blood now.

Philip woke up crying. The lust in his body scared him. The hate he saw clearly scared him. He couldn't tell if the dream was brought on by the ghost or by his own hate. He put his wrist in his mouth and bit down as hard as he could. Tears rolled across his temples and into his ears. He remembered being told he was just like them, those armed white men. Maybe he was. He knew he hated the Indians, but those others were no better. And if he really was just like them....

He leaped from his bunk and charged through the curtain into the black of the main room.

Jane sent a harsh "Shh!" out at him as he rushed past the doorway to her room toward the screen door. He didn't think to turn on the light or move quietly. Bolted out of the house and down the path to Swimming Rock. His bare feet caught on the few roots and the uneven ground, but he kept on until he almost fell down the final slope onto the flat rock.

He raised his hands to the starry sky and shouted, "Help me, God! I'll do anything!"

His last word echoed off the east cliff. The water and air were almost still and only a few cottage lights could be seen to the west. Just the buzz of crickets and the odd flutter of oak leaves.

Then his tone changed, no longer addressing the same audience, more quietly now. "I'm going to kill myself. Is that what you want? You win! You win, whoever you are. I surrender." He thought of drowning himself right then and there, but knew he didn't have the nerve. "I need to sleep! You have to let me sleep!"

"Ha!"

Philip jumped at the sound of the voice.

"Pathetic wretch! You think you have suffered enough? I am not evil by nature like the white man, but I have an infinite supply of this for you yet."

The boy collapsed on the rock, on all fours now. Then his head struck the flat bedrock lightly as his arms buckled beneath his weight.

"But you will sleep from now on. It is part of the pact." The voice sounded disappointed with this change.

Philip couldn't properly absorb what he had heard. He tried to ask for an explanation, but his faintness stalled his thinking.

The voice answered him before he could collect a question. "You work for me, I permit sleep." After a pause, the voice ended thoughtfully, "The red man puts the white to work...."

Philip felt a slow hint of relief in his aching body. Back muscles releasing their fast grip. His head throbbed from hitting the rock. He rolled onto his back, but his tired eyes just made a blur of the brilliant display of stars above.

"This pact is no favour to you. You deserve less than this. But your punishment and efforts will serve a purpose higher than the penalty fit for you. In my new work I need a tool who is fresh from sleep. You are that tool. If I were idle, your fate would be much worse." A pause for all of this to be understood. "But I am not. Sleep now."

Philip's eyes had already started to falter. He tried to say thank you, but just let out a low grunt.

"Ack! No thank yous. I say again—this is no favour! Sleep. We begin in two full days and nights. Do not thank me again, white wretch."

So close to sleep, Philip almost did it again. He fell into a deep sleep on the rock and didn't wake up until his pale skin had started to burn in the morning sun.

"Oh!" his mother shrieked when she stumbled upon him. She held the towel and soap to her nightgowned chest, and stood at the end of the path. "I didn't know you were up. It's so early." She checked her watch. "Well, maybe not so early...."

Philip opened his eyes and instantly felt his burning eyelids. He grunted and rolled over. Jane went down to the water and bathed herself as usual. The occasional gasp and shudder with the cold shock. When she looked back at Philip on the rock, he had rolled over onto his stomach, spread-eagled. She shook her head. Finished her wash, she poked him until he stirred. "If you want to sleep, go to bed, kid. You're going to burn to a crisp here," she said, touching his face with the back of her hand. She practically had to drag him up to the house. Once he was in bed, she didn't see him for the rest of the day.

Everything was on hold. Philip didn't dream. There was no voice. Even his bladder seemed to have shut down in the name of slumber, allowing the spent boy to replenish himself. He woke up only after sleeping twenty-one consecutive hours. He felt he could roll over and do it again. But the voice said, "Get up. Sleep again in eight hours. No more, no less."

"But I'm sleeping now," Philip whispered, unaware to whom he spoke as he rolled over with his face on the pillow.

"You will sleep when I say."

The voice slipped away again.

He exhaled, bellowing his cheeks. Rubbed his eyes. Better get up. He almost laughed out loud at how elementary the decision had become.

That morning Philip strolled the island paths in peace. He ate his meals in his usual stoic silence, but again—in peace. He wondered what he would be forced to do and how hard he would have to work. Maybe hacking a huge boulder until it was gravel or even sand. It couldn't be any harder than his last two weeks. Anything would be better than what had been.

For the first time in a long time, he recognized beauty when he looked around him. Took nothing for granted. The same trees, swishing in a fresh south wind which haunted him only days ago, now made him smile. Maybe it was a wakeup call. He hadn't found anything about the island he liked in the last two summers.

He walked down to Swimming Rock, took one look at the blue water, and ran back to the house to get his bathing suit. He changed in a fury and whizzed by his awe-struck mother.

That day Philip swam three times, drew four acceptable sketches of trees around the island, and came up with an idea for a new evil super hero. The Savage. Got the idea from the cover of the *Soul Catcher* book. He thought he might start reading it, but after reading the back again, he changed his mind. The words still made him shudder. The day was eight hours of heaven. He remembered now the fever he once had for drawing. It had always been a way to pass the time and avoid people, but it hadn't been this kind of safe-haven in ages, it seemed. And the trees came out right—no gargoyles, no voices from hidden places. He forgot all else.

After lunch, he handed his mother a sketch, but strode away before she could react. Then went off to enjoy the rest of his waking time.

But promptly at five, Philip walked calmly into his room, changed out of his bathing suit, and climbed into bed.

"Philip?" Jane called through the curtain. "Can I take your bathing suit and put it on the line to dry?"

No answer.

"Philip, are you in there?" She dragged the curtain open. Philip felt her eyes upon him and her silence. "You can't be serious," she mumbled. Then he heard her rescue his bathing suit from the rafter just as the first drip fell, and leave the room quietly.

Philip opened his eyes one final time, then closed them for the duration.

FIFTEEN

The Two Children

"Get up!" It seemed like only a moment later that the voice yanked Philip out of his deep sleep. His eyes sprang open and his body went tight. "Do not go back to sleep. Eat now. Then go to the site of my grave."

That was it. Philip decided not to test the power of whatever was inside him again. He got up directly. While he followed the directions, he had to wonder why the burial ground again. It made sense since that was where the spirit came from. But what horror awaited him there now? He vividly remembered the circling gulls and the dark sky of that first day. The bony spectre that buried him there one night. The churning whirlpool flashed in his mind. What if the dreams had been premonitions? It struck him for the first time that this thing he was dealing with might be the devil himself. It came from beneath the ground, certainly sounded evil. Maybe he had inadvertently sold his soul already. He began to sweat nervously as he pulled up his usual brown cords, and kicked a stray pair of underwear under the bed.

He took a peek in the mirror. Like preparing for a big date, not that he had ever had one. He found no surprises in the face he saw, but noticed that he looked quite tired and a little pinkish. The mirror would have seen more of him if he had been the least bit impressive. This was more of a moment-of-truth mirror-check than anything approaching vanity. Assume the worst, he thought. He put on his glasses. Took them off. He was no prize either way. He slipped them on again, shrugged, and walked through the curtain to the main room, prepared for his doom.

His mother stirred in her bed. His head cocked to listen. To the kitchen. He got out the milk and Frosted Flakes, and sat down at the table to fulfil the orders put upon him. He ate without thinking further, staring into space,

74

mouthful after mouthful. When he had finished eating, he walked straight out the south door. He let it slam behind him.

"Philip?" his mother called. But he did not answer.

Although nearly shaking with fright, he knew resistance was futile. The beads of sweat grew on his brow. When he got down onto the bedrock shore, he looked up at the low ceiling of clouds. His eyes closed for a moment and his fluttering lungs breathed in deeply. A final breath. Turning back toward the burial site, his mind filled with all the excuses to never go back. He felt sure that something hideous must be waiting there. He wished he could sprain his ankle on purpose, so he couldn't climb the little incline. But he didn't know how to do that. At a loss, Philip pushed himself up one ledge of rock, over the boulder, and under the oak branches.

And there it was.

Awkward. He found himself looking around as if for a seat at some tense family gathering. The mound of still fresh earth seemed to spy on him through the thin layer of twigs and leaves he had piled on top of it. He checked for seagulls but found none. Okay, I'm here. Although the voice said nothing. He felt he should sit down where he was. He looked beneath his feet and cleared away a few twigs. He sat on a spot of bedrock, his back to Swimming Rock and the water, looking directly at the grave.

His brow furrowed with confusion as he realized for the first time that he more than regretted his dig. For this brief moment, Philip felt a strange sense of guilt he couldn't explain. He tried to let it go, but it lingered. What had happened to his grandfather's grave was no less a violation of deserved peace. So much of his concern over the toppled rocks had been for his own well-being and status with his mother that he had barely thought of Grandpa Frederick. He looked at the grave in front of him and realized that, in this case, he had been the violator. Guilt gnawed at him. He had disturbed the peace.

Finally, the voice came. "Reflection often comes too late. People should respect the dead. Grave robbers. Gold diggers. If you had dug deeper, you would have found more valuable objects. You might have been rich. That is what you want, whether you say it or not." A pause. "The white man is a seller of things. A swindler, a thief by nature. The element is deep in his blood. Your blood.

"This is where I was buried. It was 1783 by your calendar. I did not die in battle, but of your smallpox. Many of us died that way. All but by the very hands of your infectious ancestors."

Philip laid his head back onto the ground with his hands beneath it, prepared for a story. My smallpox?

"That was how I died, although I know you do not care. This disease was a great weapon of your ancestors, especially later on. That is your link. That, and the fact you have disturbed me." Philip heard and felt a dissatisfied huff. "I will not explain myself any further. There will be only instructions and direct orders. You have no choice in any matter. If I tell you to swim, you swim. If I tell you to sleep, you sleep. If I direct you to draw your own blood, you find a knife. Consider yourself fortunate that I have found a use for you. Your service begins now. There are many loose ends to be tied." A pause. "Go to the east end of this island and stand on the fourth rock north of the south-east tip. You will look across to the cliffs, which hold deathly secrets. Go! Now!"

Deathly secrets! It was all Philip could think of as he hurried through the early-morning spider webs stretched across the path to the east. The fast-growing undergrowth grabbed at him as he pushed past clumsily. At the clearing at the south-east tip, he slowed down to count the points of land. One. Two.... There! Sure he had counted right, he went back to check anyway. He ploughed through a large, green-leafed bush and ducked underneath the brittle, dead branches of an old balsam. This was the rock. It had to be. A slanted mossy point.

Deathly secrets....

Philip gazed across at the cliffs. They were orange with lichen except near the water line where a black band about four feet up ran the length of the shore. He had drawn pictures of them before from another point to the north. Today they looked ominous, evil.

"Kneel!"

Philip obeyed the command.

"Among the trees at the top of the second highest ledge.... Locate it with your eye!"

Philip scanned the landscape nervously.

"No! To the right! Yes, that one."

Philip's scalp bristled at the thought of someone else looking through his own eyes.

"Beyond that ledge, maybe twenty man's lengths, are the graves of two dead."

Philip felt a chill run down his spine and his torso went erect. He held his palm tightly to his temple and echoed, "Two dead?"

"That is what I said. Two dumb Injins like me, you might say. I do not care where any dead whites lie." He laughed. "The dead have been waiting there for over one hundred years. You must find them and help them."

"Help them? They're dead!"

"Silence!" the voice boomed. "Do not speak of things you know nothing about! I too am dead to you. But I am far from gone from this place."

Philip noticed a pause that seemed a little too long and thought he might ask—

"Silence! Do not speak unless spoken to!"

The boy's mouth hung open in surprise.

"I know all your moves. Even the ones you are unaware you are about to make. Listen carefully: The two dead have not made the journey. These are a young boy and girl killed by two Englishmen, your ancestors. At this time your rail line was being constructed, and the workers suddenly infested the land. On one of your days of rest, two English men hunted for deer in the woods. One of them saw movement and fired. The two men followed what they thought was an animal deep into the woods. But the sounds they heard and glimpses they saw were not of a deer, but of two young, terrified children.

"With the water in sight, the older girl found a place they could hide. Some of the whites had even been kind to them because they were so young. They did not understand these shots, but feared for their lives. They hid beneath a fallen cedar bough, in a hole between two great white pine roots. They would have survived had it not been for the white man's heavy feet.

A white man fell into the hole while he searched for them.

"Always discovering something, that white man. That same idiot found America while looking for India! A lucky, undeserving stumbler, he was and is.

"Outraged that they had unknowingly been tracking Indian children and were now completely lost and without reward, one aimed at the girl's groin and fired his gun again. After the initial shock of the blast, the other shrugged and said, "If we kill them while they're young, we won't have to deal with them later." He wasted no time in shooting the shrieking boy through the head. They left the girl to bleed to death. She died embracing her dead brother one full hour later. You will know them as the boy Mudjeekawiss and the girl Zaugitau, children of the Anishinaabe. My people. Both were destined for greatness, but Mudjeekawiss was to follow his great name and become an important leader during a difficult era. They were never found by their band or family and received no proper ceremony or passage."

The spirit paused. "This is how you will be useful. You will perform the last rites of these people. You will do so for these and many more. This is your service."

Philip stared at the cliffs, shaken by the brutal story and a new responsibility beyond all imagination. The horrific dreams played in unison in his head. They made some sense now, though still overwhelming. He shifted to sit down and swallowed hard on that taste of vomit creeping up his throat. "I–I can't do a...ceremony. I don't know a—"

"Fool! That is why I am here. I teach you. I would do it myself and let you rot if I could, but it is not possible. I am no longer a man. I need a physical presence. The words must be spoken, actions acted, mide bags collected. You are the one."

Philip lurched forward and threw up onto the lush green moss. Lumpy brown liquid rolled across the strands of moss and then eased itself down in between. He coughed, choking on the bitterness. A tear formed in his eye. There didn't seem to be any means of escaping this. He shook his head wearily.

"Weak child! You had better toughen up. You will be useless to me like this. Get straight!"

Philip wiped the vomit from his lips and dried his eye. "'kay."

"Listen. I have great vision of the past. I see how Mudjeekawiss and Zaugitau died. No other Anishinaabe knows. I never knew them when I lived on this land because they lived here after my lifetime. But I do know them now. I know their pain. They are in a limbo stage and have been for too long. They must move on and join the others in the Land of Souls. But they cannot get there from where they are now. Not alone. You are the guide. The ceremony and duties will do you more honour than you deserve. But this is unavoidable. I have to give you this honour in order to accomplish my goal. Your act of idiocy may serve me well yet."

The voice paused long enough for Philip to gather himself. All of this death and murder and afterlife was too much to absorb.

"Get the canoe. We will go over there now."

Philip hesitated.

"Go! Get the canoe. There is no time to waste."

Philip scurried up off the rock, then down and around onto the path. The north path brought him past the beach and boats. Needed to get to the house first, but hoped to avoid another scolding. His feet moved quickly across the roots and rocks, briefly forgetting their clumsiness. The house was empty. Lifejacket. Paddle. It had to be fast. Philip moved as efficiently as he could, and ran back down the path to the beach.

Out on the dock, he stopped and looked at the canoe. He realized he hadn't used it since he and his father had taken camping trips with it three summers ago. It didn't feel right to be using it again, especially alone.

However, he forced himself to jump off the dock onto the beach. The untied canoe hissed across the sand as he slid it down into the water. Paddle in hand, he jumped into the canoe a bit late as he pushed off, dragging his foot in the water behind him. He glared down at the soaked shoe as he pulled it into the canoe, sailing cockeyed out into the bay. Swore under his breath. He struggled to move to the middle and sit on the bottom as he remembered was correct. Or was it to kneel? Both ends of the canoe looked the same. Checking them again, he realized he had no idea how to manoeuvre the boat on his own. He would try. He picked the paddle up off the canoe bottom and dipped it a little too gingerly into the water.

"You do not know how to do this, do you?"

Philip just swished his paddle around in the water, looking down at the slightly blurry, rock bottom. The canoe spun slowly around and drifted toward the cliff wall of Blueberry Point. What was he supposed to say?

"You have no skills. That should not surprise me. All right, boy, bring the canoe back to shore and we will use your devil motor boat."

"No. I can do it." Philip believed in himself for a moment.

"Bring the canoe back. I have no time for you to take two hours to cross a stone's throw of water."

Philip argued no further. He pulled the canoe to shore by poling the ground with his paddle. The voice waited silently during the ten-minute ordeal. Finally, Philip pulled the canoe up on the beach and tied it to the tree again. Almost glad not to have to use it. Wasn't ready yet. He climbed across the top of the old dock, prepared the fishing boat and sped out of the bay toward the cliffs.

Philip approached the cliffs and slowed the motor down until it faltered and stopped. The cliffs seemed a good deal higher from directly below. He could feel a damp cold radiating from the dark rock. Strange black holes and

crevices seemed to lead deep into the shore. He let the boat drift and waited for instructions.

"The dead have been buried by time!" boomed the voice. "Buried! That
means we have to land! Drifting will not do. Unless you can scale a rock face,
you had better bring this tin boat around the point to where you can climb
out. Have you no mind?"

The voice stopped, waiting for ignition. Philip guided the boat carefully between the two reefs that guarded the swampy back bay. Blinked back
the tears, trying hard to satisfy. When he leaned over to check for depth, he
suddenly realized that he had not asked his mother's permission to take the
boat. Better not hit anything! He gunned the engine to build enough
momentum to drift to shore, a trick he had learned from his father. Then
turned the motor off and tilted it up out of the water. As the boy stood up
to move forward to the bow for landing, the boat struck a ledge just below
the water's surface, and sent him stumbling forward. His wrist twisted under
his weight on the boat bottom and he grazed his head on the hot aluminium middle seat. Now the boat drifted away from shore. He hated that. He
swore at his wrist and this boat that refused to co-operate. Then grabbed one
of the oars and poled himself to shore again. This time Philip stepped out
onto the ledge before the boat slammed into it, soaking his other shoe. Swore
at himself this time. He grabbed the painter and lifted the bow out of the
water, resting the keel on the rock. The sound of the grinding sand between
the boat and the rock made Philip shiver. He looked around for some kind
of tie, but found nothing. Finally, he picked up a rock and wound the rope
around it as he had seen his father do on occasion. Three more rocks
piled on top of the first would hold. He looked at the mooring proudly
when he was done—he had been quite resourceful. And the ghost had not
scolded him.

His surroundings seemed foreign. The land seemed very different as he
stood on it now, never having actually set foot on it in all the times he had
passed by. Immediately inland from the ledge underfoot were two more
ledges, which he guessed he would have to climb to get to the place he was
supposed to go. Just ahead grew a clump of brambles. He wondered if there
were raspberries somewhere in there. To his left, more water and then the
island—a little peninsula hid his docking area from the channel. He turned
to check the boat again. It seemed to be behaving well enough. The water
was calm. Beyond the boat, he looked deep into the bay, which he recognized suddenly as the swamp he used to visit with his father. He stood on

the shore. This was just one of many little inlets down the sides of the bay. Directly across the main bay stood the withered beaver hut. It looked a lot less exciting than it had when he was little.

The spirit interrupted the daydream. "The more you move on your own, the less I will torment you, white boy. You know which direction to go, so go!"

Philip took a step forward toward the brush.

"No!" shouted the voice inside his head. "Do you not recognize the poison leaves, child?"

Philip twisted up his face as he looked closely at the shiny, drooping leaves that dominated the green patch ahead. Recognized the stuff now. Just didn't see it before.

"Move!"

The outburst almost sent the boy headlong into the poison ivy. He quickly checked for a way to pass it. He had pants on, but he didn't want to challenge that thunderous voice again.

He skidded down the inclined rock onto a reedy, algae and debris-lapped beach that wrapped around the back of the little inlet. He clamoured up the dirt bank at the other end using old roots to steady himself.

Inside the clutter of thin trees, the mosquitoes found him, burrowed into his hair and pierced the skin of his feet through his socks, humming intolerably all the while. A few more steps inland left him disoriented. He turned around and found he could barely see the water through the thicket. He tried to edge his way uphill to his mysterious destination, but lost his balance and toppled backwards onto a thatch of dead wood with a loud crack. He saw that he had been walking on a false bottom, just a thick layer of fallen branches and saplings. An eerie crackle accompanied each step as Philip tiptoed across the treacherous layer. It sounded like a fire snapping and cracking.

After a good fifteen minutes of trying to keep his balance and peeling spider webs from his face, he stepped up onto a mossy clearing where he could see through the trees better. He groaned when he saw that he stood only twenty feet from the water. Then slithered down the other side of the strangely placed tabletop slab and pushed farther into the jungle-like woods. Every part of him itched with mosquitoes, the heat, and his own sweat. In amongst these trees, the air didn't move and the sun seemed all the more intense. Next came a patch of juniper that pricked him through his cords and socks.

Slowly, boulders and rock clearings came more often. And finally he found himself looking up a steep bedrock slope, covered with white moss and the occasional bush or mangled old jack pine. He exhaled with relief and climbed onto the rock.

He trudged up the incline in the direct sunlight, the dried moss crunching underfoot. Wild flowers grew from the crevices and the bees and wasps whirred about busily. Gradually, more jack and white pines presented themselves. He hopped over the rocks and rotten logs as nimbly as he could and watched for a view of the island. As he neared the top of the bluff, the breeze took the edge off the heat on his back, still covered with twigs and bits of spider web. With a few more paces, Philip stepped down onto a carpet of pine needles and felt the cool shelter of the canopy of pine branches above. It was as if someone had drawn a line, and the heat and bugs were not allowed to cross.

The spirit told him to veer left and keep going. Philip felt himself drawn toward where the cliffs must have been and where he might be able to spot the island.

"That is not where we are going. Turn right now. Go!"

What a jerk!

"Call me what you like, but do what I say and be prepared to face my wrath. I am not your tour guide. What you will be doing here will dwarf any view you hope for or any selfish wish you hold. Putting your thrill ahead of these people's souls is a sin that should be punished."

Stupid Indians! Bunch of drunk idiots running around town. Who the hell cares about two dead Indians? The kids were probably crooks anyway. Philip's heart throbbed violently as he raved inside.

"I will not discuss your thoughts now. I care about these two people! That is all that matters. There is much work to be done."

Philip felt invaded, but also now a more familiar pang of guilt in his throat and stomach.

He headed inland a few more paces. The voice told him to straighten his path and keep walking. Up onto a ledge where his wet shoe crunched into more white moss. The trees were craggy and covered in a dry white growth. Little prickly bushes grew between the moss-covered bedrock slabs. Then Philip's path dropped down again, and the white pines towered above a dark orange needle carpet. He found two more small drop-offs and ended up in a valley of sorts. To his right, another clearing sloped deep into the leafier, lusher woods below.

"Wrong way! We are near to the destination. Turn toward the deep wood and walk fifteen paces down the slope. You will find holes in the ground. It is there that we will start. It is there that Zaugitau and Mudjeekawiss lie."

Philip took his fifteen paces. When his foot struck a thick root, he knew he was there. There were no bones. For a moment, he disbelieved the whole story. No telltale skull. Either they were properly buried or this joker was way off. The kids had hidden in this tiny hole with a cedar branch over them.... But where was this cedar tree? Philip looked around and saw none. Felt the cool of being at the border of the sheltering lush forest, as he looked up toward the hot dry slope.

"It is not that simple," the voice said mockingly.

Philip waited for the inevitable speech.

"This happened in your 1876. Things change with time. Even the simplest child knows that. People die. Trees die and forests recede or burn. Rocks fall. Ice carves out the shorelines. Do not assume you know something then when you look at it now. Once the cedar grew in these crevices. Although your beliefs are irrelevant, your disbelief angers me. The bones cannot be seen because years of pines needles and earth have collected on top of them, the wolves, the birds and insects have picked at them. To satisfy your grave-digging, mistrusting soul, I will show you one bone. One. Then we will move on. We are not here to unearth the dead. We are here to help them. I do not like the idea of you touching my people's bones like you did mine. Your brothers have done far too much of that already. But I want you to see what was done."

Philip squatted and reached down into the needle bed in front of him. He ran his fingers back and forth through the needles. He shifted forward and tried again. Now he foraged almost frantically, although he hoped to find nothing. The hole was shallow and yielded nothing. His hands probed more deeply into the earth nearby. He wanted to kick at it with his feet, but thought he might get in trouble for that. Occasionally, his hand would hit something. A root. Then a rock. His heart leaped at each contact he made, his fingers always investigating and discovering the object's identity. Deeper now. There! He hit something hard again. He brushed the area clear and saw a yellow-brown that couldn't be rock. A familiar colour. He knew right then, and started digging around the object with his uncut fingernails. The piece was quite long, just over half a foot. He paused occasionally to see if he could grab it. Finally, he got his fingers beneath it and yanked it free.

Only when he held the bone in front of his eyes did he realize the implications. It had to be a human arm or leg bone. Too short to be his. It was the perfect size for a kid, though!

This meant he was not crazy. All of this was real. Not a dream. The proof stared him in the face. A foreign part of him yearned to forage for more, but the rest made him throw the bone back to the ground.

He heard the spirit chuckle at his nervousness. "Do you see? We drunken Indians know a thing or two, white boy."

Philip felt he might throw up again. A murder had happened here. A double-murder, like on the Detroit news station. It didn't matter how long ago—it scared Philip. The bone lay amid the disturbed earth and needles now. Philip realized there were probably a hundred more floating in the earth only inches below his feet. He couldn't believe he once dug up a grave hoping to find something.

"Now you have found your bone, grave robber. I trust you are satisfied and your doubts are calmed. The bone would be called a femur by your doctors. It belonged to Zaugitau, if you care to know." After a closing pause, "Now, our work can begin."

Philip braced himself for the next instructions.

SIXTEEN

You Are My Voice

"Put the bone back into the hole. You will touch no more of these. You are no Anishinaabe." A pause. "Now you must put together a mide bag for each child and perform the Ceremony of the Dead. The mide bag will lie with the body. Then Zaugitau and Mudjeekawiss can complete their journey as they were meant to."

The voice paused again as Philip gingerly picked up the bone between his thumb and forefinger and dropped it down into the hole near his feet.

"You must also remember the children. You must mourn their deaths, for few did that when they went missing. You will—"

"Wait a sec!" The weight of responsibility was too much already. And for what?! "You want me to perform a... blessing?! And... And remember people I never even saw? You're crazy! Let me guess—the blessing is in some hooga-haga language, right?" He began breathing quickly, and held his head in his hands. Then burst again, "What the hell do you expect me to do?! I can't—"

"Exactly as I say!" interrupted the spirit. "You are a mere tool. All I need is an entity with some motor skills. What little you have will do. I have tried to do this without a physical being. It cannot be done. When I was not scaring you out of your soiled sheets in my rage of twelve days, I was trying to help my people. But I could not touch them. I can move water, fire, earth, but I cannot make a mide bag or sing. I cannot fully be in your world. You are my hands. You are my voice. All you must do is to listen and follow. I am afraid that you may have to care as well. My mourning may not be enough. We will see as we begin. Do you understand?"

Philip pulled his hands from his face and closed his eyes, tilting his head up toward the sky.

"Understood?!"

"Yeah," Philip answered in his weakest voice.

"The mide bag will help the children make the journey. They have been travelling for a long time. The mide bag is a gift to the spirits. The bag will be filled with tobacco. Tobacco was once sacred when we were pure. The mide bag is an offering. I do not think the white man is buried with any gifts for the spirits, only objects he does not want to share. His greedy god might likely only accept the dollar bills as an offering. But the greedy family a white man leaves behind would rather keep that money for themselves." A derisive snicker. "These two children should be buried properly with possessions, clothing or moccasins, but we did not know them, nor do we have access to their belongings. Totems will be impossible to replace.... But we will give them food and shelter for their journey. Now we must find Saemauh. Tobacco." A pause. "Your mother does not smoke it?"

"No." Philip wanted to be helpful to avoid trouble. He tried to think of where he might find cigarettes. "Hey! My grandfather smoked. He rolled his own. Maybe I could try to find some in the attic."

"Good. But we will need a large amount. There are others to be helped exactly so. Unless you find a great deal in the house, you will need to find a way of getting more. Not cigarettes, tobacco for a pipe. Check for tobacco when I let you go, but go to the portage soon."

"The portage?" the boy wondered out loud.

"Rat Portage! Misnamed for muskrat by your kind. Kenora, you fool!"

Whatever you say! Philip thought bitterly. What the hell was Rat Portage?! Then he remembered the law about kids not being allowed to buy cigarettes, but pushed the thought away. He shifted to the other puzzle. "What about this song thing?"

"I will tell you the words and you will say them. You can sing in tune?"

"I'm not sure. I guess. I don't know."

"My kind of song will be different than one of yours. But I will teach you. The song will last a long time, especially for those who have waited so long."

Philip grew excited. "Teach me now!" he said. He waited hopefully. "Come on, teach me." Like it might be a way out of this gloom. Waited again.

"Tell me why it is that you will speak to no one, hide from all contact with your kind, yet you would make demands of me who am mightier than any mortal you know? Did my storm blowing the roof off your house fail

86

to convince you of my power? Do you ask too much because.... Ack! I do not care to know. You will demand nothing of me, boy." Then after a pause, "Now is not the time to teach the words. You would only forget. When you have the mide bag and tobacco, we will return and you will perform the rite. Do not ask anything of me again."

Philip thought about the spirit's unfinished question. Did he care? Did he really want to know something?

Philip also found himself surprised at the spirit's taking responsibility for the roof. Although he had been sure the ghost had been involved, it was even more frightening to have it confirmed. His thoughts soon drifted back to himself. Why could he ask the spirit questions when he wasn't supposed to, but couldn't speak to normal people? There was something to that question. But he found no answer. He tried to feel around inside himself to see if the spirit was still there. But he had the distinct feeling of being completely alone. He thought of whispering hello, but it might only provoke abuse. Perhaps that was all for the day and he could just go back home. Was there something he was forgetting to do?

As he stepped up one ledge to make his way back, he caught himself turning around to say goodbye to the bones. How stupid! He shook his blonde head, grimaced at his foolishness, and turned to begin the battle back through the brush. He looked at his watch. Four hours had slipped by like nothing at all. It was well past lunchtime.

SEVENTEEN

Offering

Philip checked furtively across the table to see if his mother was preparing to ask him where he had been. If she had known he had taken the boat again without permission, there would have been a real fuss. A second violation would not go unpunished. But she just ate silently along with him. Today he had stuff to tell, things to say, answers to give, but nothing he would dare reveal. She pecked at her sandwich and asked no questions. Sort of spaced out. Hadn't even given him trouble for being late.

The rhythm of their crunching food was drowned out by a sudden downpour.

"Ho-ly!" Jane shouted. She sprang up, licked the mayonnaise off her finger, and ran to the north door in a panic. Philip listened to her rustle on a plastic raincoat and scramble into those useless duck boots. He turned to look out behind him to the west as a mist of rain blew in through the screen.

After the door slammed, Philip contemplated helping his mother. She certainly wouldn't expect it. She was too good at playing the martyr to ever ask for help. Always tried to make him feel bad later. What the hell, he shrugged. He jumped up and ran to the door. He put on his rubber boots and his father's old slicker, and headed out.

"Christ!" he heard his mother say as she wrestled with the west shutters. He peeked around the corner, then ran around the east side of the house to the south end. The rain ricocheted off his plastic hood, rang in his ears. He stood in a rapidly growing puddle beside the concrete step. He reached up to start closing up the south side. Slid the wooden pole out from beneath the shutter and let it crash down. A similar crashing came to him through the roar of falling water from his mother's work around the corner. He moved over and let the next shutter drop. He turned and found his mother staring at him from behind the heavy eavestrough stream, soaked and amazed. He smiled at her as he hooked the bottom flap over the last shutter.

"Well, give me a goatee and call me Shakespeare! You're making yourself useful!" Another stab, he told himself. But he couldn't help laughing, melting her further. She laughed too, shook her head, dodging the small waterfall, and led the way inside. Philip followed with a strange but good feeling. And felt uncomfortable with it.

Just inside the door, they both shook themselves off and removed their jackets and boots. He could feel her trying to catch his eye, so he looked at the ground. Picked up his boots and carried them to the north end of the house in silence.

His sudden shift had caught her off balance. He felt her eyes still on him as he walked. Heard her step through the curtain into her room. "Oh, what a mess I am!" Must have been looking in the mirror again. But she only half meant it. She was always waiting for someone to tell her she was beautiful, then put on another layer of make-up to improve the chances. He wasn't going to do that. It was the same thing with that garden, except no one ever came to look.

Philip found his way into his room as well and spent the rest of the day on the top bunk, throwing a tennis ball up toward the high slanted roof. He pushed the exchange with his mother out of his mind.

After dinner, he suddenly remembered: Tobacco! He needed tobacco for the dead Indians. And tomorrow! He wouldn't dare ask his mother. She didn't smoke and thought it was disgusting. He could hear her now. She would probably quiz him, try to make him admit he was a smoker. Combing the house was the only way to find an old hidden stash. He pretended a casual stroll around the main room of the cabin. Eyes active, scaling the high shelves at each end of the room for some clue.

Tobacco. Tobacco. Tobacco. But Grandpa Frederick and his pipe were firmly entrenched in his memory. That special smell. It still lingered in the curtains. He wished Grandpa Frederick was still around. He could picture the old man's face emerging from behind a pipe's initial puff of smoke, sitting in the rocking chair. And watching the fireplace flicker reflected in the man's eyes.

Tobacco. Had to keep himself on track.

He pulled a chair from the dinner table to the set of shelves in the corner of the room. He stood on the chair and tried to juggle the contents of the top shelf to see each object clearly. Moved things around or down a shelf.

A can of coal oil. A jar of rusty nails. The roof must be leaking here too. Or perhaps they really were that old. Four unused ant-traps. He held them against his chest with a forearm. A clam shell. Then another. Everything coated with dust and strung together with cobwebs.

Then he spied the words Black Cat and Camel. Cigarettes! But when he pulled one of the curious flat tin boxes off the shelf and pried it open— more nails. The others, just screws and bolts in them. No tobacco. He picked up the bottom box in the pile and laughed as he read, "It's toasted!" beneath Lucky Strike. It struck him that the box was green and yellow, the wrong colours for Lucky Strike he was pretty certain. Maybe it was so old it was actually worth something, or maybe just old enough that the colours had gone sour. He paused atop the chair and gazed around for another possible source. Laid the box back on the shelf. We worked it out—nine years had passed since Frederick Caplan had smoked here. Ancient history. There was no tobacco here.

But Philip's eyes found the chimney and followed it up. Of course! The attic! How could he have forgotten? He flew off the chair and climbed the rock mantle and ladder to the attic, grabbing the flashlight next to the fireplace on his way up. At the top of the ladder the old attic fear came back to him. Stretching from the ladder to the platform had been a struggle for him when he was younger, and he hadn't even tried it last summer. Even now he felt himself quiver as he looked down at the hardwood floor below. He deserved a slap for even stopping to think. Maybe it had actually been easier then. His mind flashed to what Dr. Southland, that therapist guy, had told his mother when they had thought he was out of hearing range. That Philip had "regressed" since his father's death. Regress meant moved backward. He remembered looking it up to be sure.

He lunged for the platform, just to stop his thoughts.

The attic was the only expanse of the house where spiders ruled uncontested. His mother scoured every corner in her view so well that this was their only refuge, aside from the high shelves he had already gone through. It was dark up there except for the small ventilator windows at the north and south ends of the house and whatever light came up from the ceilingless bedrooms. Darker now with the ventilator shutters still closed from the shower at lunch and the sun nearly set. Philip relished the idea of probing through his grandfather's relics and wondered why he had never done it before. Still, he had to concentrate on tobacco.

With the weak flashlight straining in one hand, he rummaged through the cottage's history. Old cracked rubber flippers, lampshades, wooden cheese and butter boxes. None of it had been touched in years. His mother didn't care about all this stuff. She and Grandpa Frederick had had some kind of falling out Philip had never had explained to him. She liked the island more than she liked her father. Uncle Dixon had said she just liked the idea of sitting on a million dollars. But of course, he might have been jealous, preferring the island to the Winnipeg city property he had inherited. Uncle Pete had the other half of the island, officially, but he had barely ever returned from B.C. since the funeral.

Philip wondered if he had been the first one up here since his grandfather. Then he remembered rafter-jumping with his father, piggy-back style, clinging to a bare freckled neck.

An old wooden orange crate filled with assorted smaller boxes hidden beneath a blanket. He threw the dust-darkened blanket aside and began opening the boxes: playing cards, marbles.... Then he found a beautiful old, carved wooden box with hinges. It reminded him of the urn he had found at the grave. It had to have been Frederick's. Inside, three extraordinary tobacco pipes separated by browning tissue paper. He recalled the one in the middle, made partly of ivory. He removed the box from the crate and looked beneath it. A large, round tin. He pulled it out. Player's Navy Cut. Philip felt very proud of himself for a moment, and opened the can. The unmistakable scent hit him. Tobacco! And quite a bit of it still!

His mother called, "Philip?"

Should he say anything? He would get in trouble if she found out he was hiding from her. "Yes. Up here," he answered stiffly.

"Oh, hi." She walked over to the opening in the platform and looked up the ladder. "What are you doing up there?"

"Umm. Nothing. Just looking at some of Grandpa's old stuff."

"Oh." The curiosity long gone from her voice, she ducked out of sight again. He knew that would get rid of her.

He looked up at the roof with a smirk on his face and caught a glimpse of his father's old baseball cap. It was an almost woolly, dark blue Detroit Tigers cap. Somehow it had ended up hanging on a nail up in the attic. He flexed the visor and pulled it down onto his head, pinning his unruly hair back away from his eyes. With a real smile on his face, he finished putting things back in order and climbed down the ladder carefully with the tobacco under his arm. At the bottom, he froze with the sense his mother was sitting in the chair directly behind him. Explaining the tobacco would not be easy. Holding the tin to his stomach, he turned to check the chair. No one! Relief. He stole quickly into his room and hid the tin in his dresser.

He sat on his bed and thought about tomorrow. No doubt he would have to go back there. What would he have to sing or say? None of this made sense. And he knew it hadn't even started yet. He hoped the tobacco would somehow satisfy. The spirit had not spoken for hours. Philip still wasn't sure what that meant. The thought that it might be gone forever rushed past him. But he was quite sure the voice would wake him tomorrow. He hadn't caught a break yet.

Philip looked at his watch and rolled into bed fully clothed. He slept undisturbed, as promised.

EIGHTEEN

Ceremony

5:45 am.
Sunrise.

The spirit woke Philip and told him to bring the tobacco, two rags, two precious pieces of nature, and two arm's-lengths of string.

Philip did not delay. He went about gathering the materials, putting them in a plastic bag. Fatigue tugged him towards the bed again, but he resisted, closing his mouth around the yawns. Not quite sure what could be precious from nature, he picked two clamshells up off the beach as he was about to leave. Time was a factor. He could feel the suggestion he hurry. By six o'clock, he was pulling the ripcord on the outboard motor just off the beach in the still bay. He retraced his path from the day before, but just as he was about to land, the spirit interrupted.

"Not yet." The surprised boy turned the tiller suddenly, jerking the boat out of its straight line. "Go to the back of this bay. We must pick something up before we begin."

Philip followed the directions carefully, no longer tired in the crisp morning air. The boat headed directly for the wall of reeds, the plastic bag of assorted requested objects flapping about under Philip's foot. All he could see were the tall pale green reeds and the woods far behind them. One tree in the middle of the back shore drew his attention. It looked as if it had been split by lightning. The bright yellow, splintered wood from the inside of the trunk stood out against the peppered dark green and white band of woods. Above it all, a sky steadily becoming quite blue.

"Slow down. Pull in beside the rice and bulrushes."

Rice? He slowed the boat down and then swung the bow around to come parallel with the bank of reeds. Wild rice, he remembered when he shut off the engine. But it did not look like any rice he had ever seen.

"The souls need sustenance for their journey. We should not use your white, processed foods unless we have no other option. We cannot harvest Manomin now, but the bulrush roots are ready."

What?

"Rice must be winnowed and pounded, but the bulrush bulbs need only be picked." The spirit paused.

Philip used the time to remember what the bulrush looked like.

"Anakun."

"Huh?"

"Nothing for you, fool. Find the bulrush stems and reach down into the water to find their roots. Pick only ten. They will not keep long out of water."

Philip hesitated, looking over the edge of the boat into the layer of brown muck just below the water's surface.

"Do not try my patience."

No more prompting necessary. His hand entered the thick-looking water. The roots held on stubbornly. The boy fought hard, provoking a great stink with his churning. By his sixth bulb, he had greatly improved his efficiency. Soon he had ten onion-like bulbs with thick green stems sitting in the bottom of the boat, and he had forgotten the repulsive smell hanging in the air.

He started the engine again with the feeling he had actually learned something useful. If he got stuck in a swamp, he could survive. Although another look at the bulbs made him wonder if they were really edible. He veered into yesterday's inlet just before the outermost lip of the bay where the sun was just starting to hit the water over the woods backing the swamp.

After he had docked the boat without wetting his feet, he put five bulbs in the bag, pushed himself into the dew-wet treacherous jungle, up the hill and to the site with minimal guidance.

"Cut the string in half," ordered the spirit almost immediately after Philip had found the spot.

Philip grew indignant. "You forgot to tell me to bring scissors."

"I forgot nothing!" The spirit shouted inside his host's head. "There are other ways to cut...."

"Well, I didn't bring a knife either." Philip started to lose his cool.

"Confounded imbecile! What were knives once made of?! You think that before refined steel nothing was cut?! Did we sit about wishing we could cut string? Did we have string? Surely those horrid white history books taught you something!"

"I could use a rock?" trying to recover.

"Then do so!" roared the spirit.

Philip felt the old tickle in his nose, but held in his tear. He busied himself searching for a sharp rock. He spotted a sharp-edged, hand-sized slab lodged in a crack in a nearby rock ledge, and pulled it out. After a couple of experiments, he held the string on the top of the ledge and dragged the rock across it. When the string broke, he laughed with excited satisfaction.

"You did not measure the string for even length." The spirit left a dissatisfied pause. "But we have no time to backtrack for perfection. You must start thinking from now on.

"Now. Lay the rags out on this rock ledge. These will be our mide bags. We should be using skins or bark for them instead of cotton, but Gitche-Manido will see that it is well enough this way. Lay a small handful of Saemauh on each rag. You will give each child one of the shells. The smaller is for the younger boy...." Then a pause for perhaps a second thought. "But do not include the shells in the bags. Now pull the corners of the rags into the middle and tie them with string. These mide bags will not be perfect, but will serve the purpose. The problem will be understood."

"What problem?" asked Philip as he carefully piled tobacco on the first rag. "Understood by who?" Wondered in the back of his mind how the spirit knew he had found the tobacco last night, if he had been watching....

"You are here for a finite amount of time. That is the problem. Even if I keep you here until the weather grows cold, I will not finish all I must. Things will be done respectfully, but without wasting time."

"There are that many more?"

"It is your chore to correct all of this. It is my duty. Each night I dream of the souls travelling endlessly, never finding their place. When the sun comes up, I know where their bodies lie and how they came there. They all died missing or without mourners and have never found a home."

It made no sense: Saving dead people? Still, he finished pulling in the rag corners and began the tying process. It was difficult. His hands were not bad, but they fumbled the first bundle and dumped it onto the ground.

"Fool! This part is simple. There never was an Anishinaabe as clumsy as you, boy. Is that another gift of the white skin or are you an anomaly?"

What's an anomaly?

Philip looked down at the tobacco on the ground with the rag on top of it. He wasn't sure if he should pick it up or begin again.

"Pick up the rag and fill it with new tobacco. Do not let it fall again," the voice boomed.

A now shaking boy tried again. It seemed weird to have this Indian using English words he had never heard before. If he had really lived that long ago, would he know any English at all? They were supposed to be stupid, but this one was quickly proving to be the opposite. Philip moved especially slowly, trying to avoid the fits of clumsiness he knew too well. Carefully pulled in the corners of the bundle and gave it a twist. He wrapped the string around the top and tied a bow. More sure of himself. Glad he had his glasses.

"And now the other!"

Philip started to rush, but slowed himself down to avoid another disaster.

"Do not drop it!"

Thanks a lot! the boy couldn't help thinking.

"Now the ceremony begins. We will combine the ceremonies into one since the children died together and were of the same family."

Philip knew he couldn't handle whatever was next. Just felt it.

"You will hear the song in your head as you hear my English words now. Do not concern yourself with the meaning. You must know only that the words are necessary. You must sing with conviction. Repeating will not be enough. You must mourn for the people. If you do not care enough and it becomes a problem, I will make you care by force."

Philip shivered at the thought of the spirit's using force again. "But how can I sing with feeling if I don't even know what the words say?"

The spirit seemed to reflect on the question. The long silence gave hope to Philip. Maybe he would get credit for his good question....

"Ack! Nonsense. Do as I say. You would not understand if I told you. It is above you. Your kind has never had respect for the light and dark of life and death. I would not waste my time and contaminate its importance by explaining it to you. That is all."

Philip waited, shot down again, but confused as to how it happened.

"Now you will listen. It is a chant. You will listen well and repeat what you hear. Then you will perform the rite as I instruct."

At first, the sounds came to him faintly. Like a man's voice, but it rose and fell in an unfamiliar way. The sounds didn't ring clear, everything muddled together. When Philip realized his eyes were closed, he opened them quickly to make sure the sounds weren't coming from someone standing right in front of him. The voice rang more real than ever. The tones reverberated in his head, soothing his nervous, cramped heart.

The boy jumped when the voice spoke English again. "Did you hear those words? I will repeat them slowly. You will listen."

The droning chant began again for a few seconds and stopped.

"Repeat it."

Philip heard the short section again, but it still seemed unintelligible. He knew he had to try. But it sounded all wrong with Philip's squeaky, untrained voice. Even before the sounds hit the air. All wrong. Worse when his ears heard the real noises that followed. His voice could not imitate these somehow flawless foreign words of the one inside his head. He tried again. Worse this time, having forgotten the original sound. He could feel the spirit wince within.

"Enough!" Then the spirit sang the phrase again.

Just musical grunts to Philip, impossible to relate to. Although they should not have been difficult to imitate, again and again Philip's efforts fell short.

"Stupid, useless child! Your incompetence will ruin all my plans to help my people."

Then Philip heard no more. He could tell the spirit had left him again. He sat on the ground like a scolded house pet with the mide bags at his side. Crap! He couldn't do anything right. Crap! He sat and waited, bending and twisting a twig until it gave way.

An hour later, with the sun almost directly overhead, poking through the seams between the treetops, the spirit returned and spoke. "Now I will try something different. It may not work. It will take more energy from me than from you. You must empty your mind of everything but the children. Zaugitau and Mudjeekawiss. Do not think at all. The boy and girl are all we will have room for. You must grant me total control."

Control?! Philip shuddered as he pictured himself walking around the island as a crazed zombie.

The voice continued, "Everything must go loose. Lie down. Relax your body. But do not sleep. This is still work." Like the doctor telling him to let his tongue go soft so she could pull and prod it. He never did that quite right either.

97

He lay flat on the ground, eyes closed. His heart pumped frantically, somehow even more out of his control than usual. Slowly, it calmed as he sank into the needle bed. Thoughts of his mother, his father, the grave. When they came, he pushed them away. Had to keep a blank screen. Maybe he was trying too hard. Concentrate without concentrating. He thought of what would happen when the ghost in his head would take over. Maybe he could escape the whole thing if he just ran. But he kept pushing all the nonsense away, waiting for someone or something to make a move.

His fingertips began to tingle. His toes felt strange as well. At first, like they were asleep. The tingling mounted until it ran through his whole body. Very faintly, he heard a humming he recognized. The trees spun above him, the streams of sunlight swirling. The hum grew louder and more defined. He squeezed his eyes shut again and gripped his head in his hands. A pain held him paralyzed. Then he recognized the sounds from earlier, but now it was his own voice that made them. The more he thought, the more pain he felt. He listened to himself. It sounded so different from his previous attempts. It was him, but it wasn't. He couldn't feel his lips moving, yet they were. Time was a lost idea. Didn't matter. Just empty yourself, he coached. He pushed it all away again and the pain faded slightly. And gave way to more pleasant vibrations. Let it happen. Philip lay face-up with a mide bag in each hand. He felt the rhythm of the chant pump through his veins, like an irregular heartbeat. Beneath the sound of his voice, the sound of rushing water.

There were new feelings coming. He knew the spirit was inside him, but his insides felt more crowded than usual. There was more than just the spirit who spoke to him inside. He tried not to think about it, but soon he felt a distinct swelling in his chest. It grew there. The boy and his sister. Philip knew. The tingling grew warmer and his voice rang louder. Philip felt somehow connected to the world and the land as never before, yet more detached from reality than he ever imagined possible. Stop thinking, he scolded himself. He could feel something pushing his hands together over his body. He tried to release them from his own power so they might do whatever was intended. They shook violently. But the force trying to manipulate them couldn't seem to do it alone. Philip began thinking again. His head throbbed from it. Where did his hands want to go? The pain deepened. He looked at his clenched hands, still pointing past his feet, just above the ground. The hole between the roots! The mide bags had to get there. He forced himself to sit straight up. His whole body shook. All his joints locked. He rolled forward, falling down onto his elbows. Gravity held him tightly. He gathered all his strength. Now or never. He threw himself toward the hole, landing with his hands over the edge of the root, dropping the mide bags down into the earth. Facedown, the words still coming out of his mouth into the soil. He tilted his head back, resting his chin on the packed dirt and pine needles. Each movement was like another stake being driven into his torso. The pain faded as his muscles relaxed.

There seemed now to be yet another presence inside him. Terrifying. But beautiful. Immense. It seemed to envelope him from the inside. The two other presences faded, swallowed up by the more mysterious one. Then it too slowly faded. Soon it was only the boy and the spirit again. Philip instinctively pushed some dirt and needles into the hole after the mide bags as his own chanting tapered off and the tingling cooled. He felt the space in him increase again.

Completely alone now, he turned his head to the side and fell asleep.

NINETEEN

Four Days on the Path

When Philip woke up two hours later, he remembered a dream of a great black bird. The bird was even bigger than the one from when the spectre had buried him alive, yet it didn't inspire an ounce of fear in him. He felt it still in his heart somehow and could still picture it soaring above him. That was all he remembered.

After he let the dream go, he wondered at his present position—facedown in the middle of the woods. Slowly, he remembered that strange sensation and the sounds that had come from inside him, but not really from him at all. He wondered where the spirit had gone. He wanted to call it, but feared another scolding if he said the wrong thing. Maybe he was supposed to go home again.

"Boy. You are awake." The voice sounded strained and weak. "We cannot continue this way. I cannot work through you in this way again. Your soul is too heavy."

"What do you mean? My soul is heavy?" His back up again.

A pause. The spirit might have been deciding whether the question deserved an answer. "You are not happy. I do not care. But this makes the ceremony difficult. It is hard to make fire with wood that has been at the lake bottom. Rotten wood is soft, heavy, and weak."

Philip found an uncomfortable truth here. He lowered his defences. He did feel heavy, more often than not. And he always felt weak. As if for the record, Philip stated, "I wish I were not so heavy."

"Your happiness is no concern of mine. You get what you deserve. Any suffering a white man encounters is the result of a debt not paid."

What a load of crap! "Why do you hate white people so much, you dumb Indian?! We give you all of that reserve land and—"

100

"Silence! Ignorant wretch! Do not try to sell your Nazi propaganda here!"

"Nazi?! I'm not a frickin' Nazi! Canada helped stop Hitler!"

"Rubbish! The white man only put Hitler down because he turned on his own kind. The Jewish people were just white enough to merit intervention. It was a white problem."

"But he hated blacks too and—"

"Enough!"

Philip lost his fear and self-consciousness in his anger. He had just studied all of this for a project in school last year. Then he was sure he had the winning hand. "And how the hell do you know about Hitler if you've been dead so damn long?!"

"I have witnessed all of the world's story since my death. Every sick joke. Every war. Every wasted life. The fall of the Anishinaabe."

"That's such bull! And who the hell are you talking about? I've never even heard of that stupid tribe!"

"Say nothing more or you will wish you too were dead." A harsher hiss of the spirit's breath, fierce and ready to wreak havoc. Then it eased. "This debate is over."

Philip knew he had crossed a line and that the spirit's threat was real. But the damned Indian was just plain wrong. He should have been thankful that the whites came and brought—

"The white man changed our ways by taking our feet out from under us. He changed our ways to a dependency on him and his vices. He changed our ways by force. Your history books are not written by the Anishinaabe, my people, the Ojibway, to you. They are written by white men who discovered a place that we knew well and called home. They are written by men with unacknowledged guilt, trying to save face. This land is and was Anishinaabe-aki!"

Philip fought the mysterious urge to believe every word. The spirit was crafty with his words. Spell-weaving words. Who was more like Hitler? He could remember Mr. Parks talking about how Hitler was a master speaker or…some word starting with an R.

Philip tried to exit the topic. "So, did we do it? Did the song work?" Suddenly, genuinely excited to know the result of the strange ceremony.

"They are well on their way. But I did not finish. The work was too hard and I needed a rest. Even you needed one, although you did nothing."

Nothing?!

"There should be a fire, but we cannot do this. We do not have the time, and it would be unsafe to leave it burning in these dry days of summer. We will leave food and shelter that will last four days. Put the shells at the top of the hole as totems. Pieces of the land are as close as we will get to totems for these people. Get the bulbs from your bag. Build a small wigwam with sticks. The bulbs will go in the wigwam, just in front of the hole."

Philip found this last bit a little much, but obediently started walking around the site, looking for twigs. He gathered a few in his hands, each about eight inches long. Wondered how many he would need? "I can make like a triangle, right?"

"Yes. It need not be detailed or weather proof, but it must stand for four days."

He laid out the skeleton of something like what he would have called a teepee. It fell repeatedly until he figured out how to use the little knots and bumps to hook the first three twigs together. He laid a few more sticks carefully across the structure, but then remembered the bulbs. He tried to shove a bulb in between the slats of the wigwam, but succeeded only in toppling the whole thing over. He started over with a frustrated sigh.

"There," he finally announced, with the two bulbs safely inside the structure.

"It is good." But the spirit was not through. "I cannot do what I did this time again and again. You must shoulder more of the burden. At the very least, you must feel kinship with my people you still hate. I am not hopeful, but I will make sure you try."

"I will." Philip surprised both himself and the spirit with the certainty in his voice. He would try.

"Now. Carry the flame of the young boy Mudjeekawiss and the girl Zaugitau in your bosom for four days. You will return here each day and check the supplies you left and make an offering—more food and tobacco. That is all. Now. Go. Eat."

Philip's eyes widened. Back again tomorrow and then twice more?!

He made his way down to the water, thinking about all that was said and resisting a temptation to poke fun at the word bosom. He jumped into the boat and drove back to the island. When he arrived, he stood on the dock looking out across the water, wondering if what had just happened was real. It had to be, he decided, because there seemed to be nothing else. Blueberry

Point hid the cliffs from view, but he knew they were there. He turned and headed up the path to the house.

"Where were you?! I was worried sick!" His mother met him at the door of the house, a scowl on her face.

Really? Philip was sceptical.

She pressed her palm against her forehead and clenched her eyes shut. "The boat was gone. You were gone. You could have been anywhere! You think you can just come and go as you please? This isn't a country club...or...a...a hotel or something!"

You could never tell what you would get from her. He cowered slightly. When she yelled, he could really see her for what she was: heartless and mean-spirited.

She turned to walk back into the house, then stopped and turned. "You're doing the dishes after lunch and dinner too! We'll talk about this later."

Ooh! Big deal. But why punish him? What would she care if he disappeared? All she ever did was complain about him anyway. Heartless and mean-spirited. The words were just right. Then it dawned on him that this might well spell the end of his use of the boat for who knew how long. He couldn't let that happen.

Without trying to warm her up at all first, he asked, "Can I still use the boat tomorrow?" Probably should have done it differently, but he felt he must challenge her hardness, dare her to say no. He would take that boat one way or another, he had decided by the time he had asked the question.

After a long stare directly at his still-deferring eyes, she finally answered, "First, you do the dishes. Next, you do the toilet. Then you regain boat access."

For all her hard-heartedness, she had never made him do chores. With the boat's use now secure, Philip let his anger sweep over him. This was a real rip off! "But Mom, you can't—"

The spirit swooped in. "Shut up, fool!"

"Can't what?" Jane, smug at Philip's aborted protest. She had no clue that he had been interrupted in mid-sentence by a third party. His sudden silence seemed to satisfy her.

Philip's head spun from the unexpected interjection, bombarded suddenly from both sides. He would do the toilet and dishes without another word. The boat had become essential.

After finishing the dishes, he walked down to the outhouse with a pair of work gloves on. They were gross and smelled like poop and chemicals from doing the job each week. For all those weeks, this was to be his first try at it. Guessed that wasn't too bad, really.

Once on the path, the spirit laced into him. "Never speak to your mother in that tone. I do not care what she says or what you think. It will only cause problems for our work."

The boy stopped to listen, leaning on the outhouse door. Why was he on her side?

"Move!"

The voice sent him whirling back into action. He lifted the top half of the chemical toilet off the receptacle tank. Lowered it to the floor. Then he struggled with the heavier lower half, and dropped it awkwardly into the wheelbarrow just outside the door. Could hear all the juicy crap swishing around inside. Gross! Now he remembered how far he would have to push the tank. A six-foot deep hole on the other end of the island served as the toilet dump. It had been his father's last bit of work on the island. "You can't just dump a chemical toilet anywhere," he had said the week he had started to dig in five different unsuccessful spots around the island. Something like five, anyway. Most of the island was so rocky that there weren't too many options. The old outhouse had been full and the composting toilet his father wanted to buy was sold out. Nobody knew it then, but with the chemical toilet and dumping hole, Bruce Reddy had saved the day for the last time on the island. He had dubbed it "The Coal-Hole." And no one had bothered to buy the composting toilet after that.

Philip sweated with the heavy wheelbarrow over the roots on his way around the island, the spirit harping at him on and off. A couple of times he almost tipped everything over as he tried to shake off the mosquitoes gnawing on the backs of his arms. He had to turn around and drag the whole contraption over the largest roots. Along the south path, past the point where the path nearly fell into the water, past the open grassy slope leading to Grandpa's grave, and into the thicker brush again. Then a sharp left, toward the middle of the island onto the greener, more freshly cut "Coal-Hole" path. At the pit, he lifted up the old wooden plank, supporting it on his shoulder, and tried to pour the tank's contents away into the ground. Its weight sent him stumbling and made him partially miss the hole. The black-green sludge splashed onto the level ground, and soaked his shoe. He groaned, and took a careful step backward and almost slipped into the hole himself. The tank fell to the ground and another spray of sludge shot up out the opening with the impact. The plank slammed back down over the open hole. The tank produced a low gurgle and almost toxic smell sifted into the air. Gross!

Philip swore. Then whined, "What am I going to do?"

"You are not a baby. You are dirty. Clean yourself. Go!"

But the boy just stood looking down at himself, flustered. Then he ran out onto the south path again and down Sumac Rock to the water's edge. He peeled off his still clean t-shirt and shuffled down the sloping bedrock into the shallow water, shoes on. He let himself fall forward into the cool wet. That water made him feel secure again. After a few minutes of soaking, he waded up onto the shore and did his best to wring out his shorts without removing them. Checked the contaminated shoe, and swished it around again in the water to make sure. Then he saw something white in the water. A flickering down on the bottom.

The bar of soap! From the other day! It had somehow drifted downshore. Was it a sign or something? Forget it!

He dripped up the path to the pit and finished his job. Carefully poured the rest of the sludge out away from his now water-soaked but clean shoes, legs spread widely. He brought the tank back down to the water and started filling it to rinse it out as he had once seen his mother do.

"Fool!"

"What?" What now? The soap?

"You mix your filth into the water of the lake. If that were meant to be, your father would not have made a hole on land."

"What the hell do you want me to do? And what the hell do you know about my father?! I have to rinse this out. And I know my mom does it like this." Behind all this he wondered if the spirit did know his father. They were both dead, after all.

"Think is what you should learn to do. I told you not to cross your mother. I never told you to follow her folly. Think!"

The next few moments seemed especially allotted for Philip to work out a solution.

He used his time as best he could. Then he had it. "I'll use another container to fill it up."

"Yes. And then?"

"What do you mean?" Just missing it.

"Ack!" The spirit lost patience. "What will you do with the foul water?!" Philip shrunk beneath the rage. "Um. I'll...ahh...bring it back to the house and, uh, pour it down the sink?" But that couldn't be right....

"That is not necessary, idiot."

"Put it into the hole?"

"Better. Now, move."

The boy followed the instructions without further incident. He stole back to Swimming Rock and grabbed a plastic drinking cup to use for rinsing the tank. Everything was over in twenty minutes, the cup back in its place. When he arrived back at the house, he found his mother reading some women's magazine on her bed. She seemed to have forgotten all about the punishment and whatever lesson she wanted to teach him. She nodded at his appearance, and went back to her article on how to improve something or other. Like he could have ignored her orders and just gone off again. Just as he pulled his curtain, she called out. "Wait!"

He stopped and re-traced his steps back to her doorway, ready for just about anything.

"Okay, Philip. I see you like to play with the boat. You may use the six whenever you like, but you must tell when you go and when you'll be back. And it must be reasonable. Otherwise.... Well, it just won't work and you'll be stuck here. Am I being fair or am I being fair?"

He bobbed his head ambiguously and gave her what she wanted, "Fair." What she said actually did impress him, aside from the last typical bit asking for credit. He put together a quiet thank you, so she couldn't call him ungrateful, then turned back towards his room.

The spirit spoke before he could manage a clean fall onto his lower bunk. "The day is now yours. Do not waste it away. Think of the children and understand your luck at being here today. Tomorrow morning we will return to Mudjeekawiss and Zaugitau with more food and the continued ceremony. Be well rested." And he was gone.

Philip slept for a good hour, then awoke, wondering if there was some good luck to his being here as the spirit had suggested. He supposed it was better than staying in Thunder Bay except that it brought everything back. He wished his memory of other summers here wasn't so crisp. He wandered around the island. Lonely, but not quite depressed.

As promised, the next morning Philip was pulled from his slumber early. He spent a good couple of hours at the gravesite beyond the cliffs in the dehydrating sun, giving his pale skin a raw pink hue, but was set free again afterwards. The ceremony was performed through him again, and things were slightly easier because the bag and wigwam had been made. He did some drawing that afternoon, but nothing was worth finishing.

The next two days seemed to be carbon copies of the last but with cloud cover. He made the trip, made sure the wigwam still stood, placed another bulb for the children's journey, somehow sang the words he didn't understand just by clearing his mind. Although it seemed the same each day, there was comfort in having a job to do and knowing he would be free once it was done.

Before bed on the fourth day, he asked his mother if he could take the boat out early again the next day, just for good measure. She agreed. And he slept soundly again, looking forward.

TWENTY

Migizi

"First look at the map on the wall and then follow my instructions. Find the island where this house stands. Use your finger."

Philip took a good look at the map above the table, but could make no sense of it. Started to look around Kenora, upper right corner. His brain was still filled with sleep. He glanced at the clock on the coffee machine— 5:49 am!

The spirit gasped in disbelief. "Do you not know which island this is? How is this possible? Does a white child have no sense of adventure or curiosity?"

Philip shrugged. Some did, but not him. His dad had been that inspiration. That was that.

"Find the words Grouse Inlet with your finger." Philip felt the spirit almost exploding inside him as his finger skimmed across the old map, then zeroed in on the title. "Now move your finger down slightly...stop! There!"

He had found it! He felt a sense of wonder as his eyes scanned the map with respect to the spot beneath his finger. The lake was huge! He had never really considered its size before. He lifted the finger and looked at the tiny oblong shape below. A cross even marked the west reef.... The rest of the map slowly started to make sense to him. The open bay to the west. Misty Bay, where the mainland shack was. The swamp bay behind the island. White Partridge. Above it all, the black line of the highway....

The spirit intruded again. "Focus! Now move your finger slowly down and right.... Stop! The island just to the right of your finger—mark it. Mark it. That is where we go now."

It seemed a bit far from his own island, if the scale was at all right. He wondered if going there was such a good idea. What if the motor broke down? Or a storm came up? His heart sank further when he remembered he had no choice in the matter. He concentrated on the destination, lifting his finger just off the map. Stepped away with his eyes fixed on it, fumbled on the desk below the shelves for a pencil. Then circled it soundly.

"Take the map off the wall."

Philip hesitated.

"Ah, yes. Your mother would notice..."

"I know!" he blurted out loud, then slapped a hand across his mouth for silence. He leaped across the room, landing hard on his heels, and opened the lid of an old butter box now used as a coffee table. Maps! His father used to keep laminated, waterproof navigation charts in there. "Got it!" he declared as he pulled a few maps from the box. Ignored his mother's shushing and opened the maps, giving them all cursory once-overs. The hard laminated paper banged about loudly as he hastily unfolded and flipped the detailed sheets of yellow-coloured land and blue-and-white swirled water. Their scales were all larger than the one that hung on the wall. They each highlighted a different part of the lake. Philip found one titled Shoal Lake-Clearwater Bay and brought it over to the wall. He held the new version up over the wall chart with the point of the pencil, and scanned it for familiar formations. He circled an island he thought was his own, and then a moment later, circled another. The pencil barely showed. He pushed harder to make a dent in the plastic. He checked it twice. Sure, but didn't want to make a stupid mistake. "Is that it?"

No answer. But then, an almost incredulous, "Yes. Yes it is." Some of the harshness gone from the voice. Almost tender. As if Philip weren't quite as stupid as assumed. Another moment of silence passed before the voice sounded again. "Be sure to bring string, tobacco, bulbs and berries if you can find them, and a rag of some sort. Also find something for an honourable, wise old man. This gift should not be a white man's trinket. Once again, it should come from the land. Soon we will need more tobacco. I will tell you the story of this man on the journey. You will need to know it to perform the ceremony."

Ceremony?! You're joking! Why would he even want me to try that again? Although no one had been around, the last four days of this kind of thing had been highly embarrassing.

He gathered the materials and found an old, fabric satchel to put them in. It had probably been Grandpa Frederick's. It might be a long time, so he took a can of 7Up from the fridge for the trip. His father's Swiss army knife. He made sure to grab a lifejacket before he headed down the path. But he still needed some kind of present for an old man...an honourable, wise old man. Maybe someone like Grandpa Frederick. But Indian. He surprised himself with the generous thought, since no Indian could be anything like his grandfather.

He walked down the path slowly. Engrossed in the search for something to offer, he didn't think any more about the long distance to travel. But he found nothing. From the dock, he gently tossed the satchel into the stern of the boat and the can inside it clanged against the boat bottom. He untied the ropes and began pushing the bow down the beach into the water.

A present.... Still needed to find one.

He looked down as the boat finally slid free and his eyes found the perfect thing. On the beach right at his feet lay a piece of driftwood. Shaped like a whale or a dolphin, about the size of his hand. He bent down and picked it up. Stepped around the bow to the lapping edge to rinse the sand off. The wood felt wonderfully smooth against his palm and fingers. Cool, wet, soapstone-dark now. Perfect. Too perfect for a dead Indian, really. He tossed it lightly into the boat. Ready for launch, he lifted the boat off the sand again and pushed off. One foot in, one foot dangling. The keel grazed the sandy bottom once with his weight-shift, then the boat floated free through the few reeds into the deeper water. As he stepped away from the bow, the flat bottom of the stern slapped down onto the water's surface, sending ripples in all directions. He tilted the motor down and pulled the ripcord.

With the motor running, Philip swung the boat around and began the journey, surprising himself with his dexterity and borderline recklessness. He had been so cautious and uncomfortable in boats just days ago. And hadn't ever enjoyed them, except with his father.

The island's shelter abandoned him as he rounded its east tip. The wind gave the aluminium boat a broadside shove. Small, tight waves made the boat's bow bounce like a rubber ball. Soon the boat settled into a somewhat sporadic rhythm all its own, the metallic bounce and vibrating rivets in the warming seats. The sun shone hot on Philip's neck as it peaked out above the trees behind the swamp. He could almost feel his skin starting to sizzle again. Had to remember sunblock next time. Once he had consulted the map and found a straight line of travel, the spirit spoke.

"Many years ago, on the island we will see today, lived an old medicine man. This was before my time. Before the fur trade changed us forever. Before it had reached this far west, in the second half of your 17th century.

This man was very important to his clan and other people of the area. His knowledge of both the land and spirits was vast. His true name was Mishi-Coocoocoo, but many called him Migizi instead. Migizi is Wise Eagle. They gave him that name because when they did not find him at his camp, instead they found a great bald eagle perched on a dead branch near the top of the tallest white pine on the island.

"One of the first things of note the Saugaushe, your people, did on this lake was to kill this great man.

"Mishi-Coocoocoo had journeyed north and west a few years earlier with a small group of Anishinaabe who had young children and needed to be clear of danger from other nations pushing this way. The whites pushing west made the Iroquois push west before them, both with the motive of furs. The Sioux came up from the south. This wise man had already begun telling the people of the ending of the world. He said that neither the Iroquois nor the Sioux would be the cause. He talked of a time when the hunting grounds provided to the people by Gitche-Manido would be swept away. He knew many things.

"My people thought the English killed Mishi-Coocoocoo because they knew how important he was to the people. They said the English knew his death would weaken the Anishinaabe. That is what we learned in the stories of my lifetime. But the murder was more shameful than that, for it was an act with no motive but ill will.

"The white men landed on the island in birch bark canoes they had stolen. They were not soldiers or the religious cloaked people, but the typical renegades who had pulled ahead of most of the whites to lay claim to whatever fortunes lay westward. The five men saw the smoke coming from the island of Mishi-Coocoocoo and thought to pillage a camp. Despite his wisdom, the medicine man was unprepared for the attack. The bullet gave him no time to recognize that this was the first wave of the newcomers who would destroy the world as he himself had predicted. A bald eagle continued to roost on the island for many years, until it too was shot by a white trader."

The story slowly crept up Philip's spine. It tarnished the image of his ancestors as discoverers, just as the dreams had done. He hated the story, but couldn't disbelieve it. The spirit seemed to be a lot of things, but was no liar. Philip turned the boat into the mouth of a large and deep bay with a growing sickly feeling in his stomach. He slowed and checked the map. Just one point down and to the right, he figured. He was surprised by how quickly he had travelled what he had thought was a full day's journey on the map. It was the farthest he had ever been from the island alone, or with strange company for that matter. His heart pumped with still unfamiliar excitement. He was actually doing something! There had been a difference in his life in the last five days.

The building wind and waves pushed him from behind now. The boat kept a new, slower rhythm, rolling on top of the waves. Toward the back of the bay vertical white lines striated the green-black of the unmolested forest. Birches. The very end of the bay was so far away that it was a blur below the blue sky. As he rounded a tip of land to his right, he found the island that was his goal. The map really worked. And it was so easy!

Once he had circled the island without finding a docking spot, the spirit directed him to a tiny beach just barely visible on the north side. The voice complained that Philip had not found it himself. He must take on more responsibility, it reminded him gruffly. He pulled the boat out onto the short pebble beach just six feet wide. With the boat tied to the most accessible tree trunk, he looked up to find only dense woods. No path. He didn't dare ask for more help. He picked up his satchel, put the driftwood whale into the side pocket, and slung it all over one shoulder. The only option seemed to be to charge through the bush. His father had always said it was better to stay on the paths if he could. It was better for the trees, especially the scrawny little ones you might really trample. By the end of the last four days at the first site, he had almost made a path through the wild brush. Again this time there was no other option, so he took his first step with a clear conscience. Something in the underbrush scratched at his legs. Might have been thistle. He concentrated on parting the branches that all seemed poised to gouge out his eyes, ignoring the ones that poked his stomach and scraped his bare legs. He stumbled on unseen roots and bushes, and fell down once with the loud snaps of dozens of twigs beneath him.

After what seemed a long distance, Philip stepped up onto a clearing. The ground was mossy, but hard and dry. Must have been bedrock just beneath it. The sun streamed down on his reddening neck again. He suddenly realized that more trees stood on this island than his own, although it was half the size.

"You must go through one more layer of wood before you come to the right place," the spirit announced.

Philip wondered which way, but dared not ask. He narrowed it down. It couldn't be back the way he had come. He walked across the clearing and peered into the trees: water there too. Opposite that side, the trees almost melted into black, thick and wild. When he checked the remaining end of the clearing, he saw light through the trees to the right. He began pushing through, hoping he had made the right choice.

As he scrambled and broke twigs and branches in his way, he remembered that the spirit could read his thoughts. This spirit must have followed all of his reasoning as he figured out which direction to try. No scolding or interruption. Philip found it strange that someone so impatient could bear to let him waste all that time. It didn't make sense.

"Now we are here. Now we will begin."

The voice jolted Philip back to the here and now, to this second, smaller clearing. He tried to remember what he had done last time. All he could remember was digging up a bone. But he was not to do that again. His bag dropped to the ground. He bent down to untie the flap, knocking his knees together. Pulled out the old tin of Player's tobacco. Then the string, the bulbs, the rag. He checked for the whale in the side pocket and put it on top of the rag on the ground. What else? He spread the rag out and sprinkled a small ration of tobacco from his hand onto the middle. There seemed to be very little left, a detail he had missed in his excitement the night before. Had he used too much earlier? How to cut the string came back to him. The roll of string would certainly last a lot longer than the tobacco. He spun himself around, trying to locate a cutting surface or a tool of some kind. The land was very different here compared to the woods up on the cliffs. Not so high. Flat, mossy, almost field-like right here. No ledge like he had used last time. But a small, perfect skipping stone next to his foot seemed to lie waiting just for him.

A sudden flash of his father skipping rocks swept through his mind. He had always made it look so easy. Philip had tried and tried, and finally succeeded once or twice, but never could master it. And hadn't tried since.

He held the rock tightly in his hand and dragged his mind back to the present. Keep moving and no one will bug you. Spinning again, he found a patch of bare, flat bedrock near the bush he had come through. He sprang over to it excitedly and began using it as a chopping board. He sliced at the string with the rock-knife. Once he held the cut length in his hand, it struck him that he had a knife there with him, at the bottom of his bag somewhere. Stupid. He brought the foot-long piece over to his mide bag in progress, moved the piece of driftwood to the side, and began tying. This stuff was almost fun! He almost giggled out loud. The tying was difficult, but easier the second time. He did it all without instruction until—

"Stop." The voice was calm, but stern. "Do not finish tying the mide bag yet. I have told you the story, have I not?"

"Yes," Philip answered, puzzled.

"Then why do you smile and laugh? Have you not yet learned that the same evil lurks in your blood? The evil which flowed in the veins of your ancestors? Are you not sorry about this death? The mide bag must be prepared with the heart. In a case where a person has been killed so unjustly, the heart must mourn." Slowly less aggressive. "Your heart is able only to feel sadness for itself. Perhaps you must learn slowly. But still, you must learn…" The voice tapered off.

Had the spirit given up? Philip's mind went back over the accusations of racism. A Nazi? Before he let himself feel sorry, he reminded himself that Indians were stupid. They are, he decided. They are. Still, he finished tying the mide bag while thinking of the old man. He felt no real pity, but tried to please the voice in his head.

"Now we will try again," said the spirit, apparently satisfied. "You will repeat the words after me. Repeat them with the same tune this time. While you do this, dig a small hole for the offering. Listen…"

The suddenly familiar tones echoed through Philip's head. He remembered the near euphoria and great pain of the spirit taking hold of his body each of the last days. The words stopped for a moment. Philip was supposed to repeat them now. The spirit hadn't asked him to try again after day one, but now it was as if he was supposed to have been studying for some kind of test. He gulped and tried feebly. All wrong again. But the spirit seemed to be giving him a chance this time as he seemed to recite a second piece and then pause.

"K'neekaunissinaun, k'd'ninguzhimim."

Philip tried again.

Then he heard, "It's no use. Gitche-Manido would not recognize it."

Before he could respond at all, he felt the spirit swish out of him, so quickly that his body swayed. Alone. But only for a moment.

With another sudden rush, the voice warned, "Brace yourself, boy!"

Philip could feel the tingling begin. He felt sad that the song was yet another thing he was no good at. But realized in a moment that the spirit planned to do just as he had been doing. The pain in his head quickly reminded him thinking was exactly what he should avoid. He tried to paint a blank canvas. He knelt on the ground and tried to relax his body. Feet and hands trembled. Soon he found himself trying to put the mide bag into the

114

earth. His hands searched for a hole that didn't exist. His eyes could see there was none there. The spirit's control over his body was incomplete, but powerful. Again, Philip had to fight the power to help its cause. He concentrated until he gained control of his right hand. Pain coursed down his spine. Effort grunted through the foreign words. The hand began digging a hole in front of him. Never before had an act been so deliberate, so conscious, so painstaking. Beads of sweat ran from his hairline into his eyebrows. Not only was he digging, but re-teaching himself each movement as if he had never done this before. He could taste the salt seeping between his lips into his mouth, his jaw clenched shut. Everything vibrating.

When the hole was dug and the mide bag dropped inside, the pain eased its grip. A tingling replaced it as the spent boy relaxed his muscles and let the spell caress him. The strange presences graced him again. But were one less this time. Fleeting, but compelling. He put the whale on top of the grave.

When he remembered the bulbs, he had to cross the threshold again. The pain seared through him as he reached into his satchel and grabbed hold of two. When he remembered the wigwam, he knew he didn't have the strength to go and find sticks with the spirit taking so much of him. Again, he relaxed. He would bear the consequences. The tingling came back, soothing the muscles that had worked so hard. He felt as though he were hovering above the ground. Still kneeling, he was not front-heavy enough to fall onto his face, but his folded legs prevented him from leaning back at all. He swung back and forth like a baby in loving arms.

The sounds and tingling stopped and Philip caught himself as he fell forward.

"Did we do it again?" he asked, still high on the adrenaline.

"I did it. And now I tire. The old man is well on his way. Still, I must provide shelter for him. Make a wigwam over the bulbs."

Philip felt unappreciated. "You know, I had to dig that hole myself. During your prayer thing. I had to fight all your...stuff. It's not that easy, man!"

"Rubbish! You did nothing. You are just the means through which I work."

But that wasn't right! He had dug the hole himself! He looked at the dirt under his nails. Frustrated, but more tired than anything, he wanted desperately to sleep. Right there. It seemed he was already out of practice in this new game he was playing—the last three days hadn't required him to do anything more than clear his mind for the spirit to work. Now he was back to digging, building and being forced to try to sing like in some mad music class or something.

"We go now. No sleep. We cannot risk your mother's disapproval or punishment by staying away too long. Do not forget this medicine man named Mishi-Coocoocoo. Keep him with you even if you do not love him. We will return to him tomorrow." He paused. "Go now."

Philip turned to pick up his belongings from around the clearing. Slipped the new cutting rock into his bathing suit pocket. He peered into the trees around him to find the side of the clearing he had entered from, tried to piece the puzzle together in reverse. He started through the thick growth and soon saw through to the other clearing. Out in the open a second time, his sense of direction abandoned him. He stepped onto a large boulder and turned to see he had missed the beach by about thirty feet. Loser! He could see the stern of the boat sticking out from the inlet. Not wanting to risk losing himself by heading back to the clearing for another attempt, he scaled the shoreline toward the boat and soon found himself standing on the beach, relatively unscathed.

Another perfect skipping rock lay right next to his foot. He felt like giving it another shot. He picked it up and tried to skip it. One clumsy splash. He had completely forgotten how to do it. And who would teach him now? No one. There was that other new rock in his pocket, but he didn't dare try again. He tried to think only of the ceremony he had performed and performed well, whether he got credit for it or not.

About to swing the bag into the boat, he remembered the 7Up and smiled to himself. Satisfied, he pushed off, popped open the can and took a large swig. Looking at this thick, bushy tuft of an island from out on the water, he noticed no particularly tall tree for an eagle to perch on. Wondered about how much of these stories was true.... But he remembered challenging the lack of cedars at the last site too.

The sun had moved quite a distance across the sky. He checked his watch again and headed for home. Retracing his steps was still a challenge. Everything on the map upside-down this time. Once out of the long bay, he put the map down and headed straight for home.

That night he finally let his mother put cream on his sunburn.

TWENTY-ONE

A Familiar Wise Man

"Wake, my child." A rough old hand lay lightly on Philip's head. "Drink this herb water. And sleep again."

He did as he was told, up on one elbow, and tried to focus his sleep-filled eyes. The head that hung over him eclipsed the sun. Only wrinkles and kindness were detectable in the mysterious silhouette. The water was warm and had little bits floating in it, like Chinese tea. The warm liquid felt good as it went down his throat into his stomach. Tasted like a tree. After two sips, he tried to identify his surroundings. Outside. A strange, flat clearing. A smoky fire with a pot on a tri-pod hanging over it burned to his left. He tried to sit up, but his body was too weak. On the other side stood a strange looking hut or tent. Wigwam?

The silhouette appeared again. "Do not move. You must have patience. Your breath must become dry again."

"Where am I? Who are you?" A panic struck Philip at hearing the strange voice again. As he finished speaking, he realized they were both speaking a language quite other than English. Words he shouldn't have been able to understand. But he understood them all.

"Do not be afraid. A young brave found you on the sandy beach and brought you to me. Drink again and sleep. Your heart is still heavy from the water." The voice was phlegmy and rasping, like that of a man maybe too old. The words sounded familiar.

"Sandy beach.... I don't— I mean—"

The figure brought a finger to his lips. "Shhh. Trust. Sleep will help to heal you."

Philip closed his eyes after sipping from the strange bowl again. The smell of the broth and the smoke seeped into him, caressing his body, easing his mind. Just as he was fading from consciousness, he felt the soft flap of a feather and a quick burst of wind. The beating of wings was the last thing he heard.

TWENTY-TWO

The Legend of Mong

Philip awoke peacefully just after dawn. He felt he might have had another strange dream. He knew it had been no nightmare as a great calm seemed to hold him safely. Had he dreamed of the old man for the fourth night in a row? He looked out the window. The sky was a white sheet. Maybe cloudy or maybe the sun hadn't turned the sky blue yet. The weather this summer had been a lot better than last year. As boring as the island could be outdoors, indoors, under pelting rain for an entire summer was a thousand times worse. The extreme wet of last year's July hadn't helped soothe his pain at all either.

He sat up and swung his feet around onto the cool floor. Today he would swim. Swimming had been a forced activity since last summer—his mother insisting he wash—but today he couldn't wait. Like the day he first made the contract with the spirit. The unfamiliar true desire to swim. He had swum each of the last few days because it was hot. Just jumped in and out to cool off. He slipped into his suit, grabbed the towel off the hook and headed for Swimming Rock. At the end of the path, he stopped and looked out across the water. Mirror still. He found himself thinking, beautiful. Seagulls guarded the Big Whale, one of two little islands that resembled the ocean giants just over a hundred metres off shore.

He stepped gingerly down the escarpment onto the rock. Let his towel slip off his shoulders and stepped down ledge after ledge until he was waist-deep, ten feet from the shore. The shocking cold didn't grip him as roughly as usual, but the water heightened the feeling of his sunburn for an instant before it soothed it. After one last gaze around at the stillness, Philip broke the surface with his thin chest. His body's redness soaked the lake in like the earth of a too-dry potted plant. In a mounting good feeling, the boy's mind wandered to the old man who had nursed him last night. The old man had made his heart glow. He remembered clearly now, still somehow warm. The warmth gave him power. As he treaded water, he turned to look back at Swimming Rock, then again to look out to the Whales. It might not be that hard to swim out there, even for a weakling like him. He felt a compulsion. With broad, gawky strokes he pulled himself away from the comfort of the island. The new energy in him made the trip quite short despite his terrible form. In a few minutes, panting fiercely, he was just inches from the sloped shore of the closer Little Whale, the hump of rock that was the smaller replica of the Big Whale. The feeling of touching it was gold. Suddenly fearful this power might desert him and leave him stuck there, he pushed off again and headed for home.

After a larger than usual breakfast, Philip picked up his satchel and checked his inventory. Today was day nine by his count, so there would be some new twist to things if there was any rhythm at all. He wondered for a moment if he would ever set foot on the two sites he had worked on. Why would he? He didn't know those people? Yet still he wondered. He hoped for some instruction soon, but was not prepared to wait for it. It was past the time of the usual morning call of 5:45 am, and he was ready to make a move.

He went to his mother's rag bag in the utility room and pulled out a few good sized pieces of cloth. If this was to be his new business, he might as well keep a good supply of materials. The jack-knife hadn't been much use thus far, but it made him proud as he slipped it into his pocket. Maybe he would use it for something important today.

What else? Tobacco? Check. Bulbs? Check. Ready. He thought to pick some berries for good measure if he had time. He had harvested enough bulbs for a few more days yesterday in the back swamp.

"Bring three stones."

Philip felt like greeting the spirit upon his morning arrival, but what do you say to a voice inside your head?

"And make sure you have at least three rags with you. The remaining tobacco must last all of today. Three bags' worth. Then you must get more. Food as well. We will deal with three more souls for the next four days. You do not have enough."

Philip realized the spirit was all business and did not respond except by following orders although part of him wanted to complain that he should have been told to collect more bulbs while he was doing it yesterday. He did notice the we instead of I in the spirit's talk. Mildly flattered that finally the change had been made. He picked up his lifejacket and began walking down the path toward the boats. Then he remembered his mother. She was still asleep, so he could hardly ask the permission he was supposed to. Maybe he would just go, risk it. But the spirit had warned him about angering his mother. He walked back to the house and wrote her an unusually cordial note.

About to shove off from the beach, he remembered the stones. He looked just next to the boats and bent down to pick up three stones nestled in the sand. He held them in his palm, wondered what they were for.

"Those are pebbles!" The voice was angered. "I said rocks!"

"No. You said stones. Stones!" Philip answered instinctively.

"I said rocks!"

"No, you didn't! I heard—"

"Silence! Do not question me. Rocks. Three rocks. Rocks are larger."

Philip knew he had heard right. Knew that he was right. Was suddenly quite tired of being bullied. A heated frustration crept over his skin. "Fine!" he retorted under his breath as he whipped the pebbles into the water. Rocks! What the hell?! Philip looked up at the bank and spotted three good-sized rocks, each the size of a softball. One at a time, he waddled them over to the boat and lowered them gently into the bow. They still thundered against the aluminium as he let go of them.

"And three gifts. These can be fine stones. We will make them into personal gifts later."

'These can be stones.' What crap! Philip's face went red with anger, but he ran his fingers obediently through the sand until he found four good stones. He pushed the rock-laden bow out onto the water and motored out of the bay. With the boat moving across the mirror of water, he forgot his frustration and stole a moment to enjoy the perfect morning. He felt excited at getting up early with an adventure to tackle. The feeling still unfamiliar and new.

As he passed behind the island, he remembered again Zaugitau, Mudjeekawiss and Migizi. The spirit had said to keep them in his heart, and he was surprised to find that he actually was. Or at least as close as he could get to it.

Almost at the farthest mouth of White Partridge Bay, he slowed down suddenly. No instructions on where to go from here. He turned the throttle down to SHIFT, and the boat's wake increased momentarily as its little hull sank into the water. He tried to remember any clue he had been given at the beach, but his mind just drifted back to the old man. The sound of his fading yet strong voice each night. Bits of the dream came to him....Then it clicked—Migizi's island was the very island of his dream! He had met the wise man face-to-face! Four times now....

The three rocks rattled against the boat bottom, derailing his train of thought. Philip turned to look over his shoulder as the boat hovered in mid-channel. The old man's island was now indistinguishable against the back of the bay, or maybe it was behind a point of land from here. He felt sure he was still the only being awake. Or the only person anyway, glancing up at the two grunting ducks swooshing by overhead. It was both early and mid-week, so all the Winnipeggers were in the city. Most of them anyway.

As he gazed around, still somewhat lost in thought, he noticed the birds circling above the channel ahead of him, beyond the mouth of the bay. Circling gulls again....Without another thought, he charged for the circling mess of birds. It was his only clue. It had certainly meant something that day three weeks ago! Although he had been the one to draw them, if he remembered correctly.

As he approached the birds, he began to think their circling even more strange. There didn't seem to be anything to circle. No tree. No dumb kid digging a hole. Maybe they were hovering above a reef! He jerked the throttle down to SLOW, and bolted up onto his feet. But the water was dark and deep. The swirling birds rose to accommodate him, but didn't scatter in their usual way. Philip wondered if they were now circling him.

"Good." The voice, pleased. "This is the place."

"But there's nothing here," Philip whined. Crashing through brush to find new places had started being fun, but now he sat in the boat almost within view of his own island. There was little to it.

"Think about what you say."

"It's just water. I don't get it." Philip looked up, the gulls seemed to have evaporated. The wheels began to turn. "You mean—you mean there's dead people underwater?"

"Many. But here there are three. They do not lie together at the bottom, but they died together. All at the same two sets of white hands. The water is deep. The bones are covered only with thin moss at the bottom as flat rock offers no burial."

The spirit had struck a chord. Philip felt suddenly sad for the three people below. He thought again of Wise Eagle and how he had been killed for

no good reason. And the two kids. It all made him angry and confused.
"How? What—"

The spirit needed no more prompting, and began weaving a most incredible tale....

"On a day much like this one, with quiet waters and a sky of low clouds, three young Anishinaabe journeyed to check their fishing nets. Two were brothers. The other was a more experienced fisherman. All were less than sixteen-years-old. The youngest was only ten.

"Only the very young men would fish in these times, for big game animals still abounded and the fully grown men stalked them in the woods. Moose and deer were not rare as they are now. It was the women who checked the nets, as well as the younger or frail men. When the big game had vanished, the other men began to fish. But this is no matter now.

"As the braves paddled across this channel, a canoe of white men approached them. The young Anishinaabe saluted the approaching canoe, but their greetings were not returned. They knew these men were white by the way they moved. But they had yet no fear of the Wamitigoshe." The spirit was courteous enough to explain: "These common whites came mostly to speak of their god. The other whites with the sharper tongues, the Saugaushe, were not so harmless, but still rare. They were unruly and concerned only with what the land had to give them. Your kind. The kind that killed the other three we have helped on the path as well. It was the autumn of 1765 by your calendar."

Then his vigour increased. "Before the young men could flee, the canoe of the white men charged them. Negik, the fisherman, manoeuvred out of harm's way just in time. The whites spoke a strange language the Anishinaabe braves could not understand. They knew only that these had to be the sharp-tongued type.

"The whites wanted the young men to lead them back to their camp or village, so they could scout it and take from them what they pleased, or simply trade with them if the village was too big to pillage. However, Negik understood that these strange and hungry-looking men wanted to know where to find fish. He told the others what he thought and they agreed. Negik motioned for the whites to follow, and the Anishinaabe canoe resumed its course. The two whites grew angry and shouted obscenities in your English. First, they seemed to argue with each other. Then they followed the canoe. They called the attention of the braves and pointed them in the opposite direction where they had seen smoke the night before. Mong laughed in his friendly way and shook his head. The net full of fish was still ahead. Within a short moment, the front man drew a musket from the bottom of the canoe and shot the youngest brother, Wauh-Oonae, behind the ear. The blood flew upwards and out onto the water. The older brother, Mong, turned and leaped on top of the dead boy."

"For one short moment, the white men stopped to realize what they had done. The one holding the gun swore loudly. But he transformed any guilt he felt into a ball of hate as he hurried to reload his gun. I can feel his fleeting regret, but it was quickly forgotten.

"Negik tried to spin the canoe around from the stern, but it turned slowly because Mong lay grieving upon his brother in the middle of the canoe. 'Get up or we too will die!' cried Negik. Mong sprang up and paddled. Tears covered his face and rage filled his body. But the whites closed behind them. The white man in the bow stopped paddling and shot again. The bullet hit Negik in the back. He fell forward, but still paddled, leaning on the thwart in front of him. Mong knew Negik had been hit by the sound of the grunt and his heavy breath. But he did not dare to turn around or stop paddling. There came another shot. The canoe grew heavy under Mong's paddle. His two companions were dead. He turned to face his foes and dove into the water.

"Beneath the two canoes, he removed his clothes. He let them float upward. He looked up and saw the silhouettes of the canoes against the white sky. He saw his leggings jerk on the surface as the white man's bullet pierced the water's surface and the leather. The white men's canoe moved over to the lump of clothing to prod for his dead body. Mong saw one of the killers whack the water angrily with his paddle. But he could not rejoice at having caused them frustration. Two Anishinaabe were dead.

"He needed air. From two body lengths down, he rose to the surface as far from the canoes as possible. He pushed through the surface with a gasp.

"'There!' said the gunman. He fired once more, and the stern man steered the canoe toward Mong's position. The young brave ducked under again. He knew he had at least another minute if he conserved his energy. He thought to outrun them underwater. He gathered his bearings, turned toward the nearest shore and swam as efficiently as he could. Above him, the whites still scanned the surface. They could not let him escape. They knew these red people could be angered and were very dangerous in large groups. Mong rose to the surface without being seen. He renewed his breath and readjusted his course. He felt he must get away for the others who did not.

Revenge crossed his mind. The water was dark and the algae stung his eyes. His fatigue made him break the surface sooner this time. He gagged on the water.

"'There he is!' shouted the stern man who spied the boy's sputtering.

"'Go! He's headed for the shore! Cut him off!' He threw down his gun and began paddling.

"Mong ducked under again. But his own choking had not allowed him to hear the men. He was unaware of having been seen and continued on his course. But the canoe moved much faster than he could swim and, suddenly, he felt a stir in the water and the shadow pass over him. He did not understand how it was possible. He tried to double back, but he needed to rise again. By the time he reached the surface, the whites had passed, checking all around them. Then the stern man spotted him. Mong stayed at the surface for a few moments to gather his strength. The canoe turned and headed directly for him. As the bow man raised his gun, Mong ducked. He heard the great crack through the surface. He remembered the weapons of the whites were slow to reload, so he took another breath.

"'There he is again!' cried the stern man. 'Get him!'

"Mong went under again. The gun did not go off this time. It waited for him. He had to stay down. He hovered just deep enough to avoid being seen. The white man was ready for him. There was no hope to reach the shore or the other canoe. So the young brave decided to charge the white men's canoe. This was the only possible way. He treaded water directly under it. Slowly, he eased himself up to the surface. He tried to make a plan. He came up from the stern and allowed only his lips and nose to break the surface. He felt that the whites had not seen him. He played the game for a few moments. They would either give up or figure him out.

"'There!' he heard one shout.

"The canoe rocked as the bow man staggered to turn around. The man said, 'Red bastard! Load your gun too. We'll get him. Get ready to club him with your paddle.'

"Mong sank below them again. But he knew he could not last. His heart pounded.

"Then he rose up toward the canoe. He punched the canoe on one side, then ducked underneath it as the whites leaned over. He pushed the other side up a little bit. As the whites tried to compensate by stepping toward that side, he grabbed the gunwale and pulled down with all his fury. The canoe capsized. From the air pocket beneath the canoe he drew the breath he needed. He knew they would find him if he stayed even another moment, so he ducked down and swam toward the other canoe.

"But a hand grabbed his foot. He pulled away, but another body stopped him. He struggled beneath the surface. He pushed and punched to be freed.

"The white men held him under until he lost his fervour. Then the stern man held him as the bow man bashed his head and face with the butt end of a paddle. He had almost escaped, but had had too little strength left...."

Philip realized the story was over. The here and now felt less real than the struggle he felt he had just lived through. He had no response. Mong had been so smart, but so unlucky. Philip could barely believe the young man hadn't escaped, that there was no happy ending for this hero. His mind still dodged bullets from beneath canoes.

The spirit spoke in a more detached, sobering voice. "We have drifted. Bring us back."

Philip started the motor and brought the boat to where he thought they had begun. A nudge from inside told him to shut the motor down. He moved to the front of the boat and grabbed his satchel. From inside, he pulled three rags, the small pebbles, the string and the tobacco tin. He opened the tin and sized up the meagre amount remaining. It had to go three ways. And he needed a little to sprinkle for three more days as he completed the ceremony. He carefully laid out the three rags on the middle aluminium seat. Tiny, even rations of tobacco on each. With a glance just below the foremost seat, he realized what the big rocks were for. Pretty smart. The spirit seemed to think of everything.

Philip unravelled about seven feet of string from the spool. He forgot about the jack-knife again and cut the string with yesterday's skipping rock, leaving a scratch on the aluminium seat. With one end, he tied the rag together. He moved to the bow and picked up one of the heavy rocks. He looked at the rock in one hand and the mide bag in the other. Slowly, he began wrapping the rock with the mide bag string. Five times one way. A half-hitch. Then three across. There was no more string suddenly. Philip loosened the wraps and passed the mide bag through them, then pulled them tight again, binding the bag to the rock. This one was for the youngest. Philip tried to remember his name, but could not. He did the same for the fisherman. The spirit scolded him, demanding he pay better attention and show more respect. They were Wauh-Oonae and Negik. But for Mong, whom he could never forget, he took more time. He already felt close to him. He wished he could be so brave and smart. He knew that this boy had been exactly his age, a better version of himself. Maybe it was their unluckiness that bonded them together. Before he finished this last anchor-bag set, he kissed it. Mong.

The spirit took control of Philip's body again as the rite began. Philip struggled to throw the weighted mide bags and totem stones overboard while his voice made the wondrous, incomprehensible noises. Even as he fought the spirit's power to do what he had to do, he listened intently. The ceremony hurt less this time. Maybe it was because he knew better how to free his mind. Or maybe it was because he felt true remorse. No shelter was needed for those under water, so there was no wigwam to worry about. He threw one bulb each into the water, along with the rest of his blueberries. They floated, but the spirit said not to worry. Philip barely noticed as the first huge drops of rain pounded down on him.

The calm surface became a blur of activity. The rainfall was so thick that it hid the land from view. The rain crashed onto the lake, and even more loudly against the aluminium boat bottom. Philip sat unmoving, this time not overcome by the depression that always came with rain. A certain peace came with floating alone on the lake, protected from people by the weather. Safe. Surrounded by a falling grey-white curtain. He sat there immobile but not unhappy. Continued the chant which kept him warm. It crossed his mind that this was better than being burned to a crisp for a change.

That afternoon, once he had returned to the island, he thought of Mong and didn't do much else. The story still held him spellbound.

TWENTY-THREE

Brimstone and Treacle

The next morning he swam to the Little Whale again, this time climbing up onto the great rock to look around. He then made off for the site of the water grave for day two of the ceremony. His only thoughts were only of the three men. The words came in their strange rhythm and pattern of highs and lows. He recognized them better each time, almost knew where they were going.

"K'neekaunissinaun, zunugut ae-nummook..."

The sounds were as soothing as ever and somehow less alien. The urge to join in grew in him, but his mouth and voice were already singing. A forced spectator, although he shook and perspired.

"K'neekaunissinaun, mino-waunigoziwinning k'd'weekimmigoh..."

And the chant went on. His body shook and a hum built beneath the words. Louder than usual.

Then there were more voices.

Philip opened his eyes, the words still pouring out his mouth. "K'neekaunissi—"

Just ten feet from him, Max and Rupert stood in Rupert's idling speedboat, staring directly at him. Philip managed to stop his voice, ending in a curious mumble.

"Whatcha doin', Mr. Not-Reddy?" asked Max with his eyes squinting sceptically. "Masturbating? Friggin' loser!"

Rupert laughed. "No, man. He's speaking in tongues!" And roared at his own wit. "Aren't you a little far from home, Mr. Holy Roller?"

Philip felt himself disappearing although he wanted to shout that this wasn't far at all. He had been even farther a few days ago. But his head

128

tilted down. Eyes grabbed at the floor of his boat. What a coward he was! Angry with himself, he forced his head up to make eye-contact with the boys. Just for a second. He would get them somehow, some day. He swore it. But what could he say or do to them really? His eyes fell back down to the rivets on the boat bottom, where they belonged.

"We own this here lake," said Rupert in an exaggerated tone.

Max laughed his admiration.

Rupert went on, imitating some cowboy villain from a movie he must have seen. "This here lake ain't no psycho-church, boy. If you talk all crazy like that.... Well, we'll just have ta sink yer boat." He grabbed one of two fishing rods that were leaning against the side of the windshield and waved it at him threateningly.

The two boats bumped.

"Hey, check this out," Max offered. He leaned over into Philip's boat and slapped him soundly across the head.

Rupert's mouth widened with surprise, impressed by his sidekick. He laughed and took his turn. The boys each took another turn and shouted with the energy of violence. Rupert gunned the engine, pushing the bow of Philip's boat sideways. The boys circled Philip, shouting all the obscenities they could think of. Max barely missed Philip's head with an empty root beer can. The wake from their boat wove a treacherous swirl around and beneath Philip. He watched the wake, but did not raise his eyes until the boys tired of the game and raced away, hooting and hollering. Philip wondered where Franny was. Maybe she didn't like fishing.

The boat eased its rocking motion as the churning faded. The can bobbed cheerfully ten feet away. No other boats. Still pretty early. Philip was alone. Almost.

"What was that? You fool!" The spirit's voice was too loud, somehow booming in his ears although it did not pass through them. "Where is your pride? When will you take a stand? They hit you and you turned to stone! I felt it. It was not heroic self-control."

The spirit was right: Philip was no pacifist hero. He would have retaliated if he could. But those kids were so tough. He had no chance. He didn't bother trying to defend himself from the spirit's words either. Got what he deserved, every time.

"Pathetic," the voice grumbled. "They hit you!" Still incredulous. "They knew you would do nothing and that is why they did it without fear. They will do it again. They are nothing at all, but to you they are Mishi-naubae."

Philip did his best not to cry. Things had been not too bad for the last week, and now it was back to square one.

"Ack! Put the boat back where it should be and we will finish this before you melt. The Anishinaabe do not strike each other in anger, but you would tempt anyone to do so. You are the essence of frustration." A pause. Then another burst. "And pick that cursed can up out of the water."

Another boat passed him, a family staring.

If only he could have resisted the temptation of the mound in the first place. He always had before. Philip looked at the near-empty can of tobacco sitting beside him. What kind of crap is this?! Sprinkling tobacco into the water like some kind of witch doctor?! What is that?!

He wanted to curl up into a little ball and sleep until he felt better. Dad had taught him to sleep when he got upset—things always looked better the next day. He seized the can with every intention of tossing it over the side. "Man! Screw this!"

But then came a laugh. Not the scornful tone of the spirit or of the boys. Something completely different. The boy turned to catch a glimpse of a loon as it dove out of sight. It left a tiny, swirling pool behind. The widening circle of waves disappeared atop the larger lake swell. Then the laugh again. Straight ahead another loon. Philip could see its mouth move with the laugh. A sharp black beak opening and closing fast, almost vibrating. A big bird. It seemed to look directly at him. Just as its friend came up, the one staring at him went under. Philip waited, betting on where it would turn up. A few seconds passed.... On the other side of the boat! It must have swum right underneath him! Philip smiled with wonder. Both loons laughed together. Mesmerized him. Maybe they mesmerized the spirit too. No words were spoken. They were so close now that he could hear the slurp as the surface closed over as they dove again. Down, up again so near to his reach. Laughing. Almost beckoning.

After a full fifteen minutes, another boat whizzed by and both loons decided it was time to leave. They flapped their wings vigorously and rose slowly off the water, turning gracefully around a point into a bay. Out of sight. Laughs still sounding.

Philip sat for a moment, feeling somehow saved. He started the motor and brought the boat back to the approximate original spot. Without thinking, he said out loud, "That was neat, eh?"

After a few seconds, the voice responded. "That was not neat. You do not see all of what it was. It is difficult to believe."

"What? What is it? Magic or something? Did you do it?!" Growing more excited.

"No, I did not. I cannot explain it. Do not worry about this thing. It is only good."

Philip realized that was all he was going to get and tried to be content. His heart still beat excitedly. It was something special. He tried not to think of the loons while he finished the ceremony. But their joy lifted him and made him sure the ceremony was working.

As he headed for home, he made a quick detour further out into the open to rescue the bobbing can.

TWENTY-

FOUR

Good Will

At lunch, Philip remembered he had to convince his mother to go to town very soon so he could get his hands on some tobacco. The amount he had left was a joke. But it would never work. She only did what she wanted to do. Usually that was messing around in the garden while still trying to look like a movie star. She hadn't said a word when he had returned late for lunch. Hard to tell if she hadn't noticed he was late or if she was silently ready to kill. The notes must somehow satisfy her, he thought.

He finally thought of an angle and gathered the courage to try to talk her into it. Told her the small boat was almost out of gas. He was shocked to hear her suggest going to town all on her own. "We need vegetables and fruit anyway," she said. "And topsoil, of course. We'll go tomorrow."

Philip smiled at how easy it had been, but couldn't help being a little suspicious. His mother suggested an early start, and although he usually worked a ceremony to start the day, he figured the spirit wouldn't care if he knew this meant more tobacco. He could get out on the lake in the afternoon. Besides, there really was a shortage of gas now anyway.

Philip appeared to have the rest of the afternoon off once again. He swam playfully at Swimming Rock despite the still grey sky. He stopped for a moment and looked out over the water, thinking of Mong. He thought Mong would be a good friend to have. Then he swam to the Whale for the second time that day.

That night, with his head propped up on his arm, Philip drew Mong beneath a canoe, fooling the murderers. A lithe, agile Indian dream. Mong would be forever what Philip thought of bravery. He was no Mong himself, but he was quite happy with this latest drawing. Maybe his best yet. By the time the drawing was done and the lights out, Philip had worked himself up into such a state that he could not sleep. He longed to hear one of his father's great stories. He missed him so much sometimes that his boy heart felt physical pain, but tonight he just wanted a story. Without thinking it through, he whispered to the spirit, "Will you tell me another story?"

No answer.

"Hey!" he whispered a little louder. Wished there was a name he could call. "Are you there?"

"I have told you no stories."

"No. I know. But—I mean—I believe they were true, but could you make one up so I can sleep. I thought since—"

"Ack! Do you think we are friends?! I owe you nothing." The spirit was gruff and impatient. "Needjee you are not."

The shattered boy made no sound. A tear welled up from his eyes and rolled down his cheek and into his ear as he lay in his bed in the dark. A patter of rain started on the roof. What a fool he was! He caved in so easily. Too fragile. He swiped away the tear that stung his ego more than his skin.

"Once there was an old man named Grey Beaver. He lived many, many years before this time. He was wise and respected throughout the land, but his three sons had grown up to be troublesome. They refused to give their father or the legends of the land the proper respect."

Philip held back his thanks and dove headlong into the story. He was no longer in his bed with dried tears on his face, but somewhere altogether other. Perhaps the spirit had a heart after all.

A few minutes into the story Philip slept.

TWENTY-
FIVE

Have No Fear

Philip heard the brisk swish of the curtain from his half-sleep.

"Good morning, Sunshine. Let's get going."

He stirred and forced his eyes open to look up at his mother. It must have been a very late night. He felt it pounce on him now. Couldn't bear to get up even though he could feel it was well past the usual time he began his work. His muscles were amazingly sore from his newfound hobby of real swimming.

She watched him as he closed his eyes again. "Come on, Philip. I want to leave within the hour. Your breakfast is ready. And it'll be cold if you don't get a move-on." He could feel her still watching him. "Philip. I'm not closing the curtain again until I see you're sitting up."

God! "Okay, okay!" he barked. He sat up and looked angrily at his mother through the haze of sleep. She smiled an exaggerated smile and closed the curtain, leaving him to get dressed.

The sky had cleared overnight. Out the window it stretched infinite blue. He must swim! The urge seemed to grow in him every day. He stood up with sudden energy and traded his underwear for a bathing suit. Put on his flip-flops and grabbed a towel.

"I'm going swimming first. Bye," he called out as he left the house.

With Philip already out of the house, Jane peeked around the doorway of the kitchen. "Swimming?!" she shouted, as if she had never heard the word.

He didn't really care what she thought, although he guessed she would be happy he was getting clean. For the first time he thought she might not like him swimming so far away. The water called to him and he came.

134

At breakfast, he was quiet as usual, but cracked the occasional smile. The swims to the Little Whale were his secret. And it was a good secret. There was nothing weird about it. He tried to ignore his mother who kept trying to catch his eye, trying to trap him into talking again. But she went ahead and spoke anyway. "Okay. We're leaving in ten minutes. When you're ready, you can start carrying down the coolers. Oh! And put on some sunscreen or I'll have to do it for ya!" She smiled, mock-threatening.

He made sure to grab his wallet once he was ready. Buying the tobacco was his only thought. Then he would have enough for the others, however many more there were. Maybe buy two containers of the stuff. He dried his face on his sweatshirt sleeve, wet from a reckless tooth-brushing, and caught a glimpse of himself in the mirror. He squeezed a gross-sounding dose of factor-30 sunblock onto his hand, and started rubbing it into this face and neck. His face looked more tanned than he could ever remember, the burn from a few mornings ago fading. All that time outside in last few days. He could remember his father telling him when he was a little kid that if he got enough sun, his freckles would all come together and he would be a beautiful golden brown. It hadn't quite happened yet. His finger ran across his standard deep, painful pimple, this time on his right temple. Some things never changed. There was always another one on the way. That was why he avoided the mirror most of the time. He adjusted his glasses and pulled on his cap. Forced a smile and said out loud, "Who cares?" He slapped his pocket to check for his wallet, ready with forty dollars and change inside. He had money because he rarely spent any. As mean as she was, his mother even paid for all his video games, which he had lost interest in some time over the winter anyway. Tobacco couldn't possibly cost more than that. Ready for anything.

He followed his mother's directions and carried one empty cooler in each hand to the big boat. He woke the bilge pump which then gurgled and spat the rain of two days ago out the side drain hole. His next trip: two empty jerry cans for the small motor gas, oil already in the bottom. Noticing the oil, he felt a bit silly—he was the man, but his mother was the one who had taken over the job of measuring out the oil for the gas cans. It had never bothered him before. Hadn't thought about such details.

When he came back up to the house, his mother was about to lock up. "Wait! I forgot something!" He rushed toward her. Jane rolled her made-up eyes jokingly and swung the door open dramatically for her son. He charged in and grabbed the old satchel. It would hide the tobacco on the way home. Now back out past his mother without a word or a glance.

An early morning mist hung thickly on the lake as they approached the communal dock on the mainland. Jane made the big, old fibreglass boat come to a graceful but sudden stop near the old dock. Philip did his usual job of cushioning the landing against the bedrock shore. His job was to sit on the bow and fend off any potential hard, fibreglass-threatening landings, but he often just ended up pinching some part of his body. Mother and son lugged all the tanks, coolers and packs up the steep path to the car.

With the car packed and the dew still streaking the windows, Jane Reddy backed up and turned around to face up the road. The little Toyota engine conquered the first steep hill in its high-pitched first gear. Jane rode the ruts to the left to avoid gouging the undercarriage against the rocky, median-like rise that ran the middle of the road. The light car jerked and rocked over the old lumps that gave the road its character. They both gritted their teeth in wait for the inevitable bottoming-out just past the Melons' place. The road smoothed out and became almost dangerously soft and wet. Cars had been stuck along here more than once. Then, at last, the relief as they turned left onto the paved wonder of Grouse Inlet Road, better taken care of than most city streets. The car bucked as Jane tried second gear, a week out-of-practice, then roared to tackle the steepest hill on the stretch toward the highway. She gave a tentative honk at the crest, something Bruce had always done. From then on, the car swished easily around the curves offered by the road, most of the trip downhill. The road crossed the old highway where adolescent trees grew successfully through the cracks in the sinking pavement, then led up a final hill to the Trans-Canada. Two trucks rushed past, shaking the little Toyota, which then turned right to follow. The first green sign: "Kenora 19 km."

Jane looked over at Philip's intent expression in the passenger seat. "Why do you suddenly actually want to go to town? I usually have to drag you, or I just leave you behind."

"I dunno," he answered, hiding a smile. "Something to do, I guess."

"You've really taken to that boat, eh? Like old times." She stopped. Then more cautiously, "I mean, you're spending a lot of time going off places. Have you made a new friend?"

"Umm, no. Just exploring. There's lots of nice bays and islands I never saw before."

"Maybe I'll go with you some time?" Her lack of confidence with him suddenly obvious.

No answer. His face prickled. No way!

Jane put her hand on his knee briefly. That either meant she took back her stupid question, or she was pushing the envelope. Philip leaned the knee slowly out of her reach.

The car whizzed by the assorted mysterious roads and lily pad lakes. Philip tried to forget his mother and followed the old highway below to his right with his eyes. It seemed to lead right through a swamp. Maybe that was why they built a new highway in the first place—the road had sunk down into the goo. His view was blocked out by a close, thick stand of evergreens. They gave way again.... Some cheap-looking mini-golf place.... Trees.... A lake with nothing but a raft smack-dab in the middle.... The by-pass turn-off.... Billboards appeared every few seconds as they neared town: one for McDonald's with "McDeath" spray-painted in black over it... "Gayle's Motel"... "The MS Kenora Ship Tour"... "This is Pepsi country!" All looking very old.

Every thirty seconds, another hardware-lumber yard-type store. One on the left, one on the right. All the same. He wondered how they all did business? ...The ridiculously slow speed limits: 60, then 50 km/hr! The Reddy Toyota easily doubled that. Passed the Keewatin turn-off: "Town of Keewatin (Population 2000)." Philip guessed they would go in to pick up the mail on the way home. Not that he ever got any.

Soon they came to the construction site. The sun had crept up into the sky and burned in through the windshield. It seemed at least one of the bridges along the highway was always under construction. Philip peered out the window at the water below, shielding his eyes. Every few moments another powerboat passed beneath him out into Safety Bay where, if the water level were just ten feet higher, all of the low-slung land would be completely submerged. At least his island had something to it. He stared at the wake of each boat that passed. The woman in fluorescent orange standing in front of the car shifted her weight from her left to her right and flipped her sign to yellowy-green: SLOW. Like on the throttle of his six-horse motor. Everything seemed somehow connected to his new work. The car lurched forward, following the procession across the now single-lane bridge.

Along the glinting lake, past the Dairy Queen and Norman Motel. Down through Norman, past the bus station, a car dealership and up by the Husky. Then another bridge. This one with four big cement pillars boasting artistic black steel outlines of Indians holding spears and arrows. Philip wondered if the man inside his head had ever looked like one of them.

137

Finally, the flat of the Habourfront. Husky the Musky, the big fish statue. And all those boats and planes. The Kenora town centre loomed just ahead and to the right. A strange mix of old and new buildings. On the back of an old building was printed in huge faded letters A.T.FIFE & CO, bricks missing from the E. The highway became Main Street with a sharp turn to the right. The buildings hid the water except for occasional glimpses. Town seemed exciting today, a new experience.

On the steps of the library sat four Natives. Ojibways, he guessed, or whatever that other word was. It was only 9 am, but there they were, in party mode. Must have been drunk. A white family of five walked by them, chipper and well-dressed. Just down the street, the Reddys came up behind a Native family walking down the street. A mother and three kids. The mother was kind of fat and soft, and sported stretchy sweatpants with cheap, worn-out jogging shoes. The kids looked like their clothes came from the Salvation Army. The older boy and girl wore glum looks. The little one seemed playful, picking up stones off the sidewalk. It was like the little kid didn't seem to get it yet.

Philip leaned back into the car and let his head fall back onto the headrest. The sun couldn't warm him through the window anymore. Poor kid.

Jane stopped the car at a red light. "Should I let you off here? I have to—"

"Yeah," Philip interrupted, still dazed, but understanding the question. He opened the door before the car had come to complete stop, grabbed the satchel and stepped out onto the curb.

"We need to decide where to meet," she shouted after him. "I'm going to Safeway and a couple of other places. I should be done in about two and a half hours." She reached into her purse and opened her wallet. "Here's five dollars in case you get hungry."

Philip leaned in to take the crisp blue bill. Someone honked from behind as the light turned green.

"You know where the liquor commission is? How 'bout noon?"

"Okay," Philip answered and stepped back from the car.

Jane Reddy drove off, leaving her son to his mission.

He put the satchel on his back properly and checked for his wallet again. He paused, realizing he was no longer alone as he had been on the island, and slowly began walking down the street. Already the sidewalk teemed with the Saturday bustle of tourists and shoppers. Saturday was a big day in Kenora. He glanced behind him. The woman and three children had almost caught up to him because his mother had stopped so long to let him off. He turned away to continue down the street, but found himself frozen.

It seemed like hundreds of people were around him again. They passed him in both directions. He stumbled forward, his old self again. The island had sheltered him from his people problem to a great extent. That was the island's one positive contribution to his life. Until recently. This was supposed to be some side effect of losing his father, according to Doctor Southland. Philip would deny the whole thing, but his dizziness wouldn't let him. His heart pumped feverishly. His lower lip quivered. He was surrounded, but alone. He needed help. Or time. Something.

The voice sounded just in time. "Forget your fear and think only of your goal. No one here will hurt you. Go. Do not hesitate any longer, or you will never move from where you stand. And you will fail." A tone of understanding in the voice. "Go."

The boy fidgetted in his pockets for a moment, gulped very consciously, and clenched his fists by his sides, forcing his legs to work the way they were supposed to. He wondered for a moment how much of this fear the spirit inside him could feel. Each step required great effort, but was easier than the last. Walking in the city had been hard for a while now. The last days in Winnipeg. All of Thunder Bay. And now here. He rarely looked at anything but the tops of people's shoes. After four weeks in a row on the island, even tiny Kenora was a shock.

After one successful block, he felt a sense of accomplishment, however silly. His progress astounded him. The family had only just passed him by, the youngest child examining him closely. He couldn't remember it being this easy for a long time! And so much better than just two minutes before. He forced himself to forget about the walking and just start working on his task.

He scanned the storefronts as he walked, looking for a clue that might lead to tobacco. Gift shops. Some kind of store with surfing stuff. Bookstore. More souvenir shops. They might carry the stuff, but he wasn't sure and didn't want to try any more stores than necessary. He stopped in front of a craft store. A customer brushed by him, setting off the door chimes. Philip didn't relish the idea of having his entrance announced. He moved on.

He happened to glance across the street and saw a Native man sitting with his back against a storefront wall. Their eyes met. The man wore a dirty black-and-white baseball cap with a faded Harley-Davidson decal on it. His jeans and jean-jacket were almost brown with dirt. His seemingly black eyes were set in a face darkened with stubble and sun. Behind his ears, hair flowed gracefully down onto his shoulders. Philip's first thought was if the man was drunk or stoned or something, just knowing he was an Indian.

He watched as the man grunted loudly and struggled to his feet. Might have been under thirty years old, but looked a lot older, badly worn. He began to weave his way across the street. A driver honked impatiently and raised his hand in disgust as the man staggered toward Philip, eyes still unwaveringly on him, the only part of the man that seemed solid. Philip suddenly grasped that he was being approached specifically. His brain said, run! But he only stared back into the man's almost too-dark eyes. Soon the smell of alcohol and body odour sifted into the boy's nose. He had never stood this close to an Indian before. He felt a finger poking at his chest.

The man's eyes rolled as he opened his mouth. The teeth he still had were rotten, brown and yellow. He coughed, then spoke. "Why're you're starin' at me? I ain't no bum." He laughed and then choked, starting a coughing fit. Rough. As if a vital organ might shoot out of his mouth at any moment.

Philip just watched.

When the fit had passed, the man stood up straight and tried to compose himself. Pitted face, now Philip could see. And his eyes were a very dark brown, not black. "Listen, Richie-Rich. I'm a derelict. I know it. But I'm gonna make good. Came to this town from Grassy. You know it?" A hiccup to finish. Caked white saliva collected at the corners of his mouth.

Philip had never heard of it.

The man laughed, "Sounds better than it is. No grass up there." After another moment, "I don't ask usual, but sport me a dollar?"

"No. Sorry," Philip answered without thinking. Instinct.

"Tha's okay, eh." The man grabbed the boy by the shirt and held their faces together, nose to nose. A man walking by hesitated to see if Philip needed help with the drunk, but then pretended he hadn't noticed and walked on. "You're a good boy. Not scared. Many people's scared or have hateful hearts." He pushed Philip's head back and wobbled off.

Philip felt a goodbye hanging off his tongue, but it stayed there. Philip realized it was the first time he had looked into the eyes of an Indian. Couldn't help feeling they weren't so bad. He had certainly seen enough of them up and down Main Street and around Langside back in Winnipeg. But this one gave him more of a compliment than he had heard for a while. And...wait! He felt no fear now! Or at least not the usual incapacitating amount. Like a prophesy. Not afraid! He remembered looking the man straight in the eye without flinching. Philip watched the man stumble around the next corner. Should've given him that dollar.

Okay, let's do this, he coached himself back to the task.

But the voice came. "You have seen a piece of truth. Do not forget it." Then an empty moment for his host to absorb that truth. "How much paper money do you have?"

"Forty. Maybe forty-five," Philip whispered.

"That is not much. We will not be able to buy leather for the mide bags, or any other extras. Gitche-Manido will understand. Go and buy what you can."

Who was it that would understand? Philip shook his head and started walking again, then stopped at the Marlboro poster. There! Perfect! He stood in front of a variety store. It was perfect until he saw the black and white sticker on the door: UNDER 19? FORGET IT! He remembered the sign now from other stores, but he had never really paid it much notice. If they wouldn't sell him cigarettes, then would they really want to sell him a can of tobacco? He wondered quickly how the kids at school managed to get the cigarettes they smoked in the parking lot. Did this roadblock in the mission mean he was off the hook? Or just in serious crap? The spirit's words flashed in Philip's memory: "Forget your fear and think only of your goal." No choice. He would get what he needed somehow. Just take it? Say he was older? That would never work. How about: "Hi, I need tobacco for a ceremony for dead Indians." He shook his head and pushed the store door open. Cringed as the unexpected bell sounded overhead.

Just inside the door, scanning his new surroundings. To his left, the cash and the man behind it, arms folded. He gave an almost undetectable nod in his new customer's direction. Straight ahead, a glassed-in fridge. Two kids pointed at drinks through the pane, trying to decide. On the right, a few aisles of food and magazines. Philip headed for the magazines. He looked for one for a fourteen year-old. MAD was as close as he could get. He held it up, pretending to read, while actually examining the man behind the cash over the top. The store-keeper seemed more concerned with the two kids now at the slush machine.

Philip took a moment to study the tobacco area. The man stood between him and the wall-full of cigarettes and tobacco cans. He would never sell a kid like him tobacco. How do the kids at school get it? He had seen them mix it with their hash or whatever it was. Couldn't imagine asking the man for a can of the stuff. Couldn't imagine speaking to the man in the first place.

Philip's eyes attached themselves to a blue can on the back wall. It had to be tobacco. Had to be. If only he could just seize it with his eyes and teleport it from the store. His underarms dampened and sweat moistened his forehead. The man glanced at the plotting boy who clumsily pretended to read the magazine again. Then picked up another. In Thunder Bay, you got yelled at for reading instead of buying.

The store-keeper was nearly bald, with bushy grey sideburns. Wore a red golf shirt that had been washed too many times. A potbelly just above the counter. Seemed to decide once and for all that a boy like Philip was no threat, and glanced down another aisle where an old man stood with one brand of canned beans in each hand. Philip inched toward the cash.

Suddenly, a scream came from the slush machine. And another. Then giggles and plastic cups bouncing on the floor. The man flew out from behind the counter. He shouted as he darted toward the two kids throwing slush at each other. "Hey!"

Philip sprang to life. He dropped the magazine on the floor and charged the counter. Magazines and chip bags whizzed past his field of vision and he heard nothing more. Without hesitation, he stepped around the counter and candy shelves, and grabbed the blue can. He looked over his shoulder. The man was yelling at the two boys, holding each one by the shirt. Philip still had time. He put the can in his satchel and grabbed two more. Too much! He let one drop. The man turned at the sound of the crash. Philip dashed from behind the counter with one can in the satchel and one under his arm.

The man released the boys and bowled over the old man making his way to the cash with his beans. The slush boys' mouths dropped—somebody was stealing for real. The man crashed into the door as it closed behind Philip. The bell rang like crazy—customer leaving. Philip sprinted down Main Street, his corduroy pants rubbing loudly. It felt like he was flying. A giggle crept out from somewhere inside him.

"Stop, thief!" the red-shirted man yelled after the boy. After a moment's hesitation, he was running as well, an effort in his old loafers and too-tight slacks. Philip looked over his shoulder. The man was gaining on him. Philip dodged between two parked cars and ran out onto the street.

He heard the honk, screech and thud before he felt any pain, as a car struck him from the side. It sent him flying forward onto the road. He lay facedown for a moment, knowing he was caught. He heard a woman's shriek. The sound of the loose tobacco can hitting the street. But no more footfalls of store-keeper loafers.

Philip sensed two people hovering over him. When they touched him, he stirred and pulled away. The girl told him it was okay, to just relax. He spied her from under his arm. Another Native. A man's voice came from above him, but he couldn't see the speaker.

Where's the man?!

His fluttering eyes searched the asphalt toward the sidewalk. He heard the can speed up its slow roll across the street, then hit the far curb.

Where is the red-shirted man?

The searching eyes stopped on the tops of two large loafers just ten feet away. He could feel they belonged to the store owner. On reflex, he bounded up and ran across the street, narrowly missing being hit a second time as the cars had started to move again. The tobacco can lay there waiting to be scooped up in front of the sidewalk.

The people who had gathered around stood dumbfounded as the boy they assumed fatally injured limped speedily out of sight with his loot under his arm. "He just got up and..." remarked the shocked white man, standing beside the victim's rightful place on the asphalt.

Philip slipped around the corner, hung there a moment to see if he was being followed.

Nothing.

He wondered for a moment what must be going through his victim's mind. He was usually on the butt end of this kind of deal himself. The day of the surfboard came back to him for a moment. But a strange and powerful feeling overcame him, as he rested his hands on his knees and gasped for air.

TWENTY-SIX

Thinking it Through

"Idiot!"

The boy heard the voice, but started moving again at a slow jog to make sure he was safely away from the scene of his crime. Again, the voice assaulted him. Philip slowed as he came to an alley, and found a van to hide behind. He leaned forward with his hands on his knees again, panting. Hip throbbing. He closed his eyes and let out a whimper of fatigue. Huffing and puffing.

"Boy!" The spirit was livid. "I told you not to do anything to jeopardize this project! You deserved to get caught and you might have been killed. You left yourself open to too many possibilities." A pause for Philip to reflect. "Why do you refuse to think before you act?"

"But you said to get tobacco. Go for my goal. You said it!" Philip was in the right here, still high on adrenaline. Besides, he had been successful, got two cans of the stuff. He stood up straight and stretched out his back. Took a quick look at his chafed palms. It looked like he might have a few pieces of road imbedded in his skin. His lungs still heaved from the run. He put the second tin into his satchel. "I'm only doing what you say," rebellious in his tone.

The spirit offered no response at first. Then, "You run faster than I thought you could." More a statement of fact than a compliment.

Philip laughed, letting down his new facade, briefly pleased with himself. "I run faster than I thought I could. I was scared. Not like people-scared. I was afraid of something more. Like death or something. You know? I ran for my life." Looked down at his heavily laden satchel. "I stole this stuff. Stole it. Me! Just like that." He slung the bag over his shoulder and gave a quick glance each way down the alley. Just like that.

144

"Do not gloat about what is not good," warned the spirit. "It would be yet another trait of yours I cannot bear."

But Philip didn't let the slight touch him this time.

The newly-wanted criminal lurked about on the opposite side of town until it was time to meet his mother. He stiffened and slipped into a drug store once as he spied a police cruiser down the street. If they were looking for him, they weren't exactly doing a thorough job. He moved on, still smug about his deed.

He sat on a cement block in the liquor commission parking lot with a can of 7Up he had bought at The Chip Truck. Just outside the store, a white man and two Indian women sat on the paved step underneath the "No Loitering" sign. One of the women kept poking the man in the stomach, and then they would all laugh. Philip looked around him to see if the police might be coming to shoo them away or attack them. In the Peg, the police sometimes had to remove them from storefronts. It used to be funny to watch them get shoved around after they refused to leave. He had only seen a couple of times, really. Now he hoped he would never witness that again.

An old woman, maybe Indian, intruded on Philip's frame of the derelicts as she shuffled diagonally across the parking lot. She was round, leather-faced and wore a kerchief over her head. Never lifted her eyes from the ground. An Indian.

The sight of more sad-looking Indians sobered him completely now. Why had he hated them so much? Maybe it was different in Winnipeg. But it wasn't. The people here looked just as awful, if not worse. Although it wasn't all of them, he noticed. It was like they were either really good or really terrible. He remembered thinking in his first horrible month in Thunder Bay last fall that at least there were no Indians in town, or very few that he saw anyway. Everyone hated them in Winnipeg, or at least it seemed that way to him. Although he couldn't remember his father ever talking about them, his mother had made her views clear. The more he thought of it, the more he seemed to remember a fight they had once had over exactly that. But now these people seemed like sick children to him. Somehow even less than just harmless, like they might disintegrate all on their own. And it all led back to Philip's own ancestors, according to the spirit. It seemed more believable now. His eyes drifted back to the people just in front of the store.

"Indians." Philip remembered learning how that was the wrong word for these people. It had been called wrong in school, at least. It never mattered before. Aboriginals. Natives. Ojibway. First Nations. Those were the names he was supposed to use now. He had heard it all in school but had dismissed it. Indian sounded way off now that he thought about it. Maybe there was no correct name....

He tilted his head back and drained the last drops of drink down this throat. Waited.

A few minutes later, a well-dressed, primped, very white Jane Reddy came through the door of the store. She tossed a dismissive glare at the drunkards now bellowing gibberish. She hated them. Philip could tell.

He hated her. Almost on their behalf now.

"Hi, Philip," she smiled. "Did you have fun?"

He could tell she didn't believe he could have fun. Suddenly aware of the pain in his hip and brought down by all the thoughts swimming in his head, he only scrounged together a weak, misplaced, "It's okay." His high of just an hour before was officially gone.

They walked together toward the Toyota parked near the lot exit, Jane carrying a brown paper bag like the Natives did. But somehow that bag didn't make her look like a drunk....The ride home was silent except for her complaints of hunger, more irritating every second. Why the hell didn't she eat in town? But she always said fast food was disgusting, that she didn't know where it had been.

Along the highway, down the road, into the boat, across to the island without a word. An even more distant Philip noticed no bridges or billboards. He was wrapped up in these Natives, emotionally flattened despite his success in town. Sandwiches for lunch. Philip felt better on the island, away from the people he couldn't seem to ignore anymore. They depressed him. Some of their ancestors were murdered. The thought shook him. It seemed to him that they still grieved. And his own ancestors had been the killers....After lunch, he waited impatiently for the voice of the one strong Native he knew.

"White boy!" The deep, harsh voice welcome now.

Philip smiled eagerly and sprang up off the rock where he sat, looking over the water. More boats today, the weekenders were out in full force. But that didn't matter. He would do whatever was asked, and do it well! A relief to have the spirit back.

"Get your things. There is much work to be done."

The boy entered the house through the north door and reached into the rag bag hanging on a nail, pulled out a handful of old underwear and sheet bits. He wondered for an instant if his mother would notice the missing rags. When the bag was empty, she couldn't help but wonder. Eventually, he would have to replace them. But not now. The satchel was heavy and bulging now. He stopped and thought for a moment. He pulled out one of the new cans of tobacco and lifted up the dresser curtain to find a good hiding place for it. Behind a can of marbles on the bottom shelf. He shuddered at the thought of his mother somehow finding it. Not so easy to explain. And the truth would be the least believable option. He tilted the Chinese checkerboard so the can was hidden from every possible angle. There. He checked the satchel for materials, threw in the roll of string, the rock and the knife. With nearly empty old and one new tobacco cans, the bag bulged again. He was ready. Just needed to hit Blueberry Point for a half-hour to collect some berries.

On his way out, he picked up another 7Up, still warm from the store shelf. He walked down to the beach and dropped everything at the end of the dock, then marched up the hill to the blueberry patch with a margarine container. The berries were at their peak early this year and were hard to resist eating right off the bush. On his way back down the path, the spirit sent him into the bush for chokecherry twigs. Philip had to laugh at anyone who would eat sticks, but reminded himself that the spirit knew best. When he finally arrived back at the beach, he saw the full jerry cans behind the tree just before the dock and remembered the gas tank needed to be filled. He packed the twigs and berries in the satchel and threw it and his lifejacket gently into the bow. Only then did he see the water in the boat bottom. Damn! He went straight to work bailing.

Then back to the shore to get the gas. The can was heavy! He struggled to slide it along the dock, then just barely heaved the can off the dock, trying not to let it hit the boat bottom too hard. The boat swayed slightly with the swell of the bay. Usually Jane filled the boats and took care of them, at least this summer and last, but if he was going to use the boat, he had better wake up. He was the man, after all. He tried to remember how his mother did it. Or better yet, his father. What he remembered best about his mother was the constant complaining about her smelly hands afterwards. His father, on the other hand, had been simply pure grace in every movement. Philip tilted the can carefully. Too full, the first spurt of gas hurdled the tank completely, onto the floor. Then again. The sudden messy bursts came more frequently until a steady stream established itself. Now the gas was making it in through the tank opening without a problem. He wondered how much he had wasted. Then the tank started to overflow. After he had corked up the over-filled tank, his brain processed the forgotten funnel he saw lying next to his feet. The old frustration sneaked up and spread through him from its banished corner. He was so stupid! His skin prickled with the feeling.

He thought of himself again. His life. His problems. And his thumb went right for the big red pimple on his temple. Tongue ran over his braces and the canker sore. He sat there for a few moments, lost, before he rallied himself not to sink any further. Okay, let's go! He pushed the boat off and started the motor in one fierce go.

As the boat gathered speed, the voice came. "You did not come to that tobacco honestly. If I had the choice and you the time, I would not permit its use. It is stolen."

"But they would never have sold it to me," Philip protested. "Look at me, damn it!" Philip pulled roughly at his t-shirt as if he was gesturing to someone standing in front of him.

"Yes, but I do not approve. The tobacco is also of the white world, as are you. I do not approve."

Philip grew angry. "Man! What the hell am I supposed to do?! Stupid racist! I don't have to do this any—"

"Ack! Silence! You are the last bigot who should use the word racist against another. Choose your battles wisely. And, yes, you do have to do this. You understand that already."

The discussion was definitely over. Philip felt the guilt the spirit intended for him.

"Remember the good people walking the path, waiting for us to help them."

Philip knew what that meant, despite its obscure sound. I brought you here to teach you about life, he replayed it in his head. There had been another dream last night he remembered suddenly. A yelling match between him and the spirit. They had been deep in the woods and that was how the spirit had silenced him. I brought you here to teach you about life.

Philip and the spirit performed the third day of the ceremony for Mong, Negik and Wauh-Oonae. Philip dumped the last remnants of Grandpa Frederick's tobacco out onto the water's surface. Then pulled out the new can. The blue colour was so intense compared to on the old, faded can. "MacDonald Export Medium," it said. Heavy with fresh tobacco. He looked at the can carefully, sealed with a band of plastic around the rim. He laughed as he read out loud, "Smoking during pregnancy can harm the baby." And there was some blond lady with a Scottish hat. He snickered and wondered how her baby was. Then broke the seal on the can and forgot the joke. A different smell came this time. A good smell. Fresh. And the stuff was moist as Philip reached in with his fingers. The strands of the offering rode the tops of the waves. The early August long weekend boats passed by and people did stare at the raving Reddy boy, but no one bothered him. He thought to himself afterwards that Franny, Rupert and Max must have been heading to Max's place or whatever this weekend. That was the best luck of all!

The next day Philip and the spirit finished the ceremony in their usual morning time slot. When they were done, Philip tried to ask the spirit for his name, but there was no response. Where does he go? He was totally gone! Just like that. He let the boat drift and unfolded the map. Wondered where he would be going tomorrow.

TWENTY-
SEVEN

A Change in Place

P hilip dreamed of the loon that night and each night following. The
inexplicable interest it had shown in him made him smile. It strength-
ened him. Every day presented a new challenge, and although the degree of
difficulty varied, each one seemed easier than the last. Philip could truly feel
the sadness of each tragedy he tried to right, but the work brought a joy he
could not explain. Something was loosening its grip on him. But something
that had very little to do with the spirit, whatever had held him for the last
year or more. Free time became a commodity. To be spent wisely, never
wasted, never just an opportunity to be bored. Having the island to himself
for an entire summer became a good thing. The days all began early, with
important work, but ended with a calm the boy had not felt in a long time.
A satisfaction that comes with pushing oneself. He had earned his free time,
and it was his to spend. The swimming made the outside and inside of him
stronger as well.

On the evening of his thirteenth day working for the spirit, he ran out
to his father's front cliff with his pad and pencil. Tired from being out on the
lake all morning and only somewhat grudgingly helping his mother put the
new topsoil from Kenora into the garden in the afternoon, a new energy
took hold of him as he began to sketch. As the sun slowly sank beyond the
line of trees across the water, a loon swam close to shore. Maybe the same
one from out on the channel. He wasn't sure, but pretended it was. It had
come to visit him. Philip sketched the lines of the bird roughly on his page.
Then the ripple lines on the near-still lake. The loon began to take shape on
his page, surprising its creator with its beauty. He filled in the black head and
body with the hard rhythm of his pencil. A slick patch of dark grey. Left a
white spot for the shiny eye. An image of the boy Mong popped into his

head. Darting underneath the white men's canoe, fooling them. Underwater like a loon. Philip stared at his work. Slowly, the idea emerged and unrolled itself for him.... This drawing could be for Mong. It could be his totem drawing. The spirit had said that was the one important thing missing. Philip didn't know if the spirit meant a totem pole or something else, but he knew he couldn't make one of those. But he could do this.

He taped the finished drawing to the wall in his room that night just before bed. The word Mong printed neatly below it. Staring at the rest of his empty wall, he realized what he had to do. Every soul needed a totem, something from him that represented them. Something he made on his own. Something extra. That would show he was committed. He wrote down the names of the souls he had chanted for, sounding them out from how the spirit had spoken them. Counted six, plus the four young men whose ceremony he had begun that day. He would start catching up on drawings the next day. Too tired tonight, he got ready for bed and nodded a good night to the new bird posted on his wall. But from his bed he could also see on the dresser the spine of *Soul Catcher*. Remembered how it had appeared. He stretched across the room and pulled it to bed with him. He opened it and began reading.

As the days passed and drawings accumulated on the wall, things opened up between Philip and the spirit. The extra contributions were never mentioned, but the spirit softened slightly in his manner. Philip could feel the difference, but reminded himself he was doing this for his own reasons. Not looking to get out of any work. Not trying to impress. But because he wanted to. Doing at least a drawing each night allowed him to slowly catch up to the progress he and the spirit had made.

He knew his mother was monitoring the budding collection of drawings on his wall. Said they were good a couple of times, which meant nothing. But she began to smile at him sickeningly often, looking all dreamy. Like this meant he was recovering from the illness she thought he had. He didn't let it bother him too much, happy that she was mostly smiling and not asking too many questions. His silence with her had not changed much, except that he was around less often than before and caught himself being almost helpful once in a while. She told him it was great to see him wearing his glasses again, and it didn't annoy him as much as he expected it to. She had started to cough a funny cough too.

The morning sun of the sixteenth day shone in on the drawing-plastered wall. Four pencil sketches. Hung with bits of masking tape at the top corners. A loon. A detailed flower. A bald eagle. A sunrise. Names were printed below each sketch. Each one was a gift for a specific person, soul. The one for Zaugitau conveniently covered the mirror. Philip was on schedule to catch up within the week.

"Boy! Wake up! It is time. Today we go one more time to the Crow Rock site. Bring food for yourself as well as supplies. We must start now."

After a good yawn, his lips cracking painfully, Philip began scraping the sleep from the corners of his eyes. Out his window he could see it was another bright day. Today he would wear sunblock and something for his lips, which seemed to have got toasted yesterday.

The loon had come around again during the night. They had swum together. Philip felt beyond a doubt that the loon was male. That this loon was just like Mong, and not so unlike himself. That idea was enough to shake him from bed. Sat on the edge and nodded good morning to his friends on the wall. He stretched back the waistband of his underwear to check the bruise on his upper hip from the accident in town five days earlier. Still a bit greyish, with yellow around the outer edge. He left it and dressed himself. Packed his bag and made himself a peanut butter sandwich to satisfy the command to bring food. After the last couple of days, he knew he would need it. He knew the routine now and double-checked that he had a food source for the souls and tobacco to offer. Leaving a note for his mom had also become a steady part of the routine and kept her from being on his back. Philip had learned to bring an extra can of gas after running on fumes on the way home from Crow Rock just three days ago.

Philip unfolded his trusted map and scanned for the words Crow Rock. He had almost memorized the route, but the chart still gave him a thrill. This would be his last day doing the ceremony there.

He thought about the spirit's story of what happened. That it had been in retaliation for something the Sioux had actually done to the whites. That a few angry Frenchmen would just go and kill four Indian men innocently drying meat on the shore. They weren't Sioux, and it was way farther north on the lake. But it also seemed pretty weird that twenty-one white men had been massacred earlier that summer in the first place. The spirit hadn't explained that part but had said it happened pretty far south in what he called Pequonga. But in examining the chart, Philip found Massacre Island, where it was supposed to have happened, was just north of Big Traverse Bay. Despite all the details of the story, what stuck in Philip's mind was what the spirit had said about history. That Philip could find information on the massacre of the whites in 1736, but that he would never find anything about the massacres that occurred in retaliation or before that no matter how hard he looked because it was only Anishinaabe or other First Nations who died. Philip wondered suddenly if anything he had ever read had been true. And thought for the first time that the twenty-one white men that were killed might have done something terrible to deserve it, only no one wrote it down.

At the red buoy, he knew which side to choose without referring to the map. Figured it out the last two days with one of his father's old sayings, along with a growing knowledge of the lake's channel systems. Still, he slowed down from time to time to check his direction. The spirit had definitely left him on his own, as he routinely did on these journeys. Perhaps he had gone on ahead.

By the time Philip checked the map one last time to find he was almost on top of Crow Rock, some dark clouds had changed the sky's mood considerably. The air went cool. Philip suddenly saw the murder in his head. The sounds came to him as if he had been there. Gun blasts. Then silence again. He was getting close. The souls were Shaudae, Amik, Numaegos and Waussee. None had been older than twenty-two years.

The familiar words came out of his mouth and swirled around him like rushing water. Somewhere inside he sang along, knowing exactly how the words twisted and turned. How the music flowed high and low.

"K'neekaunissinaun, kego binuh-kummeekaen.

K'neekaunissinaun, k'gah odaessiniko..."

The joy the words might bring if they had no meaning was swept away by his remorse for the murdered men. His heart was theirs one last time.

When the ceremony was done and the food and wigwam laid out, Philip noticed the changed sky. A complete and angry black now. The wind howled in the woods behind him, much cooler than before. He wondered for a moment how he had missed the transition. But two hours had passed. Time seemed to move faster every time he performed the ceremony. The water lost its blue tint, reflected only the soot colour above. Philip felt an initial shiver. He had to get home! He nodded a goodbye to the men and began pushing the boat off the shore.

"No. Stay here. You will not make it home before the storm."

Philip scowled at the spirit's voice. He couldn't stay here! "I can make it if I leave now!" he declared, just barely convincing himself.

"Stay!"

"Forget it! I'm gone!" Philip pushed the bow off the rock into the water. He leaped clumsily into the boat, almost falling overboard. He pulled the ripcord and started the engine. No problem. Stupid spirit.

A lightning flash over the opposite shore!

Philip's eyes sprang wide with it. Second thoughts. It had been a true fork, neon brightness. The thunder came a few seconds later. He remembered a longer delay meant the storm was not yet on top of him. He sped away from the site up-channel as fast as he could. Could feel the spirit's anger, but pushed on against it and the increasing chop.

More lightning. This time the thunder followed more promptly.

Couldn't back down after taking a stand. No way. He ducked his head down out of the wind and stepped firmly on the satchel strap as it hinted at jumping ship.

Another flash. This time a sheet. And a crack that pounded into Philip's ears. The waves uncomfortably large now.

His boy-heart raced and his eyes darted about at the chaos surrounding him, both panic-stricken. He needed somewhere to land immediately. Finally, his eyes fell on a nearby point of land. He jerked the boat toward it and ducked his head down again. Sped toward the rock at full tilt until the last few feet. Depth was no concern. The motor was up before he had even switched it off. Just as he hit the shore, the first hard pellets of rain began to fall. They clanged viciously against the aluminium. He pulled the boat up onto the shore and tied it to a small balsam. As he scrambled back to get the satchel, the spirit said, "Stay dry at all costs." Philip thought about mooring the boat better, but decided he had better actually start listening to orders, and bolted for the heavy brush.

Safe under a canopy of pines, he looked back out at the water. The lake crashed against the shoreline in big rolling waves. The boat rolled and slammed against the rock as the water pulled out from beneath it. Should have pulled the boat higher out of the water. But he wasn't to get wet for some reason. He turned again and looked into the woods. He could see a rock face not far off. He wanted to go there, but felt the boat should be watched. Only the occasional drop made its way through the thick layer of branches. Above the low layer, he could make out the flailing tops of trees. Philip listened to two huge white pines creak and whine against each other at some point out of his view. On the path to Blueberry Point there were two trees that did the same thing in a high wind. He wished he were back there.

Finally, he allowed himself to realize he was lucky that he had stopped when and where he did. The lake thrashed about with a wrath reserved for special occasions. He sat down on a fallen tree trunk to wait out the storm. Watched as the rain slowly filled his boat and pinned it more solidly to the shore.

Hours passed and he felt himself getting hungry. The storm kept circling back at him.

After another hour of sitting, arms folded, head on his knees in an attempt to sleep, Philip reared up to see that it was getting dark. Darker than a storm could make it. The sun must have been setting! Better get back. A moment of panic. But the rain and wind still swirled out on the water. His heart sank when he realized he might be stuck there for the night. He tried to put the thought out of his mind. Surely that couldn't be the spirit's intention—just to leave him here. He would starve. He would freeze. Maybe both. He rubbed his thin arms briskly. Tried to ward off the chill stalking him in the damp air. Back at the island, it sometimes got cold at night. He remembered being shocked at the cold bite in the air a few times when he had to pee just before dawn. But here he had no house. No nothing! He shook his head in disbelief. No real sunset, but Philip definitely felt the darkening with every passing minute. His watch read 8:55pm. He thought of his mother and swore. He would get it from her tomorrow. For sure. But first he had to survive.

"Go to sleep now before it grows too cold. Go pull off six cedar boughs. Put them beneath you and over you to stay dry and warm."

Philip reacted now to what he had all but known already. "We're staying here?!"

"There is no choice. You cannot navigate with a flashlight even once the storm stops because you have none. You cannot leave now because the waves are too large. There is no decision to make."

"But what am I going to eat? Wait! Can't you direct me with your powers?"

"I will not waste my energy for your comfort. You will not eat. It will teach you humility."

Philip slouched lower on his log. He hadn't heard harsh words like these in the last few days. They hurt him now more than before. They meant more. But no tears came this time. I brought you here to teach you about life. It came back to him again now. He looked around for a place to set up his bed. He tried to think like a man of nature, like an Ojibway.

Anishinaabe. It had to be dry. And smooth enough that he could sleep. He decided the big thing was not make it in a trough where the rain water might collect. Very smart. Holding himself back from asking for help, he searched the area for the supposed cedar source. Once he had found a stand of three trees, he painstakingly pulled and twisted, all the way right and all the way left, the first bough off one of the trunks. He ran his hand across the soft green of it. As he attacked the tree to take a second bough, he remembered his knife and smiled. The next five boughs came with a great deal less effort than the first. As he walked back to a high, flat spot he had found, he wondered why hurting the tree was suddenly okay. He would never forget how the spirit had intervened when he had attacked the white pine with that rock. With the boughs arranged next to a rotting barkless log, he tested the materials and found a bed of pine needles and cedar boughs was not as uncomfortable as it sounded. His eyes eased themselves shut slowly, tired from so many long days travelling the lake to perform the rite. But the creaking trees and whistling storm kept him from sleep.

As the night grew colder and darker, sleep became less possible. The spirit was right, as always. Philip looked at his watch. Two hours had passed slowly. An intense, frightened boredom grew in him. His stomach rumbled again. He wondered when the spirit would start telling him the tricks the Indians—Natives—used to survive and build fires. But nothing came.

"Can I make a fire?" he ventured.

"You may if you can." Sounded like an English teacher.

"Can't you tell me how? Or can you start it? Should I rub some sticks together or something?"

No answer.

Philip went hot. He had wanted to keep going to get home way before sunset. The spirit had put him in this position and kept him here, so he should help get him out of it. Or at least make it tolerable. He tried to think of something to make himself feel better. Then he remembered why he was here in the first place—the dead. At least he wasn't dead...yet. He folded his arms and looked up into the blackness of the natural canopy.

In the third hour, Philip started to shiver. He rubbed his arms vigorously, pushing the goosebumps down. Wanted to talk to the spirit. He could feel that he was there with him now although silent. He needed anything to keep his mind off the cold and the endless frightening possibilities out here. Without a real plan, he tried to start something.

"Um. Hello?" he tried, raising his eyebrows in wait for a response.

After a few moments: "I am here."

"I was wondering. We never really, well, talked. I mean, I know you, but not really. I have some questions. And maybe if I understood better, I could—"

"I will help you no more tonight."

"No. I know. I just want to talk to you. Just talk."

"Nonsense. You don't talk, you hide. Even if you could talk and listen like a real person, why would I talk to you?"

"I don't know, but I help you, right? So you could explain some things to me, maybe...." A hopeful tone.

"You have no father. I am not your father. I have no wish to fill that role. Do not try to adopt me. Do not pretend that I care for you."

The boy gritted his teeth to shield himself from the stab. "My father has nothing to do with this," as calmly as he could manage. He tried not to sound too desperate. "Just give me one hour. One hour. And then I'll leave you alone, I promise. Please. One hour."

"Did you not once complain that I talk too much? This was not wise. I speak when necessary. I do not speak when it is unnecessary. You must learn many things from me. Therefore I use many words. Still, I have not forgotten your complaint."

Philip remembered it too well. Maybe again just the day before yesterday. Swore to himself, Never again. "I'm sorry. But please, can we talk now?"

One last try: "Please?"

The spirit seemed to be deliberating. A good ten seconds later, he answered, "Granted. But I do not promise to satisfy your every curiosity."

TWENTY-EIGHT

Q&A

Philip feverishly tried to file through all the questions that had piled up over the last weeks. His memory betrayed him. He sat up, hoping to shake things into order. Then one came...

"How come we only do the ceremony for people who were killed by whites? Aren't there any people who died and, like, weren't murdered? You know. But still need help?"

The spirit sighed deeply, astonishing his host who had never heard his breath before. "There are many who died unnoticed because of the shuffle to move westward. Some never received the proper ceremony. Some clans were exterminated in a matter of days. No one was left to mourn for them. This happened in wars between tribes, also at the hands of the whites and the diseases they introduced. But you are only connected to this in that you disturbed me and you are white. There is not time for you to help save all of my people." He paused. "Any soul who dies at the hand of the white devil must be purified before it can move on in peace."

Then it didn't make any sense to have a white kid carry out the ceremony, did it.... But Philip nodded, already overwhelmed by the raw volume of knowledge that was suddenly at his disposal. There was still so much more to ask. He tried to block out the wind whistling in the trees above, the hiss of rain. "Where do you go sometimes?"

"That is not a clear question."

"I can feel when you go away from inside me. It feels different. Bigger. Or more empty anyway. But you go and come back, and I don't know where or why. It's weird."

The spirit seemed to be deciding whether to answer the question. There might be a line that they should not cross or information that a white boy simply should not know.

Philip shifted on his cedar bed, pulled off a twig and started to twirl it. Ready for a refusal, he tried again. "Like when we're in the boat.... Or when I'm in the boat, I guess. Sometimes you're there and sometimes you're not. And even before, on the island, at the beginning, when you were meaner.... Sometimes I could feel you weren't there at all."

The spirit finally budged. "When you violated my grave, I was set free. But it was no happy freedom. I was ready to wreak havoc like spirits do when the white man ploughs their gravesites to make parking lots. When I arose, I was angry with all that had happened to the world once beautiful. I had known of it, but had never seen it. From where I was, I could feel all the negative change. This is how I knew of the Nazi movement. The clearcutting of the world's forests. The pollution of this lake. And the state of the Anishinaabe. I knew who was to blame. But something pushed me out of this pure rage. Soon I had a sense of where certain people lay who were still in need of passage. I flew over the lake like the raven to find them. When I go away, I am looking for them, finding them, speaking to them. I learn when I disappear. You would not understand. Sometimes I need rest. Your English is not my language. It takes great energy to do what I do now. I am using a vessel that is not my own."

Philip stopped himself from gushing "Wow" out loud. An image of an angel-bird flying high above the lake, seeing all. From eagle height, but black in colour. He could barely believe the spirit would tell him all of this. But he could not let his awe waste time.

He asked questions he had never thought of before, and the spirit was courteous if not complete in his replies. The new level of conversation not only satisfied his yearning to know, but kept away the better part of the cold. The spirit told his boy of the four lakes that made up what was now called Lake of the Woods. That Clearwater Bay where his mother's house stood was really Clearwater Lake. It made a lot of sense—the map showed that the big lake was hardly a unified body of water. And how the name Lake of the Woods came from a mistake, a simple mixing up Mis-tic and Min-es-tic. They did not even go back and correct it. And Lake of the Islands would have been the better name—probably a million islands made the lake the labyrinth it was. Philip wondered at every word of every answer until silence beckoned the next question.

"You keep saying the history I learn is wrong or something. Like someone faked it. Or we tried to make it sound better, white people. Umm.... I get it now how the Indians—I mean Natives—that I see are like that because we came here. Like it's our fault. But I don't get why. They could go to the reserve to live, right? They could live like the old way. And not drink. So how did the reserves get started?" His brain ready to burst. "Oh yeah! And what do you call Indian people. Like, Indian is the wrong name 'cuz that guy thought he was going to India, right? I mean people who—umm... have redder skin and that? Who are they...really?"

A silence. Just the shrinking waves against the shore. The wet hiss around him.

A thoughtful voice broke it. "You tie your questions into knots that need to be untangled. But these questions are not bad or wrong. I would not have expected them from you. Not in the beginning.

"Your simplest question I will address first, although I will not solve your problem. We have been called many things since the arrival of your people here. None were right. None were wrong. Some of the white fools who study such things rationalize that the word Indian can still stand because it can stand for indigenous and means aboriginal Native, what the original peoples of this land are. Whether the first white man here called us Indians by a mistake or not is not important. All these words are wrong because they assume we are one nation. Because you stole this continent, all the people whose land you stole were one. But it was never so. Now is the first time such an idea would be useful. It may be the only way to regain any independence. And it may even be starting to happen. We will see. A wise man of your time said it well when he was asked about the correct term: It does not matter what you call me—I will still be an Indian. A word or name is just that. Nothing more. People waste time when they fight over such things. A name for a people who never were one. My people are the Anishinaabe. You will call us Anishinaabe because that is who we are."

Another pause. Philip waited. Didn't notice the steady rush of rain had faded to a light patter. This flood of knowledge made all his work even more worthwhile.

"The term History is well named in your tongue. A story that belongs to someone. The person may write it the way he or she chooses. The fact that it is not a true telling of what happened through the course of time shows that the conscience of the writing-people is not clean. What you learned was not altogether false, but badly stained by the winner's pride and guilt. Yes, the whites came and traded with us. Yes, they gave us new tools and ideas. Yes, we surrendered much of the land by ink. But it was nonetheless an invasion. None of what they brought improved our lives in the end. They turned us into dependent, weak infants over a mere four hundred years. They forced us to relinquish our culture and our way of life. The Anishinaabe had never experienced an invasion of this magnitude or kind. Our resistance was unsure at times. We saw the short-term benefits too clearly. It was not a battle against another tribe. It was a disease that came from outside and inside. We could not see this early enough.

"The earliest contracts surrendering land to the whites were voluntary. The English flashed their toys, alcohol and the easier way of life we had grown accustomed to through the fur trade. Many of the tribes traded their rights to the land for these things. But the contracts were hollow as all promises were soon broken. And when their offers were rejected, the English eventually seized the land by force. Some groups who rejected the offers claimed the land was not theirs to sell. The Anishinaabe knew they were merely keepers of the land, that it could not be owned. The English did not understand this truth. Nor did they care for our role as the middlemen in the fur trade. We were an obstacle, no longer an ally. A large number of leaders resisted the white man's heavy bargaining hand whether out of respect for the earth or wisdom about the end result. Later, when the peoples learned whites would take what they please regardless of any dealings, resistance became less popular. Arriving at the best deal was the goal. They insisted on pushing us together, as if huge stretches of land could be under one chief's rule.

"The old land contracts still create problems today between the whites and the original nations, as you have heard. We are reduced to claiming tracts of land. We pretend ownership, a concept introduced to us by your culture. These English brought about the long prophesied end of the world, the theft of the sacred hunting grounds.

"The reserves you ask about are not the lands we kept from the whites. The reserves are the pieces of land given back after the whites created a nation directly on top of nations that already existed. Small, less desirable, spent, remote lands were thrown upon us to pacify the few weak cries of injustice. When even that land became too desirable, reserves were simply moved to another location. In our weakened state, we could do little to fight for better. We were levelled by a genetic weakness for alcohol and by generations ravaged by the small pox and tuberculosis you introduced. Our will faded further under the forced acceptance of your god and schooling.

Soon the whites passed a law that all our young had to attend special schools. But these schools taught the children to ignore their bloodlines and mother tongue. These schools ignored the teachings young people needed to live as Anishinaabe or any other people. Great skills passed down for many generations were all but gone by the middle of this century.

"A return to the old way is not an option. The reserves are either too small or unfit. But worse than that is the fact that a self-hating alcoholic cannot learn the old ways because he has no will. More importantly, there are none left who will teach him."

The boy ignored time and pushed on with his questions. Rarely felt such motivation toward a goal. Leaning forward now, elbows on knees, crossed-legged, concentrating, trying to retain all the new information. If he could just know it all....The spirit answered patiently into the night.

"A name to call me? You should not call me at all. I call you. You have no reason to know my name." The spirit's voice rang hostile for the first time in the session.

"But—but I feel like I know you well..."Trying to entice the spirit back into the open.

"You know nothing of me, boy! Nothing!"

Philip was suddenly incensed by the spirit's harsh tone. He gathered up his new heat and anger and retaliated in full. "You know, I'm doing everything you ask me to and I don't even complain anymore. And I like doing it, even! And you can't even freakin' tell me your freakin' name?! Screw you!" Philip's brow furrowed in the now colder darkness, teeth clenched tightly. "Screw you!" He shook his head in frustration. Still warm with rage. A single raindrop fell on his head from the somehow stiller space above. Maybe the rain had stopped. If only it were still light, he could go home.

"I did not know you had this fire in you." He paused. "You may call me Tikumiwaewidung. That is who I am now."

Philip uncovered his face and relaxed his tensed fingers. He felt like he should ask what had just happened. Despite his outburst, he had never expected an answer. The name was so complicated. Hard to remember. He panicked, wondering if he would ever hear it again. Searched the blackness for an answer.

"Tikumiwaewidung."

Tikumiwaewidung. He could remember that with a little work. He felt proud to know the spirit's name. Spoke it out loud: "Tikumi... wae... widung."

"That is my name to you. It is the name I took when you disturbed me. Now you know it. Do not abuse it. But it does not sound right coming from you. You may say Manido. It means simply Spirit."

"Okay," Philip breathed, still caught up in the feeling. Manido. He repeated both new names in his head, hoping they would stick. Maybe he could squeeze in a few more questions....

The spirit grunted consent, slightly annoyed.

"What is a Kreechy Manitoo?"

The spirit laughed derisively. Then softened slightly and corrected the pronunciation. "That's Gitche-Manido, boy. He is the everything. He is no man, but a force. Your word He cannot describe Gitche-Manido. Nor can She or It. All-knowing and all-powerful. Gitche-Manido makes many decisions that affect this world and more. A mystery. A great mystery. The ripples on the water and the cold bite of winter. These are Gitche-Manido. The name is Great Spirit in your tongue. Your people and our modern storytellers spell the name Manitou in books. The earth and its animals belong to Gitche-Manido. The water belongs to Gitche-Manido. That is why any dealing of the land is by nature impossible. You need know only that The Great Spirit is to be respected and is responsible for everything you are and see. This name is not to be abused."

"He's like God. Does he have a beard?" Right away, Philip realized what a stupid question that was.

The spirit exhaled audibly again, disgusted. "Your notion of the supernatural is as unworthy and degrading as your entire culture! This god of yours cannot exist in the way you imagine. Your god is a story. Perhaps he has a hairy face and smells as bad as his kind. But this god is a white issue I prefer not to speak of. We were once forced to believe it."

Philip meant to say something, but missed his chance.

"Your people did not understand our ways when they found us. They did not like what they could not understand. Soon they made many of my people forget about the natural law and The Great Mystery. They erased parts of our history. They tricked us into depending on their trading posts. And they tried to erase what we were as a people. You too would have done the same. I still feel that lack of understanding."

Philip dove in. "No, I wouldn't. I wouldn't make you believe in God if you didn't want to. That's not fair." He desperately wanted to convince the spirit and himself. "It's not right. And now that I hear you tell me all this stuff, I think—"

"That is enough. Your hour is over. Now you must sleep."

Philip felt like protesting again at first, but he could feel a new, unangry warmth coming from Manido that made him somehow satisfied without an answer. And his watch made it plain that his hour was long over. He pondered the pleasant feeling in his chest as he rolled over on the forest floor and pulled two extra bows of cedar over him. He breathed the cedar and surrounding pine scent deeply into his lungs. A soft chorus of swishing needles and odd drops of old rain lulled him to sleep.

TWENTY-NINE

A New Day

Philip slept hard for a few hours, then awoke for no reason he could find. Eyes suddenly wide. The blackness startled him as did the cold, wet presence of the tree trunk beside him. His body convulsed. He felt cold and hungry, yet nowhere near unhappy. The cedar brushed lightly across his face.

Why did he feel this way? He slid his hands down into his pants to warm his fingertips. An old Winnipeg Reddy trick. He felt smart. Somehow loved. Not fazed by the cold. There was no logic to it.

But when was the last time he had woken up in the middle of the night with a pleasant feeling? Not after a terrible dream? He was convinced he would make it through the night. No animal would devour him. He would not freeze. Slowly he drifted back into sleep, the hiss of rain on the lake starting slowly again, soothing his ears and his heart.

He woke again with the sunrise. The rain remained only as puddles down on the shore and the occasional drip from above. The air colder than ever. He bolted upright. His breath clouded in front of him. Toes ached with cold. He crossed his arms and rubbed them furiously, stamping his feet. The sun! Warm up in the sun. Again, he felt smart. He wondered if he would have thought of the idea even a week or two ago. Perhaps. It was hardly genius. But today every movement, every thought felt so good. He hurried down to the shore where the powerful sun made the rock look bright white. The water had been transformed from the crashing black of yesterday to a serene, beautiful blue. The sunrays blasted him with heat. His burned skin welcomed the irritation after the cold night. He smiled solidly, pulled off his shirt, and lay himself face-up in a spread-eagle position. With his eyes closed now, he saw his father. That peaceful red beard. The smile. The face looked a little older than he remembered. Philip made it that way, the way he would have looked today. Just the face, looking at him proudly.

Then he remembered all the problems with talking to people and how used he was to that feeling. His heart sank back to its usual level. There was nothing to be proud of. His little fantasy didn't mean a thing.

"Are you there?" he asked without much hope.

"It is only I," the spirit answered knowingly.

Philip tried to push away the confusion. "I'm hungry. What can I eat here?"

"Nothing."

"Nothing? But isn't there roots or berries from the ceremony. Or I could eat—"

"You will not touch that food! It is not for you!"

"I didn't get any dinner last night. And this is an emergency, right?"

"No. Tribesmen once went on vision quests where they ate and drank nothing for many days. You have eaten in the last day and you are not injured in any way. This is as close as you get to a vision quest. Have you not felt the gains? You will eat later." That was final.

"Manido." The name he could pronounce.

The spirit grunted, "Yes."

"Nothing." Philip smiled. "That's your name. I remember it."

Another grunt, maybe slightly amused.

Philip lay down again and relaxed. He let the sun touch him and shielded only his eyes with his forearm. No hurry.

A few moments later, the spirit spoke. "We must return to the island soon. Your mother will not be pleased. Empty the boat of rain water."

Philip cringed at bailing the boat—always bailing a boat. Then almost cried out when the thought of his mother sank in. He had completely forgotten. How would he explain this? More than just missing a meal.... He tried to throw the idea out: Who cares?! Checking his watch, he thought he might be able to make it home before she woke up....

Who was he trying to fool—he cared, and a lot. Pissing her off would only hurt their plans. Funny, it barely occurred to him last night.

7:30 am.

He tried to calculate the travel time. Sometimes she slept past ten o'clock. He could say he got in late last night.... It might work. He got up off the rock and hurried over to the boat where he groaned out loud. Almost full to the gunwales. The whole lake was in there! No way he would get back in time. Who cares? he tried to convince himself again. Then, to prove he felt that way, he offered, "Hey, let's help a new soul on the way home. Someone near here. We're here anyway, right? C'mon." He put his shirt back on, ready.

"That would be unwise."

"C'mon. I'm screwed anyway, right? So why not get something done before I'm actually grounded."

"Your attitude concerns me." He paused. "You have been more willing in these last days, but you have become reckless. This enthusiasm is not connected to your desire to help my people. It is just spite for your mother. It is disrespectful. You have become your own main concern once again."

Philip listened hard. Manido was easily in the right although he had started to feel for these people. The drawings were proof of that. "Okay. I understand." Lying slightly. He paused before one more go at it. "But you have me here. I'm willing and excited. It doesn't matter why. Take advantage of it! C'mon!"

"In the interest of the mission, we must get to your mother as soon as possible. I feel already that she is not pleased. She still has control of you, you will agree. We must have access to this boat, and she has the power to limit that. Every moment we waste jeopardizes our goal."

Philip stopped himself from saying she wasn't that bad. Didn't like to think of her as anything other than an adversary. He pulled off his shoes and stepped into the cold water in the boat. Feet ached instantly. The sun had just begun its work at taking the cold edge off the replenished lake and boat-full of water. The bail floated next to his speckled, pink-burned calf. The stern lurched with his weight, sending a flow of water from the bow over the stern seat almost up to his knees. He grabbed the margarine container and began bailing vigorously. He recalled the last time he had bailed a really full boat, when those three assholes had come by to pick at him like vultures. He looked up across the water just to be sure. He was indeed alone. Thought for a moment that if he had frozen to death last night, he might not have been found for days. And if the boat weren't there as a clue, his body might never have been found. Like the people whose souls they were saving. The occasional pang of hunger rattled his stomach, but otherwise he felt content. In less than half an hour, the work was done.

He brought his satchel from last night's bed, still wet, and placed it in the bow. Untied the painter from the balsam and checked around him to make sure he hadn't forgotten anything. Laughed at himself. What did he have to possibly forget? He struggled with the now lighter, empty boat and laid it gently into the water. Looking to his left and right now, he tried hard to remember exactly where he was. Somewhere not far from Crow Rock except for yesterday's idiotic attempt to beat the rain. He couldn't have made it far. But in his panic, he had lost his bearings. In the new day, he recognized nothing. He pushed off and gracefully jumped into the boat. Sat on the damp rear seat and pulled the laminated map from the satchel. A red buoy bobbed not far ahead and to the left. He looked up to the sun for help. Then found Crow Rock and the nearby red buoy on the map. Smiled. No problem.

Philip started the trusty motor and accelerated confidently. Once at full speed, he turned to look back at the strange place he had spent the last night. Couldn't really locate it. The sunlit wooded shore looked flat and uninteresting from out here. The idea of an almost-comfortable cedar bed next to a log somewhere in there seemed impossible. His secret.

By the time home base came into view, it was past ten o'clock. As he turned the corner into the mooring bay, Philip almost threw up at the sight of the OPP boat pulled up on the beach. He swallowed hard as he slowed the engine to a crawl and prepared himself for whatever might follow.

THIRTY

Old Hostilities

"Philip!" Jane shrieked as her son crept cautiously in through the north door. "Where in hell have you been?! I was so worried! Where were you?!" She ran to the boy standing dirty in the doorway, satchel crusting dry over his shoulder. She grabbed him and held him close, too close. The sickening smell of perfume. "Oh, Philip," she cooed softly.

Philip barely listened, eyes on the two cops clad in dark blue shorts, light blue shirts, trying to look severe for him. One held a note pad. The other just stood there tugging at his moustache. Suddenly, Philip was being shaken violently by his shoulders.

"Where?! Where the hell were you?!" She looked straight into his eyes. "I went out in the big boat to find you. I didn't know where to go. I had to call the police." She motioned to the men standing behind her—one rolling his eyes and bouncing on his tiptoes, the other finishing a cup of coffee.

Philip felt a little guilty, especially at this unusual showing of affection by his mother. He knew she would notice he stayed out all night, but her made-up eyes said more than that. They were wet with concern. Still, what could he say?

"Little shit! Little selfish shit!" She whispered harshly. Half to herself, but directly into Philip's ear. She threw down the arms she had held so tightly.

Philip shuddered, overwhelmed with an unprecedented mix of feelings. Unwanted tears welled up in his eyes. Annoyed. Relieved. Confused. Maybe he hadn't given her enough credit. Maybe she wasn't all bad. But he shouldn't get carried away....

"M'am?" one cop intruded. "I think we'll be going now. There's no work for us here. Thankfully, of course. I won't even bother to file a report,

169

if that's all right with you." Looking at the dirty boy now. "You're all right, eh? Everything cool?"

The boy nodded back, looking down at the big, black shiny shoes pointed at him.

Jane nodded too. "That's fine. Thank you."

The other cop forced a look directly into Philip's eyes as he walked by him toward the north door. Moustache stinking like coffee. "Stay out of trouble, kid. Be nice to your mother. She's a good woman." He looked back at Jane as he said it.

Yeah? How would you know?! Philip's eyebrows slid down to frown at both cops' feet as they left the house. The door closed behind them. He looked up at his mother who was fixing her hair. Had she looked good enough for them? They seemed both to be wondering the same thing. Then she stopped, and remembered her Philip problem.

"Philip Reddy, you've embarrassed me in front of those nice men. Half the lake thinks I'm crazy, out there looking for you last night. I'm going to ask once, nicely: Where...were...you?"

Philip tried to think of an explanation. "I was over at the Emerys' place." So uncertain, he almost posed it as a question.

"Liar! I was there. They think I'm crazy too. Not just you now. Me! Where were you?! Lie to me again, and I swear, I'll smack you."

Philip shuffled his feet. She wasn't lying. He shouldn't either. He had never seen her so angry before. Not so sure he liked it after all. "You wouldn't believe me."

"Tell me!"

"Okay. Like.... Well.... I went on a trip to explore down near Crow Rock Island in the morning. And, well, I was gonna come back, but it started to rain and—"

"Damn it, Philip! You're lying again!" She reached and grabbed him by the chin, digging her nails into his flesh. He pulled away. "Don't pull away from me, young man!" She reached out and slapped his face.

The sound seemed to echo even in the small space of the cabin. Then the low drone of the OPP boat leaving the beach in the background.

Did she really just slap me?!

His ears rang and his mind whirred. She never hit him. The slap went deep inside him to a place he didn't think could be touched. His stomach turned on its own emptiness, and his eyes began to water again. Somewhere out there she was saying sorry. Telling him nothing mattered except that he was all right.

He was only faintly aware as something built inside him. It started to boil. First in his stomach. Then up through his heart. And into his throat. High and rolling. He clenched his teeth, still staring at his feet. She might have still been speaking, but it didn't matter. Slowly, he realized what was happening. His fists clenched by his sides. He was going to pound her! That was what was going to happen. Just pound the crap out of her. Slowly, his eyes rose to meet hers. As they met, he locked hers in. He was quite aware now that she had stopped talking, and the look on her face was hardly anger, but fear. He stepped back from her, ready. The corners of his mouth pulled down with hate. They both stood unmoving, not even breathing.

No.

Philip could not tell if it was the spirit or himself, but something kept him from doing it. But he wanted to. More than anything.

He lowered his eyes and tuned in again. She was still apologizing, a wreck. "Are you okay?" she asked too many times. "Are you okay?"

He closed his eyes to stop the tears. One slipped out. He nodded faintly. He waited, but he didn't get what he badly wanted. She made no move toward him. No move to touch him or hold him gently. Maybe she just didn't want to anymore. Maybe he had pushed her away too many times. Instead, he heard her speak from even further away. "You can do last night's dishes since you made me miss them. Then you can trim the path around the island." She was angrier than she was sorry.

Should have hit her, he thought. Eyes open now. Red. His father would never have left him there without a hug. His mother was just plain crap. He dropped the satchel on his bed and began his chores. He attacked his work with his anger. Wanted to ensure continued use of the boat. Jane watched him for a moment as he used the dish mop on the tall glasses—deep, down to the bottom, then around the tops.

The worst thing was that he had been trying to be nicer lately. Not shutting her out quite so much. What a waste! What was he thinking? He knew what never showing up last night must look like, but he had told the truth. He had made every effort to do the right thing. Written a note that morning. Even got off the lake responsibly. Didn't she remember the storms that had come through here last night…. Hadn't she considered that he might have been wind-bound somewhere?

What?! He glared at her.

She left the room, not getting it. Had herself a little coughing fit.

By mid-afternoon, he had finished all that had been laid out for him. The sweat dripped from his peeling forehead. He pulled off his glasses and rubbed his eyes as he rested for a moment. Some of the frustrated energy came out in swings of the scythe. His acne burned in the salt. His arms and legs ached. A new sore on the inside of his lip rubbed against his braces. And the mosquitoes were drawn to him as if he were a beacon. Yet he kept on.

After finishing his route around the island, Philip went down to the water's edge to cool his burning face. Just hoped his mother wouldn't stop him from using the boat. That was really all that mattered. If she was going to be like that.... He splashed away all the irritation, at least for a short while. Felt so good. He yanked off his shirt and shoes, laid them on top of the scythe and clippers, and jumped into the lake. The water was arrestingly cool from last night's rainfall and the stir of the storm, but he felt he could almost fall asleep in it. The sun shone down on him, as welcome as it had been at the start of the day. Looking at the shore, he realized that the lake level had already risen noticeably from the great rain.

He just needed the boat and everything would be okay, the quest could continue. She could be the biggest bitch in the world as long as she let him have the boat. But he couldn't let her know just how important it was or she might take it away out of spite.

He leaned back in the water to float, but suddenly he was upright again. In shock, for a moment he had to struggle to stay afloat. Could hardly articulate what he had realized in that moment. "Manido? Manido, I'm only here for another couple of weeks!"

The spirit had been with him all day. "Yes," he responded, deadpan.

"How many more souls are there? Are we going to finish?"

The spirit didn't say anything more for a few minutes. Maybe he did not understand. Maybe he was figuring it out. Maybe he was fiercely angry again. Finally, "We will do what we can."

"You're not angry?" Philip asked in disbelief.

"I am not pleased. But I know we cannot continue this forever. The distances to travel will soon be too great for this boat. I can only demand of you what you can give. Your mother controls access to the boats and your presence here. I must respect that. We will do what we can."

Philip treaded water easily again, relaxed by the spirit's response. Yes, he was sure now. It seemed so clear. The spirit—Manido—was his friend. He smiled to himself. The harsh words did not come often anymore. It was only logical. Manido was his friend. All he needed was the boat, he thought again. He would ask about it tonight. Do anything for it. He felt good again, closing his eyes, absorbing the sun. He did his best not to think about all of this being over so soon. In less than a month school would be in full swing. But not now. Not now. He forced the smile back on. The lake rocked him like a baby. He looked around at the far shore, a set of reefs. Over to the west, he saw the edge of the Little Whale. Very far from where he was. He looked again at the dolphin-shaped reefs which were also pretty far and began to swim.

THIRTY-ONE

Half?

The sun streamed in Philip's window waking him early and easily. Last night he had read more of the book that reminded him of Manido, but put it down when it became uncomfortable. After a day or two, things with his mother had seemed to be back to normal. Not a word about the boat. She must have felt guilty or something. She also seemed a little sick. Maybe she didn't have the strength to be too mean. But he wouldn't dare forget what she had done, actually hitting him, then saying she was sorry but not meaning it. Promised himself never to forget. He made his sandwiches quickly, packed his satchel, and left the island at 7:30 am. He had missed only one day of work, when he had gotten in trouble for being away all night.

The light fishing boat skimmed across the calm, dark water. The sun slowly took the edge off the cool morning air. A clear sky again. Philip's only company was the gang of gulls and cormorants standing on the reefs he passed. The occasional caw. But it was the book that bothered him now. Crazy Katsuk reminded him all too much of Manido. The awful Manido who had haunted him earlier on. The spirit had definitely put the book on his bed for a reason.

"Manido?" He waited. The boat headed toward a faraway end of the bay.

"Yes, boy. You have a question about the book."

"Yeah. I was reading it last night. And I just wondered, I mean—you're being nicer to me now, but you could change your mind. And, well... I need to know if you're going to sacrifice me or something. And—"

The spirit laughed wholeheartedly.

Philip had never heard such a sound. He felt he might burst out as well, but mostly out of shock.

"No. I do not plan on sacrificing you." Still barely able to control himself. "That book was meant to frighten you as were the other events of those first days. I knew the face on the front cover would scare you. I have not read such a book. I know only that it is a book of the white man. One must be wary of its truthfulness."

Relief cooled Philip from the inside out. "No, well...," he began, trying to justify his question, "You see, Katsuk is really this Native guy called Charles. Then a bee-god stings him and he has to sacrifice an innocent white kid to sort of make up for all the innocent Anish—wait!...no, whatever tribe he is—all the innocent ones the white man killed. So he kidnaps him and, well, that's where I am."

A silence. "That is an interesting idea. I will change my plans."

Philip tried to laugh, hoping Manido would join in. Nothing at first. Then a thoughtful chuckle.

"That was a joke, right?!"

"Yes. You should hope so." A pause. "Still I am intrigued by the idea that a white man would write such a story. I am certain the book is full of falsehoods. But this premise sounds almost respectful of the culture the white man destroys. Perhaps the world cannot be viewed completely and accurately from the Path of Souls." A guarded stop.

"The Path of Souls? But I thought—"

"The Land of Souls. The Ojibway words are very similar and easy to mistake. The Land of Souls. That is where I have been."

It must be strange to come back from heaven, Philip thought. There had been some pretty bad movies about that. He shook himself back to the present. Checked the map for the one reef left to worry about.

Today he would complete the ceremony for Kinozhae in the hidden loop of White Partridge Bay on the Indian reserve. The story of this man bothered Philip. Did Kinozhae really deserve all of this work and bother? There had to be a soul somewhere more deserving of the ceremony, especially with the limited time left and supposedly so many lost souls in the area. This man had been no innocent child or bystander. He was a traitor to his people. Philip hadn't liked performing the initial ceremony three days ago, nor did he like the idea of going back again. The reserve set him on edge too. And it wasn't just that Kinozhae didn't deserve it, but Philip had come to take the ceremony very seriously and hated to perform it without love. His resentment finally crushed his appreciation for the glorious morning.

"Okay, listen," he started as the boat passed a small island surrounded by reeds. "You know I want to help you, and I like doing it, okay? But—but I just can't do this for him. It's not right."

"I have explained to you that you do not make these decisions."

"Yes. Yes, you have, but—"

"You should not argue. You do not know enough."

"Okay. Well, convince me at least. Tell me enough! So I can do it for real. I don't want to do it and not, like, really mean it. Don't you get that?"

"You have made your point," the spirit said coldly. "Now listen.... Kinozhae made many mistakes. Some of these were costly to his people. Unlike many others we have helped on the journey, he was never lost, nor did he die alone. He received no ceremony because he was not entitled. He was a weak man. I told you how he deserted his people for the English. He did so out of fear, weakness and greed."

Philip started to laugh.

"Why do you laugh?!" boomed the spirit.

Philip stopped in order to speak. "When did you turn into such a dork? You hate whites. You hated me. And you hated them when you were alive, for sure. Why would you ever help someone who helped them? It doesn't make any sense!" That sounded good! he thought.

"When I found that Kinozhae had not made the journey, I too thought to leave him to suffer indefinitely. I found the place where he died, learned his story and went on to find others more deserving. But I have learned something. He too has learned it. For almost two hundred years, he has been trying to cross the river on the Path of Souls. He has cried long.

"And I dared not say it before—" The voice seemed to choke, and stopped.

The engine droned on as Philip followed the channel down to the end of the bay.

His brow creased with confusion. "What?"

The spirit let it out. "Even in your infinite ignorance...you, white child, have taught me something."

The boy turned the engine throttle down, as if it might help him hear better. What on earth could he have taught anybody?

"You have taught me there is forgiveness. I could forgive your deed and your heritage. You could forgive mine. This happened in a very short time. And now I can forgive a man once greedy and weak two hundred years after his crime. And I can hope that Gitche-Manido can do the same. If not, I will accept it. But I will have done what I feel is right. If only I too were forgiven...."

A cold sweat prickled beneath Philip's cap. His eyes and nose tickled. He realized then that he couldn't remember the last time someone had trusted him, confided in him, for real. At the same time, he could feel a mysterious sadness in the spirit. Why would Manido need to be forgiven? And who's supposed to do that? Me?! Can't he tell that I don't have a problem with him?

The boat resumed its speed, planing on the rippling water. The sun blasted Philip's vision from the east.

Philip could go through with this ceremony now, but he couldn't help wondering about Manido, suddenly silent. The kind words echoed in his mind. He had taught the spirit something. The idea seemed absurd. But the more he thought about it, the more it seemed possible.

The boat buzzed past a ramshackle house on the left bank. A figure stood motionless on the deck and watched him pass. Philip noticed the house for the first time. For the first three days it had been camouflaged. No road seemed to lead there. No dock. No clearing of brush. Just a house.

The bay opened up again as Philip approached the end. Big, new houses along the wide ear-shaped left shore. Satellite dishes too. He hoped they were rich Natives, but couldn't help thinking they had to be whites who had somehow bought the land. Purposely didn't ask. Didn't dare look anywhere directly for very long for fear someone might see him and wave him off. Just the idea of an Indian reserve made him nervous, especially now that he knew how only land not otherwise useful had been given to the Natives. If he could just get through unnoticed one last time, he promised never to come back. He made this promise to himself and the people who lived here. They had been bothered enough. How could they not hate whites? Philip let his head sink down between his shoulders as he neared the narrow passageway at the end of the wide-open part of the bay, where he would come closest to one of their houses. The boat squeezed between a reef-island and a mowed grass shoreline. Another satellite dish. And a jeep. He rounded the wooded corner that always looked like the very end of the bay from a distance, and entered the final secluded pocket of White Partridge.

This hidden area was a marshy lake of its own, with narrow bays going off in every direction. You could forget how big this lake really was. His landing cove came up to his right. He pulled up the motor and pushed the boat through a patch of reeds, poling the soft bottom with one of the old wooden oars until the boat grounded onto the shore. He pulled the bow up onto the tiny, gritty beach, then looked across the water to another reedy channel which led to Mackenzie Portage Road. He had studied the map again last night. If he had had more time, he might have adventured down there just to see if the map was right. But this was all business. He prayed no one would find him. He would complete the ceremony. Then he just wanted to say a few final things to show he believed more fully now in the man he was trying to save.

He clambered up the eroded, ant-infested bank onto the grassy bluff. Pushed into a thicket of strange berry trees, crushed large orange mushrooms underfoot. He found the wigwam intact. From his pack he pulled a margarine container of berries and one bulrush bulb. He thought to make up for any lack of enthusiasm he had shown earlier, adding extra pieces of bark to the wigwam, spreading more tobacco than usual.

His ear twitched. A twig breaking? He turned around, but saw nothing. Forget it. Turned back toward the grave and spoke.

"K'neekaunissinaun, ani-maudjauh.

K'neekaunissinaun, cheeby-meekunnaung.

K'neekaunissinaun, kego bin—"

A pair of shoes appeared in front of him. He looked up to find himself face-to-face with a young Native man. A huge headset blared heavy rock music into the hidden ears, but Philip could hear a good deal of it.

An Ojibway! An Anishinaabe!

The young man's mouth hung open. "What the...?" His eyes went big above the few thin whiskers decorating his still boyish face. On top of his head, an L.A. Raiders cap held back his shoulder-length hair. He gripped a drumstick tightly in each gloved hand. They looked like some kind of driving or biking gloves. He must have been air-drumming to the music on his headphones. At least that meant he hadn't heard Philip's chant.

Philip stared right back at the stranger. He couldn't think of anything else to do. Soon he noticed the man's eyes had shifted down to the grave between them. He had pulled his headphones down onto his shoulders, in awe. "What's that? Looks like a teepee." Looked back up at Philip, who responded by looking down at his feet.

Wigwam. It was a wigwam. But he didn't respond out loud. His heart raced with excitement. He half-expected to be attacked or shot. But the tall, t-shirt and jeans-clad man just stood there. Just as dumb as Philip. Not quite.

The wheels began to turn behind the stranger's eyes. "Isn't this still...? You know you're trespassing, eh?"

Philip gave a hint at a nod, the downward part. Trespass. The T word. But the man didn't seem to care. "So, what's with the teepee? Whatcha got in the bag?"

Philip remained frozen, as the guy stepped forward and reached for the satchel. He opened it, grunting to himself as he sifted through snack food and rags. Then his eyes lit up at the tobacco.

"You wanna smoke? You got zig-zags?"

Philip could barely believe what he was hearing. It bordered on being funny. He had expected a bully by the size of what he saw before him.

"Hey. You're not deaf, are you? Or a mime? A mute?" The questions cautiously asked.

Philip cracked a smile.

"Okay, so where's the paper, man?"

Philip felt he could almost talk to this guy, but not quite. He's not dangerous, he told himself. He reached out for the can without looking up. After he had wrestled it from the man's hand, he opened it up and sprinkled some on the wigwam. Then, without thinking, he held out a pinch for the young man. The Indian turned up his palm, and Philip laid the tobacco there.

The young Anishinaabe man laughed a warm smile. Philip could feel its heat, but got scared and bolted back toward the canoe. He whispered his final words to Kinozhae as he ran from the site. From behind him he heard shouting, something about not having to run. Philip skidded down the slope to the water. Fought with the boat to push it off into the bay again.

The new friend appeared at the top of the ridge. "What did you say when you ran before? You said K'neekaunissinaun, right? You said that. I heard that, right?" he called.

Philip stopped, half in, half out of the boat, and looked up at the man's curious expression.

"It means brother, right? My Grandfather used to say it sometimes. Other old-time words like that too." His face grew even more puzzled, "How the hell do you know that tongue?! Are you half or something?"

A rush flooded through the white intruder as he realized someone might figure out what he was doing. For a split second, he longed to speak to that grandfather to find out the meaning of each of the words he had used and sung in these last weeks of the summer. But he had stayed there long enough. Wasn't ready to ask the guy standing there right now. Pushed the boat free of the bottom with the oar.

The Anishinaabe drummer watched as Philip back-paddled the boat out of the reeds and into the main pocket of the hidden bay. The white boy looked up at the nodding man. At first he thought the man was bouncing to his music, but his eyes were in the here and now, headphones still around his neck. Philip stole one more quick glance as he started the engine and pushed toward the main bay. The man raised his hand to wave. Philip wished later he had returned it.

Alone again, underway. He saw that his worst fear had finally been realized—he had been discovered. But he was no worse off. The young Anishinaabe man must have at least had some idea of what he was doing, that it was a ceremony. Couldn't really have figured it all out. It was far too complicated. Too impossible. Philip shook his head in disbelief, and headed back out toward the main lake. As he sped out into the open part of the bay, he saw a canoe with two more people in it—probably Anishinaabe. Feared looking at them directly, but he could see their outlines clearly and that they stopped paddling to watch him pass. They did not wave, but watched intently. Maybe because he hadn't waved back to the drummer. It was all connected. Maybe they too thought he was half, almost one of them. Was that a good thing or a bad thing despite his distinct white-man looks? If only he had a twenty-horse motor so he could speed by, forget them. Just wanted to be out of there. He leaned forward to streamline the boat against the slight headwind.

He stared at the bottom of the boat until he thought the men would be out of sight. His eyes rose above the vibrating bow again, just in time to catch sight of the reef-island rapidly approaching. He jerked right to avoid it, sending his satchel off the seat, the tobacco can clanging against the aluminium. Then readjusted for the channel out of the bay. The frightened boy gasped, broke into sweat. Stupid! A reminder of how much trouble his cowardice could cause. It didn't matter that he had missed the rocks, but that if he had crashed on them, it would have been only because of fear. Freakin' fear! He suddenly felt as low as he had at the beginning of the summer. He knew it was weird to roller-coaster up and down every minute like this, but he couldn't help it.

Now he couldn't stop obsessing about the rocks. Wanted to whip himself. Brooded all the way out the long bay. He couldn't shake what he was. He was unaware of any tear until one rolled down his cheek. He tried to think of all the souls he had helped in order to forget about his destiny to always fail. There had been eleven. And he had been told the jobs had been done successfully. Found it hard to believe today.

The spirit made himself heard. "Do not do this to yourself now. Go home. Rest. Tomorrow, we will perform one last and important ceremony."

Philip couldn't move. It would soon be over. All of it, the work. Would it be an accomplishment to be proud of? Or would the end of it just be another loss he would have to deal with?

"Go home. Enjoy the day. Tomorrow will not be easy. I feel a resistance building itself against us. It is more than just limited time."

He went home as he was told, but could not enjoy the day.

THIRTY-TWO

Winonah, Stanley and Jack

"Listen to this story now, for you must understand it well before we begin tomorrow. The day will be difficult. Listen well and start building the will to push through the trials."

Philip lifted his hand over his head to turn off the lamp. Singed his hand on the hot bulb. He lay on his back, staring up at the berth above him, cloaked in fresh black. Didn't like the sound of the next day. But Manido's voice was welcome after an unfamiliar afternoon of moping around the island.

"Almost seventy years ago this fall but well after the lake level changed, my own Great-Great-Grandchild and her two little ones were murdered at Shoal Lake. They were innocent. The act was as cowardly as ever committed by a mortal.

"Many years earlier, the white man had begun raping what many call Poplar Island. He did such damage to much land all around the rest of these waters. He did it without respect, thinking only of the precious stones and ores he might find. The gold mines on Shoal Lake represent his world of taking without asking. He used poison agents to help his work without concern. He left everything in ruins. The white man had found out about the gold in the earth and had decided he must have it.

"One day, near the summer's end, Winonah and her two children canoed over to the island which had grown quiet in the last few days. They lived only one portage from the island where the headframes stood. Winonah and her people still lived mostly in the old way—trapping, collecting wild rice and fishing. Sometimes they would sell the harvested rice and fish in order to buy other supplies. But they were not ignorant of the ways of the new world. Winonah remembered her father telling of the moose he had once taken on the very island which had been made strange with booming white craft. It was off limits. It had become the Bon Courage Mine. Property of Keating Prospectors Ltd. Winonah remembered well how the sign had changed and the work had stopped and started over the years. As a young girl, she had read, Dorsett Gold Mining and Reduction Company. Then Poplar Island Gold Mining Company. The signs had all looked different to her, yet they meant the same thing. They meant that this land was being beaten.

"She had learned not to take the white man's exploits lightly. She spared no detail in warning her children about them. On this quiet day, she decided to show her children what the whites had done to the island. She believed her children should see the nature of this other people. She knew that soon enough Stanley and Jack might attend the white schools as her friends' children did. She knew the old way would become unclear by the time they grew up. This is why they went by these Saugaushe names and kept their Anishinaabe ones close to their hearts, for their family only. Before the white world brainwashed them, she wanted them to be on their guard. Many others in her clan had grown to accept the whites over the years. She knew better. I am very proud of who she was.

"As they paddled past the great mound of rock removed from deep below the ground, Winonah told the children of how it got there. She told them it was not supposed to be there. The small family landed on the island where the shore was soft and flat. She told her children to walk in the quiet way because the workers had a camp not far from there and might be about. Winonah had her suspicions that the mine had been closed yet again. She had timed her visit so that her children might learn what this was before someone else bought it and work began again.

"They passed by strange buildings as they walked onto the island. Trees had been cut and the earth had been upturned. Winonah remembered how the trees had disappeared over the years. She kept her children within arm's reach as they passed the great mountain of rock which had grown each year in Winonah's memory. She was wary of what might lurk on this land turned inside out.

"Then young Stanley let out a cry. The family stood in front of a gaping hole. It seemed there was no bottom. Thick cables disappeared down in the darkness and a machine hung above from a metal frame. Winonah pulled her curious children behind her by the shirts. She could barely believe what she saw. It was not a cave. It was what you call a shaft. It went straight down like a large well, but there was no water to be seen in it.

"A spiteful, drunken voice came from behind them. It said, 'Hey, little squaw lady. That's a big hole to fall into.' It was a drunken miner. He laughed heartily with his two friends. The family turned around together to set their eyes on the three creatures. Winonah held her children close to her. She knew something was terribly wrong.

"'This land is not for you, little lady. You're gonna hafta pay a toll.' He laughed again looking back at his partners while nodding and undoing his belt.

"The men threw Stanley and Jack down the shaft, then raped my Great-Great- Granddaughter. She could hear her broken Stanley's screams from the bottom of the hole. The fall had killed Jack instantly. When the men were done with Winonah, they threw her down the shaft as well. She fed Stanley the blood from her own body until she died. He starved to death with his broken neck.

"These men had no fear or care. They were angry white men who had been told their jobs were no more. The mine was closed. No one would find the bodies. No one would miss three Indians.

"Only you know now where they lie."

Philip felt his stomach turn. Suddenly nauseous, he envisioned it all happening. He leaned over the edge of the bed and heaved his dinner violently onto the floor. He was quite sure Manido was right—no worse crime had ever been committed. The last of his vomit dripped into the puddle. He wiped his mouth with the back of his hand and rolled back to the middle of his bed. That all too strong sense of guilt and shame. And a very real acidic burn in his throat. He let his forearm rest across his eyes and did his best to sleep. But his dreams were filled with blood again.

THIRTY-
THREE

Ash Rapids

The bitter aroma of last night's vomit did its part to wake him. He had to scrape the last bits of it off the floor. The boy could feel the weight of Manido's family on his shoulders, and became determined to do all he could to help. After a less-than-enthusiastic swim, he made a lunch, packed his satchel, and left a note for his mother. Today would be his longest day for sure. Even after eating, his stomach felt nervously empty. Down at the dock he filled the gas tank and put an extra gas can in the bow of the boat. Somehow knew everything would be against him. Including the waves. He had been warned. It was part of the deal. He sat on the dock and squinted at the map as the morning sun shot at him through the trees of Blueberry Point. He scanned the messy route to Shoal Lake as he lathered his raw neck in sunblock. His finger stopped on the name Ash Rapids. An immediate knot in his stomach. Shook his head, wondered if it could be done all in one day. This was the summer's last push. Philip's stomach somersaulted again with the thought that his adventure was almost over.

The trip seemed to take even longer than the map promised. Philip often found himself slowing down to find landmarks on the unfamiliar route. Overly concerned with the shoreline and buoys, he missed virtually all of the breathtaking landscape flashing past his eyes. As the waves increased in size, he pulled down his Tigers cap and pushed his glasses to the top of his nose.

Finally, the rear-heavy aluminium boat swung into a bay the map indicated should mark the transition from open water to narrow passageways. Navigating between the green and red buoys, he slipped into Ash Bay. The entrance itself was deceptively narrow, but then the water opened up again so that the waves were again a factor. He passed an orange-red post standing on a rock. The rock would have been lethal without it. The bay

185

seemed to stretch forever in every direction. He had to check the map again to see if he was still on course. He let his gaze fall right, across the bow, where he found a mess of buoys and tall markers toward the back of the main bay. It looked even more chaotic than the map showed it to be and refused to sort itself out as he approached.

Only when he was two hundred feet away was he able to differentiate between the obstacles. They were indeed in sequence, although the posts still appeared to be side by side. If they're the same colour, I can't just go between them! he thought, remembering his dad's lessons. He slowed as he passed the first red buoy on his right. Checked the map every few feet. Was he on the correct side of the buoy? Yes. He checked again nervously. Okay.

The rapids were up ahead. By the looks of things, he would have to climb the rapids to get to the waterways that led to Shoal Lake. The map seemed to take these rapids very seriously, a sign that he should too. He slowed further, letting the boat drift a bit. Examined the map more closely. Next to the passageway was written in red: (SEE CAUTION) (VOIR ATTENTION). To the lower right of the normal scale was a magnified version of each set of rapids. The depths, markers, buoys, the dotted-line channel all laid out. Below in more red ink: CAUTION: Very strong currents exist in Upper Rapids. Depending on the lake level, the flow can be in either direction. Philip wondered how he had missed these warnings when he studied the route the night before. He gulped and laid the map down.

The direction of the current became apparent after he had motored a little closer to the passage. The water moved toward him, independent of the wind which hit him broadside. He sent the engine down past SLOW. Ahead, swift water churned in a narrow channel. Even fifty feet from the actual rapids, the current slowly pushed his bow to the side and into the wind. The wind spun the boat further, pointing it back toward home.

The boy let out a low whine. He grabbed the map and spoke the name aloud. "Ash Rapids." He swore quietly and cut the engine, already beaten. The boat drifted as he studied the map for an alternate route. But this was the only way to Shoal Lake, except for two crazy portages from the end of Pelican Bay. The dotted lines on the map led into small lakes, then directly to the top of Shoal Lake, exactly where he wanted to be. No rapids. No huge open-water. But on his own, the other routes were not options. No choice to be made here at all. He looked back at the pitiful six-horse motor that powered his boat. Again, a twenty would have been a lot better. But he had to try as is. What if I hit bottom? Checked the depths again.

In the distance, the buzz of another boat. Surprising to hear a motor so early on a weekday morning. In another moment, the boat was visible around the same corner he had passed fifteen minutes earlier. A bass boat bouncing solidly through the islands guarding the entrance to Ash Bay, approaching him almost directly. A crusty looking fisherman gave Philip a wave as he sped by, heading up toward the rapids. Philip raised his hand hesitantly as he looked on. The boat slowed slightly against the current, and was gone around the corner in a few seconds. The hum faded as quickly as it had come.

It was possible. It was even routine. Philip shook his head at what a fool he had been, and started his own motor. The boat gathered speed as Philip gunned it.

As he approached the rapids, he could feel the boat's progress slow versus the current. But a moment later he was half-way up the rapids. He was grinning with the thought of success when his eyes caught sight of the bottom. He jerked the tiller away to escape the rocks. Too suddenly. The boat lurched off course. He lowered the throttle in a panic, and the boat was held completely still for a moment. Then his eyes widened as the water caught the bow and swung it downstream. The boat drifted toward the fixed green marker he had just passed. Philip yanked the motor up out of the water just before the bow struck the marker's cement base. The crash sent Philip forward. Palms flat on the metal seat. The boat bounced off the obstacle and slid back down the rapids outside the channel, scraping the bottom. Into the still water once again.

He let out his gasp of breath. Sat with his head in his hands, breathing hard for a few moments, trying to recover. He turned to look at the insurmountable current. This motor was pitiful. He glared at it. Gave it the finger. Face twisted up. Maybe if the rocks had been just far enough down. Maybe if he hadn't flinched, just gone straight....

Forget it! It hadn't even been close. There was no point in trying again. Shoal Lake was supposed to be his biggest challenge and he couldn't even get there to face it!

Maybe this was part of it, the great challenge. He half-hoped so.

What would the true Anishinaabe do now? If they had come in a canoe, there was no way they could get up the chute to the next level except by land. A portage? But he knew he had far more than just the weight of a canoe to worry about. And he was a weak white boy, all alone.

He knew what he had to do. It just seemed impossible. He bit his lip. Nothing left to do but try. A portage of some kind....

THIRTY-FOUR

Shoal Lake's Fury

Philip got the motor going again and rammed the boat into the rocky shore at the base of the rapids. A little reckless now, having half given up already. He tilted the motor out of the water and walked to the bow. The boat rocked side to side as the keel grounded against the bottom under his weight. He stepped out onto the slightly inclined rock and pulled the bow up over the land's edge. It was like a beach, but made of solid rock. Upstream, the bank followed a more tilted plane of bedrock that leaned toward the swift channel. Easy to walk, but impossible to drag a boat over without it sliding into the water or tipping right over. He would have to scout the rest of the shoreline, find out just how far he would need to go to safely put the boat in again, provided he could move it at all. A few steps further, with a dodge of an old, leaning oak branch hanging from above, he was relieved to find the other promised piece of still water and a decent launching pad. He would have to drag the boat about fifty feet. Maybe not so impossible. His heart raced as he dashed back to his waiting burden.

He lifted the bow further out of the water again and pulled the rope over his shoulder, turning to face upstream. The stern floated easily ashore. A good six feet of progress with ease. Then the underside of the stern struck the shore and Philip's frail body jerked backwards with the sudden resistance. Cold flushed through him as he stared resolutely up the shoreline. He refused to turn and face his grounded boat. With his arm cocked awkwardly behind him, he pulled like a good horse on a broken carriage. Squinting, holding his breath for power, about to burst, he finally made the boat budge. A sickening grind of metal on rock. His feet slipped and he collapsed facedown on the warm rock. His body felt relief, but his mind reeled. There's absolutely no way!

He forced himself up and gave another half-hearted tug. Nothing more. He kicked the old aluminium boat. Again, this time harder. Then again and again. There was nothing else to do. He looked around in a panic. Stuck, really. He almost had to laugh at how ridiculous it all was—he probably couldn't push it back into the water either! He kicked one last time and the motor swung down out of its tilted position to smack its skeg against the dry rock below.

Finally, he sat down, cross-legged next to the boat, head in his hands. If he just had the bigger boat, he could have made it up with no problem. Maybe he would try again. But he would need a charm from Manido to make that work! And Manido wasn't offering any help.

The timeline weighed heavily on his mind. He had promised nothing, but he knew what was right. It was right to finish this. But what if he simply couldn't get to Shoal Lake? What then? He felt a genuine wish not to cop out, not to be lazy or let things go. Think, you creep. You're too weak to carry the boat or drag it. What else? He needed a three-wheeler or a 4x4. Maybe Superman.... He thought hard as he sat next to the immovable boat. Turned the problem upside down, looked at it from different angles. The deeper he dug, the less he felt like giving up. He drew an imaginary sketch with a peeled beaver twig as he pondered the situation. Circles. Squares. Boats. Shorelines. More circles.... That was what he needed: wheels. Good luck! The twig dropped. It bounced noiselessly and rolled down the sloped rock until it got lodged in a crack. His mouth dropped. He busied himself with trying to figure out just what he was on the verge of. Picked up the twig, and let it drop and roll again. Placing his shoe carefully across the twig, he moved it slowly but effortlessly.... It rolled back and forth. His foot vibrated on the uneven knots. The boy's scalp suddenly moistened as he put the pieces together and clamoured to his feet.

"Rollers!" he cried out.

With new energy, he struggled up the earth bank above the bedrock. If he could just find some sticks, logs, anything that would roll. Immediately, his eye found a skinny, dead balsam, barely standing on its crumbling roots. He approached it aggressively and pulled it down as if he were a powerful beast. After he had tossed the balsam over the edge of the bank onto the bedrock, he wandered through the tall grass and berry bushes of the field looking for more. He would need at least two rollers. Then, as if someone had been looking out for him, three uniformly shaped skinned logs presented themselves in the grass. Each piece was about three inches in diameter, two-

and-a-half-feet long. By their pointed ends, he knew they were the workings of a beaver, abandoned or forgotten for some reason. He laughed as he tucked them under his arm, and ran back toward the shore. Skidded down the bank onto the rock, eager to try his cunning plan. Didn't need that sorry balsam anymore, and laughed at it leaning upside-down against the bank, its top bent over sadly under its weight on the rock, hairy roots up in the air.

Thinking it out carefully, Philip lifted the bow of the boat and gingerly slid one of the lengths beneath the keel. Then another. With a tilt of his head and one last breath of preparation, he gave the first tug on the bow handle. But it just dug into his fingers and palm. No movement at all. He looked toward the stern and remembered that the motor needed to be re-tilted. Then he returned to the bow. He leaned on the bow with all his weight, heard a gritty budging and felt the stern rising slowly off the rock. The boat wobbled strangely. He seized the moment—held the bow down, changed his footing and pushed the bow as hard as he could from one side. The contraption lurched forward away from the water. The solid drone of wooden wheels. Philip held his breath as he cautiously experimented with letting go of the boat for a moment. It stayed put. Crouching down, a step to the side, the boy could see a boat was more like a car than he ever could have imagined. He shook his head in euphoric disbelief and laid the third roller down just in front of the boat.

The rollers moved the boat like a dream. He pushed the boat from behind and replaced the rollers. Pushed and replaced until he found himself more than halfway there. He was brilliant. The rollers even resisted the sideways slope into the water, holding his intended course almost perfectly. A quick glance at the green post he had struck not long ago reminded him to stay humble. He had already passed that point, but sooner or later he would have to come down the rapids too.... He shook off the thought by picking up the roller left behind the boat and replacing it up front again.

The front roller splashed into the water, letting the bow hang as Philip eased to the end of his portage. The back roller slipped out from underneath the stern. The boat lurched forward and crashed onto the rock edge, the bow just breaking the water's surface. Then stopped moving. He let go of the boat and the tilted motor he had been leaning on, gushing relief. Looking back at the swirling mess of water, he couldn't help smiling to himself—he had taken the hard route and made it.

Wiping the sweat from his reddened forehead, he decided to move on. Another set of rapids were still ahead and with a quick glance at the map he saw there were no markers. At least that meant he couldn't crash into one. His hands found the convenient handles attached to the transom and he managed to lift the stern off the rock and into the water, just grazing the motor's skeg against the shore. Quickly, he sprang into the boat, pulled the rip-cord and gunned the motor full thrust to avoid somehow being sucked back down the chute.

He picked the map up from the floor and looked ahead for the next set of rapids: Upper Rapids. This pond was Lock Lake, the map told him. The idea of being trapped on a lake between two sets of rapids in the middle of nowhere didn't sit well with him. With a closer look at the map, he saw that the red print warning about the current was really just for this second set. So the current here was even stronger and the passage even narrower.... As the boy neared the passage, his stomach turned with the swirling at the chute's base. No alternate portage or carry-over path along a bank this time. The stream couldn't have been more than twenty feet wide. One false move would certainly mean hitting the shore, if not the bottom first. He gasped, and plunged full-throttle into the middle of the channel. He refused to look over the side into the water this time. This would either work or it would-n't. He couldn't influence a thing himself. Last-second predictions meant nothing. In what seemed an incredibly short time, he was through and back into still water again. Ash Rapids, conquered. Upper Rapids, conquered. Maybe it hadn't been a big deal. Maybe it shouldn't have been. Maybe everyone else in the world would have breezed through. But Philip still felt he had done something quite extraordinary.

As if to demand a reward, Philip's stomach began to rumble hungrily. His watch read 10:30am, as good a time to eat as any. But it seemed he had barely started.... The lunch cooler rubbed insistently up and down on his leg. Not yet, he told himself. Had to set goals and reach them, otherwise he would get nowhere. But he did slow down for a moment to reapply sunblock to his peeling forehead. He could feel the burning through his t-shirt. The sun had nearly boiled the cream through the satchel. It was hot and soupy against his skin. A fishing boat passed by and two men waved at a white-smeared Philip. Set again, he sped up, making his way to and through the Shoal Lake Narrows, buoy to buoy, island to island. He turned the map on his lap, refolded when he reached the edge of a section.

Philip didn't notice that the waves were rising gradually until the tiny fishing boat was bouncing almost out of control. The once pesky chop had somehow given way to real ocean rollers, and the narrows to a huge body of water. The boat changed angles to the water every few seconds as it rode the slow-bucking surface. Suddenly, Philip realized he was surrounded by the mountainous waves. They were coming head-on. After each one, he would ride down into a trough. Water strained to come over the gunwales. The oars shook and crashed about on the hot, vibrating seats. The rivets pulsing as if they might suddenly give way to the water. Every few waves he felt sure the boat would flip end-over-end as the wind caught the hull and reared it up so he could see nothing but the chipped baby blue of the floor. His fingers throbbed and sweated as he desperately clutched the fluttering map.

The light aluminium boat bounced and thudded wildly, occasionally completely airborne. Easing up on the throttle allowed him to steer and at least gave his windblown mouth a chance to salivate. Glimpses caught over the high-bouncing bow left him agape—the far shore was almost out of sight. This was the big time. Worse, bigger, than he had imagined. The Crow Rock trip had been nothing like this. Looking at the gas supply again, he mentally crossed his fingers. Gripped the tiller with all his power, sure he would spinout or even capsize if he relaxed for one second.

Out in the open, navigation was no longer child's play. The more distant shorelines appeared flat to his eye. Impossible to distinguish a distant island from mainland. Huge bays and islands, pivotal landmarks for navigation, could be staring him in the face and he would never know. All his energy was channelled to watching for the next buoy, but the markers appeared less and less often. And there was something odd about the Shoal Lake part of the map. It had less colour. But something more important. No blue.... It was only then that the boy's eyes widened above the bare white space. Not a single number to indicate depth! Shoal Lake was entirely white, with the occasional buoy marked in colour and black cross for a reef. It seemed impossible that it could be so badly charted. Maybe it was a misprint. He shook his head in disgust at his ever-complicating task and again strained to spot the next marker.

There. Relief as he found a string of protective islands by following the dotted line on the map between two buoys. Safe from the wicked west gale for a short while. The muscles in his body eased as the boat planed more normally on the smoother water. But this was no time to relax—this useless map listed no depths for Shoal Lake whatsoever! New tension gripped him each time he approached another cross on the map. But every time he spotted jagged rocks or a lonely clump of weeds corresponding to a cross, he exhaled with relief, for a fleeting moment sure of his position and safety.

Between the islands of this channel, the chop picked up again, funnelling through from the ocean-sized, west side of the lake to his left. Around a corner, between a red buoy and the last island of refuge, the full force of the lake presented itself once again.

A dotted line on the map showed the way north, up and around, and into Belle's Inlet. The absence of any buoys would make navigation difficult. An accident waiting to happen. The map showed a straight dotted line across the open water to a passage and then a nearly flat east shore to follow north. His eyes searched the shore, but could see no passage. Scanned his total range of vision and took a guess. Not at all sure. He knew he needed to make a right soon, but it looked wrong somehow. All wrong.

Unexpected, jagged reefs surrounded the tempest-tossed boat. The engine down to SLOW. Philip poured desperately over the map. A legitimate panic. Too many islands. Too many seagull-whitened rocks peeked up out of the heaving water. He tried to find corresponding crosses on the map, but nothing matched now. Maybe the right turn was just ahead. He sped up half-heartedly, checking to the right for what appeared on the map as a pipeline out of the tangle. Nothing. And nothing to do but keep going, looking for some sign. His mind tried to bend the shoreline to fit the one on the map, but he couldn't kid himself. After all the navigating he had done recently, how could he screw up so badly? He longed to be back at the rapids so he could try all of this again. Please don't let me be lost. Or maybe he could just turn around. But the scene behind him looked suspiciously similar to what lay in front of him. A compass wouldn't have been a bad idea. His stomach growled loudly now. His head throbbed. It had to be a right turn, so he went for the very next opening. With the throttle held at FAST, the boy headed for a huge stretch of water beckoning him between two nearby islands. He tried to find something like it on the map, but couldn't. All he could do was to head north, even if he was off.

And off he was.

He shook his head and thought, I suck! Fit to be sacrificed by any angry Native. Then the motor shuddered, slowed and shut down. The only sounds now were the wind in the boy's ears and the water slapping on the aluminium. Man! Out of gas! He had forgotten. Lifting the red five-gallon tank told the story, so empty it almost leaped overboard out of his hand as he grabbed at it. The wind caught the bow and pushed the boat forcefully toward a nearby reef-island. Philip scrambled to the bow, grabbed the smaller can, untied it from a seat support beam. Reached under his seat for the funnel. The ballooned can hissed violently as he released the air valve, explosive with the sun's heat and agitated sea. Opened the tank and inserted the funnel. He gritted his teeth, prepared for a difficult pour. The rocking boat made sure the initial stream splash directly onto the floor. The next shot skimmed off the funnel's edge onto the tank. Finally, the gasoline hit the funnel perfectly, spiralling down into the empty tank. Holding the can steady required all of his concentration. The sight of the reef over his shoulder just ten feet away made him spill another spurt. He quickly righted the can and rushed for the old green oar. The deep water went brown, and its surface broke, sucked and slurped around the rock. Then a big wave crested and hit a pocket in the reef, shooting a jet of water into the air. As soon as he could reach it, the boy awkwardly fended off the reef with the oar, the boat jerking violently in the reef's surf. As he pushed, the stern was sucked around by a trough and the motor skeg cracked against the shallow bottom, hiccupping out of the water. Philip should have been shot for leaving the motor down at all.

No option but to fill the tank and hope the motor would still run. He inspected the surrounding water for any more surprises, and went back to filling the tank. Philip pulled the bruised engine's rip-cord and it caught on the first try. Hungry and lost in Shoal Lake, he couldn't help laughing at his good fortune and decided to forgive his stupidity this time. The motor hummed contentedly and propelled him toward the passage to who knew where.

A strange, competent sensation. History's great explorers probably spent most of their lives lost. No big deal. Of course, a little help from Manido would have been nice. But doing this on his own was a true adventure: he was out here alone, no advice from on high, no commands to follow, a weekday, no help from vessels passing by every few minutes…. Somehow there was a wholeness to it.

When an apparently uniform strip of shore made itself visible to his right from behind yet more islands, Philip held himself back from celebrating. He turned to ride eastward with the waves. Closer to the shore, he became more sure. Slowly, he scanned to the right: the shore extended almost perfectly straight as his eyes skimmed it. He ended up staring directly down the strait to the south, surely through the passage he had missed so badly. A desire to weep for joy swept over him, but the journey was far from over. The bouncing boat hugged the high, wooded coastline now, squeezing between it and small islands, trying to hide from the huge, side-swiping rollers. As he travelled north, cottages appeared along the shore, atop high cliffs. Big, beautiful houses with elaborate decks, staircases and mysterious large boathouses. All deserted. Weekenders.

In an astoundingly short amount of time, Philip arrived at the first real variation in the shoreline, a point and then a bay. The map confirmed his position. He was about to round into Symcoe Bay. The name rang familiar somehow. In his detour he had to have almost crossed the entire lake, miles upon miles too far west. He had missed almost all of the intended course along the flat shoreline, and instead made a huge circle into completely unknown waters. Hoped he hadn't used too much gas on the detour to let him make it home. His blood pumped a little faster now as the journey neared its end. Minutes away now! He whispered to himself, "Just don't mess up now. Don't mess up." Giving a wide berth to yet more reefs on his left and a point of land on his right, he entered the first sheltered bay and continued toward the channel into Belle's Inlet.

A hurt expression crossed his face as the shore ahead appeared unbroken. Jumping on his map with his index finger, he shouted, "It has to be here!" Had the trip been for nothing? Only within a hundred feet did the wooded point of the overlapping right shore become distinct from the bank of green a bit further back. There was indeed a hidden passage! Another look at the map and it made sense. He hooked right and cruised through the gap, heading directly south. One island to pass on the left, then straight through. He had expected to see the headframe Manido had described, but its absence or invisibility barely quelled his bursting joy. He was here, whatever he found! The island dead ahead had to be it. Had to be. Still no buildings in view. But as the bay narrowed holding the island like a hand holding an egg, a square white sign set itself apart from the brush on the shore. Maybe....

Philip squinted and read it.

KEEP OUT
PRIVATE PROPERTY
Jarvis Industries Ltd.

Exhilaration ran through him. "Yesss," he hissed.

THIRTY-FIVE

Poplar Island

Flushed with his success, Philip passed the sign and cruised along the west side of the island. Slowly, to inspect the shore for a landing slip. The north end of the island where he had seen the sign stood high and rocky, but further along, a grassy slope tapering into the water. Just beyond the high front of the island a huge mound of dark grey rocks stretched from a peak of about eighty feet down into the water beside Philip. Looked like an avalanche that had fallen from nowhere. On its peak, a mangled wooden frame, abandoned and all but completely destroyed. He knew nothing about mining, but it made sense that you would have to pile the dug-out rock somewhere or other. Manido's story flashed back at him—this was the great heap the family had seen just before they were killed! He could barely believe it, but it had to be right.

Up behind the heap, pieces of rusty machinery and a cement foundation peeked out from behind a thin layer of poplar trees. Philip felt a chill through all the heat. Maybe too much sun. But the excitement of finding the island could no longer hold off his driving hunger. He had to land and eat immediately.

The boat parted a thin stand of reeds as it drifted toward a low, flat space nearer the south end of the island. The clearing was dry looking and free of any growth. With the boat pulled up on the muddy edge, he didn't pause for manners. He ravenously tore at his peanut butter sandwich, devouring it in just four ragged bites. Satisfied, he felt a pressing need to explore the island. Dust rose and drifted with each step. It looked almost like ash. A fire of some kind had spread and then stopped, not burning down the rest of the island. Like it had been fenced in. The trees bordering the clearing seemed healthy and framed a densely wooded area. Through the branches of a cedar tree, he spotted a small shack. Then realized it was a doorless outhouse. He giggled and walked closer, peaked inside. No toilet seat. Just a hole. And down the hole? He checked: bottles and pop cans. A lot of people had been here since that day Manido's family had died here. The wood was grey and dry to the touch, but still quite solid. He gave it a kick just for fun.

Paths cut through the bush, as if the mine were still in use. Only a few steps away from the burned clearing, he came to a forked path. Looking straight between his two choices, his eyes caught the water on the other side of the long, narrow island. He veered right instead. This path seemed even more worn as it sloped downward into a darker, heavily treed area. Had somebody moved in? Were there enough visitors to carve such a path?

A moment later, he almost collided with an unexpected house. The picture-perfect haunted house. More of that greyish wood, but this time with a layer of badly peeling tar paper. The door hung wide open, inviting anything in. All the windows were at least partially broken, many without any glass at all. He gasped as he stepped into the mess inside. The floor slanted toward the far end of the house where a warped doorframe led to a back room which sent a strange light out at him. One end of the house had sunk. Quick sand! His eyes shot down at his own feet. The floor lay somewhere beneath all these plastic bags, cans, rags, half-rolled, disintegrating carpet. Two large holes in the walls exposed clumps of archaic-looking wiring. The remaining walls looked as though they might once have been white. The creaking boards below hinted at sudden impending collapse. He stepped gingerly across the suspect floor to the light of the second room. It came from a hole in the roof. A dead cedar hung down into the room. The live cedar trees above turned the sunlight a greenish hue. The room contained nothing more than a pile of old, sodden mattresses looking about a hundred years old. But he knew they weren't quite that old. He knew too much about this strange place he had never seen. Everything covered with decaying cedar bits and pine needles. Absorbing the musty odour of the mattresses, Philip stepped backwards from the room, noticing a stairway he had somehow missed. His foot tested the first step carefully. Pressed harder now. Nothing wrong. He jumped onto it with two feet. Solid. Half way up the stairs, red spray graffiti: "Beware of dead miners upstairs." Philip did not appreciate the thought. The rest of it was mostly F-this and F-that. After one craning look, he climbed down the stairs again. More graffiti struck him from the opposite wall, huge: "I WANT CANDY BUT CANDY DOES THE WORLD." Knew what that must be all about. He felt himself about to shiver and quickly left the house the way he came in.

That was no mineshaft. He didn't need to be there at all. Candy does the world, he laughed to himself nervously. He took one last glance at the old house as he walked back up the path, and hoped never to see it again. Just find the shaft and get this thing done!

After walking up a brambly, more open hill, he found himself surrounded by impossibly huge pieces of rusted machinery. Wheels that dwarfed him lay snarled in the tall grass and bushes. Maybe wheels, maybe cogs, maybe pulleys. But certainly immovable. A good six feet across. He climbed up onto a cement foundation just beyond the first major piece of scrap. Rusty nails littered its off-white, cracked surface. There must have been another house or some kind of building there at one time, but no walls stood. Everything had vanished, probably burned. On a colossal cement block at Philip's eye level stood some kind of machine or engine, easily 15 feet tall. Its size mesmerized him. He stepped over the stray scraps and an old winch, circling the old piece, staring up at it.

FRANCIS AND CHASE
ENGINEERS
CHICAGO, ILL

He smoothed his fingers over the brown, embossed letters, then rubbed the rust residue between his thumb and fingers. He lost interest after another long moment and began wandering around the various levels of the gymnasium-sized foundation. From the edge closest to the water he could see the slagheap with its rotting wooden crown. Jumping down a level, his heart raced to see rotten beams and planks seemingly covering a hole. He lowered himself gingerly onto all-fours and looked below to see if the wood hid any depth. But it didn't hide much. Maybe it had been filled in. That 1935 or whatever was a long way back. Anything could have happened since then. He paused. If this was it, he would feel it.... Nothing. Keep looking.

He moved on, back past the monstrous contraption, off the foundation toward the north end of the island. The path still seemed too clear for his liking, although it made searching the island easier. He passed another abandoned building, definitely burned out, in the throes of slowly tumbling to the ground. The path led into the woods again, darkening.

Philip heard a laugh. He swallowed to gather himself. His throat tensed. It couldn't have been a laugh. Maybe the Indians had come back and moved in. A vision of them running for their lives out of his dream. Knew it couldn't be. Maybe it was his loon.

A moment later he found a railing of obviously new wood, still green with pressure treating. As he stepped closer, he saw the rail formed a square. A plank walkway had been built on the path side of the fenced-in square. The shaft! It had to be! Ignoring another strange noise coming from dead ahead, the excited boy raced to the rail to confirm his theory.

He kicked a few pebbles off the platform as he approached the rail. They fell into the darkness, clanging metallically. The platform and rails construction was like a boxing ring. It hadn't been built more than ten years ago, maybe for safety. What lay in the middle was the main event. Looking down into the hole, he saw the massive tangle of rust-brown sheets, boxes and cables stretching across a good twenty feet and down out of sight. It all seemed to be suspended in mid-shaft. The whole deal wasn't quite what he had expected. More of a pit full of garbage than a pipeline or a well-like shaft. But he had the feeling he had found it.

Straining to see deeper, Philip's eyes jumped at a sudden influx of light and movement. A bead of drool dropped from his mouth as three sets of shining eyes appeared out of the deep black.

THIRTY-SIX

Betrayal

"Awk, no way!" One of the sets of eyes became a voice, then a face. It grew larger as it scaled its way up the old machinery toward Philip. A kid. The voice familiar. Philip froze.

There it was—suddenly in his face, body hoisted up by the railing into daylight in front of him. Max's eyes stared him down. "What the hell are you doing here?!" Cigarette between his fingers.

Philip stepped back from the railing without a word. Max swung a leg over top and stepped up chest-to-chest with the cowering boy on the wooden platform. Stuck the filter back between his lips, and rammed both palms into Philip's chest. His victim stumbled backwards and tripped off the platform edge onto the solid ground, almost falling onto his back. With a cigarette-muffled voice, Max started in. "How did you friggin' find us?!" He poked Philip's sternum just as he had recovered from the first attack, and made him stumble again. The fresh stench of nicotine on the bully's finger made Philip gag. "This is our place, you piece of crap! Ours! Tell anyone about it and I'll personally kill you."

"That is...if I don't kill you first," calm and confident from behind. The main man. Rupert hopped over onto the platform, followed by Franny and her usual cigarette and smirk. Rupert held a huge can of beer in his hand. "Or maybe we'll kill you right now. You'd like that, eh nerd-boy?" He paused with a smile. Then annoyed, "How did you freakin' get here?"

Philip thought he might be able to answer, but nothing seemed to work as it should. An arm motioned back to where he had parked the boat, but he managed no sound. Franny grinned, took a deep drag of her cigarette. Rupert sized up the intruder and stepped toward him like a sheriff from the wild west.

"You followed us here, didn't you. Asked your mommy to put your boat on a trailer so you could be down with us. Well, we don't want your loser-ass here. Capiche?"

Philip didn't quite grasp the trailer idea....

"Did you come here to make good? To be cool? Eh, douchebag?" Rupert's bony hand grabbed a piece of Philip's shirt near the neck, arm flexed impressively. The muscle seemed to jump out of his arm. The other hand coolly held the beer. Then more slowly, "Or did you come here to get your ass kicked?" He spat in Philip's face. A big, thick gob.

Philip stood helpless, trying to blink away the mucus gluing his eyelashes together. It stank of beer as it ran down his face toward his mouth. He heard Max whooping in the background, then a high five with Franny. He thought for a split second he might cry, but it didn't happen. He wiped the spit away with his sleeve just before it touched his upper lip.

"Rupe-man, let's really kick his ass," Max suggested. He flicked his cigarette down the shaft, punched his palm once, and waited for an answer.

Everyone waited, Philip included.

Rupert turned, looked back at Max, then grinned again at Philip. Before Philip could even think, a fist hit him like a bullet. His head rang and felt toothless for a moment. He swore his jaw had flown right off. That his braces had come right through his lip. Everything hot. Surprised to still be standing, Philip looked up at Rupert who was busy flapping his hand madly about, whimpering in pain. Before he had a chance to rejoice at surviving his first ever punch square in the face, Max jumped him. Two shots to the stomach made Philip forget any claim to the Iron Jaw title. He buckled over, blood from the first strike ran slowly into his mouth. He tried to breathe, but his lungs seemed to have shrivelled up into nothing. A wheezing came from deep inside him. Everything too tight to function.

He resisted the temptation to fall to his knees as they trembled beneath him, losing power every second. Max pulled back another fist and thrust it into Philip's already bloody nose, toppling him over. Crumpling his glasses and sending them off his face. Then Rupert stepped in and kicked the reeling boy in the stomach. Three piercing blows. Philip's eyes bulged, screaming for oxygen. He rolled over onto his stomach. A tear squeezed out from between his tightly shut eyelids. He braced himself for more, tightened himself against it. Insults accompanied each kick in his ribs. The voices and thudding blurred together. He knew they were all in on it now because of the frequency and the shade from the sun. Then a hot, wet feeling came over his back and head. A foul smell. A strange liquid ran down behind his ear. Piss! He instinctively jammed his face into the shoulder of his shirt to wipe it off.

For a moment his mind cleared out and the sounds were crisp. "He's done, Franny. Turn around." Max's voice. Rupert just pissed on me! Bloody, beaten and soaked in urine.

Suddenly, his head was being yanked up with a great pain in his scalp. Through the blood, spit, piss and caked dirt, he could make out Rupert's face, upside down. "Listen! You tell anybody about us being here, you zitty punk, and we'll do way worse. Come back here again and it's down the shaft with your ass." Philip felt his hair pulling out of his scalp. Even harder now. His neck cramped up. "Got it?"

Philip couldn't move. Had a dreamy image of Franny having pity on him, pushing the boys away. He was almost delirious now.

"Got it?!" Rupert pulled harder.

Philip gasped something close to a yes.

Then they were gone, as far as he could tell. Philip lay facedown in the dirt. The muscles in his neck felt like they had been ripped to shreds. His scalp raw. Still incredulous—what were the odds of meeting them here? Even with a bigger boat, it was a long way for anyone to come. Especially if this was a regular clubhouse or something. He couldn't help wondering how it had happened.

Not long after, Philip heard the sound of an outboard taking off. He thought it might be his for a moment. It certainly wasn't Rupert's usual Bayliner by the sound of it. Disoriented, he remembered someone stepping over him, the clinking of beer bottles. As he regained his senses, his surprise turned to anger and hurt. No way was any of this ceremony crap worth getting his head kicked in over. Before his blood could really boil, the voice jumped in.

"Why did you not fight back?"

What kind of question is that? He touched his nose, checked his hand for blood.

"Why did you not do something? Anything. Even to run. Did I not tell you this would happen?"

Philip did not have the strength to argue, but he hated the spirit now more than ever. The bastard just watched those asses pummel him. Never lifted a finger. Never offered a word. The one time he really needed help. He knew where to lay all the blame. Bastard Indian!

"I thought you had grown more confident. The work you have done should have made you stronger. These were tests that make you a man. I would not expect you to stand up for the ceremony, but stand up for yourself. I do not understand....You need to rise up against your Kawaesind, your Mishi-naubae."

Then Philip mustered the strength to belt out one thing. It didn't matter that spirit already knew his thoughts. He just had to say it out loud. His lips lifted off the ground and parted, then slowly and deliberately: "I hate you."

No response.

It barely mattered. Nothing mattered. Lying soaked in another boy's urine with a throbbing stomach and bloody nose didn't matter. Being spat at. Being a zillion miles from home didn't matter. The whole summer being ruined didn't matter. He was sure he hated the spirit and sure he wanted to be home, even in Thunder Bay. No hint of friendship felt before could change his feelings now. He had been betrayed.

After another twenty minutes of rest peppered with visions of violence, the battered explorer decided to drag himself home. A long trip, but it had to be made. His heart ached along with his body. He found his misshapen glasses on the ground within arm's reach and was briefly grateful that Rupert, Max and Franny hadn't thought of crushing or stealing them. He pried himself off the ground and retraced his steps back to the boat that was just as he had left it. He dabbed his nose on his t-shirt. A bitter soldier after battle, oblivious to the simple victory of surviving. On the trip home he felt none of the fears he had felt earlier in the day. The high rollers barely fazed him despite nearly tipping the boat. No fear. He ploughed through the entire obstacle course without a thought, followed the mapped channel like an automaton. The crashing about and tricky navigation blurred until Philip found himself at the first set of rapids. Only then did he stop for a moment to consider he might not make it home. But if he had made it against the current, then he should have been able to make it down, he reasoned. And he let his new, hot numbness to emotion and pain carry him through.

Manido made an offering of peace. "You have done well. I should not have expected more. I commend you, Needjee."

"Screw you!" Philip raged. "You ruined my life! I was just fine without you. All your stupid crap! I can't believe I did any of it. And then you almost get me killed?!" The anger tripped over itself into sobbing. "Go to hell! Get out—Get out of my life!" The boy's breathing grew laboured. Then convulsions. With the motor off, the boat drifted with the stiff breeze across Ash Bay. A crying boy, holding his head to his knees. And it all fit together: in *Soul Catcher*, Katsuk turned on David in the end, despite everything. Philip had finished the book the night before. Why should it be any different here? When he had finally gathered himself, he made his way back home to Clearwater Bay.

Life was a curse.

"You're late!" Jane Reddy's voice reminded him that hell was not over. She stood threateningly in the kitchen, hands on her hips. Calming slightly, "I'll heat dinner for you. You know it's 7:45, Philip. 7:45!" She turned toward the fridge. The worn-out boy flung his lifejacket on the pile in the extension and made a break for his room. After he thought he had made it, he heard his mother again. "Oh my god, Philip!" He heard the heavy feet bound toward his room, and the curtains whipping away from the doorway. No chance to hide. He turned around to face her. She stared at him, wide-eyed. "Christ, Philip. What happened?! Your face..." She reached out, but he blocked her hand. Turned sideways. He could see the crusted blood around his swollen nostrils in the crooked hanging mirror. "Let me see," she insisted, pushing his arm aside. He jerked his head back as she touched his inflamed nose. "Philip. You've been...beaten."

"Really!" as sarcastically as he could manage. No point in being shy now. He didn't need the boat anymore. He wasn't going to be a ghost's slave anymore. "I know. Three kids beat the crap out of me. And if you don't believe me this time, then go—" Choked on himself. His finger picked at the dried blood at his nostril. He realized he must smell pretty bad too.

Jane looked shocked again. She seemed to buy it, he couldn't help but notice. But his story had never been wilder. He felt it as they both flashed back to the slap incident. A strange smile cracked her face. Not mocking. Like she could forgive any harshness from him this time. She took his glasses off his face and began trying to reshape them.

He saw her softening and attacked. "Happy?!" He looked into her eyes accusingly. Challenged her. His thumb jabbed his chest with each word, "I am a loser." Then he held out his index finger in front of him as if to lecture. "I will always be a loser. Some of this is your fault. But what I got was coming to me. And I'll get it again and again in this piece-of-shit life." He paused. Looked down at his feet. Then raised his head to her, "This is how things are supposed to be," he said, sure it was true. "This is me."

"Oh, Philip, you're not a loser." Overdoing it. A tear in her eye.

He didn't buy the act. She knew bloody well what he was, what he had become. This was exactly how things should be. This was it.

"Come here." She held out her arms.

It wasn't real like it should be, but it would have to do. He slammed himself into her, gripping her with all he had. Just this once. One time only. There was nothing else in the world for that moment.

After treating the cuts on his face and sending him down to the rock for a bath, Jane sat with her son as he ate. He knew his sadness had never been so transparent before, or at least not in a long time. Totally let go. Not since his father's death. This was where he was at, whether his mother could handle it or not. Maybe it was better that she knew. Now he didn't care. The silence sat heavily, but with a new texture. Open. Philip picked at the reheated ham and potatoes with no desire to eat. Finally, he glanced up at his mother who was wringing a napkin nervously and got up to go his room.

She probably thought this was about his father, but it wasn't. Not at all. He had been deserted again, but it wasn't the same. This deserter had done him in on purpose. Safe behind his curtain, he pondered this strangest summer as he stared up into the upper berth springs. The wash in the lake should have done him good, but now there was no life left in him. He reached up and pulled on the rusted metal wires. Thought he could still smell Rupert's piss. Emotions had never come so mixed. His anger at being put into danger and his sorrow at having failed waged war inside his head. There was more room in there now. Tears welled up in his eyes. The spirit had been outright wrong to let him get beaten like that. When he could have helped so easily. Could have started a storm or felled a tree. Or even just coached him. But maybe Philip should have been able to defend himself. He had grown stronger than ever, without a doubt. The spirit was right that he should have gained confidence with all the work, not to mention muscle from being so active. Regardless, this boy could not succeed. Not even the supernatural could bring him out of his tailspin. And this was the end of trying. This was the way things were supposed to be. Tired of crying, he stared up at the springs and mattress, looking for shapes and faces.

"Philip," he heard inside, "Philip, you need not answer. But I must tell you that you are free. I must tell you that I am sorry for trespassing on your Grandfather's grave, as I know you are for trespassing on mine. You will hear from me no more. What you have done, you have done admirably. You have completed more than I thought possible for you. More than any white man has done before. You have not failed. I have hope. I thank you. The

Anishinaabe thank you. Gitche-Manido knows you well. You will hear no more from Tikumiwaewidung. Live well, Needjee."

Philip let the silence hang for a while.

Free. Free to do what? And what was this word the spirit used for him now? He reflected back to the days before he had dug up the strange mound. He could see himself sitting at the water's edge, throwing pebbles with his wimpy arm, wishing he were anywhere else. Winnipeg, Thunder Bay, wherever. His anger and sadness left him then for a sickly, empty feeling in his stomach. Manido was not a liar. If he said he was gone, he was gone. Philip, the deserted boy. His father, and now some ancient ghost. He could see a pattern emerging. Who would be next? Even though it wouldn't have been the same thing, his mother crossed his mind. He heard her cough somewhere in the house. It didn't matter. Nothing mattered except that he stood alone again and no one in the world cared.

The August sun set noticeably earlier and left the boy in the dark before he wanted it. He didn't brush his teeth or say goodnight. Just pealed off his clothes and rolled under the covers. By the next morning, he had lost all inclination to get out of bed. He lay with the covers over his head, hoping to hear the familiar harsh voice. But he stayed there for most of the morning without reprimand. His heart ached. Nothing motivated him to move from his bed.

Finally, just before noon, he heard, "Come on, kid. Get up." His mother cheerfully through the curtain. He found himself cursing her existence once again. His old life was sucking him back into its clutches and he held no power to resist. The desire to leave this place started in him again and intensified at an exponential rate. The island had never been a lonelier place. Everything triggered memories that burned his insides. Somehow the old images of his father returned to weigh him down further. He started to count down the days before leaving. Wondered if he would make it.

THIRTY-
SEVEN

Jane and Philip

Philip went through the summer in his mind over and over again in the next two days. Old files of memories he had made fond. His heart hung heavily, despite all the flashbacks that made him laugh. He found humour in the mistakes he had made and in the comments from Manido, never appreciated in the moment. He still had something left from that time, from all the work, the strife, the friendship. But the humour made him lonely after the initial giggle, brought on longing to go back in time. Promised himself he would enjoy every second if he were just granted the opportunity to live through it all again.

After two days of mourning his loss, Philip found the urge to swim too much to resist. He started the day with a trip to the Big Whale. Climbed out onto it to feel the warm sun on his healing face. The cut behind his lip was turning into another canker. But he smiled at the brightness around him and perhaps at this freedom he had been granted. When he turned to look back at Swimming Rock, he saw his mother standing there with her arms folded. She wore a sweater and a pair of jeans, which seemed a little strange given the warmth of the morning. Philip gave her a big wave. She returned a weak one.

Philip dove off the peak of the island into the water. He could see his mother flinch with worry even then. He swam madly toward her, eager to show-off to her his new sport. All of his swimming exploits had been either too early in the day for her or while she had been busy in the garden. She smiled at him as he waded to shore breathing heavily.

"This is a change," she laughed. "You're swimming and I'm not. You are fast."

"Why aren't you swimming? You always swim."

"Your mother doesn't feel that great today. Actually, it's been almost a week. It feels like a curse someone's put on me."

Philip's mind lurched for a moment as he remembered the awesome power of Manido. But almost immediately he remembered that the spirit had been decent to him in every way and couldn't be part of doing his mother harm. "I guess I heard you cough a couple of times."

"Yeah, I'm pretty much a wreck. I think I have a fever. Aren't you cold?"

"No," he answered, drying off.

Jane started to talk, but her voice caught on phlegm in her throat. She winced and took out a tissue to get rid of whatever had come up into her mouth. She smiled at him as she took a peak at it. "Green."

"Gross."

Suddenly he realized that she probably had been pretty sick for at least a week, but he hadn't noticed because he was never around. Now he could get up at a decent time and do whatever he wanted. He noticed for the first time that his palm and fingers were raw. It didn't make sense since, if anything, they were missing the touch of the six-horse motor's throttle. Although he missed the daily trips and adventure, it was nice to know he could just stay here, that there was no pressure. Another cough brought him back to his mother.

"Anyway, I'm going back to bed. I feel like the world is ending. You're okay to make your own breakfast, right? You've had lots of practice these last few weeks. So you don't need me."

The world ending. Part of it had. And now he was stuck on her saying he didn't need her. Didn't he though? Sure, breakfast had become an easy solo venture because he had had to leave the island so early every day. But did that mean he finally had what he wanted?

Jane filled in the silence. "Aren't you going to go helling off somewhere in the boat today? It's been three days. You don't need to go where you'll find those bullies, you know." A quick gasp for breath. "I don't mind if you go. Just don't go too far."

"Do you want me to go?"

"No, Philip. Of course not. Never." She smiled weakly again.

It was then that he realized what was different about her aside from being so warmly dressed. No makeup at all. She always wore makeup. She looked pale with sickness, but this unprepared face was an even greater sign that something wasn't right.

She turned and went up the path toward the house. It dawned on him that if he lost her to some weird disease, that would be it. There was no one else. Remembered at least once wishing something like that would happen. But he was being stupid.

Over the next two days, he found a curious, positive feeling in helping his mother around the island, surprising her to no end at how useful he could be. When her energy was up, he even found himself with her in the garden, pouring topsoil, picking cherry tomatoes. The cough seemed to be getting worse, but her spirits were good. He wondered whether her smile had something to do with his being around and hanging out with her. The conversation wasn't strained the same way it had been for what seemed like forever to him. There was a loosening of things between them. She watched him swim in the mornings. He went back and forth to the Big Whale twice to start each day. At first he thought she was there just because he probably shouldn't have been swimming alone all that time, but she seemed to genuinely enjoy it and even whooped and cheered for him when he was done. Philip started helping out around the house too. He repaired an old shutter and only once smashed his thumb with the hammer. He restained the cedar siding of the cabin extension. The more he did, the better he felt. These tasks he gave to himself reminded him of the tasks he had been doing less than a week ago. They were a lot easier, but they too made a small difference in him somehow. Making his mother happy was a side-effect he could tolerate now. Her unfamiliar smile was less and less disconcerting. It was like she was getting sicker and healthier all at the same time.

It was in the morning that he missed the voice of Manido most intensely. Quarter to seven would come and go in silence, except for the laboured breathing of his mother in the next room. Quietly to himself he would mouth the words the spirit had ingrained in him. They soothed him and gave him energy somehow.

During the day his mother slept a lot. He tried not to stray too far away from the house just in case. He had a sudden occasional impulse to tear all the totem drawings off the wall, but it always passed. Although it was all over, Philip finished the drawings just the same. For all the souls except for Winonah, Stanley and Jack. He didn't feel he could or should draw them if the ceremony was never going to happen. The hours slipped by slowly as he swam, drew and did little jobs around the island. And although The Savage was a cool name for a superhero-villain, he finally finished his earlier sketch based on the cover of *Soul Catcher* and renamed the character simply

Manitou. It wasn't quite how he had been pronouncing it, but he had seen it written that way before. It became the image for the voice in his head.

He walked around the island with the words on his lips. Found the canoe at the beach and thought for the first time that he would some day learn to paddle it solo whether someone showed him or not. He twirled his silver canoe paddle necklace charm between his fingers. Farther along the path, he stopped along the south shore of the island. There was a rock beach full of skippable stones. At first he didn't dare try, but something pushed him to pick up a couple of the flattest pieces. He tried to get the right spin and action on the rocks, but neither made more than one splash. A small part of him wished he hadn't bothered, but he bent down and picked up two more. He threw backhand a few times until he got his first skip. Then tried forehand as his father used to do with such ease. A flick of the wrist. After a few tries, the first small skip came to him. A rush of power flowed through his body. Maybe he wouldn't suck at everything if he just practiced. That might even go for sports at school. Encouraged but not wanting to disprove his new theory, he left it for the day, but promised he would be back to try some more another time.

Philip noticed a difference in himself. He walked differently. He talked differently. He felt like he could almost go over to see Brant and tell him things were cool now, that he hadn't been himself last year. But he wasn't interested in that yet. Could he really have changed? And this much? Maybe the spirit had changed him somehow after all, failed mission and all. But then why hadn't this week been worse? More "regression" as the doctor had called it…. It was like the spirit had started a ball rolling and now Philip and his mother had enough strength to keep it moving….

Other knowledge sank in slowly and gave him new perspective. His father was dead. His mother was a bit of a bitch sometimes. And he had been busy digging holes. One this summer. Another for the past year and a half. They had to be dug, but they could be filled as well. Perhaps now that was what he was doing. If he kept getting his act together, he could be ready for school, he thought.

Then Friday night, a familiar kind of dream….

THIRTY-
EIGHT

Putting the Pieces Together

S tanding barefoot on hard-packed ground. He raised his head and saw that
a path made its way down into the dark woods ahead. He spun around.
The path stretched out of sight into a maze of trees in that direction too, but
on an incline. He finished assessing his situation with a check of himself—
without clothes once again. Something told him to follow the path in the
direction he had faced first. The territory didn't look familiar. The trees stood
so thick, completely blocking his vision just five feet in on each side of the
path. He could have been anywhere, yet somehow he knew which way to
go. The green leaves bordering the path reached out to touch him as he
made his way down the well-trodden walkway. The thick roof of balsam,
spruce and white pine barely allowed the glimpse of blue sky to sneak in.
He quickened his pace.

Soon he heard sobbing. As he continued, he came upon an old
weeping Anishinaabe sitting just a few feet off the trail. The old man looked
up briefly as the naked white boy passed, but seemed overcome with grief,
unable to move. The bloody carcass of a deer lay partly-eaten at the man's
feet. Blood on the man's hands as well. He looked as if he was mourning the
death of the deer. But almost more like he was crying because he had eaten
from the deer.

Something clicked inside the boy. Do not stray from the path.

He pushed on, trying to figure it out. A simple enough order or
piece of advice, but from whom? No voice told him the words. Then someone passed him walking in the opposite direction, almost knocking him
down. The boy turned around and watched as a buxom woman trudged
purposefully off and away. He hadn't heard her approaching until she was

almost on top of him. Felt an urge to yell to her that she was going the wrong way. But she was gone before he could gather his wits.

A few minutes later he found a man sleeping at the side of the path with great white tearstains on his cheeks. This man hadn't killed or eaten any deer. He had been crying for something else, and now he just slept.

As Philip continued almost blindly down the path, his heart started pumping harder for no apparent reason. Something significant approached. He felt it. His entire body rattled with each beat. Soon he saw it coming. A huge figure emerged from the tapestry of trees and brush. It came along the path directly for him, then stopped.

A big, beautiful man with perfectly straight hair down behind his shoulders, a large headdress on his head. The man's skin seemed dark and red compared to the light brown leather garments he wore. He stood not twenty feet from Philip. The boy's eyes scanned down the tall body to a pair of ragged moccasins. The moccasins had no soles left whatsoever. The tops of the soft shoes hung like skirts around his ankles, his toes plainly visible with a closer look.

Philip's heart raced. Why did the man stop? Why wouldn't he push a boy out of his way and keep going? He could sense the large man was affected, almost disconcerted by his presence. Silky black hair flung out over his shoulder as he swung abruptly around to glance back in the direction he had come, suddenly unsure of his own path. Philip could have told the man he had been wrong, that he should turn around. Although how was he to know they were both searching for the same thing? He wasn't even sure what he was headed for. Just knew this direction was right, wherever it led. Again the man looked over his shoulder, then checked Philip's face. He seemed to make a decision, and finally turned completely around and started into the darkness the way he had come. Relieved, Philip followed the majestic man.

They walked for what seemed hours, up and down hills, through a muddy area near a swamp. At least fifteen feet separated them at all times. They passed many more forlorn-looking people at the side of the path. Some slept. Others lay naked together. Philip turned his head away. None of them held happiness in their eyes.

Soon Philip heard the sound of rushing water. Maybe a waterfall. As he neared the sound, more and more people appeared, some sitting lethargically, others huffing back past him.

The path opened up: at least a hundred people loitered on the bank of a large rushing river. The water rolled high and white. Many of the people wept. Almost all appeared to be Natives, but some almost white compared to the others. A couple were actually blonde. Philip watched as a man took a running start and leaped into the churning river. Once he had broken the surface and taken one or two flailing strokes, his body simply disappeared.

The boy noticed a moment later that the people wore everything from animal skins to frayed jeans to business suits. The mix seemed strange. They did not speak to each other. Didn't seem to know each other. Some prayed, some chanted, seemed to ask for something. Almost begging. Across the water Philip saw a tiny clearing and an opening in yet a more dense wood. One woman stood dripping in the small clearing and looked back across at him and the others with a sorry expression. Turned and raised her hands to the sky for a moment. Then stepped into the bush and faded quickly from sight.

Philip's focus changed as he saw the large solemn man he had followed turn and look directly at him, hopeless. He didn't seem to want to try the river, or even pray, for that matter. He looked down at the ground for a moment. When he looked up again at Philip, his face had changed. Suddenly, he looked old. His hair was white and shorter, balding. A goatee on his face. Philip's eyes darted up and down the man's changing body. Now he seemed plumper, shorter. And the clothes he wore now were completely different. Brass buttons on a fancy blue coat.... He looked totally different, but it was the same man for certain. Despite his increased girth, he looked more deflated and hopeless now. He walked toward Philip. They brushed shoulders. And the man walked by, back onto the path to waste all the time he had spent getting here going back. But what for?! This was the place to be. Philip knew it. The perplexed boy turned to watch him fade into the darkness of the wood. Like the woman he had seen, but on this somehow unfortunate side of the river.

The mass of people at the river all stared longingly across to the other side, save for three faces whose eyes locked onto Philip. A woman and two children. They stared at him expressionless, unwavering. Somehow recognized him and expected him to know them. The children wore animal skin pants with wool sweaters, and the mother a skin dress decorated with beads. He grew more conscious of his own nakedness, although they didn't seem to notice, looking him directly in the eyes. He couldn't shake their stare, couldn't run away. The faces warped slowly until their expressions grew angry. They approached him slowly but steadily. He stepped back, stumbled and landed hard on his elbow. Pain shot up through his shoulder. He tried to get up to escape, but his desperate heels only scraped up dust as he flailed about on his back. Now their arms stretched out toward him as they took their slow zombie-steps and mumbled words he couldn't make out. Like body snatchers! Philip found himself up and running suddenly. He crashed through the dark brush, completely off the path. His vision blurred. A stick in the face. Then black.

A strange silence came in the darkness and the branches eased their attack against his tender skin. He opened his eyes, and found himself sweat-drenched and sitting up in bed.

His elbow throbbed. Must have whacked it on the bedframe. No, he remembered falling on it. Bits of his dream started to come into focus. Another Indian thing. More Anishinaabe stories. Similar to the ones from earlier in the summer, but somehow different. Maybe Manido was back. He stopped his thoughts for a moment, fumbling for the presence. Rolled his eyes and tilted his head as if to jog the spirit out of his hiding place. "Manido?" he ventured. But he lay alone with his question.

When he awoke the next morning, it all made sense. The three Indians at the riverside were the ones from the Shoal Lake mine. Two kids and a mother. He reminded himself not to think of them as Indians. They were Anishinaabe. But now everything fit perfectly—he had never finished what he had set out to do and they were mad at him. He hoped for a second that they wouldn't destroy his house or burn anything like Manido had. Were they going to besiege him? Were they here with him now? It seemed unlikely somehow.... And if they were behind this dream, they would have given it to him right away, the day he got back from Poplar Island. It had to be coming from somewhere else....

Later, while he sketched, Philip's pencil line trickled off to nothing as he drifted back into the dream. The path had been so strange. And so perfect...in a way he couldn't fully grasp. The details struck him now as if he had walked it a thousand times. But he swore he had never seen it before. And all the weirdoes crying and sleeping at the side of the path.... Worse than any street in Winnipeg or Kenora! A level of grief he had never witnessed. The sheer numbers of people didn't fit with the surrounding dense forest, not a house in sight for hours of walking. It had to be a message, this dream. These three Anishinaabe wanted something. They wanted passage.

His eyes sprung open and he found the words on the tip of his tongue. He let them fly in whisper. "Path of Souls." As he started drawing again, pieces fell together. All those people are dead. They want to get through the trials of the path to get to the Land of Souls. It all seemed so obvious. This place must be on the other side of the river. The man who changed his shape and the other people by the path were trying to make their way there, but were stuck in some kind of limbo. Do not stray from the path. Some had done just that. Others were stuck for other reasons maybe. That was why the man had turned around when he came to the river! He had been there before and knew he couldn't get across. He had been there many times, maybe....

As the elation of figuring out his dream faded, he started to pity all the miserable people stuck along the path. The trip was supposed to take four days, if what he had learned from Manido was right. And if Manido was also right about the mother and kids, they had to have been there since the 1930s!

His scalp tightened as he saw that the decoded dream presented a problem to be solved. A renewed will to help burst inside him and washed through his body. He could still do something for those three, if for nobody else. He knew where they were. Whether through simply triggering guilt or divine commandment, this dream forced Philip to act.

So he spent the day obsessing over somehow helping the Shoal Lake family, thinking of little else other than his mother when she coughed or called for a bowl of soup or glass of water. She wasn't strong enough to go to the garden at all and mostly read and slept. Maybe these people really weren't expecting anything. Maybe the dream was just his own guilt, not a call to action at all.

He started a new drawing. A doodle that soon turned itself into the family. One tall figure flanked by two smaller ones. They held one another. These were the people he wanted to make happy at all costs. He wanted to get them across that river. Before he detailed the figures at all, he drew the river in front of them, put them on the far side where they would be happy. Happy in the Land of Souls. No longer needing to haunt him. Whether they had done so on purpose, he still didn't know. The forest grew on his page behind the family. Although he knew nothing for certain, the young artist pretended someone waited for the family just beyond the trees, in the heart of this land. A father to make the picture complete. One like his.

The faces of the three lost souls met him again that night as he crossed over into sleep. They stared him down. But when he called for Manido, no response came. Maybe none of his dreams had been Manido-creations, but these certainly weren't. These demons came from his own bad conscience, he finally decided. Still, if he could just get to the mine and do the ceremony, they would disappear. He was sure of it. He would have finally helped his friend. He could move on. And so could these poor people perhaps. The mother came from Manido's own bloodline, he reminded himself. He had to find a way to help her, and quickly. He added more to the family portrait to help quell his guilt and worry.

It was all he could do. His mother had said he could use the boat again, but she certainly wouldn't want him going back to Poplar Island after what happened last time. He could lie.... But he didn't really want to do that. Plus, he would need to go there four days in a row! The door was closed on this.

That night he couldn't sleep for his mother's heavy breathing. He could hear some kind of lump of gunk slipping up and down her throat. It sounded pretty sick. Her breath would catch when the stuff got caught, and she would cough it up. She heard her swear to herself. The cough had been pretty harmless a week ago, but now it was deep inside her. Finally, he fell into the rhythm she provided with her gurgling breathing.

THIRTY-NINE

Opportunity

"Mom!" Philip blurted out.

Her face hung there above him. She smiled. She must have been trying to wake him. He remembered now a snapshot of a dream in which she was choking to death. But she sat there on the side of his bed, looking down on him, ill but quite alive. "Good morning, Philip. I didn't mean to scare you." Smiling, running her fingers through his hair. Still, she wore no makeup.

"It's okay. I was just having a dream, I guess."

"These drawings are amazing, Philip. You're getting better all the time." She looked over her shoulder at the wall, plastered with sketches. Eleven of them now.

Philip appreciated the genuine-sounding comment, but he knew there was more to this rare early rousing by his mother. It usually meant they were headed for town, but most often it had been planned days in advance. He waited.

"I've put cereal out for your breakfast, Philip." She paused. "I'm pretty sick, as you probably noticed."

Philip nodded without showing too much of his worry.

"It's not getting any better, so I think I should have it checked out. I think I'll walk-in at the hospital in Kenora and see if I can't get some antibiotics or something. If there's a walk-in clinic, I'm sure it's closed because it's Sunday. You can come with me, but I think I'll be a while. I'm sure I'll be at the end of the line and get bumped by every real emergency, but I've got to make sure it's not too serious and get some medicine for it. It feels like bronchitis or something. It's really hard for me to breathe and I ache all over."

Philip nodded, and they both laughed at how much noise she had been making coughing and wheezing the past two or three days.

"So. I would take you and drop you somewhere to shop but I could be all day. Or you could wait with me in the hospital, which is always lots of fun. Or...you could stay here."

The boy was surprised at the option. He almost wanted to go with her. There was something happening between them that he didn't want to lose track of. But it would be so boring. Plus, it was neat to think that she would trust him....

"Are you okay to go alone?" he asked.

"Oh yeah. Just don't ask me to run a marathon or anything."

"Then I guess I'll stay."

"I thought so. Believe it or not the island has a special magic when you're alone with it. I used to have that chance once in a while."

What now? He guessed he could go back to sleep, but she seemed to be thinking something through.

"All right. Here's the deal. You keep my cellphone on all day. If I'm going to be home before dinner, I won't bother calling. There's salami in the fridge and bread in the freezer. And you know where the peanut butter is. You must leave the cell on, just in case."

"In case of what?"

"Oh, I don't know. If I need to check in with you because they can't see me 'til later. Something like that. And use the cell in case of emergency. 911, right?"

"Duh. Of course. That's why you bought it." He rolled his eyes but smiled to make sure she didn't take it the wrong way.

"And you have the McGinnises' number. And Aunt Gladys back in the Peg too. Well, that settles it." She was trying not to fuss too much. Then coughed a loose, phlegmy cough. "Well, there's my cue to go." She ruffled his hair. "I'll spare you an infected kiss." She laid the cellphone on his nightstand and plugged it into the wall. Looked at him fondly for a moment before she stood up to finish getting ready to go. "The cereal's out but I didn't bother putting out the milk. Oh! And no swimming to either Whale!"

She had had it all planned. The cellphone. The milk had never left the fridge. She was okay with him staying. Philip couldn't help but be impressed. "Okay, no swimming to the Whales."

When Philip awoke again, the silence around him seemed strange. There was a stillness to the air and heat to the day already. He remembered his mother saying it was supposed to go up above thirty degrees. No cough. No creak of the floor under his mother's feet. He hoped and assumed it was just a bad chest cold that she had, but already he could feel the magic of being alone. At Swimming Rock after breakfast, he contemplated at least swimming to the Little Whale. He had done it without supervision so many times now that it seemed silly to resist today. But he had given his word and wanted that to start being worth something. It was a big deal that he was allowed to be on his own. He laid the cellphone, his glasses, the Tigers cap down on his towel and plunged into the water, staying right near the shore as he knew she would have wanted.

As much freedom as he had before, the notion that he could do anything he wanted at any time was intoxicating. It didn't change much of what he decided to do, but was nice just the same. Some work on skipping rocks. A sketch of the painted turtle that had decided to sun itself on Sunset Rock.

The phone finally rang as he was boiling noodles for macaroni and cheese. Mom!

"Hi. How are you making out?"

"Not bad."

"Well, I hope you like it because we don't have a lot of options."

"What do you mean?" A heightened seriousness in his voice.

"Well, it looks like I'll be sticking around for a couple of days. Here at the hospital, I mean."

"Are you okay?"

"Yes, I'm fine. They've ruled out hantavirus, which is what I was most worried about. You can get it from mouse poop and it can actually kill you. I just know there are lots of mice at the island."

"That's for sure." He hadn't known about the hanta disease, but was relieved nonetheless.

"So they want to do a bunch of tests on me. Nothing serious, but with my bad breathing and blood pressure that was a little low when they checked it, they say I should stick around. I figure it's easier, given what a production it is to get back and forth from the island."

The island suddenly seemed bigger as he realized what might be happening.

"So, kiddo. I have some options for you. You can come into town to stay near me. There's a hotel not far where you can sleep and hang out when you've had enough visiting me. I can send a taxi for you at the mainland. You'd have to close the shutters and lock up, but you could do that. But it would be pretty boring for you here. I tried to get Uncle Dixon to join you at the island, but Aunt Patty says he's away on business until late Thursday night. And Patty's working this week. So…. I could get him to come down on Friday…"

"What about you though? Are you going to be all alone there?"

"No, no. Gladys has already said she will come visit me. She can check on you on the way in from the Peg."

"Well, if it's going to be tomorrow, then there won't be much to check on. I can survive."

"All right. Glenn may come down to see me too. I'll call him later."

"You didn't call him yet?"

"No, Philip. You are my primary concern. Now. What do you want to do?"

Part of the boy wanted to see her right then, but another stronger part told him to take this offering and run with it. "I'll stay here. I'd like to visit, but there's no way I'm hanging around with Gladys for more than a day."

She laughed. "That's fine. You have lots of food. Bread. There are peaches ripening on top of the fridge. There's meat in the freezer, but that won't help you much. Lots of pasta on the shelf."

"Sounds good."

"Now, if we're going to do this, a few guidelines need to be established. One, still no swimming to the Whales."

"I've been good, mom."

"I know. Two, no trips around the lake. Three, keep the cell on and with you. You know who to call if you need something. The McGinnises or Aunt Patty. And I'll give you the number here."

"So I'm chained to the phone?"

She had a little coughing fit. "Sorry. Yes, in a manner of speaking. You will call here four times a day to check in with me. The calls will be at set times. If you miss one, I'm calling you. If I don't get an answer, I'm on the horn to the McGinnises and they're going to go over and check on you. I talked to them this morning before I left to say I'd be away for the day and I asked them if they would be ready to step in. I'm sure they won't mind being on guard for a few days."

"Holy crap, mom."

"Well, you wanted to stay…."

"Yes, but…. How about three times a day…."

"All right. How about 10 am, 4 pm and...ummm....10 pm?"

"Okay."

"Remember: if you miss one, I will assume the worst and you'll have company. Bev and Lloyd don't mind doing this, but they won't be happy if they end up over there just because you forgot."

"Yes! Okay, mom!" Getting impatient with the whole thing. It was getting less and less like he would be free. But it was still the best option.

They ironed out the details and Jane told Philip that she should start the calling pattern that night at 10 pm. She would confirm everything about the arrangement and Uncle Dixon then, and give him an update. She might be home as early as tomorrow, but she said it was unlikely. He told her to feel better and ended the call.

Right after he pushed END to finish the call, he realized what a gift this was. Although he felt bad for his mother, this was the chance he had hoped for.

FORTY

Plan B

That evening he used his sketching pad to make a list. A list for a trip:

sleeping bag

tent?

food—cans, cookies, apples

tobacco

He tried to remember what his father brought when they had camped together. Some of the stuff might still be stashed in the cabin somewhere. He tried to think back. Four summers ago they had left his mother home on the island and gone on a two-night canoe trip. They had camped nearby because he had been so young. But it had been so exciting just to be out of sight of the island, out in the wild. He vividly remembered cooking spaghetti on a weird little burner thing.

little stove

After dinner Bruce had shown his son how to make a banana boat: wrapped a split-banana in tin foil with chocolate chips and marshmallows and laid it in the coals of the dying fire. Philip could still taste the sweet burn on his tongue.

matches

knife

pot or pan

A lot of goddamn stuff to bring!

He stopped writing. He sighed and drew a slash diagonally through the list. Shook his head at the whole idea. He had to stay put for the calls. The time between calls wouldn't allow for a trip back and forth to Poplar Island.

But when he got up, his eye caught his own old red sleeping-bag, jammed up against the ceiling of the cupboard in his room. Then his father's just below it. He reached high and grabbed at the cinch-lace of his dad's bag. Yanked suddenly to shake off the top bag, but they both came toppling down on him. One shelf down lay the old orange tarp that came back to him suddenly. His father had used it to put the food on, and then as a shelter when he had built the fire in the rain. He remembered now that he would need rope to set up such a shelter. Maybe there was some in the Sleeping Cabin.

At the very back of the cupboard, he spied the sacred black-and-red Mountain Equipment Co-op backpack. So many straps! He pulled it out and stepped back with it into the centre of the room. After inspecting the beautiful bag, he tried it on. Too big. His eyes fogged slightly as he realized it was still sized for his dad. Should he dare adjust the straps? Ever? It should remain his dad's always! He resisted the urge to cry. Put his still-misshapen glasses on the top bunk behind him. Pulled the mystical relic off his back and figured out how to adjust the straps and belt. It was his bag now. Besides, he needed it for this trip. No one could hold that against him. His father would be happy to know it hadn't been forgotten or disposed of. Philip straightened himself, wearing the bag proudly, clips done up. It felt just right, tight against his back and hips.

At 10 pm he made the call. Jane was impressed. Still sounded pretty bad. Uncle Dixon would arrive Friday at 10 am at the mainland, and Philip was to be there. The two of them would come into town to visit her at the hospital. And if she wasn't ready to leave, he would spend the rest of the weekend at the island with Philip. If she was going to be released from the hospital earlier, they would change the plan and she would see him sooner. So it was going to be a maximum of four full days that he would be alone— tomorrow through Thursday. She sounded very grateful that her brother was willing to do this. They weren't exactly close anymore. Jane and Philip went over the call times again and said goodnight.

It was when he hung up this second time that the gift finally clicked: it was the cellphone in his hand. He could call her from anywhere!

FORTY-ONE

Back to Poplar

The next morning the house was quiet and empty again when Philip woke up. Still, he checked thoroughly before he let out too loud a hoot of celebration. Before he had even eaten, he laid out the open pack by the front door and started to top it up with supplies. He had packed most of the things on his list the night before after realizing he could go and maybe even stay at Poplar Island. Six boxes of Kraft Dinner. He broke open the boxes and poured the noodles all into one big plastic bag as he had seen his father do. Two cans of peaches. He took a long look at the cans of tuna and beans. No way! Too bad he couldn't bring a cooler with burgers in it. What else did he need? He scanned the shelves again. Then he remembered the oatmeal in the morning of his overnight with his dad. Not exactly something he craved, but he knew it would work and it would fit. He dug deeply into the dry food shelf and found a rumpled up, half-empty bag of Quaker Oats with that Amish guy on the front. Grabbed a can of tuna, just so he wouldn't wish he had it if he were lost and starving somewhere.

Kraft Dinner and oatmeal. He would survive. He checked through his list over a bowl of Frosted Flakes. He could remember putting all the items in last night, even an extra container of gas for the stove which never made it onto the list. And finally a tightly-rolled ball of rope just a few minutes ago.

But Rupert, Max and Franny worried him more than all other possibilities combined. He knew somehow that it wasn't over with them. Only fitting that they should be there again. Manido will come back to help, he predicted hopefully. But he doubted that. He sat stoic and severe at the breakfast table. Determined, ready to conquer. I am not afraid. I am not afraid. He mouthed the words over and over again. But every few times he stopped and changed. K'neekaunissnaun, k'd'ninguzhimim.

224

K'neekaunissinaun, k'maudjauh. K'neekaunissinaun, k'cheeby/im.... These words that he only loosely understood would keep him afloat. They would give him the power he needed. He unfolded the map to refresh his memory of the route. Labyrinth Bay. Shoal Lake Narrows. Into the ocean-sized expanse. Up the east shore. Into Symcoe Bay....

Symcoe Bay! Max's place! It all made sense now. He hadn't thought before now of how it would have been spelled. It didn't look right, but how else would you say it? He spoke the words. Max had mentioned that place more than once. That was why they had their clubhouse there! It made it all the more likely that they would be there again, but he also realized that they had never made the trip he had made and would make again today in the six. It was easy for them to get there. Not nearly as impressive as his journey, he thought.

Once he was completely packed, he sat down to check that he had prepared for everything. Leaving without telling his mother seemed a little inconsistent with his new commitment to being truthful. But this was something he had to do and it was something she would never willingly allow. He pulled a page from his sketch pad and wrote a note to her or "to whoever finds this" explaining that he had gone on a trip, that he was okay and apologizing for lying. With any luck, no one would ever read it. He put it in the middle of the table, weighed down by the pepper grinder.

Everything looked like it was going to work. He considered taking the big boat, but that would be harder to explain and more people might notice it was gone. He felt pretty good about his idea to add oil to a big jerry can of pure gas that was for the big boat so that he could use it in the six-horse. If his mother decided something fishy was going on and sent Gladys to check on him, he would need to get back to the island right away. Then once she was gone, he would need to get back out there. As much as he hoped for his mother's health, Philip prayed that the first family member he would see again would be Uncle Dixon on Friday morning. He now had more than enough gas to get to Poplar Island and back twice.

A last scan before the trip. He spotted his lifejacket and grabbed a slicker that might cover his bag from rain or splash. He felt very adult with the responsibility of closing the island all on his own. He started to close the shutters, but realized this would be a dead give-away that he had left the place. Today seemed like it was going to be pretty hot and wasn't windy, and he recalled the radio weather talking about a high of thirty-two again tomorrow. The simplicity of it all confused him. He could leave everything.

He shrugged his shoulders and propped the south shutter up again. He would just lock the doors, that's all. He turned on the living room light and the floodlight outside so the island would seem inhabited when the McGinnises glanced across from the mainland.

He had everything. He grabbed his backpack and as much of his other supplies as he could carry and headed down to the beach. On his second trip he picked up the orange tarp and unplugged the cellphone at the last second so it would have the longest charge possible. Put it in his pocket and locked the door carefully behind him. The water was up a few inches since his last boat ride and the aluminium boat slid easily away from the beach.

As he headed toward Corkscrew Channel across the cellophane surface, he couldn't help feeling he stuck out among the few other boats out on this beautiful Monday morning. He felt almost embarrassed. Maybe everyone could see how serious he was just by how the boat slid across the lake. His energy and excitement twisted about inside him. The other people on the lake were out having fun, but he was all business. Did it show?

He barely needed the map for the first leg of the journey, having travelled the channel before and dreamed his return many nights in a row. Once out in Ptarmigan Bay he pulled it out from beneath the seat to avoid hitting any surprisingly placed reef. The water rippled now with a light east breeze. But there were no real waves to war with this time, the wind low at his back. He shut the motor down in the middle of the bay as his watch alarm went off to remind him of his first call. He spoke briefly to his mother and assured her all was well.

Rounding the point and heading between the islands into Ash Bay, he remembered last night's dream—the rapids. He could remember whipping up the rapids as if they weren't there. With speed, true power. As they loomed larger, his stomach shook with fear beneath his confident glare. He slowed for a moment, checked around him, and looked at the magnified portion of the map that showed the crazy channel path that would take him so close to the right shore and around the black and green posts grounded in the treacherous rock bottom. But there was no question this time—if he stopped now, he could never live with himself. These rapids were navigable. It said so on the map. People did it every day. Enough of this crap! He gunned the engine to get a good run at them.

The boat slowed only slightly as it entered the fast water and Philip ascended the dreaded waters even more easily than he had dreamed. The water seemed a little less vicious this time. Maybe because of the water level change, or maybe because of his own. It didn't matter. He laughed confidently as he turned his head to see the rippling, conquered task falling behind in his own wake. He charged through the next set of rapids without worry. The water was barely moving at all. And the perfectly calm water in the labyrinth that followed nearly brought tears to his eyes. Everything would be easier this time.

And his prediction continued to ring true as the Shoal Lake Narrows opened up into the huge basin that had nearly sunk him just a week earlier—still no legitimate waves to negotiate. Philip took advantage of the good conditions and stopped often on the route to check land marks to avoid wasting his time and gas getting lost again. Still feeling conspicuous, he made his way up the straight east bank of the lake, barely able to contain his excitement. Almost there. He let out a gasp when he glanced at the cell phone screen that read "No signal." But when the cliffy shoreline dropped the text changed back to "Home" again to his great relief. He checked behind him again. Forget it. Don't be such a dork! He was home free.

He rounded into a deserted Symcoe Bay forgetting whose cottage was supposedly there. Then grinned at the site of Poplar Island directly south of him as he entered Belle's Inlet. Even the "Private Property" sign brought a smile to his face. He had been through all the hard parts. All he had to do now was remember the words and feed himself. He could do that, more sure now than ever. He did a full lap of the island before attempting to dock, remembering that those assholes must have already had their boat parked on the other side last time when he arrived. He slowly motored by what looked to have once been a large wharf. Imagined Max's boat sitting there. Philip continued around and docked the boat back where he did last time. He pulled it almost completely out of the water and into the brush beside the scorched clearing to camouflage it from passers-by. He straightened up and winced at the remembered pain of his last visit. Picked up his bag and moved on to set up camp near the shaft. He didn't need to adventure around this time. Knew what he wanted. He even knew where the bathroom was. Laughed briefly out loud.

He stood on the wooden deck in front of the shaft, and laid his bag down. Checked his watch. Maybe he could do the first day's work before he even set up or called the hospital. He could barely wait to start. And hoped for the return of his old friend. He knelt down and opened the clips at the top of his father's pack, released the plastic synch on the drawstring, and rooted around for the can of tobacco. Then he searched the area for objects to send down the shaft in memory of Winonah, Stanley and Jack. He had brought along the sketch of them as well. He wandered down to the water to find something other than the rusty old nails since they represented only the murders and murderers themselves. Then he thought of the perfect thing for a person's mide bag as he spied one—a pinecone. Pinecones held seeds and Philip thought to himself of how that meant hope and new life. He thought more deeply and with his eyes closed as he held three pinecones in his hands. The largest one was for Winonah.

But the boy's eyes blinked wide open. Without Manido, the ceremony couldn't possibly work or even be real. Even with his specially dedicated drawing to add.... As much as he cursed it right now, he was as white as you could get and couldn't very well perform a ceremony like this on his own. He shook his head sadly, thinking for just a moment that he had wasted his time coming all this way.

Slowly, he came back around. Turning back would be even worse! Maybe if I make it somehow extra-special. He remembered how Manido had cut some corners, saying Gitche-Manido would understand. But what if he cut no corners, did it all perfectly? That might make up for what he was. Adding a fire to the ceremony would be the first step. And to keep it going for the four days straight—a vigil where he would think of them and hope for their successful journey. He could do that this time since he had nowhere else to go.

And maybe a better mide bag. If it were made of bark instead of cloth! His head pounded with all its inspiration. Almost immediately, he found himself looking for birch bark on the ground. He could use the sewing kit from his father's pack to make a purse if the bark was thin enough. He grabbed all he could find off the ground and peeled more off a rotting stump. Anything left over from his work would be perfect for starting the fire.

And berries! He needed food too. Something traditional. Not anything he had brought with him. The fever for the ceremony was coming back to him with each idea that popped into his head. The words floated back into his head as he worked. Today they would come from him alone and do more than just help him get through the day.

But he stopped when he heard something that might be a voice.

His ears twitched with the sound, and he turned his head. Then came the low bubble of an engine. Outboard. How could he have missed the sound until it was so close and slow? He stalked the sound cautiously, then spotted the boat through the trees. He stepped back, bowed his head.

They had come for him. They were here again. This time on the other side of the island. He saw Max point to his badly hidden boat. Rupert. Max. Franny. They were not part of his dream here. Philip suddenly had less than five minutes to adjust to a reality he had not truly considered.

FORTY-TWO

The Shaft

A familiar panic flushed Philip as he scrambled to hide himself. He swung one leg over the railing, then the other, and lowered himself down onto a thick rusty pipe. Pulled his bag and gear after him. Another step down, squatted on a rusted platform for a moment. Thought hard. The only trace of him up there was the pile of birch bark. His thoughts swarmed around him. But those jerks knew he was here, so how long could he hide? Should he just get it over with and let them do whatever they want to him again? But it would be worse than last time—they had promised that much. Manido was not even expected this time. No illusions of how alone the boy was. Maybe I should've hidden in that old house. The graffiti flashed through his mind again. But it was too late. He would have to pass them to get there. He looked over the edge of the platform down the shaft. Rupert and Max could easily trap him down here, beat him and leave him for dead. Might as well get up out of the shaft and wait for his fate like a man. He lobbed his pack and tarp up onto the deck, then climbed up and rolled under the railing. The small platform below shook from his take-off, humming metal. He hid his stuff in the nearby brush and leaned against the rail with outward calm. Crossed his right leg over his left. Folded his arms. His heart eased its furious pounding. Either a good or bad sign.

Snapping twigs told of their approach.

"Shut up and get ready to bash his skull." Rupert's bark, easy to recognize.

Finally, he saw a blue sweatshirt through the low brush and trees as they came uphill toward him. He braced himself. Reminded himself that this was a grave site above all else, before it was any creep's clubhouse, and that he had a duty to protect it.

"Hey punk.... Hey punk," Max began calling in a mock-mother voice as the gang of three approached. Philip stood completely still as they came around the last layer of trees to face him. He just stared at them.

Only slightly jarred by his victim's apparent refusal to flinch at his appearance, Rupert began his tirade. Started with a derisive laugh, finger pointing at Philip's face. "I thought I told you this was our place. But here you are again. I don't know what you're doing here and I don't care. But I remember warning you very well. Don't you remember?" Maybe so angry he had forgotten about his Wild West accent.

Philip's jaw tightened. He hoped they could see it flex. He knew very well this wasn't a game now, if it ever had been. Nothing to lose, he told himself. Nothing to lose. "I'm not moving," he responded in a dead tone. He chanted to himself inside his head.

Rupert blinked widely and laughed again. Tried to gather up a comeback: "Well, you won't move after we're done with you. That's for sure!"

But somehow Rupert didn't seem so frightening this time. He was bigger and stronger than Philip, and had the support of two more people, but something was missing.

Max jumped into the mix: "Are you ready, loser? Ready to get your ass kicked! Ha! Reddy?"

Fear crept into the underpowered boy's body as he sized up the large, apish Max, and flashed back to their last meeting. Max certainly could kick his ass. He had already done it once. It seemed that this would have been a good time to pull out a gun, if you had one. Just kill all three of them and worry about the consequences later. Throw them down the shaft. Teach them a lesson.

Then Franny spoke for one of the first times he had ever heard. "Philip Reddy. The Dickless Wonder." Gestured toward him with her lit cigarette. "When we have you down, I'm going to stick one of these up your ass."

The words were harsher coming from her. Like she had been saving them all summer for effect. He was about to bolt. The mission was not worth all of this. His millionth second thought. He could tell them very nicely right now that he would never come back. Could beg their forgiveness. Maybe get off with a few less punches. But beating him was something they wanted to do very badly. Run, he commanded his body. But his legs would not budge.

"Get the freak!" sounded from a charging Rupert.

Philip pushed himself up and away from the railing. And just as Rupert reached out to grab him, thrust two fingers directly into his right eye.

The world stopped for an instant as Rupert let out a frightening shriek and his hands flashed to his face. The assailant, assaulted. "My eye!" he screamed.

Behind Rupert, Philip saw Max's lips mouth something he couldn't quite read, and his hand pull a jack-knife from his pocket. Philip ignored the writhing, stumbling group leader standing in front of him as he watched Max unfold the main blade and begin moving toward him. Sharp metal bent on plunging into his wimpy, boy flesh.

Now his legs were ready to move. As if by reflex, he swung over the rail and jumped down onto the rusty platform he had crouched on before. It shook precariously under his weight. He cursed himself as soon as he had landed. There was no way out of this hole. Should have bolted for the forest instead. Too late. Had to hide now. As he slithered down to the next available stepping place, he heard the thud of Max landing on the first rickety chunk of machinery above him. Faster! He stopped thinking and simply moved as quickly as he could, swinging on old pipes, slipping down the earthy walls that crumbled under his shoes. He stopped for a moment and looked above him. He saw the silhouette of Max's head looking for him over a platform edge against the daylight.

No time to watch. He turned and slipped further down the side, bracing himself against a stiff rod. Easily more than twenty feet down now. He wondered for a moment how much farther down he could go. Kept his eyes peeled for a hiding place. But it only grew darker. His very next step left him standing in ankle-deep cold water. He remembered learning about the water table in school. This is the end of the line, he couldn't help thinking. His only hope was to hide, and to do it well. He splashed across the watery bottom, slipped and was suddenly up to his neck, gasping. The water was frigid and carried a thousand-year-old stench.

He pulled himself out onto the muddy opposite side of the shaft, looking frantically for any way out of this pit bottom. A bed-sized, thin plank of some kind leaned against the shaft wall a few feet up. He crept up onto a ledge and in behind what was really a huge piece of sheet metal. Did his best to stop breathing. The earth cold against his wet body.

A few seconds later he heard Max hit the water. He called up to his cronies, "Hey, Rupe! I don't see nuthin' down here, man."

Just a moan of pain from above.

Both voices sounded strange so far underground. Static. But it would be just a matter of time before Max spotted the sheet and checked it out. "Can't see nuthin' down here," to himself. Philip looked around him for anything to defend himself with. Nothing but what he hid behind. But just off to the right, away from his cover seemed to be a hole. If there was an option, that was it.

Gambling that Max truly couldn't see nuthin', Philip inched his way out from behind the sheet and peeked into the hole. Square, framed with old wooden ties. It seemed to descend slightly. A few inches inside the frame his fingers found yet another rusted pipe, but just an inch or two in diameter, covered by a thin layer of damp earth. The hole seemed to be timber-lined. He could probably just fit—it looked no more than a foot wide and high. He checked again for Max, and heard him still shifting about in the shallow water below. Jumping up to the hole might make noise and give him away. Had to make this one chance work! Just then, he heard a shout as Max plunged into the deeper water. A swearing, thrashing rage. Without thinking again, he pushed the heavy sheet of metal with all his strength away from the wall. It rang like a gong as it bounced and rolled end over end one time and crashed into the water. The still-struggling Max let out another yelp, hopefully struck right on the head by the sheet.

But Philip had already inched himself headfirst halfway into the mouth of the hole. Rocking from side to side on his forearms and shoulders, he slowly made his way down the cold, filthy tunnel. The tunnel-long pipe dug into his right hipbone every time he shifted his weight, but wriggling was the only way to make any progress. He tried to ignore the pain. He could hear faint shouting behind him, but his own body muffled everything. No idea how close behind Max might be. He dreaded the horror movie grab at the ankle. Had to keep moving fast. As his shoulders rubbed against the walls, it came to him that Max couldn't follow him here because of his ape-like build. Simply too wide. He barely fit in here himself!

Philip went completely still for a moment at the thought of actually being safe. Already ten feet in, no one could touch him. Could just stay here until they left. That's all. They would surely have to go home for dinner in a few hours.... Then he would just have to inch his way back. He had done it! He had escaped them!

But what if they found his bag and took his food? And the boat.... Give them an opportunity to screw him and they would take it. But so far today, he was leading in the screwing department, it seemed. Maybe he could still do more.... He felt the power of Manido inside him and gently whispered a few words to help gather his strength. He took a deep breath of the thick earthy air, and slithered further down the tunnel. It might lead to another exit. Maybe he could really screw them just this one time....

After five minutes of struggling, the opaque black brightened slightly. His hands slowly appeared in front of him as they pulled him forward. Inch-by-inch, his vision increased until he could see what looked to be daylight. The tunnel ended the way it had begun. Philip's fingers gripped the bottom of a wooden frame. An open area. And daylight indeed. He eased himself down onto the sloping ground and found himself standing on an old metal rail of some kind. He looked more carefully around him—a narrower, inclined shaft. The rail had to be for bringing gold out of the mine. Or at least all the rocks piled near the water. He peered down the debris-covered track and saw only the glint of water. Turned the other way, and the daylight made him squint, but with relief, because of where he had been. His white t-shirt now claimed deep brown as its colour. His face was caked with rapidly drying mud. It flaked off his forehead onto his hand, also black with the stuff. But it didn't feel so awful, really. He fought with the cobwebs and metal scraps to squeeze around the pile-up of slag carts near the exit. Pieces of frayed cable pulled and grabbed at his soaked, heavy pants. He hoped to at least have the element of surprise over his enemies. He gave himself another quick brush-off.

Past the old wreckage, he cautiously extended his head up to spy Franny and Rupert calling down the shaft to Max not thirty feet away. Rupert was still holding his hand to his eye. He yelled down to Max again. Philip's realized his bag was hidden too close to where they stood to just grab and run away with. This would have to be head-on.

The quicker he acted, the better. He picked up a few baseball-sized rocks from around his feet and hoped his arm had somehow miraculously improved. Maybe the skipping rocks and swimming had helped. Standing straight up at the mouth of the cart shaft, he threw one rock as high and hard as he could toward his adversaries. Then another immediately following. He had overthrown by over ten feet. Surprised himself.

The two kids turned quickly to see what made the noises in the trees behind them. As they inched away from the shaft, swearing at whoever was hiding there, Philip threw one more rock over them and dashed with light feet to where they had been standing. Arms folded, leaning against the rail where they had first found him.

After inspecting the bush, they turned and clawed their way back to the clearing in front of the shaft. "I guess it was just—" Rupert stopped dead at the sight of Philip. "What the hell?!"

Franny's jaw dropped.

Philip felt the power of his surprise. His blood pumped confidently. And a rock in each pocket made him sure.

Rupert tried to gather himself. Glanced furtively at Franny, his eye still red and tearing. Then tried to strut up to Philip, to intimidate him physically. But Philip didn't move a muscle. Rupert's act wasn't working the way it was supposed to. "You watch too much TV, geek. You think you just have to stand up to the man and he's going to back off. Or maybe poke him in the eye like a stupid girl...." Franny frowned behind Rupert's back. "But this is real life and losers always get theirs." He stood only three feet from Philip. The eye seemed to be getting worse.

Still no flinch from Philip's side.

A grunt came from the shaft behind him. Then a whimper. Rupert strained his neck to see beyond Philip. Franny tilted her head to see around them both.

Now! Philip pulled back his foot and kicked Rupert between the legs with all his power. The gang leader melted to the ground. He shrieked like no man should, far louder than he had with the finger in his eye. He rolled about on the ground. A disgustingly soaked and muddied Max began labouring to pull himself from the shaft. Looked far worse than the boy he had chased. Philip stamped his foot on the deck, and Max lost his grip with one hand for fright. A gash on his forehead shone bright red through the filth, and he no longer brandished a knife. The sheet must have hit him just perfectly. Philip turned to Franny with a rock, cocked and ready to fire. She flinched.

He had them.

Slowly and carefully he said the words to the suddenly uncertain girl. "If you know what's good for you, you'll collect these two idiots and get off my island."

She tried to look tough, but it didn't fly. Rupert struggled to his feet and staggered toward Franny. Max followed, rounding Philip with a wide berth, after finally dragging himself up to ground level. Rupert could still hardly breathe and motioned for them to go. He gasped, "The kid's crazy...."

The three bullies stood united again, but their mystic powers were gone. Just a smoking girl and two badly beaten losers.

But Max suddenly seemed to find the energy to fight again, even alone. Looking grizzly, he stepped toward Philip. But in an instant, the rock left Philip's hand and hit Max in the chest. The bleeding boy grunted and stumbled backwards, then broke into uncontrollable, winded sobs. Philip reached for the last rock. "Go."

"C'mon, let's go, you dinks," Franny said in a disgusted tone as she turned away.

Philip watched, still holding the rock fast, as they faded out of sight down the bluff.

FORTY-
THREE

Finishings

A few moments after the frustrated buzz of Max's boat had tapered off in the distance, Philip awoke from a sort of daze. The rock was still ready to fire from his hand, but his mind was clued out. He tried to recap the events in some kind of order. Had to check that it hadn't all been another daydream. But the very real adrenaline still pumped in his veins. It had all really happened. And only moments ago. The echo of voices still hung in the air, quiet and empty now.

Philip looked purposefully upwards and whispered a thank you to Manido. But no answer came. He wondered for a moment if he might have done all that on his own, then dismissed the idea. When Manido had sat back and watched, the result had been very different. Maybe the spirit had helped but was still so angry or sad that he wouldn't or couldn't speak until things were set right. That had to be it. Just more motivation to finish strong, although he hardly needed it. Completely rejuvenated, he went about collecting firewood and rocks to make a fireplace for the four-day vigil.

Just before 4 pm, his watch alarm sounded, and he dropped everything. Feeling a little guilty at deceiving his mother like this, he was extra nice to her. "They're testing me for everything," she said. "Tuberculosis. Even something called blastomycosis. It's ridiculous." He laughed with her as best he could. Her spirits sounded good. She made him promise not to dig in the garden because that might be where she got blastomycosis if she had it. He smirked as he indulged her with his word to stay clear of the area as he sat next to his new circle of stones farther from the garden that she ever could have guessed.

After he hung up the phone and reset his watch alarm, he broke out his dad's sewing kit from the pack's first-aid pocket and began transforming thin strips of birch bark into little pockets. The bark he found was just thick enough to not collapse under the needle, yet thin enough that he stitched with ease. He folded each piece and stitched up the sides. After a good hour of concentrated work, he looked down proudly at three beautiful, all-natural mide bags. He paused and tried to remember his plans prior to the rude interruption by the bullies. He rescued the best sticks of firewood from the pile to build shelters for the three souls. As he lined up three tepees just outside the rail around the shaft, he thought one would be enough since they must have lived under one roof when they were alive. But doing extra was better than doing too little, he had decided long ago. Had to execute on every detail. This ceremony would be as close to perfect as possible. He collected what little berries were still left on the island, along with a crab-apple-like fruit he hadn't seen before. With a check of his rations, he decided to lay out a raw noodle for each person as a symbol of more solid foods and of giving something of his own. Then he put out a cup of lake water in front of the largest tepee—the mother could feed it to the sons. Pine cones ready. The drawing out of the folder.

With all the preparation he could think of already done, he checked his watch. Hunger bit him savagely as he read 5:32 pm. But eating now would just make him feel guilty, like he was putting this off. And he had never meant to put it off even this long! He had to start these patient people on their westward journey.

He took a few steps to his laid-out kindling and struck a match to it. The dry bark and leaves lit up instantly. Almost smokeless. It felt weird to make a fire by himself, especially with the day's heat still warm on his skin. Once he had built the fire up a bit, he walked up to the railing around the great mysterious hole in the earth. He strained his eyes as he peered down, as if he might catch a glimpse of Winonah and her boys. But he knew too well how dark and deep the hole was. Hardly mysterious anymore, really. But once it had been far deeper, he felt sure.

Pockets loaded with mide bags and tobacco, he inhaled deeply. Swung underneath the rail and down onto the first piece of machinery again. The same gong of old metal. He wanted to get as close to them as he could. Recognizing each step from the chase of earlier that afternoon, he smiled to himself. His own private, triumphant parade down into the earth. But next would be the truly special part, he promised. Just above the pool of water, he found a workable perch. Looked down and across toward the secret tunnel that had led him out of his worst nightmare. And here he was again. But it was different. Now he could feel just how close his waiting family lay. Before he opened his mouth to begin, he scraped the wet shaft wall with his fingers and smeared mud onto his face. His face should stay black while he mourned for them. He sat down cross-legged, facing what he was sure was west. His eyes started to adapt, and he made out a pile of beer cans which must have been those stupid kids'.

The first words sprung from inside him. But this time he sat up straight. This time the words sounded different. Resonated from even deeper inside him. This time his head did not spin. And there was no pain. He hoped that this difference would not invalidate the whole thing. The words came more heartfelt than ever. This time they were his own.

Instead of reeling in light-headed pleasure, Philip dove to new depth inside the chant. The words were everything he was now. They coursed through his veins, but no longer involuntarily. The power they had given him at home came back to him with new calm. The words were not intended to soothe his battered confidence now, but to perform their original purpose. Their true essence.

"K'neekaunissinaun, neewi-goon cheeby-meekunnuh

"K'neekaunissinaun, waukweeng k'd'izhau…

Time stopped while Philip's heart and body went out to Winonah, Stanley and Jack. He could feel them inside him more than he had felt with any before, Mong included. As he keened and chanted, hot tears rolled down his cheeks. He sprinkled the watery bottom of the shaft with tobacco and let the mide bags fall one at a time. Each landed on the water with a quiet pat. Every individual act done with care for each soul. His craft was a masterpiece this time.

His body knew instinctively when the day's work had been completed, and his voice followed that lead. No time had been measured or words counted. It was simply time to stop and rest for the night.

As Philip scaled his way up the shaft again, almost blind, grappling with his hands, he beamed with certainty that the first part of the ceremony had been a success. Could feel things at work.

Up above, dusk had fallen. The sun faintly lit the sky a dark blue from below the horizon. The air was still hot and close. He threw a rotten stump on the smouldering fire, then organized his materials to set up some kind of camp. Straining to remember everything his father had shown him before the light was gone completely, he strung his rope between two trees about eight feet apart. Bound the knots with the help of branches at about eye-level. Flipped the crackling orange tarp over the rope to make a version of a tent. He tried to pull out the three-year-old wrinkles and folds. Pinned the corners down with sticks hammered through the eyelets. He stoked the fire and watched it flare up for a while. The tent opened to it, just four or five feet away. Its heat was real. The back of his hand touched his cheek. The dried mud reminded him of the dead. He cursed himself for thinking of anything else. After deciding the fire was solid enough to last all night but not a threat to spread, the boy gave in to sleep.

The next two days passed more quickly than Philip could believe. Faster than any he could remember. He spent his time collecting wood and new offerings, tending the fire, cooking noodles and oatmeal on the propane stove. He practiced skipping stones down by the old wharf. Got up to six in a row with the best rocks. He performed the ceremony, sometimes down the shaft, sometimes by the fire. One day he performed the entire ceremony twice. For hours at a time, he sat by the fire and thought of them. Sometimes just staring into the flames, sometimes brushing his teeth until he started to drool. The feeling grew inside him incessantly, made him glow with generosity. Made his ears go pleasantly warm. He didn't need anyone to tell him what he was doing was good.

Only once did he miss calling his mother and she was quick to follow up by calling him. He said he had fallen asleep and apologized. During the 10 pm calls, when she asked what he had done that day, he was pleased he could honestly say he had not swum out to the Little or Big Whale. She seemed a little shocked that he was eating Kraft Dinner every night. But he reminded her his cheesy diet was only for a couple of days, and she laughed.

One morning when he made his 10 am call, he was alarmed when she didn't answer. When she called later on—right in the middle of his ritual—she told him she had been off for some test, a scan or something. She was getting some kind of treatment for her breathing and lungs while they did all their blood tests. She said she was okay and that a special "blasto" doctor had been called in, but she hadn't been told anything more. The plan hadn't changed, which was good news.

During breaks he made for himself, he wandered about on the island, looking at the machinery and the burned-out houses. Wondered what the mine really looked like before it closed, what Winonah's family had seen back then. But when he thought of Winonah, he couldn't help thinking of Manido and whether he would ever come back. The spirit didn't owe him anything, but it seemed strange that he would ignore all of what his student was doing now in his name.

And the same problem kept coming up when Philip thought everything through. Why had Manido appeared in the first place? If he had died and gone to the Land of Souls, how could digging up his grave make him mad, even make him come back? Digging up the grave shouldn't have mattered if the Land of Souls was anything like Philip believed it might be, some version of heaven. Something wasn't right with the whole story. Maybe he had forgotten a detail. But as it stood, it didn't sit well with him.

That night, he felt sure Winonah, Stanley and Jack were well on their way after three days of travelling. Still high on his day, he went to sleep on a full stomach of the tuna and bread which had not tasted quite as bad as he had expected. But as he drifted, he pondered Manido and the possible explanations once again.

In a dream, Philip found himself walking the island alone as he had done so often. Something felt extremely wrong. But the house seemed to be intact as he passed it, as did everything else. Then came the sound. A wailing that could only be human, but it rang so strange and deep, he could barely believe it. As he tried to track it down, he grew more sure that it was a grown man's voice crying out. After lapping the island, the boy realized that the sound was all around him, but strongest to the west. The gravesite! He remembered the voice from that first day! Echoing across the lake....

When Philip awoke the next morning, he felt low. The weather system had changed and the colder air seized his lungs. Manido had been the one crying last night, just like all the people he had seen along the path in his earlier dreams. Philip felt sure now that Manido had been nothing more than a ghost, one rejected from the Land of Souls. Not the god he had held him for. Somewhere along the line he had done enough wrong not to be admitted. The hole inside Philip widened further. Disappointed because he had admired someone who had been a fraud. All the talk of saving souls could hardly be taken seriously from someone who wandered like a lost bum on some path in some weird limbo world, from someone who was a lost soul himself. He saw the face of the changing Native man in his dream.

What bull! And maybe all of it was.... The whole damn story. What kind of kid would believe such total crap?!

He looked around him at his camp, all the effort he had put out. The smoke of his fire sifted into the low bank of grey in the sky, the first clouds he had seen in his few days here. Might as well pack up and go home. He couldn't be sure if he had been betrayed, tricked, or if his imagination had just gone too far. What a waste. Waste of time. Waste of everything. He rolled over and tried to curl up for warmth.

But something told him to finish what he had started. Waste of time or not, he finally had a chance to finish doing something that had been hard to do. Even just a pointless exercise like this seemed to be now. And what if he was wrong? Maybe Manido just needed the ceremony performed for him as the others had. If they could be forgiven, maybe he could too…. But he didn't have another four days to mess around with.

Finally, he decided that today there was nothing to stop him. Nobody to get in his way. He thought of all his unfinished drawings in the last two years. How he had left them, never really sure why. Everything since his father died. But why should that matter? This thing he would finish once and for all. And if it was all made up, nothing bad could come of it. He persuaded himself to believe it all again for one final day. And perhaps there still could be another explanation for Manido's absence now and his earlier mysterious presence. Who knew? He added the finishing touches to the drawing of the family of three.

He jumped up out of his sleeping bag into the frigid morning air. Slipped on his cold, dew-soaked sneakers he had forgotten to cover the night before, and scurried over to the brush to relieve himself. He grabbed a branch of white pine needles he had spotted while standing there to re-kindle the fire. With the fire breathing again, he piled some more wood on top, and sat himself close to the rising flames. Beside him, the water for his necessary dose of oatmeal started to simmer on the stove. After breakfast, he packed up his little camp, leaving out only what was necessary for lunch and the ceremony.

As he had done the first day, the boy climbed down the wreckage to near the shaft's bottom. Thoroughly convinced of its importance once again, he began his work, his song. Somewhere inside him, he was very aware that it was the last time he would need to say the words. He still didn't know their meaning word-for-word. He never would. But he knew they made for a safe journey. Kept his mind on that. The two boys and their mother walking an easy path to the river and crossing it on a log raft to the side they deserved. Tears rolled down Philip's cheeks. This strange and wonderful part of his life was ending, but the tears were also for the three souls one last time. He thought of waiting over a half-century for something, and how finally getting it would feel. The end of slavery. Freedom. Part of him felt the release of the family, the kin of Manido. Part of him felt it for himself.

The words rang longer than necessary as Philip wondered frantically if all he had done had been enough. But inside he knew it had worked. As if on cue, a first heavy drop of rain struck Philip's head as he gave his last salute and threw a dusting of tobacco down into the dark water. He laid the drawing facedown on the water and pushed the middle down until his index finger was wet. A moment later, the shaft boomed with the pelting rain on the old metal, mud and water. Philip climbed up underneath a motor casing for shelter.

It was all over. Maybe the rain would wash it away. But he thought clearly for the first time that this was something he never wanted to forget, real or not. Scaring off three of the toughest kids in the world would remain very real and true in his memory. Helping three good souls get to where they deserved to be was something that was now part of him, not just an act he had committed. All the others as well.... Fourteen souls....

He sat shivering, huddled twenty feet below the ground for two hours. Hoped he had at least stashed his bag under a tree or something. Remembered every word, every name, every dream, every scare, every site from the summer. It all ran through his mind like a film. No way could his imagination have come up with all of that. He had done something real. There was no other possibility, regardless of who his mentor might be. All the people he had helped....

With sunlight breaking through the lifting wall of clouds, Philip crouched next to the smoky fire pit to make a peanut-butter sandwich. Then stood looking into the coals, eating his sandwich. Then looked out across the water. He felt the pull back to his own island. His teeth chattered uncontrollably between sandwich bites despite the sun, everything damp if not soaked.

After he had eaten, he rooted around in the bag, luckily not left in the rain, for his warmest, driest clothes. He stripped down, then dressed dryly again, and put the slicker on overtop. Glad he had brought it now. With one last look to the shaft and one thought of the people, Philip doused the dying fire thoroughly with the pot of water he had ready. He hoisted the pack onto his back and looked at the swimming, hissing coals for a moment. This fire had served its purpose. He walked down to the boat through the drenched tall grass and bushes. Bailed out the rainfall and filled the gas tank. It was time to go.

The way home came fairly easily once he had fought the boat out of the brush and got it floating again. He laughed again as he charged through the two sets of rapids whose current had actually switched direction and was barely a trickle, as the map promised might happen. Maybe they had never been that fast in the first place. He just hadn't been ready. Now he was.

FORTY - FOUR

Second Chances for the Worthy

The island appeared strange as Philip caught a first glimpse of it as the boat entered Clearwater Bay from the mouth of Corkscrew Channel. Just being away those short few days had made a difference in how he saw the place. The boy's stomach lurched as he remembered turning into the beach bay to see the police boat the last time he had stayed out on the lake overnight. The west reef off Sunset Rock boldly stuck up out of the low water. Philip felt an irresistible desire to check the grave where all of this had started. Even just to confirm that the earth had been disturbed. Again unsure about it all.

A quick jerk of his wrist sent the boat in a U-turn back around the west reef to dock at Swimming Rock. He didn't want to wait even long enough to moor the boat in its regular place. He pulled the motor up safely as the bedrock shelves came into view below. The boat scraped lightly onto the easy incline of the rock. Philip hopped out and pulled the boat up a bit. He stepped up the slab levels to the grave clearing.

Just as he had left it—definitely once dug-up, but since then stable. He was relieved, although not totally convinced that that was the right way to feel.

But the voice was unmistakable: "Thank you, Needjee."

Philip let out a gasp. He didn't try to look around for the source. He knew Manido had spoken, that the voice was inside him. It hadn't been that long, really. The boy laughed, overjoyed at the spirit's return. Truly grateful. The familiar tone in the voice made his insides cheer. "Well, this time you didn't let me get my ass kicked by those guys." He paused. "I'm sorry I got so mad at you last time, but I couldn't do it alone."

"But then you did," the spirit countered, slightly more animated.

Philip's brow furrowed at the thought that he had thrown those rocks himself. That he had found the passage on his own. And threatened those kids so harshly that they fled for fear. Outsmarted them. And then the whole ceremony....

"I have been watching you for many days. Only watching, child. You were like Chekaubaewiss and finally beat your Mishi-naubae."

Philip's instinctive furious energy bubbled and then subsided inside. He would have felt betrayed again if it weren't for the fact that he had succeeded. And he had! Plus, this way was almost better. No, it was better.

The spirit laboured to express more. "You taught me not to doubt or hate what I do not know. Lessons you should learn while they can help you. I doubted you and hated you, but you did what was impossible for a spoiled white child to do. And you finished it without being asked. You did so alone. You saved innocent people with your care and you may have saved me."

What response could there be to this? There couldn't be any greater compliments in the world. But the bit about Manido himself being saved reminded Philip of the doubts he had had. Now he had to know. He wasted no time and started in bluntly. "You were buried, right? But you never got to the Land of Souls. What happened? I know there's more."

"I made mistakes. The worst of my mistakes was to sell my people. I will not tell the whole story. I cannot. Maybe it should not have been kept from you. But I stand by the decision to keep it from you and believe it has helped fuel a good purpose. Your respect was of utmost importance."

He went on a little further. "In my time, I knew we would be taken by the Saugaushe whether we accepted their offers or not. But I took as much as I could get. It may have been the only thing to do, but I did so with thoughts only of myself. I had heard of the peoples of the east being driven from their land less than one year after receiving white man's gifts and promises. I knew the end was coming. I am responsible for the deaths of many of my own kind. My people buried me out of respect. This respect I did not deserve. I have been wandering now a long time."

Philip could barely believe how close he had been to the truth. He remembered the dream and it made sense. "I saw you on the Path of Souls! It was you! As a young man, then an old man. I saw Winonah and Jack and Stanley then too."

No response.

Philip pushed on, thinking out loud. "You came to the river and turned back and went into the forest again. I saw you. It was in my dream." Positive now.

"Strange truths come in dreams."

Philip nodded and looked out over the water. "So what now?"

"You go to sleep. You continue to build peace with your mother when you see her. She is not well, but she will recover. You take everything you learned with you. I am proud to have known you. Your father is proud. Gitche-Manido is proud. He has accepted your work as if it were mine."

Too much to absorb and respond to all at once. Philip just tried to keep the conversation alive. "And you?"

"I think you may have opened a road for me to the Land of Souls. I have been asked new questions and am set on a steady path."

"You mean you got in because you made me save people? And Gitche-Manido liked that?" Checked to see if he had got it all finally.

"No. That was not all. Those great acts were more courageous on your part than on mine. I started them out of guilt and a lost love of my people. That is never enough. I will cross that river now because I saved you. But I saved you by letting you save yourself. And you did this by saving me."

It made sense, but it didn't. A tightly woven circle of cause and effect.

The boy jumped at an idea. "If you need me to do a ceremony for you to make it faster, I have lots of time. I'm pretty good now. And I wouldn't even have to take the boat!"

"I know it." Philip could feel a smile inside him. "All of this, it will be enough. In four days, I will be there. I have been told."

The blood danced hotly about beneath Philip's skin, warming him inside the slicker. Somehow it had all worked out. And somehow he was responsible. It still seemed impossible that he could be so important. But he was. His dad would be proud. So would Grandpa Frederick. His mother would never believe a word. But that didn't really matter very much today.

The spirit had a few more words. "I can't spell out everything you should have learned in this time. You will not grasp all of it until you are older. But keep it close to you, so you may find the pieces of wisdom in it. I hated the white world because I blamed my own mistake on it. Then I saw what it did to my people after my time. But I do not hate you. If you remember one thing, remember you did what was impossible. Everything else is simple, Needjee. My friend."

Philip waited for more, but could feel the movement turn to stillness inside his head. That was goodbye.

He whispered his own goodbye.

"K'neekaunissinaun, k'gah odaessiniko."

Manido or Tikumiwaewidung would indeed finally be welcome.

Philip's body felt strangely empty as he stood next to the grave in this more complete silence. He stepped back down onto Swimming Rock. Then tiptoed atop the melon-sized boulders out to the flat of Sunset Rock. Gazing westward down Clearwater Bay at the low sun peeking through the breaking clouds, he hoped his friend would be well received in the Land of Souls, that the other people would show him the proper respect. Surely, the people he saved would embrace him. Tomorrow he would visit Grandpa Frederick too, extend Manido's apology. Tomorrow he would meet Uncle Dixon and visit his mother. She was going to be okay. Manido was no liar. The boy breathed easily, letting these burdens slip off his shoulders. He sat down on the rock's edge to watch the reddening sun disappear, however long or short it was going to take.

From the corner of his eye, as clear as all else around him, Philip saw an Anishinaabe clothed in short skins. He turned to take in the sight. The figure stood on the farthest reef shelf off Sunset Rock, watching the sky with him. Not thirty feet away. Young and powerful. The glowing red-brown face turned from the sun to Philip. The water reflected the sun in ripples against the chest and forehead. The man and boy locked eyes for a moment. The man nodded almost imperceptibly, then turned one corner of his mouth up with a smile. He turned away again and dove into the water toward the setting sun without the slightest splash. Slid into it. Gone. West.

Philip smiled and felt pieces inside him falling into place. He stared directly westward down the Path of Souls to follow the invisible spirit. Hundreds of seagulls and cormorants performed their swirling twilight dance around three calm pelicans just south of the island. They shrieked and dive-bombed each other as if it were the end of the world. But when the fiery ball of light finally slipped behind the land, they all flew quietly off. A few followed the dimming light west and waved gracefully, shrinking, then fading into the distance. Philip watched and didn't move a muscle until the sky was black. He closed his eyes and lay back to dream.

About the Author:

Originally from Montreal, Greg Jackson-Davis spent his childhood summers in the beautiful Lake of the Woods area of northwestern Ontario. He has a B.A. in Rhetoric and Professional Writing from the University of Waterloo, and a B.Ed. from the University of Manitoba. He currently teaches middle school English and French at St. John's-Ravenscourt School in Winnipeg.

Photo by Khalie Jackson-Davis

Original cover concept: Tim Philippi

Free Book Club guides for *Digging for Philip* are available on-line at www.greatplains.mb.ca.